"In the beginning,  Red-and-Yellow Dog ...... the Horse Bringers myself."

"Honor to the Horse Bringers," Horse Stealer said. "Where did *they* come from?"

"They were sent to us out of the river by Uncle." Red-and-Yellow Dog blew out a mouthful of smoke in honor of Uncle. "Also from the Cities-in-the-West. That is what they said." Legend and reality might be mutually incompatible and both still true.

Horse Stealer understood that. "How many horses?" he asked.

"Two."

"I have talked to the traders who come from the Cities-in-the-West. They tell me there are horses there, and the horses travel with spirits who have hard, shiny skin—like me, only with shiny places. It is plain," Horse Stealer said, "that those shiny people are horse spirits. So we should send our young men together to the Cities-in-the-West and get horses from them. That is what they are there for, to give people horses."

Horse Stealer waited for them to think about it. If the horses had come from the Cities-in-the-West, someone brave or crazy enough might go there and find more. Horse Stealer had looked at that idea from the top and bottom and all sides, and it still made sense to him. And if the young men went together, then their peoples would not fight while they were gone, and the Dry River people would still get horses. It was a fine idea, elegant and springy as new grass.

Horse Stealer liked it.

THE HORSE CATCHERS
TRILOGY
BOOK TWO
Children of the Horse

AMANDA COCKRELL

AVON BOOKS ◆ NEW YORK

AVON BOOKS, INC.
An Imprint of HarperCollins*Publishers*
10 East 53rd Street
New York, New York 10022-5299

Copyright © 2000 by Book Creations Inc. and Amanda Cockrell
Published by arrangement with Book Creations Inc., Canaan, New York,
Lyle Kenyon Engel, Founder
Library of Congress Catalog Card Number: 99-96434
ISBN: 0-380-79550-7
www.harpercollins.com

First Avon Books Printing: March 2000

AVON TRADEMARK REG. U.S. PAT. OFF. AND IN OTHER COUNTRIES, MARCA REGISTRADA, HECHO EN U.S.A.

Printed in the U.S.A.

WCD   10 9 8 7 6 5 4 3 2 1

For Karen Franklin

INTRODUCTION

YOU WILL NOT FIND IN THIS STORY, OR IN ITS PREDECESSORS, any real nation of either the southwestern pueblos or the Great Plains. When important things happen, myths are made, and myth has a landscape of its own that crosses ours at will. So the people of Red Earth City, and those of the Buffalo Horn and the Dry River, are all people and no people at once. They are the ones that Coyote made up when he made up this story. Tomorrow he will make up someone new, and we will dance to that dance for a while.

Look for him, blowing dust off the bookshelves, and you may find some of the following: the trickster is a universal incarnation in world mythology, and he likes to live in an animal body—in Europe as Reynard the Fox and in Africa and the West Indies as Anansi the Spider. In North America he is mostly Old Man Coyote, boastful and crafty, creator of the world, shaper of mankind, sprinkler of the stars and general troublemaker.

Ask him his name and you will hear only an undulating song, a chorus of yelps and warbles and howls flowing across the foothills in the late afternoon light. As the wild lands retreat from our knowing, he holds them between his gray paws

1

for us. He procreates, and replenishes the earth. Because he is Life, he is also Death, and, conscienceless, he will eat what falls into his jaws.

If you drive through the desert at dusk, he may stick his head out from behind a rock: *Canis latrans*, the little yellowy-gray wolf who takes his name from the Aztec *coyotl*, with a chicken hanging from his jaws. He has survived the incursions of white men upon his territory because Coyote eats anything, including bumblebees and leather shoelaces. He likes melons, porcupines, mice and dead buzzards, chickens and leather gloves left unattended. His job in the world is to recycle everything, occasionally like a retriever presenting you with tokens you don't want: bits of embarrassing old stories, piles of bones you recognize. Paw through the scraps outside his den and you will find old love letters, broken hearts, the recipe for dynamite.

Coyote still inhabits the late twentieth century, telling new twentieth-century, and now twenty-first-century, stories about himself. And because time is fluid, he may tell old tales today, and have told today many years ago.

PROLOGUE

Horse Magic

YOU DON'T ALWAYS KNOW IT'S COYOTE RIGHT OFF THE BAT. Once he was two women selling a book on how to engage the Flow, and he brings the people in Sedona a lot of things. This time he had on a three-piece gray suit and expensive boots and he was drinking espresso in Starbuck's.

It was one of those days when the worlds cross. Most people live in at least two worlds anyway. That day the people were watching the Fourth of July parade outside the window. They could see his BMW parked next to the dusty pickups that lined the street, and beyond that, riders going by on horses with big silver-mounted saddles. The riders wore sombreros and serapes, and the women were got up like Spanish señoritas in flounced skirts. Some art gallery had a flatbed truck with big sculpture on it, metal things like Hopi kachinas. Behind them was another truck carrying Washington crossing the Delaware. The Boy Scouts had a color guard, and the paramedics had brought their new ambulance. On a day like that anything might sit down next to you.

A palomino gelding high-stepped past outside, carrying a teenage girl in a fancy rodeo outfit.

"At first they were not toys," Coyote said scornfully into

3

his espresso, and everyone knew he meant the horses.

"They still aren't, to some of us." A boy in blue jeans watched the girl resentfully. She bounced in the saddle. To desert people, horses are still how you get to where trucks don't like to go.

"First, even before that, they were magic," Coyote said, "because not everyone had them." He tilted his chair backward, and there were the horses, grazing just over his left ear. They swished their long tails in the grass, a white one and a sorrel and a spotted colt. You could see through them to the woman buying a latte at the counter, but they were there.

"Magic always makes trouble." Coyote grinned, and everyone knew how that would have been. They would be like magnets or little jars of light. People would want them, the way you want a gold bird, or the wind . . .

The horses in the walled courtyard wear leather saddles, their feet heavy with iron shoes, and they nibble at the thin straw that litters the mud floor, mouthing it past metal bits. One of Coyote's children slinks past the courtyard gate, ears pricked, and the horses shift warily on their big feet. Coyote edges past them, giving the horses a wide berth because they don't like him and their feet are hard. But there is something new to be seen here, and Coyote is watching it because that is his job. The new thing is inside the house that opens onto the courtyard. It has a sharp, acrid smell, sharper even than the smell of the horses or the strange men. Coyote noses at the door and pushes it open. The men inside are eating, leaning back in wooden chairs, their feet on a trestle table. Coyote watches them, head cocked, until they turn around. Then there is a shout, and a pot clangs against the doorframe. Coyote jumps back.

"Mother of God, did you see that?"

Another shout and a loud bang, a crack like thunder shut up inside the room. The air is filled with the new smell. Coyote flattens his ears and runs, his nose burning.

"In the beginning," Coyote said, "there were only a handful of horses among the people who lived on the sea of grass. The horses spoke Buffalo in the grass and Red Deer in the mountains. They spoke a little Dog to the ones who lived with the People. They didn't speak Coyote because they weren't wild, and they didn't come from here."

The boy started to protest, and Coyote said, "That other story is a lot of hooey. That story about horses getting loose from the Spanish, and growing into wild herds on the plains, and how people caught them. A few got loose—maybe—and someone found one of those. But not more. Those Spanish made lists of everything—they counted more things than the Maya—lists of guns and lists of wine casks and lists of how many sacks of meal. Lists of their horses, and probably lists of their boots and underwear. When you have to bring it all across the ocean on a ship, you know how much you have of things. If you have lost some horses you write it down in your reports."

"So where did they all come from?" the boy asked him, arms folded. He liked the old story about the wild horses on the plains.

"Oh, from the Spanish," Coyote said airily. "People stole them off the picket line. Maybe they bought some. Maybe they bought some more from other people who stole them." He held out his coffee cup, and a waitress came over and brought him another. They usually don't do that. "I'll tell you all about it." You could see his teeth, white and pointed in his muzzle, behind his gray mustache. His long fingernails were manicured, and his hair smelled like something expensive. Everyone wondered what was in the leather briefcase on the floor.

The boy looked as if he wanted to argue with him. But the story came up out of Coyote's espresso, rising on the steam like thin ghost horses who shook themselves into solidity so that there they were again, cropping the grass . . .

On the Grass, time has passed since the first two-legged people brought horses out of the red desert country. Now those people's great-grandchildren ride the horses' great-grandchildren.

It is still a fine world on the Grass. The tribes of the Grass are of the wandering kind, not a people to be penned under mud roofs any more than the buffalo who exist to feed them. They clothe themselves in fringed leggings and dresses of doe-

skin or buffalo cowhide, whitened to the color of milk from being scrubbed clean with chalk. They ornament their clothes and shoes with embroidery made from porcupine quills and bits of blue stone from the mountains in the west or shells from the coast. The older children mostly run naked, and the babies they carry in cradleboards decorated with colored quills and passed from mother to daughter. Their houses are tents of buffalo hide, painted with running deer or herds of buffalo, with red and yellow suns and wavy rivers.

They keep dogs for hunting companions and to pull the dog travois when the tribe moves on. Sometimes a man may own a tame eagle or a raven, and a child might carry a horned toad in a pouch and feed it bugs. When a new animal came into the world, they were the first to see what it was good for, to learn to ride on its back and make an even bigger travois for it to carry their tents.

But in such a short time the horses changed everything. They turned the world upside down just by being. Now the horse riders can kill enough buffalo in one hunt to feed them all season, and they have leisure to make songs and horse dances danced around the fires on equinox and solstice nights, under horsehead caps and horsetail banners. Now, for a while, they have time to tell stories and make art, ever more elaborately decorated dresses and shirts, intricate baskets, fine painted buffalo hide tents.

The other peoples of the buffalo grass, who do not have horses, can see these things. See and want. Their yearning for horses has grown until it is a live thing, like a weasel biting them.

1

Horse Dance

THE DRY RIVER PEOPLE KNEW THE SMALLNESS OF THEIR OWN horse herds and the numbers of the Buffalo Horn people's. At night when two of their scouts lay belly-down on the bluff above the Buffalo Horn Midsummer Camp, they could see the white and spotted hides like milk in the moonlight, the flicker of a moon-shot eye where a darker horse lifted its head. They could hear the drums of the Horse Dance.

"We could steal them now," Mud Turtle said hopefully.

Spotted Colt shook his head. "The best ones will be in the dance." Spotted Colt lay with his chin on his hands, watching the dance and thinking what it would be like to be four-legged. The tribal Old Man, old Rabbit Dancer, had named him when he became a man, but Spotted Colt had always known his father had put him up to it. His father thought it would make horses come to the Dry River herd if his son was one.

It might be interesting, Spotted Colt thought (he had been taught to think about things). You would only have to worry about eating grass and running, about horse business, not people business, which involved getting things. Ordinarily the Dry River people didn't concern themselves with getting things; there was enough on the Grass to provide anything a reason-

7

able person would want. There was the sun to hunt under and make the grass grow, and the moon to lie in the grass under with pretty girls. There were berries and onions, and turtles and fish in the streams, and enough buffalo for meat and tents and clothes. Only since the horses had come had it become clear that there was a way of getting *more* of those things.

Anyone could see that a horse could carry a woman and her gathering baskets farther than she could walk, and carry back even more than a dog travois. A horse could take his hunter to the buffalo when the buffalo changed their graze. And then a horse could run down the herd and its rider could send arrow after arrow into the humped backs and kill enough to last all season. And then there would be more time for thinking about things, and studying the skies and the sun's slow dance and thinking about why the world was made, which was the proper business of the Dry River people. That was what his father said.

Spotted Colt wriggled farther out on the edge of the bluff, counting the men in the Buffalo Horn camp. A dog that had been rooting in the midden turned its head toward him, silhouetted by firelight, and he froze. The dog seemed to be tasting the air, but unless the wind shifted, Spotted Colt didn't think it could smell him. He eyed the Horse Dancers circling around the horse-headed man at their center. The white head bobbed up and down. Old Rabbit Dancer wanted them to bring the head back, too, because it was old and holy and it would give the Dry River people horse magic.

The dog turned away, and Spotted Colt let his breath out slowly. Like the Dry River people, the Buffalo Horn fought for their own amusement when there was no other reason for it, so the young men could get a reputation. They liked fighting, and it might be well for the Dry River men to steal their horses when they were tired.

"There are a lot of them," Mud Turtle said gloomily.

"There are a lot of us." Spotted Colt felt excitement ripple along his arms. "We will get big reputations." He grinned, and Mud Turtle rolled his eyes.

Spotted Colt was always ready to do unwise things. His hair hung in two long braids, and for decoration he had added to his eagle feathers four red feathers that a trader had brought up from the south last autumn. No one knew what kind of magic they had, but Spotted Colt said it was bound to be useful if it was new, and stuck them in his hair.

Now he wriggled backward, sliding away from the cliff on his belly until he was far enough away to stand up. Their horses were tethered behind the bluff, two of the Dry River band's precious few, already painted red and black with battle paint. Spotted Colt swung up onto his and waited for Mud Turtle. Despite Mud Turtle's cautious nature and the fact that he bumped along on his stallion's back, he was a fine trainer. Mud Turtle talked to horses. Stolen horses followed him.

The gray coyotes who lived in dens at the foot of the bluff saw the rest of the Dry River men waiting up the valley, while the Buffalo Horn horses shimmered in their rope paddock. They pricked up their ears with interest. When the two-leggeds got their weapons out, there was usually something to eat left over afterward.

Down below, the hide tents of the Buffalo Horn people dotted the grass of Midsummer Camp, glowing like cones of light with the fires inside.

Anything might come out of a night like this, Dances thought, while the little Horse Dance fires winked like eyes all along the riverbank, and in their center the great Horse Fire threw undulating shadows along the dance ground. The coyotes sat in the tall grass outside the camp, watching, but the dogs ignored them so long as they stayed out of the midden, which was the dogs' property. There was not a lot of difference between the coyotes and the people's dogs anyway, except that the dogs were tame.

In the center of the Grass there was a thin line between the wild lands and the tame, like the line between being a child and being not a child. The cloak of wildness hung in the air, shot through with stars. You could wear it if you knew how, Dances thought. She shifted her feet in the grass on the edge of the sacred ground, even though this wasn't a woman dance. It was hard to remember the things she was supposed to do and not to do on a night like this. Her eldest brother danced by, capering solemnly at the center of the pattern, and she clamped her hands resentfully to her backside and glowered at him to let him know she was too old to be smacked like a baby. *You should be sorry,* she thought at him.

Freckled Rat glared back at her from under the horse-head cap. She was also too old to paint a person's feet red while he was sleeping, so that he woke up and scared himself to death. And it was Horse Dance night, which made it worse, playing tricks at an important time. The spirals tattooed on his cheeks seemed to frown at her, too, from under the horse's teeth.

Dances took her hands off her backside and stuck her fingers in her nose and made a face at him, but she did it after his back was turned. Freckled Rat was an important Horse Dancer, the oldest of her brothers, who were all descended from the Horse Bringers on both sides. Because of that he got to wear the Horse Mask, which had been made from First Horse's skull when he died. It used to be a silky white, but it had yellowed with age, and now it had bald places where the hair was rubbed off. That didn't matter. It was very holy and magical, and if Freckled Rat cursed her while he was wearing it, no good might come of it.

The old men were playing the drums, patting out the rhythm with their fingertips, quietly at first, then louder, like hoofbeats coming over the ground. The women swayed on the edge of the dance ground, singing the Horse Song.

"That was mannerless," Cactus Wren hissed in Dances' ear between verses. Dances sniffed rebelliously and Cactus Wren frowned. Cactus Wren, who was married, took it upon herself to discipline Youngest Sister when she needed it, which was often.

Youngest Sister favored Cactus Wren with a baleful sideways pout. Four of Mother's babies had died between the oldest four and the youngest two, so that the older ones were all grown and important now and all thought they ought to annoy her when they had nothing else to do.

The music spun the dancers in and out of the fire and smoke and made Dances forget Cactus Wren. The other dancers circled around Freckled Rat, feet stamping, heads tossing, leading their horses into the spiral of the dance. The horses' hides were painted with suns and wavy lines of water, all the things that made life grow. The Horse Dance was about growing more horses, increasing the herd of First Horse's children.

Dances' brothers jumped up on their horses' backs. The fire glowed off their eyes, and all their manes and hair were tied with sweetgrass and grain. Only Freckled Rat was dismounted, and as the pattern spun around him, it became harder to tell who was horse and who was rider, who four-legged and who two-legged. In the dance, all were Six-Legged, First Horse-Bringer.

If she closed her eyes, Dances could put herself into that wild spiral, riding on someone's sleek back. It was like sitting on top of the wind. Dances rode better than anyone but her brother Blue Jay, and she couldn't imagine life before the horses came. She would hate to be a Tortoise person, or any of those foot-to-earth hunters who didn't have horses. Only the Buffalo Horn people, Dances' people, had horses—except for the Dry River people, who stole horses.

It had not taken many generations for the horses to dance themselves into the life of the Buffalo Horn people, not many years to become six-legged. The descendants of the Horse Bringers were as important among the Buffalo Horn as Red-and-Yellow Dog, the chieftain, stamping his big feet in the Horse Dance, or Eats Air, the shaman, his thin arms raised to the flames of the Horse Fire. More so, maybe, because their position was hereditary, but anyone might be chieftain or a have a vision spirit teach him bear magic. Because she was a Child of the Horse and could ride any of the wild colts, a lot of boys would want to marry Dances, just as they had Cactus Wren.

Dances sniffed.

Cactus Wren was respectable now, but she had gone walking with all those young men while she made up her mind, and lovesick boys had sat outside their tent all night playing the flute.

Dances herself had been a woman just since last year, and boys' fathers were already talking to Mother about her. Mother was too old to be reliable, Freckled Rat said, and the family ought to let him handle matters, since Father was dead, but no one listened. It didn't matter if Mother forgot where her tent was or called her children by the wrong names; she was still Eldest.

Dances patted her feet to the hoofbeats in the drums. She didn't want to get married anyway. Not yet. She wanted to go on an adventure first, the way Great-Grandmother Wants the Moon, the Horse Bringer, had done. Women didn't have adventures, Cactus Wren said, and every time she did, Dances brought up Great-Grandmother Wants the Moon.

"That was in the far-off times," Cactus Wren told her.

"It wasn't. Old Grandmother Weevil remembers her."

"Old Grandmother Weevil is older than Mother and Aunt Blue Heron combined," Cactus Wren said. "She remembers Coyote putting up the stars."

Blue Jay, who was Youngest Brother, trotted by on his black horse and winked at Dances just before he melted into the spiral of the dancers again. Cactus Wren clucked her tongue. No one disciplined Blue Jay, either, and he encouraged Dances. They were like twins, a year apart, allied against their older siblings.

Rebelliously, Dances thought of the girl who had killed the Flying Head, and the boy who had saved his people from the Man-Eagle Monster. According to the people from the cities who traded meal for buffalo skins, there were still monsters in the west country. They ate people and made people work for them, so it didn't seem to Dances that the world was so old that nothing new happened in it.

Only in Great-Grandmother Wants the Moon's time, horses had come up out of the river. Dances tipped her head back so she could see the stars. They were bright because it was nearly dark-of-the-moon, and they looked like a far-off village, like somewhere you could go. She hung her head down her back, nearly overbalancing, and imagined riding up the trail to them, to see who lived there.

Cactus Wren poked her, and she flailed her arms. "Pay attention! Uncle will see you."

Dances made herself look dutiful. The horses thundered by, galloping around and around the Horse Fire until it looked as if their tails were made of sparks. The Buffalo Horn people's Uncle had brought them the horses. He was very powerful, but he was also always hungry and you didn't want him to think about you. He carried a big club, and when he roared, the earth shook. Eats Air, the shaman, who had bear magic and knew these things, said that when you heard the horses galloping, you heard Uncle's voice. Aunt Blue Heron said when you heard yourself shouting at someone, that was Uncle's voice, too.

The sleek bodies pounded past, and Dances thought that if she leaped into their midst she could catch Blue Jay's hand and he would pull her up with him. But she knew if she did she would disgrace everyone, and they would have to start the dance all over again and Eats Air would make her stay in a brush hut and purify herself by being hungry for a long time. She had had to do that only last moon when she had slipped into Freckled Rat's tent and tried on the white horse-head.

The horses circled the fire like living thunder. She yearned for them. All around the dance ground the women and the old men sang, calling to the long-legged colts who lived in the sky, telling them to come live among the Buffalo Horn's herds. Finally the horses slowed, and their great bodies gave off a warm steam in the cool air. It was like a storm passing overhead and diminishing, all that energy slowing, slowing, rippling into a heavy stillness, the air still sharp with where it had been. The circle of women parted to let the riders through, and the old men's drums pattered into stillness.

Dances knew she couldn't talk to Blue Jay until he had taken off his dance paint and put Black Water Horse back into the herd, so she waited restlessly by the young men's tent for him. When she saw Cactus Wren, she ducked behind the tent.

It wasn't respectable for a girl who was old enough to marry to be hanging around the young men's tent like a slut. That was what Cactus Wren said. Dances crossed her eyes at Cactus Wren's back and slipped out of the shadows again as Blue Jay came up, his rope bridle in his hand, with three of the other young dancers. Boys who hadn't married lived together in tents of their own, while girls stayed with their mothers. Dances' mother got up in the night sometimes and Dances had to find her, but she didn't think she would like living in the boys' tent—it smelled even from outside.

The other young men went inside, and Blue Jay put his finger against his lips and ducked in after them. He came out again with a ball of yucca soap, and they walked away from the boys' tent with Blue Jay tossing the soap from hand to hand. Dances sat on the riverbank and listened to the water splash over the stones while he scrubbed his face. Blue Jay had no tattoos on his cheeks yet, but Dances was sure it wouldn't be long before he earned the right in a fight, maybe with the Dry River people, and then she would be allowed to have them, too, because she was his sister.

Clean, Blue Jay sat beside her, and they listened to the river and the snorts and snuffles of the horses in their rope paddock. The night air still seemed thick with magic. After a moment Blue Jay croaked like a frog, and the frogs in the reeds answered him, all at once, in little peeps of consternation.

Dances laughed. "They think you are a big frog, come to take their frog wives."

"Why is Freckled Rat so angry with you?"

"Oh." Dances studied the shadows of her toes, tucked in her good quill-embroidered shoes, thinking of the best way to tell him so he would appreciate it properly. "I had some red paint left over from the robe I'm painting for you. That bright kind that's sort of blood color. Freckled Rat was asleep with his shoes off and his feet sticking out from under the blankets. His tent flap was wide open. I thought he would wake up when the brush tickled his feet, but he didn't, so I painted them all the way up his ankles."

Blue Jay snorted.

"When he woke up, he thought someone had cut his feet off. You should have heard him roar. Then he was embarrassed and pretended he hadn't." .

"He said he lost his temper and smacked you."

"He did," Dances said resentfully.

"Well, now he's sorry for that. His wife's going to have that baby any day now—have you seen her? She looks like a melon—and now he thinks he's going to be a bad father because he can't keep his temper with you. He thinks you ought to be married."

"I don't want to be married. You aren't married."

"Fine Day would marry you. So would Spotted Snake."

"Field Mouse would marry you," Dances retorted. "I don't see you taking her brothers a horse."

"She has two brothers," Blue Jay said. "I'd have to give them each a horse."

"I have four brothers," Dances said.

Blue Jay chuckled. "So it's a wonder anyone wants to marry you."

"They don't have to give me horses," Dances said. "Lots of people give buffalo blankets and things they get from traders."

"No, but I have to give horses," Blue Jay said. "That's because we're the Horse's children. People expect it."

"You just don't want to get married." Dances was satisfied with that.

"Not now," Blue Jay said. They listened to the night some more. The people in the camp were making going-to-bed noises, and Old Grandmother Weevil's granddaughter came down the path to the water to fill a skin jug for her.

"I have to make Mother some sleepy tea," Dances said, remembering. "She asked me before the dance and I got it from Aunt Blue Heron." She patted the pouch that hung at her waist, over her doeskin dress, yawning. "I don't know why old people can't sleep. I always can."

"You could sleep through the Big Thunder," Blue Jay said. "You snore, too."

"I do not!"

"You don't snore as loudly as Fine Day." Blue Jay compared remembered snores. "He sounds like bears fighting."

"Maybe I used to snore," Dances conceded. "When I was small. I don't now."

"Oh."

"I don't!"

"Fine Day wouldn't mind. Maybe you *should* marry him."

She swatted his ear. Blue Jay laughed and grabbed her around the middle to tickle her, but her shriek was cut in half by the sounds from the camp. They sat up, hearts pounding, frozen into immobility. Hoofbeats drummed past, and angry shouts rose over them. The silhouette of a horseman crossed the dying Horse Fire.

Blue Jay jumped up, dumping Dances in the rocks. "Stay here!" he shouted at her over his shoulder.

"I won't!" She pounded through the darkness after him. Between the tents, men were running back and forth with

spears and bows, and there were men she hadn't seen fighting
with them. *Dry River people!* Dances thought.

Blue Jay snatched up his spear, which was the only one left
in the young men's tent. Fine Day and Spotted Snake and the
rest were all fighting the Dry River men, and he ran after them.

There was a mêlée around the horse pen. Someone had cut
the rope, and the horses were milling loose. The Dry River
men, on their own horses, were trying to drive the loose ones
up the valley. A horse careened past Blue Jay, and he caught
its rider by the foot and pulled him off. The man landed with
a thump on the ground and knocked Blue Jay down with him
while the horse neighed and swerved away.

Spear in hand, Blue Jay clawed his way to his feet before
the man could get off all fours. He drove the spear through
the Dry River man's back while the man was still on his hands
and knees. Blood spurted out of the hole. It splashed his face,
sticky and warm, and Blue Jay staggered back, gagging. It
was in his eyes. Another Dry River man rode at him, and Blue
Jay turned and ran, scrubbing his arm across his eyes. The Dry
River man laughed at him in the darkness. Blue Jay turned
murderously, his spear leveled. The Dry River man guided his
horse expertly past the spear's end, tapped Blue Jay with his
own, and vanished into the herd, snapping a rope at the loose
horses. Blue Jay threw his spear after him and a horse stepped
on it, cracking the shaft.

The women and children were running among the herd now,
hacking at the Dry River men with spears and knives and
trying to catch the horses. Blue Jay saw Dances on her red
mare, herding the loose ones back. A Dry River rider galloped
by, the foam from his horse's mouth flecking the dark air.
Cactus Wren, on foot, threw her belt knife at the rider. He
swayed, the blade sticking out of his shoulder, but he didn't
fall.

The invaders were yipping like coyotes, chasing loose
horses and trying to run down the Buffalo Horn fighters who
were still on foot. Freckled Rat was mounted now, the rein in
his teeth and his bow drawn, but it was hard to aim in the
darkness without hitting the horses.

In the camp a tent had caught fire, and as Blue Jay watched

openmouthed, another one exploded in flames. Rolling Bear, who was war chief, shouted an order, and the youngest men left the horses and ran for the tents. Blue Jay cursed, tripping over tent poles, his belt knife in his hand. He blundered in the darkness, ran across a rope, and fell flat, sprawling on his face, chest hurting. When he stood up again, Fine Day and Spotted Snake had found three men setting fires and were chasing them, dodging between the tents.

The invaders' torches bobbed ahead of him as they tore open tents. Blue Jay caught up to one when the man stopped to fight with Grandmother Weevil's granddaughter, who was swinging a piece of firewood at him. Blue Jay jumped on his back and hacked at his throat with the belt knife. The Dry River man sprawled on the ground, fighting Blue Jay's hands, and the granddaughter stuck the fallen torch in his hair. The Dry River man shrieked as the flames engulfed his head and Blue Jay sawed the stone knife across his throat. He and the granddaughter looked at each other over the body, breathing hard. Then the edge of the tent behind her went up in flames, and she ran to beat it out with her hands.

Blue Jay ducked through the flap into the smoke and dragged Grandmother Weevil out by her feet. The granddaughter upended a cook pot on the flames, which sizzled and went out, leaving a charred hole in the hide.

Beyond the tents, the Dry River leader gave a sharp shriek like a gull's. The Dry River riders turned their horses, hooves pounding away into the dark. They left two of their dead behind, and another lay with his head on his horse's withers while Spotted Colt led him in a gallop up the valley. They were driving five horses ahead of them and two of their own, riderless.

The Buffalo Horn rounded up the loose horses while the bereaved wailed and washed their dead in the thin dawn light. The Dry River dead they put outside the circle of the camp for the obliging coyotes. The Buffalo Horn ghosts drifted among the ashes and the wreckage of the camp while the Dry River spirits fluttered in little circles, confused, above the churned-up ground.

Grandmother Weevil sat beside her charred tent and directed her granddaughter to stack their belongings outside where they could be inspected. The granddaughter piled her possessions around her, and she poked at them with a stick and sniffed them for smoke until she could hardly be seen among the buffalo robes and dresses, the heaped medicine bags and sewing boxes, the family cradleboard and her bed of straw and turkey feathers. The bed was blackened at one end and smelled of burned feathers.

"So many things," Dances' mother said, looking across their fire. "Should we look at ours, do you think?"

"Our tent wasn't on fire," Dances said. She poured her mother's sleepy tea into a gourd cup and scrubbed at her face with the back of her hand because she was still crying.

"But you never know what has happened," Mother said, worried. She rubbed her hands together. "Your father wouldn't have let this happen." She had been awake all night, thinking that he had been in the fighting.

The Dry River men hadn't found the horse head, and Eats Air had put it up on a pole. He and Aunt Blue Heron were making prayers to it, apologizing. To Dances it looked angry and afraid, like an abandoned child.

"I thought you had forgotten to come back," Mother said now. "All that commotion after the dance."

Dances closed her eyes. She had tried to find a spear and help, but it was like running through a bad dream, and the horse she was riding had stumbled over the body of a boy she knew. This wasn't the kind of story adventure she wanted. "They were stealing our horses," she said to Mother. "I told you."

"No, you didn't," Mother said, sipping her tea. "That was Cactus Wren."

"It was me." Dances didn't know why she argued with Mother. It didn't do any good, and it was easier not to, Blue Jay said. She wiped her eyes again. None of her brothers had been killed, or even hurt, and when Freckled Rat had found her with a muddy face, crying over the body of the boy, he had picked her up and taken her to Mother.

Now she watched the faint white smoke that sifted in little wisps from the dying fires and wondered if she could see the dead people's spirits in it, and where they went. North to the Hunting Ground of the Dead, the old men said. She wondered what the horses thought about it all.

The horses rolled their eyes in the dark and shivered because they didn't like the blood. They could smell it on the wind, and it frightened them. They swiveled their ears at the noises in the grass and waited for people to come and find them again.

2

The Peccaries

BEYOND THE GRASS, IN THE RED DESERT COUNTRY, WERE THE Cities-in-the-West, where people didn't live foot-on-trail like the wanderers of the Grass. They lived properly, as civilized people should (Green Gourd Vine's mother said), in great communal houses of clay and stones, three and four stories high. All the doors were on the second floor, off the flat rooftops of the first. Occasional stairs zigzagged up from the first-floor roofs, and in between, ladders leaned against the walls. The women of Red Earth City washed their houses' outer face with a final coat of slip mixed with chopped straw so that from a distance the city glittered like mica in the sun. Some said that was what had drawn the pale kachinas, but no one really knew.

Beyond the walls were fields full of squash and sun-colored pumpkins, maize, beans, melons, and rows of cotton that the men wove into shirts and blankets. The women made pottery painted black and white and ground the maize into meal. The year was divided by the Bean Dance and the Maize Dance and governed by the wisdom of Turquoise Old Man in winter and Squash Old Man in the summer. In Red Earth City, things were still as they had been since the Ancestors came down

20

from the cliffs, but lately the pale kachinas had come to dance on the edge of the world, and stories were beginning to be told of them that disturbed the Two Old Men.

Green Gourd Vine was in the kitchen with her mother and Five Clay Pots, her mother's best friend, watching the men from Bean Canyon going down into the kiva below with Turquoise Old Man and Squash Old Man. Their faces were solemn, like a shadow drifting hawk-shaped across the flat courtyard.

"Come away from the window," Cattails, her mother, said, "and stop gawking. You'll fall out."

"I want to know about the pale kachinas." Green Gourd Vine hung out the window, her stomach resting on the sill.

"Tch!" Five Clay Pots made a noise with his teeth. "Don't talk about them." He smoothed his skirts. "Come here and I will teach you to make flat bread so thin you can see through it."

"They are living in Bean Canyon City," Green Gourd Vine said.

Five Clay Pots made a sign with crossed fingers. Cattails shook her head disapprovingly at her daughter.

"That won't keep them away," Green Gourd Vine muttered. She wanted to see one, a horrible fascination like looking at a snake. The pale kachinas were living in Bean Canyon City now, like rats or bugs that had got in the kitchen, and no one could make them go away. No one knew where they had come from. They had just been there one day, riding on horses, which the Red Earth people had begun to see once in a while since the first ones had come and been driven away because they made people crazy. There were rumors that in other places they had killed people, but that had been in the Grandfathers' times, and no one was sure now. Then they had gone away, and now they were back.

Five Clay Pots was pouring maize batter onto a hot stone griddle. "Like this," he said. "Quickly, quickly, and flip it before it burns."

Green Gourd Vine sighed and knelt down by the fire. She thought her flat bread looked fine, but Five Clay Pots could make his thinner than anyone's. Green Gourd Vine thought soft men like Five Clay Pots had some unfair magic that made them better women than women were. He wore his thick black hair knotted into elaborate squash blossom puffs on either side of his face, like Green Gourd Vine and Cattails. The cotton blanket over his shoulders and his long skirt were embroidered with bright red and yellow squash vines, and he wore a fringed red sash around his waist. He embroidered his clothes himself, and they were more beautiful than anyone else's. Sometimes he had a husband, but mostly not. He liked best to live alone, next door to Cattails and her family. Five Clay Pots slipped the flat bread from the griddle and rolled it into a thin flute shape with quick twists of his fingers. He handed Green Gourd Vine the bowl of batter. "You try it."

She ladled a circle of batter onto the griddle. When the edges were solid, she lifted it between fingertips and burned her fingers. The flat bread flopped in a crumple like an old squash blossom while she sucked her fingers.

Five Clay Pots sighed. "It is necessary to keep your mind on the task at hand."

"I don't see how you can," Green Gourd Vine said, still sucking her fingers. "Don't you want to know what they're saying?"

"No," Five Clay Pots said, lips compressed, then relented. "We will be told, child."

"Hush!" Cattails said. She and Green Gourd Vine both reached for the bowl of batter again at the same time. If you talked about something, you might call it. Better not to.

The batter spat on the griddle.

"The child may be right," Five Clay Pots said. "They haven't gone away because we didn't think about them. Now they are in Bean Canyon."

Bean Canyon was a comfortable distance away. Green Gourd Vine's father, Squirrel, had been in the cotton field, mending the irrigation ditches, when the Bean Canyon Old Men had come. He had gone into the kiva with the Buffalo Horn's own Old Men and the Holy Clowns and the priests of the kachina and medicine societies, because if the Bean Canyon Old Men had come all this way, it was important. But Bean Canyon was a long way away. They all told themselves that when thoughts of the pale kachinas crept into their heads.

Cattails burned her own fingers on the griddle, and Five

Clay Pots shook his head. "It is not a day to teach the child when you burn yourself."

"I'm not a child," Green Gourd Vine muttered rebelliously.

"Only to us, dear." Five Clay Pots patted his wrinkled cheek. "The older we get, the younger you look."

"She's old enough to marry, and I don't know what we'll do." Cattails shook her head at the bright air outside the window, as if encompassing the immediate world in her gaze. "These days, who can find the right young man?"

"You wouldn't want relatives in Bean Canyon." Five Clay Pots sighed, commiserating. Red Earth girls brought their husbands home to live with their Red Earth in-laws, but the connection meant you owed the husband's relatives something in bad times.

Green Gourd Vine kicked the wall under the window, to which she had returned. "I don't see how I'll ever marry anybody here. We're related to half of them." The complicated matrilineal clan system that defined the families of Red Earth City didn't allow marriage into the father's clan, either, and the clans were large. There were only four in the city, which left two to pick a husband from. Red Earth adolescents had always married into and out of other cities, but in these times no one wanted to stray into the path of interesting events. No one was sure what the white kachinas were, but no one thought it good to have them in their house.

"*Mother!*" Green Gourd Vine's younger sisters and little brother pattered up the clay stairs outside and slithered down the ladder from the roof. They landed on the kitchen floor with a thump.

"Gently." Five Clay Pots caught Mouse by the collar of his shirt. "Slow down. You will fall in the fire."

"There were peccaries in the bean field. We drove them off with sticks, but one bit Toad."

Toad stuck her leg out, exhibiting a bleeding ankle.

"Tcha!" Cattails ran for her medicine bag.

Five Clay Pots inspected the ankle while Magpie and Mouse watched. "They are getting bolder. Nasty things. There never used to be so many of them."

Green Gourd Vine took Toad in her lap while her mother

cleaned the bite and rubbed a salve of pine pitch and yarrow on it.

Toad sniffled and bit her lip. "Nasty old things," she said. "They snuffle at you, and when you hit them with a stick, they poke their toothy old snouts at you."

"You need a longer stick," Green Gourd Vine told her, cuddling her.

"Is anyone in the bean field now?" Five Clay Pots asked.

"Yes, lots of people," Mouse said. "Some of the men came when we shouted, and they shot two of the peccaries. The others ran off."

"If it isn't monsters, it's peccaries," Cattails said. "Where are these things coming from?"

That evening the grown men went into the bean fields with bows, because the peccaries liked to eat at sundown. Raising any food was a constant battle with the animal people. Coyotes stole the melons and the green maize. In drought, the deer came down from the mountains and ate them, too. The Red Earth children picked bugs off the vines by hand and smashed them between stones. They frightened the crows off with rattles and flags of cloth. The peccaries ate anything that wasn't poisonous, and they knew the difference.

At dusk a coyote who had come by to see if the melons were ripe saw the peccaries rooting in the bean field. He backed up a little and lay down with his nose on his paws to watch. Pretty soon the two-legged people came out of the city, and the coyote flattened himself further into the shadows of a cottonwood seedling that had sprung up in a cleft where the irrigation channel ran around a big rock. The peccaries snorted and snuffled through the bean hills, and an arrow whirred through the dusk. A peccary squealed and raced out of the beans, tail up, the arrow sticking out of its shoulder, flapping as it ran.

Coyote watched the other peccaries tearing up the beans with their sharp hooves as they bolted past. Something seemed to be running with them, but he couldn't tell what it was. It floated, like a transparent white cloth, just over them. The men shouted and threw stones.

Coyote sniffed the air. There was a faint acrid odor on the

wind, like the smell after lightning. He sniffed again and asked a small spider spinning her web in a bean vine, "What is that?"

"Something to stay away from," Spider said. "You'll singe your nose."

"It's something new," Coyote said. "I ought to go look at it."

"You looked at it in Bean Canyon." Spider dropped down on a line of silk and scuttled along the edge of her web, attending to a fly that was struggling in the strands. "It made a big noise," she said over the wrapped fly. "You ran away with your tail between your legs."

"I was only surprised," Coyote said. "It wouldn't frighten me again."

Spider's web was bigger now, gleaming milkily against the sky, and the men chasing the peccaries in the bean field were far away. Her legs straddled the world. "You brought those pale people here," she said.

"I didn't."

"Desire brought them here. Covetousness. Appetite." Spider took a few more turns around the fly. It made a neat package, like rolled flat bread. "Their desire. But yours, too."

"I didn't want *them.*"

"You gave their horses to a human person. Now all the human persons want horses."

"They don't want those pale things that came with them."

"You don't get to pick and choose. All thread gets woven." Spider let herself down a bit farther on a milky strand, and Coyote backed away a little. She was much larger than she had been in the bean vine.

"I don't remember making those pale things when I made the world," Coyote said sulkily.

"Maybe you made things you don't know about," Spider said. "Or maybe someone was somewhere else, making another world." She busied herself with the spokes of her web, adding three new ones to strengthen it, hooking the ends to stars.

Coyote sighed, a long breath out past his teeth. Grandmother Spider spoke for everything that was woven or braided or twined, and so the weavers of cloth and the weavers of baskets were particularly her children, but her web held all of

Life as well. Her tarantula children ate scorpions unafraid.

"Can't you make them go away?" Coyote asked her. "We could keep the horses."

"Those people you gave horses to are making war on each other over them now."

Coyote scratched a flea behind his ear, digging his back foot into the fur. "That isn't my fault. I gave the horses to the city people first, but they didn't want them. Anyway, the Grass people kill a lot of buffalo when they hunt with horses, and they're grateful. They leave me good things."

"They kill so much that now they are wasteful. When human people are *hungry,* on the other hand"—she gestured gracefully with three of hers—"they throw rocks at you, and your pups don't even get bones."

"That's what horses are good for. So there is always dinner. That's why I gave them to the human people."

Spider patted the rolled fly. It had stopped struggling. "My people put by for later. And my children catch dinner as soon as they're hatched," she added.

Coyote noticed there was an egg sac hanging on the stars of the Seven, just past the scalloped border of her web. It looked vast, bigger than the moon. He edged back a little more. "How big are those, when they come out?"

"The children of the Grass will go on leaving you things to eat," Spider said, ignoring him. The wind from the stars swayed the egg sac like a cradleboard in a tree.

"I take what I find," Coyote said complacently, thinking of buffalo offal and bones with the marrow still inside.

"The others will feed you, too, if they stay here. You may find things you haven't seen before in your dinner."

Spider's voice was tart, and Coyote flattened his ears. "Are *they* going to live here? I don't think that would be good."

"They're edible," Spider said. "You'll get used to them."

Green Gourd Vine went out with her mother and Five Clay Pots halfway through the night, to take her turn standing watch for the peccaries to come back. Growing food was the men's job, just as grinding and storing it was the women's, but when there was trouble, everyone came. Peccaries were stubborn, snouty, and greedy. If they found something they wanted, they were worse than grasshoppers. The women carried baskets full of rocks.

They didn't need torches. The moon was full and hung in the western sky like a round window. The beans and squash and maize looked ghostly in its light, the leaves whispering to themselves. Green Gourd Vine picked a rock out of the basket and stood between the bean hills, waiting for the snort and snuffling that would be the peccaries coming back. On a night like this, she thought that anything might come out of the waters of Stream Young Man, who flowed on the edge of the fields, or out of the black desert to the south, or maybe over the red hills that rose up in the east like the last wall of a many-roomed house, before the land grew wild in the Grass.

A rustling in the beans caught her ear, and she turned, rock in hand. It wasn't a peccary. It was a moonlight-colored coyote, eating beans. Tendrils of vine hung from its jaws.

Green Gourd Vine threw her rock anyway. "Listen to the Grass," it said, and was gone.

3

Something Wrong with the Wind

THE GHOSTS STAYED. FOR FOUR DAYS ONE WOULD EXPECT that, and the Buffalo Horn did all the right things, cutting their hair, and weeping, and slashing the calves of their legs. They built biers among the trees for the four men who had been killed and wrapped them in their tents while their families moved to new ones. Two had been married, and those men's wives each cut off two of their fingertips, howling and wailing around the biers. Eats Air cut the dead warriors' horses' manes and tails, too, and tied the long tail hairs to the poles of the biers. Rolling Bear cut the scalps off the Dry River men so that they couldn't go to the Hunting Ground of the Dead with the Buffalo Horn people—and in retrospect, that might not have been a good idea—but it seemed that no matter what they cut, it didn't snip the threads that bound the ghosts.

On the fourth day the dead were supposed to make their way to the next world, but Grandmother Weevil saw one with his head in her cook pot. Just the head, looking up at her. She thought it was the man her granddaughter had killed. She hit it with a log, and the hot broth splashed up and burned her face.

Rolling Bear found one sitting outside his tent, playing the flute, or so Rolling Bear said, but no one else heard it but Rolling Bear's daughter, which frightened Rolling Bear into burning the tent and moving to a new one. The ghost came with them. He was the boy who had been courting Rolling Bear's daughter.

Eats Air saw two of them—he couldn't tell who they were; they looked like smoke and he could see right through them—fighting each other by the midden, rolling on the ground with their hands in each other's eyes, rolling through the piles of bones and ash and broken shoes with holes in the bottoms.

Blue Jay saw one riding Black Water Horse. He shouted at it, and Black Water Horse turned and trotted toward him, and the ghost fell off into a pile of bones under Black Water Horse's hooves. When Blue Jay looked at it, it was fading into the grass. By the time he got Eats Air and Aunt Blue Heron to look at it, it was only a pile of cat bones.

Blue Heron, who was so old she had stopped bleeding and saw visions now, knelt and sifted the cat bones through her fingers. Her cut gray hair hung in her face—the youngest dead boy had been her grandson. "This was somebody," she said. "This is not a good place anymore."

Blue Heron and Eats Air went away to talk with Rolling Bear and Red-and-Yellow Dog, who was chieftain of the Buffalo Horn this season. In the morning the Buffalo Horn moved on, leaving the biers in the trees. The Buffalo Horn might come back to this place, but it was unlikely. They were a wandering people, and often a camp was not used again even the next year. Sometimes the relatives of the dead would come back, when the bodies had decayed and been cleaned by the eagle people. They would set the skulls in a circle, and after that when the Buffalo Horn passed by they would stop and talk with their dead, and wives would tell husbands the news and hold their grandchildren up for them to see. This camp they would leave alone.

It didn't matter. The ghosts trailed after the camp like lost children. Blue Jay found one riding behind him on his horse. The Dry River ghosts followed them, too, and sometimes when you found one in your soup or your blankets, you couldn't tell which it was. Red-and-Yellow Dog's wife found a rotting fish in his bed, and black mold appeared in the meal that had been bought for buffalo hides only two moons since.

The Buffalo Horn moved yet again, but the ghosts followed after, tumbling through the air and rustling the tall grass. At dusk they fell through the smoke holes into people's tents.

Spotted Colt saw them in the Dry River camp, not just the man he had led home on his horse, who had been dead when they got there, but the two they had had to leave behind, and others he thought might belong to the Buffalo Horn. They danced around the horse herd in the dawn, bones capering in the thin red light, until no one would go out there even when old Rabbit Dancer and Spotted Colt's father, Horse Stealer, who was chieftain, told them to.

Then Horse Stealer's best mare died foaling, and when they cut her open they found what should have been twin foals but was instead a tangled mass of eight legs and two heads. The old women took it away and buried it, and Horse Stealer moved the Dry River camp into the next valley.

The ghosts came along, the same ghosts who were living in the Buffalo Horn tents and leaving black rot in the meal. The mother of the Dry River man who had come home dead on his horse disappeared. In the Buffalo Horn camp, Rolling Bear's daughter walked away one morning, following her ghost, and they found her a day's ride up the valley, naked. They were bringing her home when Horse Stealer's emissaries came over the ridge from the east, carrying green branches in one hand and pipes in the other.

Rolling Bear drew rein. All the men around him had tensed, reaching for their bows. Eats Air held up a bony hand to shade his eyes, squinting to see if they were more ghosts. The feathers in his hair stuck out like wild wings.

Black Water Horse whickered when he smelled the Dry River horses, and Blue Jay thought that if they were ghosts, they were riding real horses. He smacked Black Water Horse's neck with his palm. "They are not friends. And not someone to go running off with."

Rolling Bear lifted his daughter, who was wrapped in a buffalo robe, onto the front of Eats Air's horse and motioned to Blue Jay and Freckled Rat to follow him and the rest to stay.

Three of Horse Stealer's men came down the ridge and waited for them. Blue Jay could see a little flurry of movement along the ridgetop, as if there were more up there. Rolling Bear waved to their own men to come a little closer, and the movement ceased.

The Dry River men had bare faces, and hair in braids wrapped in otter fur. There were yellow suns painted on their shirts.

"We have come to speak with your chieftain," the oldest of them said in the sign language that the people of the Grass used between tribes.

"Why?" Rolling Bear didn't look receptive. The tattooed circles on his cheeks looked closed and angry.

"We will speak of that to the chief."

"I am war chief."

The Dry River man thought. "We do not wish to speak of war. Therefore, we wish to speak to all your chiefs." He nodded at Rolling Bear for politeness' sake, to make sure he understood that this included him.

Blue Jay thought Rolling Bear might agree. Peace talks were not unheard of. In the old days, before the Buffalo Horn had horses, there were peace talks whenever different tribes wanted to hunt together or trade. But the Buffalo Horn wouldn't sell or trade their horses, and now they mainly traded with the city people in the west and not so much for things that other Grass peoples had. Rolling Bear compressed his lips in thought. Blue Jay stared at the Dry River men and wondered if any of them were the one who had counted coup on him and laughed. It had not been a good fight; it had not been the way fights were supposed to be. It was hard to say what they wanted now.

"Our chieftain will come with us and speak to yours," the Dry River emissary said.

Rolling Bear nodded at that. The Dry River man lifted his green branch and pipe, one in each hand, and turned his horse around with his knees. The three trotted back toward the ridge.

"What do you think they want?" Blue Jay hissed to Freckled Rat, as they rode back to where Eats Air was waiting with the others. He knew better than to ask Rolling Bear.

"You will know when they tell you." Freckled Rat frowned at his unseemly curiosity.

Blue Jay looked over his shoulder at the Dry River men. He thought he saw a ghost on the back on one of their horses, arms around the rider's waist.

"The Old Men say that our dead cannot leave us," Horse Stealer said with his hands. "They say the spirits have told them it is because we are fighting so much." He took a puff from the bone pipe laid across his knees, so they would know what he said was true, and handed the pipe to Red-and-Yellow Dog. They were in Red-and-Yellow Dog's tent.

Red-and-Yellow Dog sucked in a mouthful of smoke and considered. The Buffalo Horn people always fought. They were warriors. It was their business to fight—otherwise, how would the young men get a reputation? But he had found a dead toad outside his door flap this morning, and Eats Air had said something was wrong with the wind. Red-and-Yellow Dog hadn't understood that exactly, but Eats Air said it was blowing from the wrong place and wouldn't let dead people go where they should. Red-and-Yellow Dog's wife said it was because too many young men were dying; fighting was one thing, but so many getting killed was another, which was true. The Buffalo Horn warriors fought for sport, to count coup by touching the enemy and riding away. To show bravery was not simply to kill. Red-and-Yellow Dog blew the smoke out slowly and handed the pipe to Rolling Bear. Rolling Bear knew that, too.

"Why is it that our people fight?" Horse Stealer asked.

"Because you steal our horses," Rolling Bear said.

Horse Stealer nodded. "We would not fight otherwise?" He made it a question.

"Not so much," Red-and-Yellow Dog said.

"We are not going to give you our horses," Rolling Bear said.

"If we thought you were, we wouldn't have to steal them," Horse Stealer said wryly. "War is not the only way of the Dry River. We are people who think much. But horses are important now. Time will not go backward in this world. So now we must have horses, too."

"Not our horses," Rolling Bear said again.

The two men beside Horse Stealer opened their mouths at the same time, as if they were about to say something. Horse Stealer heard them breathing in and looked at each of them quickly, turning his head like an owl, until they subsided, frowning silently. "They do not remember that you do not understand our speech," he said in sign talk, his expression bland. After another moment's stillness, his hands asked, "Where do horses come from?"

"From other horses," Red-and-Yellow Dog said. He looked at Horse Stealer as if he were ignorant.

"Does this man have children?" Rolling Bear asked out loud.

"In the beginning," Horse Stealer said.

"In the beginning were the Horse Bringers," Red-and-Yellow Dog retorted. "I am a child of the Horse Bringers myself."

"Honor to the Horse Bringers," Horse Stealer said. "Where did they come from?"

"They were sent to us out of the river by Uncle." Red-and-Yellow Dog blew out a mouthful of smoke in honor of Uncle. "Also from the Cities-in-the-West. That is what they said." Legend and reality might be mutually incompatible and both still true.

Horse Stealer understood that. "How many horses?" he asked.

"Two."

Horse Stealer shook his head and made a tutting noise with his tongue. "Do you allow your young men to marry their sisters?" he inquired of Red-and-Yellow Dog.

Rolling Bear's brows jerked together, and his hands came up in an angry gesture. Red-and-Yellow Dog said quickly, "No. Do the Dry River?"

"Certainly not," Horse Stealer said. "We know, as the Buffalo Horn know, that is not good. It is not good for horses, either." He sat back, hands folded, to let that notion sink in. When Rolling Bear stopped glowering, Horse Stealer said, "I have talked to the traders who come from the Cities-in-the-West. They tell me there are horses there, and the horses travel with spirits who have hard, shiny skin—like men, only with shiny places."

Red-and-Yellow Dog considered that. The Horse Bringers had told of such creatures being seen just before they found First Horse. That was part of the First Horse Story. But no one but Grandmother Weevil was old enough to have actually heard it said by the Horse Bringers themselves.

"It is plain," Horse Stealer said, "that those shiny people are horse spirits. So we should send our young men together to the Cities-in-the-West and get horses from them. That is what they are there for, to give people horses."

Red-and-Yellow Dog and Rolling Bear stared at him. "Together?"

Horse Stealer waited for them to think about it. If the horses had come from the Cities-in-the-West, someone brave or crazy enough might go there and find more. Horse Stealer had looked at that idea from the top and bottom and all sides, and it still made sense to him. And if the young men went together, then their peoples would not fight while they were gone, and the Dry River people would still get horses. It was a fine idea, elegant and springy as new grass. Horse Stealer liked it.

Red-and-Yellow Dog put his head out through the tent flap. "Go and get Grandmother Weevil," he said to Blue Jay.

The other people who just happened to be outside the chieftain's tent went back to what they had been doing and tried to pretend they had not been listening, or trying to. When everyone spoke with their hands, you couldn't hear anything, Dances thought peevishly, trotting after Blue Jay to Grandmother Weevil's tent.

Mother called to her as she went by, but Dances pretended she hadn't heard Mother, either. She wanted to know what the chiefs and the Dry River chieftain were doing. The Dry River men who had ridden with him sat on their horses outside Red-and-Yellow Dog's tent, faces impassive. When Blue Jay came back, hustling Grandmother Weevil along, with Dances pattering behind, one of them said something to another behind his hand, and they both laughed silently, like coyotes.

Dances hopped from one foot to the other, waiting for Blue Jay to come out of Red-and-Yellow Dog's tent. When he did, she took him by the arm and dragged him away from the Dry River riders.

"What do they want with Grandmother Weevil?"

"I don't know."

"Yes, you do. They just said not to tell."

"They didn't say not to tell. I just didn't hear. They were asking her about Great-Grandmother Wants the Moon and Great-Grandfather Six-Legged. Then they saw me and said to go away."

"What did they want to know?"

"What was at the Cities-in-the-West. If the Horse Bringers were old and crazy when they told that story, or if it was true about the monsters, how they always said First Horse was a monster's horse."

"There was a Horse Bringer who was crazy," Dances said. "But he wasn't old. That's in the First Horse Story. He married a horse woman and had children in the herd."

"Hush!" Blue Jay said. The Dry River chieftain was coming out of Red-and-Yellow Dog's tent. The Dry River men outside sat up straighter. The Dry River chieftain looked around him, hands on his hips. He seemed satisfied. Red-and-Yellow Dog and Rolling Bear looked intent, as if they had lightning in their hair. Dances wondered what the Dry River chief had done to put it there.

Grandmother Weevil hobbled out of the tent, and all the chieftains made gestures of respect to her because she was old and knew things that no one else did.

The Buffalo Horn people began to gather around the chieftain's tent. Women put down their sewing and tucked their crawling babies into cradleboards or put them on their hips. Men who had been on the hunt turned and rode home. Some whisper in the air said there was news. Red-and-Yellow Dog waited for them while they gathered around him, coalescing like gathering dusk.

"We have made a treaty with the Dry River," Red-and-Yellow Dog said finally.

That whispered through the air until even the young men coming home from the hunt heard it, like a faint insect singing in their ears, and were outraged.

"This is a horse treaty," Red-and-Yellow Dog said. The Dry

River men smiled on their horses. They had known what Horse Stealer was coming to propose. They watched the Buffalo Horn young men roll the idea in their mouths.

"We have left too many of our young men on biers. Our old men, too. Their spirits have said this to me." Red-and-Yellow Dog sighed. The spirits had whispered in his ear all last night. And he had seen their bones dancing in the air over his bed while his wife slept. "They say there has been too much death for these horses. But they also say these horses have come to us and they are ours, so we may not let other people take them."

The Buffalo Horn nodded uneasily at that.

"There are horses in the Cities-in-the West," Red-and-Yellow Dog said. "All the traders who come this way tell us they have seen them, and seen the horse spirits who travel with them. It is as the Horse Bringers first said. Grandmother Weevil remembers this. So now we will send two of our young men, and the Dry River will send two of theirs, to find these horses and bring them back. Then we will fight for sport again, and the ghosts will go to the Hunting Ground of the Dead and not trouble us."

A collective intake of breath sucked a hole in the air around the Buffalo Horn people. "Which young men?" Freckled Rat demanded.

"That has not been decided." Red-and-Yellow Dog and Rolling Bear spoke at once, but their eyes lingered on Blue Jay, who rode better than anyone in the tribe and was a Child of the Horse, and unmarried, besides.

"I will send my son," the Dry River chieftain said with his hands. The Buffalo Horn people nodded their respect at that.

Dances' eyes narrowed. They were going to send Blue Jay and leave her here by herself. Blue Jay was going to have *her* story adventure. Her top teeth bit down hard on her lower ones. They were not going to do that.

"They're going to send you!" Dances looked fiercely at Blue Jay.

"Of course they are." Blue Jay's eyes were wide with the prospect. He looked at Dances and his face fell. "They will send me without you," he said mournfully.

"Take me with you."

"You're a girl."

"Yah, he has eyes to see," Dances said scornfully. "I ride better than anyone but you. And anyway, that's only because you're older. A little. Who caught Eats Air's horse after the Dry River men came, when he was afraid and nobody else could catch him? Who trained One Blue Eye Horse to pull the shaman's travois without kicking, and who is the only person One Blue Eye Horse doesn't bite?"

"Who can ride any horse in the herd besides me?" Blue Jay asked Red-and-Yellow Dog.

"Who speaks the horse talk better than anyone except Blue Jay?" Red-and-Yellow Dog asked the Buffalo Horn women.

"It is not respectable," Grandmother Weevil said.

"She should be married," Red-and-Yellow Dog's wife said.

"I don't trust those Dry River men," Mother said. "They have no morals."

"Who can pick up more sticks from the ground at a gallop than anyone except Blue Jay?" Red-and-Yellow Dog asked the Buffalo Horn men.

"That will insult the other young men." Spotted Snake looked insulted already.

"She is already willful enough," Freckled Rat said.

"It is not natural," Rolling Bear said.

"And who is Blue Jay to tell us what we should do? Young men should do as they are told."

"Blue Jay won't go without her," Red-and-Yellow Dog said to Eats Air and Blue Heron.

Eats Air knitted his hairy brows together. "The world is turning itself upside down when young men tell their elders what they will do."

Aunt Blue Heron made a noise that might have been a snort. "Young men have been telling their elders these things since First Man's son told First Man he was old and had hair in his nose. I am an old woman who remembers Eats Air telling his father things that were rude and made his mother cry."

"I remember and am ashamed," Eats Air said crossly.

"Who will take care of Mother?" Cactus Wren demanded. She jabbed her needle forcefully into the sole of the shoe she was sewing for her youngest son. The sunlight spilled through the smoke hole and the open door flap of Mother's tent and made a warm red-brown puddle on the buffalo rug. Mother was snoring gently through her afternoon nap.

Dances bit her lip. "I don't know." She was hardly audible. It was the thing that she knew they would think of next, the one thing that couldn't be answered. Someone had to take care of Mother, and Cactus Wren didn't look as if she would volunteer.

"I have three children," Cactus Wren said before anyone could mention her name. Her baby girl was burbling happily in her cradleboard, hung from the center pole over the cold hearth.

"You aren't going to go off and leave me alone?" Mother opened her eyes in a snap like the lid flying off a box. They had thought she was asleep. "And go to the west and never come back?" She began to wail.

"Certainly not." Aunt Blue Heron put down the handful of quills she was weaving into the toe of the other tiny shoe and sat on the bed. She put an arm around Mother and closed her eyes for a moment. Then she said, "You will live with me, in my tent."

Dances' mouth opened in a round, surprised circle. Mother looked at Aunt Blue Heron, puzzled. "With you?"

Aunt Blue Heron nodded. "It will be like when we were young." Her eyes slid to Dances and she chuckled. "Maybe I will find you another husband."

"When we were girls," Mother said, "remember how you wanted to marry that boy from the Dry River people? And Father said you couldn't?" She sniffed. "And then he married you to Three Black Dogs instead, when *I* wanted him. Remember?"

Aunt Blue Heron sighed. "Yes, dear. But you can tell me about it if you want to."

"But they are going to send my babies after those horse

spirit monsters. With those men from Dry River." Two tears slid down Mother's nose.

"And you will be remembered forever," Aunt Blue Heron said, "because you are their mother."

They lit a Horse Fire in a newly cleared dance circle, and the Buffalo Horn men danced the Horse Dance to send the Horse Seekers off.

"And we will put our mark on your face, before you leave," Aunt Blue Heron said. "To bring you back to us."

Dances touched her chin with her fingertips and breathed hard.

No one was quite sure how it had finally been decided that Dances would go with her brother Blue Jay, but it had slowly crept into the knowledge of the Buffalo Horn that this was so. Partly it happened because Aunt Blue Heron took her sister to live in her tent. And partly it happened because Blue Jay fought Spotted Snake when Spotted Snake said woman magic would make the horses and the horse spirits hide from them. Woman magic was dangerous and powerful—no *man* could bleed every month and not die—so men stayed away from women before they hunted or tried to see visions.

"Yah, the horses will smell her and run away," Spotted Snake said. "Why not take your mother, too, and Grandmother Weevil on a travois?"

Blue Jay knocked Spotted Snake down and sat on him, and Fine Day had to pull him off. That was a scandal, fighting with a tribe brother from the young men's tent, and Red-and-Yellow Dog made them spend the day tied together with a rope, so that Spotted Snake had to come along while Blue Jay washed Black Water Horse for the Horse Dance.

Spotted Snake didn't like horses, and they didn't like him. The Buffalo Horn didn't own enough for every man to have one, although some people, like the Children of the Horse, had several. He leaned as far away from Black Water Horse as he could while Blue Jay scrubbed his hide with yucca soap and rinsed it with creek water from a hide bucket and a gourd dipper. Black Water Horse snorted down his nose and blew spray at Spotted Snake.

"You'll have to get up behind me while I take him where

there's better grass." Blue Jay grabbed Black Water Horse's withers with his free hand and tugged with the other at the rope that tied him to Spotted Snake.

Black Water Horse rolled his eyes, and Spotted Snake balked. His face darkened. It was shameful for a man of the Buffalo Horn to be afraid of horses.

Blue Jay waited only a moment, not long enough for Spotted Snake to shame himself publicly. Then he put his fingers in his teeth and whistled like a peewit.

Dances was farther down the creek bank, washing End of the Day Horse, even though they wouldn't dance in the Horse Dance. She whistled back.

"He doesn't like to ride double," Blue Jay called to her. "Will you take him to grass for me?" He held out the rope hobbles that the Buffalo Horn used to make sure their horses didn't wander too far.

Dances looked Spotted Snake up and down and grinned, because Blue Jay could have meant the horse, or Spotted Snake, or both. She swung herself up on End of the Day Horse, bridleless, and when they got to Black Water Horse, she clucked at him to follow her. Blue Jay tossed her the hobbles. She rode away with them dangling from one hand and Black Water Horse trotting behind her.

"Woman magic," Blue Jay said admiringly. "Other people's horses don't follow me."

"Yah, it is a trick," Spotted Snake muttered.

All the same, no one said anything more about woman magic. One of the Horse Bringers had been a woman and the horses said they *liked* women, Spotted Snake admitted grudgingly, as Blue Jay poked him in the back with his finger, when they went to see Red-and-Yellow Dog to ask to have the rope taken off.

Freckled Rat even beckoned Dances into the light of the Horse Fire when the dance ended, and put his hand on her head. His face loomed over her, hidden under the white horsehead. A whole buffalo calf was roasting over the fire, and the smell made Dances' stomach growl. The smell twined the air like vine leaves.

"Go and call the horses," Freckled Rat chanted.

"Go and call the horses," the people answered him. The old men beat their thin fingers on the drums.

"We send you out."

"We send you out."

"We send you out to call the horses."

"We send you out to bring back horses."

Horse Stealer and his son Spotted Colt, and Mud Turtle the horse talker, listened impassively, sitting by the guest fire on the edge of the dance ground, in the place of honor. Six Dry River men sat with them. If the Buffalo Horn wanted to send a girl, that was their privilege, but Spotted Colt and Mud Turtle sighed and shook their heads. A woman of the Buffalo Horn brought them pieces of roasted buffalo meat and camas bulbs cooked in the hot ashes, and they ate disapprovingly.

Dances whirled in a wild spiral around Freckled Rat, arms outstretched, making her own Horse Dance. The fringe on her doeskin dress spun out in a wave around her, and her black hair flew loose, shooting little sparks of triumph.

"If I had a sister that spoiled I would feed her to the wolves," Mud Turtle said.

Spotted Colt chuckled. He bent his head toward Mud Turtle and whispered in their language, "I talked with her brother, hand talk. He says they are Children of the Horse and all horses speak to them. He says the horse spirits blessed her when she was born, and him, too, and they are people of legend, and children of people of legend."

Mud Turtle snorted. "She said the same to me, all boastful, when we were tethering our horses, and bragged that she can ride anyone's horse. It will be like traveling with Coyote."

Spotted Colt tore off a piece of meat with his teeth. "We will be a long time with them." He swallowed. "If she can call horses, so can you. See that you call more of them than she does."

The dancers had abandoned the dance ground now, leaving a litter of sweetgrass and trampled grain behind them and the Horse Fire burning brightly in the empty center. Old Eats Air came to stand in front of the fire, his wild hair and bony legs silhouetted by the flames.

The Buffalo Horn settled in a ring around him. The panting dancers sat down cross-legged, their horses' reins looped through their fingers, unable to speak until they had washed the Horse Paint away. Their wives brought them food. Mothers settled babies on their laps, and Freckled Rat put a blanket around Dances' shoulders and sat her down between Mother and Aunt Blue Heron. He sat beside them, the horse mask still on his head, some unknowable thing looking out from the empty eyes.

"Once there were the Horse Bringers," Eats Air said, and the Buffalo Horn shivered expectantly. This was the heart story of their people, told often enough in four generations to have the holy magic of legend, the tale of the Horse Bringers and First Horse and how they came to change the world of the Buffalo Horn.

The Dry River men stopped whispering among themselves and listened, and not only for politeness' sake. The Horse Bringers had changed their world as well.

Once, in the days when the people had only dogs to carry their belongings for them, when Hole in the Sunset was chief of the Buffalo Horn people, a war leader named Long Arrow was coming along. They had been hunting buffalo, but they had not found any, and he was very tired.

While he was resting, Uncle came along. "Go in the water," Uncle said.

Long Arrow came to the waters of a large river, the Buffalo Trail Water, where the buffalo went down to drink. There were no buffalo there, and Long Arrow's hunting companions complained that they were tired and thirsty.

"Wait," he said. "There will be something in the water for us."

Long Arrow walked down to the edge of the water. While he was looking at it, someone stuck his head up out of the river. "What do you want?" the someone said.

"I am looking for a secret power," Long Arrow said. "I am looking for what is in the river."

"Well, come with me," the someone told him. He had two heads. One of them looked like a human person, but one of them was very long and bony looking, and white as a cloud. The someone went under the water, and Long Arrow followed him.

When they got to the bottom of the river, there was a woman there. She said, "Who is this that you have brought?"

The someone said, "He is called Long Arrow, and he is looking for a secret power."

"Well, this is a good place for him to have come," the woman said. "Do you see all these animals in the water?"

Long Arrow saw fish and ducks and mud turtles and eels.

"Ask for my other head," the someone said to him.

"Yes, I see them," Long Arrow said. "I should thank you for giving me one of them."

"Which one do you want?" the woman said.

"Give me the white head on that someone's shoulders."

"Oh, that is of no value," the woman said.

"No, that is the one I want."

"Well, it's not worth anything."

"I think I would like to have it."

The woman told him a third time that the head was of no value, but Long Arrow insisted. Four times he asked for the head. The fourth time, the woman said, "You are wise. My husband will take you to the surface of the river. Don't look back, and the head will follow you. We will follow you, too, but you mustn't look at us until you are standing on dry land."

The someone took Long Arrow to the surface of the river, and Long Arrow did as he was told. He did not look back. He walked up out of the river and saw his hunting companions waiting for him. When he got close to them, their eyes opened wide like frog people's, and they ran and hid behind a bush. Long Arrow looked back and saw that the someone and the woman were coming up out of the river. As they rose from the water, the someone's other head came off. Now Long Arrow saw that it had a body of its own.

The body on the other head was white and four-footed like a deer, but it had round hooves that weren't split. Its tail was like a human person's long hair, and it had the same kind of hair growing up the back of its neck, and falling down between its ears, down the front of its long, bony forehead. It stopped on the riverbank and snorted at Long Arrow's hunting companions.

"This is a new animal," Long Arrow said to them. *"Come out of the bushes."*

"What is it?" they said to him.

"It's called a horse," the someone said. He looked just like a man now, with only one head.

"You should take us to your camp," the woman said, and so Long Arrow did that.

At the camp the river spirits told Hole in the Sunset, who was chief that season, their names. The male spirit was called Six-Legged, and the female was Wants the Moon. Now the people in the camp were not afraid of the horse, and Hole in the Sunset gave Six-Legged his daughter and his niece to marry.

Six-Legged showed the people how to ride on First Horse's back. Many fell off, but eventually they learned how to do it.

One day the people asked him, *"This horse, would it be any use in pulling a travois?"*

"It is fine for that," Six-Legged said. He showed them how to make one for First Horse to pull.

Then one day when they were hunting, the people asked him, *"This horse, would it be of any use to us for hunting buffalo?"*

"That is what it is best at," Six-Legged said. He showed them how to drive the buffalo with First Horse and how to shoot them from its back.

But there was only one of it, only one of First Horse. *"Well, it is a male,"* everyone said. They could tell that by looking at it. *"If it is a male, there must be a female somewhere, otherwise why have that?"*

But no one knew where Horse Woman was.

Then the woman spirit went to Long Arrow and said to him, *"There will be a big storm. Go down to the river again after it and you will see something standing in the water."*

"Is this right?" Long Arrow asked Uncle, because it was Uncle who had told Long Arrow to look in the river the first time.

"Why not?" Uncle said. They could see his face looking down at them over the mountains. The sky shivered when he spoke.

That night a big wind came, and the people heard some-

*thing calling to them out of it. In the morning the ground was
full of broken branches. Long Arrow went down to the Buffalo
Trail Water. When he got there he saw a horse standing in
the river with its head down, drinking. This one was red-
brown, like a person's skin, and Long Arrow saw that it was
Horse Woman.*

*He held out his hand to Horse Woman. She came to him
and let him climb on her back. So he took her back to the
camp.*

*First Horse and Horse Woman had many colts. Six-Legged
and Wants the Moon, too, lived among the Buffalo Horn for
many years, and their children's children are the Children of
the Horse.*

The story hung around Eats Air like a robe of stars, shimmering in the clear night air. The Buffalo Horn and the Dry
River visitors sat in silence, caught in the telling, reliving the
far-off days when horses had come out of the river and
changed the world. The four who were leaving in the morning
would change it again, by finding the land where First Horse
had come from. Old men would talk of events as dating from
"the year that Blue Jay looked for where the horses live." Old
women would remember their girlhoods in "the year that
Dances rode to the horse country." Even if they never came
back, their journey would be a pivot point in the wheel of
years.

Freckled Rat spread the calendar hide of the Buffalo Horn
out on the ground in the light of the Horse Fire, and Eats Air's
apprentices, Dances' middle brothers, Thistle and Jackrabbit,
brought him his brushes and paints and a horn full of water.
The hide was a year old, and at the center was the ice storm
of last winter, many black drops falling out of a cloud. Next
to it Dances could see the buffalo hunt in which her father
had been trampled, and the eagle that had sat for three days
in a tree above Red-and-Yellow Dog's tent before he was
elected chief. Next to that came the three babies born to Rolling Bear's sister last spring. None of them had lived, but they
had held magic in their little hands for a short while.

Now Eats Air began to paint horses, and Dances saw time
spiral out around herself and Blue Jay. Eats Air painted four

horses. On three of them he put men with spears and shields, and bows slung over their shoulders. Two of the men carried the sun-faced shields of the Dry River, and the third a round shield with a buffalo bull painted on the cover. On the fourth horse was herself, with her long hair flying out. Dark figures that might have been the restless ghosts floated in the air overhead.

While he was still painting, Grandmother Weevil scuttled into the firelight with a skin bag. Freckled Rat beckoned to Dances and Blue Jay, and Cactus Wren gave Dances a little push with her fingertips.

"Me?" Dances wasn't sure. The old men were drumming again.

"No." Cactus Wren was scornful. "The mouse in the grain."

Grandmother Weevil beckoned to Dances, too, so she stepped into the flickering light. Freckled Rat spread out a buffalo hide for her to sit on.

Grandmother Weevil was taking little pots of charcoal from her bag and laying them out beside a row of bone needles on a piece of doeskin. She crouched in front of Dances and poked her head back. "Tilt your chin." Bony fingers pulled the skin over Dances' chin this way and that, examining it, while Dances stared at the sky. When she was satisfied with her inspection, Grandmother Weevil stuck her needles in her mouth and clamped them between her gums like a fan of porcupine quills. She dipped one in the charcoal and jabbed Dances' chin. Dances winced. Grandmother Weevil jabbed her again. "It's very likely you won't come back," she mumbled around the spare needles. "This way they will know you are ours in the Hunting Ground of the Dead."

Yah, Dances thought, *I won't die.* But she bit her bottom lip because the needles hurt. The drums vibrated in the flickering light and made the air hum like bees. Dances gritted her teeth and stared at the black sky and stars, determined not to squawk. The needles stung and stung her, tiny red-hot pinpricks. She closed her eyes because the firelight and stars made her head feel swimmy.

"That's not the way it was," a voice said out of the drumbeats. Behind her closed eyes Dances could feel the air stretching tight until it reverberated like the drum skins. She opened them, and there was a coyote sitting by the fire.

"That isn't all of it," she said to the coyote. The First Horse Story had multiple layers, too much to tell in one evening.

"Two-legged people never tell things the way they happened," the coyote said. "I'll tell you how it really was."

"Eats Air just told us." Dances felt irritated with it. The First Horse Story was the most important story of her people. It didn't seem right to have a coyote changing it.

"There are always different ways for things to happen," the coyote said. "People leave messes behind them. Then they get up and turn into stories." The coyote had gotten bigger, and she could see its teeth glinting in its dark mouth, like a little piece of the sky. Nobody else seemed to notice it. It had a low, growly voice that sounded like sand on fur.

Grandmother Weevil's fingers were pricking their way like nettles over Dances' chin, tapping out the holy pattern of the Buffalo Horn: two curving half-moons with a fan of lines like a waterfall between. The coyote's eyes were yellow. Its tongue hung out of its mouth. It seemed to be waiting for her to say something.

"How would you know what happened?" Dances asked it.

"I was there. And that Uncle of yours didn't have a thing to do with it." The coyote made a rude noise. "You people pay him too much attention."

"He's our Uncle." Dances was shocked.

The coyote had found a rib bone that someone had left and was gnawing on it. The dogs flattened their ears at him, but they didn't say anything. Dances didn't think the people could see him.

"This is how it happened." Coyote's teeth scraped along the bone. "This is how Horse Woman came out of the tornado."

It was the woman and the man who caused the storm. They did it the way you people always do, fighting over who had the right to stick it in who, although it's beyond me why that's so important. Of course, women are always happy to have me . . .

Anyway, Hole in the Sunset had given two wives to the man called Six-Legged, but all the woman had been given was a new tent. She sat in the new tent and grew angry, until one day she took First Horse away.

"Where is my horse?" Hole in the Sunset roared up and down the camp, looking for it. Long Arrow had found the horse, but somehow it had become Hole in the Sunset's. These things happen.

The woman, who had not been named Wants the Moon by her first people for nothing, went to Hole in the Sunset and said, "Horse is not here because you do not honor me properly. You have given two beautiful wives to my husband, but you have given nothing to me."

"We have given you a fine new tent and a new dress," Hole in the Sunset said.

"I cannot sleep with a new tent," Wants the Moon said. "And that was my husband."

"Well, what do you want?"

"I want what he has."

"You want wives?" Hole in the Sunset thought that maybe she wanted help with her work. He scratched his head. Or maybe she was a warrior woman, although she didn't look like one.

"No, I want husbands."

Hole in the Sunset blinked at her. He was not a man with a natural gift for new ideas, which was as it should be. New ideas are like opening an egg that has lain in the sun a long time or catching a rattlesnake. They are best left to people you can afford to lose.

"You have given my man two beautiful young wives," the woman said. "Even though I am carrying his child. So now I want two beautiful young husbands for myself."

Hole in the Sunset said, "That hasn't been done before."

"Horses have never been done before, either," the woman said. "That doesn't mean a thing is not a good idea."

"I suppose it can be done." Hole in the Sunset wondered what would happen if all the women wanted two husbands then. He asked his wife, and she said it would not be so.

"It would be too much work," his wife said. "Even if they are beautiful."

Hole in the Sunset wanted his horse back, so he called two beautiful young men and told them to come and be the river spirit woman's husbands.

The woman turned around to the river then and whistled, and First Horse came back up out of the water. Then there was a big wedding feast for Wants the Moon and the Young Husbands, just as there had been for the man and his wives.

That is where the trouble began. When Six-Legged found out about two more husbands, he was angry, and he and the woman called each other bad names. Then they fought each other.

"Slut!" Six-Legged grabbed the woman by the hair.

"Follows-His-Cock!" Wants the Moon clawed at Six-Legged's hands. "Sticks-It-in-Anything!" She made an obscene gesture at her crotch.

"I'd just as soon stick it in a beehive as in you!" Six-Legged roared back, yelling in her face. "Slut Old Woman! Rattlesnake Old Woman!"

Wants the Moon drew back her fist and smacked him in the ear. Six-Legged grabbed her by the shoulders and pushed her while she kicked at him. The wind began to blow up a storm around them. Six-Legged cuffed her across the mouth, and she sank her teeth into his palm. The wind whipped up dust spouts around their feet.

"Slut!"

"Prick!"

They were spitting in each other's faces now while the wind whirled around them both in a dark cloud. The sun went behind the dark funnel that was boiling up in the sky. Its light shone a queasy gray-yellow and turned the leaves on the wind-whipped trees upside down, white as bones.

The tornado lifted the camp into the air and smashed it down. It broke tent poles and bones and threw even buffalo into the air. An old man blew by, smoking a pipe, and a woman who tried to hold on to her gathering basket was sucked straight up into the sky and dropped in a lake on the other side of the mountains.

The storm threw the river spirits, still fighting each other, into the middle of the Grass. When they looked around them, they were ashamed of what they had done.

"We must find a present for these people to make up for it," they said.

They looked around, and it was there that they found Horse Woman, being led by a crazy man. She was a red horse, brighter than the sunrise. "Horse will like this," they thought, and so they took the red horse back with them, and also brought along the crazy man.

The Red Horse that had come out of the whirlwind was crazy, too, but First Horse didn't care. When he saw Red Horse, he began to snort and dance, and he pulled up his tether.

When First Horse and Red Horse coupled, their magic shook the world. Even Grandmother Spider felt it. The sun stayed all day at the top of the sky. New grass came up in the snow moon, and canyon wrens hatched orioles. Old men thought about lying with their wives again, and young men played the flute for their sweethearts outside their tents all night. Old women turned to their husbands in the dark and smiled, the flute song singing in their ears. Married women got up and stared at their faces in puddles of water, and thought of men they had loved long ago, not their husbands.

There were many babies born to the Buffalo Horn that season.

First Horse and Horse Woman had many colts, too. But the baby that Six-Legged and Wants the Moon had been going to have together died in the storm. So they had children with the Buffalo Horn people instead.

"I know," Dances murmured. "We are Horse Children. The crazy man married a horse, too, and had children in the herd."

"She was crazy from living with him," Coyote said. "She trampled him to death."

"I don't think that's right," Dances said. "She had colts with him. All red horses are his children, and the spotted ones are First Horse's. My End of the Day Horse is one of his."

"How do you know?" Coyote grinned around his bone. He had cracked the end and was licking the marrow out.

"Because it's in the story," Dances said fretfully. It was important to her that it had happened, proof that magic was not so far away.

"Everything's in the story," Coyote said.

"There now, I'm through," Grandmother Weevil said. "And who were you talking to? It will be your fault if the lines are crooked."

Dances opened her eyes. Her chin stung as if it had been scraped raw. She didn't see the coyote.

They left in the morning just as the sun cracked open the sky. Eats Air had talked to the spirits with Rabbit Dancer, who was the Dry River Old Man, and they both said that this was the day. Spotted Colt and Mud Turtle came out of the guest tent and Blue Jay out of the young men's tent. His chin and cheeks were tattooed now, too. The tight spirals made Dances think of the whirlwind in Coyote's story. She didn't remember him very well now, in the daylight.

They had eight horses, one apiece to ride and four spare horses to carry packs that were tied in hides and slung over their backs. The tent poles, lashed to the pack sides, would drag on the ground, but it was quicker going than pulling a travois. Dances was riding End of the Day Horse, and Blue Jay Black Water Horse, and they had picked Gray Cloud Horse and Bites If You Aren't Careful Horse for the packs. She didn't know the names of the Dry Water horses.

Eats Air put on his bear mask and asked the sky spirits and Uncle and the bears to watch over them. The Dry River Old Man shook a long pole at them and muttered words that Dances and Blue Jay couldn't understand. The pole was topped with feathers and strips of badger fur. Dances crossed her fingers at it just in case.

Freckled Rat held the horse mask up on a pole so it could see. He put his hand on Blue Jay's rein. "Listen to the wind. Pay attention."

"I will." Blue Jay looked impatient. Black Water Horse danced impatiently under him.

"Young men don't pay enough attention," Freckled Rat said.

Mother stood outside her tent wailing. Aunt Blue Heron took her by the arm. "You will be famous. You will be Mother of the Horse Seekers."

"They won't come home!" Mother said. "The Grass will eat them!"

"Hush!" Aunt Blue Heron dragged Mother inside her tent.

Dances looked over her shoulder, hoping that no one else had heard her. If you said things, you might call them. The more people who heard you say them, the more likely they were to come.

Fine Day and Spotted Snake had come to give Blue Jay Spotted Snake's spear and Fine Day's war club, so that something they owned would go on the adventure, too.

Field Mouse edged up to End of the Day Horse and Dances. "Maybe you will take this." She held up a skin bag, and Dances looked inside. "It's a stone I found. It looks like a bird, so I think it must be magic." Field Mouse spoke with her eyes down. She was too shy to look at anyone.

"You should give it to Blue Jay," Dances said.

Field Mouse's face reddened. "You're his sister," she whispered.

Dances closed her hand around the bag. "I'll keep it. It can look after us both." If Blue Jay was going to marry, Field Mouse would be good, Dances thought. She was too shy to make herself more important than his sister. Dances frowned at Grandmother Weevil's girl, who was over by Black Water Horse giving Blue Jay something, as bold as a magpie. That one had better marry someone while they were gone. Dances kicked End of the Day Horse in the ribs, and she broke into a trot. Black Water Horse followed, leaving the girl standing alone.

They slowed to take the packhorses' leads, and the Dry Water men fell in beside them. The Grass rippled ahead like a lake. *We will cross on our horse boats*, Dances thought. She wriggled her toes and breathed the ripeness of midsummer, a soft, dusty grass scent humming with the bug people's voices. The Grass spoke to them, too, whispering dry words to the horses' feet. A ripple in its surface caught her eye, and Dances squinted and saw the coyote sitting in the yellow-green grass, its eyes the color of seed heads. It got up and trotted beside them.

"Go away," Dances said. She didn't like it following her.

"You're in my house," the coyote said.

Dances looked to see if any of the men were listening. Spotted Colt and Mud Turtle were talking to each other in their own language, laughing. Blue Jay rode silently, ignoring them. "This isn't your house," she hissed at the coyote.

"Any house is my house," the coyote said. It slowed its pace, watching the stream bank upwater from where the Buffalo Horn had camped. A young rabbit was there, eating blue flowers. The coyote flattened itself, and the waving stalks closed over it. When Dances looked back over her shoulder, she could see a ripple moving through the grass toward the stream.

4

The Flute Player

IT TOOK A DAY TO RIDE TO WHERE THEY COULDN'T SEE THE
smoke of the Buffalo Horn camp. At dusk, when the sky pur-
pled and grew shadowy, it was easy to imagine that the smoke
was just hidden in the twilight, that in the morning it would
be there, rising like a friendly voice into the sky.

But in the morning it wasn't there, and the Grass stretched
like a living hide, like a river of yellow-green whispers, as far
as they could see. It was hard not to feel smaller than the
jumping mice who lived in the shadows of its roots.

The Buffalo Horn traveled mostly together, and if not, there
was always a meeting place, a time to come together again,
to coalesce, all the wanderers spiraling in on the Midsummer
Camp or the Winter Camp like the patterns in a dance. Here,
she and Blue Jay were all there was of the pattern, Dances
thought—a small, beating heart. Dances stood with her arms
around herself in the dawn, sniffing the wind that blew off the
grass. She had pulled her buffalo robe around her against the
cold, and its smoky smell caught in her throat.

Mud Turtle came up beside her and stood looking at the
Grass with her. "The world is bigger these days somehow than
when it was first made," he said with his hands.

Dances nodded her head.

"That's all right," Mud Turtle said. "More room." He shifted his shoulders inside his shirt as if it were too small and were now somehow growing bigger.

Dances looked at him curiously. By the standards of the Grass people, the Dry River were solitary folk. They splintered easily into family bands, kept themselves to themselves to look for graze and hunt for deer and rabbits. Once or twice a year they converged and then dispersed again, spiraling outward, she thought, while the Buffalo Horn spiraled in. This one was a bulky-looking man, broad in the shoulders, yet oddly narrow from front to back, like a slab of rock. He had thick black eyebrows and a nose that looked like someone had hit it.

"There was a coyote in the camp," Mud Turtle said. "After our food. I threw rocks at it and it ran off."

"I saw it yesterday. It talked to me," Dances said, to see what he would say to that.

"They do that sometimes," Mud Turtle said. He slapped his belly. "Where is our breakfast?"

Dances waved her hands at him. "I need water," they said.

They had settled it last night that she would cook, since none of them knew how to do anything more than burn some gruel and rabbit meat on the hunting trail, and they would put her tent up for her and take it down again, and bring water. If they killed anything, she would clean it. It seemed reasonable to Dances. She didn't want to eat Blue Jay's cooking.

Now Blue Jay and Spotted Colt came out of the men's tent yawning, and the four of them stood and watched the sun pour flame over the bluffs in the east where they had left their people.

"Sunrise," Blue Jay said out loud, pointing at it.

"Sunrise," Spotted Colt repeated. Then he said it again in the Dry River language. They were different and yet not, if you listened carefully, Blue Jay had decided. Like two ways of saying the same word. He repeated it after Spotted Colt.

"What are you doing?" Dances asked,

"Teaching each other to talk." Blue Jay pointed at Black Water Horse and said, "Horse," and they both grinned because that was the same in anyone's language. That was the word that the Horse Bringers had given them. If you took it apart,

the pieces meant something like "Big as an elk and tame like
a dog," in the language of the Cities-in-the-West. That was
what Grandmother who was the daughter of Wants the Moon
had told them. Grandmother had known the cities speech and
had taught bits of it to her children and grandchildren. Blue
Jay said he wasn't sure he could talk to a person from the
cities with it. He would probably say something wrong and
insulting. That was what the hand speech was for, to be sure
of what you were saying.

Mud Turtle went down to the stream near their camp and
brought back a full water basket while Dances put more wood
on the fire. She poked ten smooth river stones into the hot
coals at the heart of it, and while they heated she stirred up a
mush of maize and buffalo meat in her cooking basket. When
the stones were hot, she took five of them out with bone tongs
and dropped them in the basket. The mush steamed around
them, its smell floating out on the air.

Blue Jay tried to dip his fingers in it, and Dances swatted
him away with the tongs. "It isn't hot yet, Greedy." She took
the cooling stones out and put hot ones in.

Blue Jay ruffled her hair and went to pull down the men's
tent with Mud Turtle and Spotted Colt.

Mud Turtle sniffed the breeze appreciatively. "Maybe it was
not a bad idea, to bring a woman."

"That's because you don't cook any better than you ride,"
Spotted Colt said to him.

"I am not built for horses," Mud Turtle said stolidly. "They
understand me when I talk to them. That is enough."

Blue Jay had no idea what they were saying. He tried to
hear the words as corruptions of his own speech, to pick out
the familiar under the cloak of alien sounds. He narrowed his
eyes. They had better not be talking about his sister.

The coyote came back when they rode on. Spotted Colt saw
his ears sticking out of the grass just ahead of them and
drew his bow and an arrow from the bag on his back. He
kicked his horse forward, but the coyote had vanished.

"You won't shoot him," Mud Turtle said.

"I'll shoot him next time I see him."

Mud Turtle lifted his shoulders in a shrug.

"I'll shoot him," Spotted Colt said to Blue Jay and Dances with his hands.

They didn't argue with him.

"Why won't I shoot him?" Spotted Colt demanded of Mud Turtle.

"He's decided to come with us."

"I don't want him." Spotted Colt nocked the arrow again.

"He likes to come along when people take unwise journeys," Mud Turtle said.

"Who said it was unwise?" Spotted Colt bristled.

"He did, I think."

"Well, I'm going to put an arrow in his rear."

The coyote's head popped up again from the grass. There was something in its mouth. Spotted Colt drew his bow, and the coyote dropped whatever it was and disappeared from sight. Dances got off End of the Day Horse to look. It was Spotted Colt's spare shoe, with the toe chewed off.

"This is the best way to go," Blue Jay said. "Along this bluff, and then northwest."

"Better graze for the horses," Dances said. "That is what the horses say."

"That is where the Red Bow people live, and there are only four of us," Spotted Colt said. The Red Bow people were vicious, and no kin to either the Buffalo Horn or the Dry River. They traded acorn meal and maize and things they had stolen from other people sometimes, but they were as likely as not to be slave raiding.

"We have horses," Blue Jay said. "We can outrun Red Bow people."

Spotted Colt slapped his hands together in annoyance before he began to talk with them. "There are only four of us, and one of us is a woman, even though she thinks highly of herself." He gave Dances a supercilious look.

"Four of us makes us easy to hide." Blue Jay folded his arms. It wasn't really about the Red Bow people, it was about who was leader. He unfolded them. "I am a Child of the Horse."

"I am a chief's son."

"My sister is a Child of the Horse."

"My aunt is an armadillo," Mud Turtle said disgustedly. "But she isn't here."

Blue Jay's eyes narrowed. These people thought themselves too important. He stroked the new lines on his chin—*they* didn't have lines on their chins, and their braids were wrapped in otter fur instead of horsehair—as he and Spotted Colt faced each other. "Eats Air and Red-and-Yellow Dog both said I was to be the leader."

"Rabbit Dancer and my father said I was to be."

"The Buffalo Horn do not take orders from the Dry River!"

"The Dry River do not listen to fools!"

Their hands flashed, a little dance of anger and rival importance. "Yah!" Spotted Colt said out loud and kicked a clump of grass. He swung up onto his horse and set it off at a trot, along the bluff. The others followed.

At first they were like a village that was having a feud, two tents and eight horses and four people who rode with their lower lips stuck out. At night Blue Jay slept in the men's tent with Spotted Colt and Mud Turtle, but otherwise he kept himself to Dances' company. Then the dead who lay between them, forgotten in the excitement of departure, of the adventure, began to name themselves, pointing bony fingers at the Dry River men. The Dry River dead whispered in Spotted Colt's ear, too, bone whispering on bone, a dry rubbing like snakeskin. "These are the enemy," they said. Dances began to watch the Dry River men from the corner of her eye as if they might steal something.

The only one willing to speak to all of them was Mud Turtle's dog Laugher, who hadn't been supposed to come but who caught up with them anyway on the third day, racing through the grass with her tongue hanging out. She was a little gray dog with a fluffy ruff and one bent-over ear. She fell into line beside Mud Turtle's horse, looking pleased with herself.

"It's a wonder the coyotes didn't get you," Mud Turtle said. She hung her tongue out and laughed at him. She was pregnant. They would find that out when her belly began to swell in less than a moon.

When they stopped at noon for water, Dances whistled to her to see what would happen, and the little dog came up to her and stuck her muzzle in Dances' hand.

"She doesn't like strangers." Mud Turtle looked disgruntled.

"She likes me," Dances said haughtily.

She didn't like Red Bow people, though. When they stopped again for water, she found traces of an old fire and growled at it, the hackles rising on her back.

"The dog knows," Mud Turtle said.

At the edge of the bluff, Blue Jay turned his horse southwest, away from the Red Bow people, but he didn't say anything about why.

At night Blue Jay thought that he should not have given in, even though Dances said that the dog had been right. At night it was easy to listen to the dead and hate the Dry River men. In the daytime it was harder. Boredom poked at his anger like a sharp stick at a water bag, letting it out in little drips of loneliness and tedium. There was nothing to do but ride and watch Laugher tunneling through the long grass like a mole, her tail sticking up like a flag, and the hawks soaring overhead. Mud Turtle and Spotted Colt knew a guessing game played with four fingers that the Buffalo Horn played, too. They began it and, grudgingly, Blue Jay joined them—casually at first, and then in a kind of fierce competition, for wagers. After Spotted Colt and Mud Turtle had lost too many things to Blue Jay, though, they grew angry and wouldn't play.

While they rode, Dances tried to teach the Dry River men some of the cities talk that she remembered from Grandmother. Blue Jay joined her sulkily, and they taught each other Dry River words and Buffalo Horn words until they had a sort of mixed-up language that they could all speak.

"Dry River women don't ride horses," Mud Turtle said disapprovingly to Dances.

"I am a Child of the Horse. Buffalo Horn women ride better than you do," Dances said, watching him.

"Horses listen to me," Mud Turtle said, bouncing along beside her on Morning Star Horse. Morning Star Horse had a white star in the middle of his forehead. Otherwise he was black all over, like Black Water Horse. Dances had learned their names now. Spotted Colt rode a speckled gray named Rainstorm Horse, and the other two were Grasshopper Horse and Killed a Snake Horse.

"It is just a trick of the ear to talk to the animal people," she said. "That dog says it is nearly time for her puppies." Laugher was trotting along beside them, round-bellied and unrepentant.

"They will be trouble," Mud Turtle said, talking to the dog. "Yah, you slut."

Ahead of them, Blue Jay and Spotted Colt drew their horses to a halt so quickly that End of the Day Horse and Morning Star Horse walked into them.

"What is it?"

Blue Jay held up a hand for her to be quiet.

"Somebody out there." Spotted Colt squinted his eyes, trying to see. It was midday and the heat shimmered off the Grass. They had seen no one but an antelope since they left the Buffalo Horn people, except for some rabbits and sandhill cranes that they caught. But there were trade trails here that crisscrossed the Grass. The four had been riding along the top of a ridge, above a wide, flat valley with a snake of green water running through it. Now there were men below them, five tiny figures dressed in white, like good hides that have been cleaned often with chalk, or else the white woven cotton cloth that the city people made. Either way, it was odd to see them alone here, since it didn't look as if they were hunting. The white sun danced on their white clothes, but Spotted Colt couldn't see any weapons. That was odd, and maybe wrong. He edged his horse back from the top of the ridge, looking over his shoulder. There wasn't anyone behind them, following.

The people in the valley looked up. Spotted Colt could see them freeze, all movement stop. He raised one hand slowly. They pointed at him, speaking to each other. Their movements were jerky and wild. Spotted Colt waved both arms in a careful pattern that said, "Greetings. We mean you no harm. We are trespassing here for only a little while. We will do no harm."

The people below didn't speak back to him. They ran frantically along the riverbank, like white ants. Once one stopped and picked up a rock from the ground. He turned and threw it at the four on the ridge, a panicky, hysterical gesture of terrified defiance. Then he stumbled after his companions.

"Those are crazy people," Blue Jay said.

"They think we are witches," Spotted Colt surmised. "It's the horses. They have never seen horses."

"Everyone has seen horses," Mud Turtle said.

"Here between the Grass and the cities, maybe not. Why else would they run?"

"Maybe they are afraid of us. Maybe they don't understand sign talk." Dances fluttered her fingers at Spotted Colt. "Maybe you talked too fast."

"Those were City people. Did you see their clothes? Cloth weavers." Blue Jay was scornful of anyone who would spend his time at a loom, making things to wear.

"Then they know sign talk," Mud Turtle said. "They just don't believe it."

They could still see the five tiny figures scurrying through the grass. In their frightened flight they looked more like ants to Dances than ever. Small white bugs that you could reach out and squash. "Why wouldn't they believe us?" she asked. *Someone lied to them last time*, was the thought that crossed her mind.

They watched until the white figures were out of sight in a stand of trees near the river, and then they followed cautiously. What is afraid of you may also be a thing to be afraid of. That was what Horse Stealer had always said to his son, and Spotted Colt knew it to be a true thing.

There was no sign of the white-clothed people when they descended the slope into the valley, except for the flattened grass that marked their going. "We will camp here a day or two and let them get ahead of us," Spotted Colt said, and no one argued with him.

"Maybe they are the ghosts we left behind in the Grass," Mud Turtle said uncomfortably. "Maybe they want to come with us."

"Yah, keep thoughts like that to yourself." Blue Jay peered into the twilit trees, but nothing moved there now.

In the middle of the night, Laugher had her puppies in Mud Turtle's bed. He woke to find her nursing five of them.

"Now what will we do with them?" Spotted Colt demanded, glaring at the puppies.

"I have thought already. They can ride in the pack on Killed a Snake Horse. I will leave it open at the top, and she can feed them when we stop."

"They are half coyote, more than likely," Spotted Colt said, disgusted.

The coyote that had followed them might have thought so, too. They saw its gray ears peering around rocks and trees as they moved on, never coming into the camp, but paralleling their path. Only when their tracks intersected and followed those of the white-clothed people for two days did it vanish.

The trade trail through the valley had taken them past the edge of summer, into the chill of Leaf Fall. "We will have to make a Winter Camp soon," Spotted Colt said in the evening, looking at the low sun through the ragged leaves of a cottonwood. "Maybe as well here as anywhere." For reasons he couldn't name, he found himself reluctant to follow the white-clothed people any farther. There was something wrong with them.

"There's a moon of good travel weather left." Blue Jay turned in a circle, looking behind them. "And I don't like it here."

"There are caves in the mountains just to the north," Dances said. "Eats Air drew it for me with a stick. I think this is the place."

"And there is a trade trail through this valley," Blue Jay said. "Which any fool can follow. And there will be some good place for Winter Camp on it, or it would not be a trade trail."

"We should have waited until spring," Mud Turtle said gloomily. "And then we wouldn't need Winter Camp."

"No, we could have lived at home, with the ghosts!" Blue Jay snapped.

In the morning they moved on, diverging by common agreement from the trail that the white-clothed people had left. No one wanted to admit that the white-clothed people had frightened them simply by being afraid themselves. Fear was contagious, like lung sickness in a bad winter. The horses felt it. They were like still water that someone had dropped a stone into, and their riders' fear rippled under their skin and along their flanks until they snorted and threw up their heads at the slightest sound, and Bites If You Aren't Careful Horse took a piece out of Blue Jay's thumb.

"Yah! Motherless!" Blue Jay punched Bites If You Aren't Careful Horse in the nose, and she flattened her brown ears back.

They were following a cold, shallow stream that flowed out of the mountains in the west. A Leaf Fall wind was in the air, blowing the horses' manes up and driving great drifts of yellow leaves before it. Dances chased her cooking basket across the grass with Laugher's puppies, their eyes open now, bumbling after her. The basket tumbled ahead of them, end over end, bouncing and half windborne. Dances caught it and took it back to wash. She could see little brown fish in the clear eddies of the stream. A heron was stalking them farther down the bank, with one black eye on the humans. Dances scrubbed the mush from the tight weave of the basket. The people of the cities, she had heard, made clay pots to cook in, but who could carry clay pots on the trail? Clay pots were heavy, and broke. Grass people traveled light, like the turtle people digging into the mud at the bottom of the stream, their winter lodges on their backs. Beyond the horizon the Buffalo Horn would be settling in for the winter, harvesting the squashes planted last spring, cutting new thatch for the earth lodges of Winter Camp, sweeping out the floor. Here, Blue Jay was tying the rest of her belongings into a pack while Spotted Colt stood looking away into the red cliffs that jutted from the other, western, horizon.

They had come nearly to the edge of the Grass, where the land broke more often into rocky bluffs and hillocks, and the grass grew shorter and was interspersed with desert shrub and chaparral. The air was dry and the landscape looked bleak to Dances, red as raw skin instead of green and yellow. She had stubbed her toe on a cactus retrieving the basket, and when she sat down by the stream to pull the spines out of her shoe, the puppies climbed in her lap as if they too were looking for a lost nest. She pushed them off, and Mud Turtle came and stuffed them into their pack. They rode with their paws on the open mouth of the pack now, looking out, big ears sticking straight up like little tents.

"I told you they were half coyote," Spotted Colt said. "Look at those ears."

"I want one," Dances said. "Mud Turtle says I can have one."

Blue Jay and Spotted Colt still pushed and shoved for the lead, but Dances and Mud Turtle had formed a partnership born of their mutual ability to hear the animal people. When Rainstorm Horse said there was a stone in his foot, Dances told Spotted Colt, and he didn't ask her how she knew before he checked.

"Well, that is something you are good for," he said, prizing the stone out with a stick. "And cooking. Maybe somebody will marry you when we get home."

Blue Jay's back stiffened, but he didn't say anything.

Dances wondered what it would be like to be married to Spotted Colt. It would make Blue Jay mad. And anyway, she would rather be married to Mud Turtle if she had to marry someone. He wasn't as handsome, but he was comfortable. He wouldn't want to come and live with the Buffalo Horn, she supposed.

"You can't get married and look for horses, too," the coyote said. She saw him that night, nosing around the spot where she had cleaned the rabbits Blue Jay had caught in a snare. Laugher and the pups were gnawing the bones. She slipped a handful of offal she had been saving onto a rock out of sight of the fire, and he licked her hand. His tongue was hot and left her fingers stinging like nettles.

In the morning they knew they had to find a Winter Camp. The air had a bite in it that made her think of the coyote's tongue. By midday they came to foothills threaded with leafy canyons where the low sun touched the cliff walls when the floor was in shadow. The walls were striped red and yellow, gaudy as a butterfly.

"Here," Blue Jay said. "There will be caves in the walls maybe. Eats Air says the deer climb up where the piñon pines grow, and eat their nuts. We should go where they go and eat them."

"Or eat the nuts," Mud Turtle said. "If we can't catch deer."

Blue Jay turned around with a snarl. He had tried to run down a deer from a band of a buck and three does that they had found yesterday. Spotted Colt had said not to, because he had seen prairie dogs popping their heads up while the deer zigzagged over the ground, but Blue Jay hadn't listened. Black Water Horse had put his foot in a prairie dog hole and was still lame.

"We have dried meat," Spotted Colt said. "That is what it is for, for winter." The Buffalo Horn and Dry River had sent them off with nearly a whole buffalo calf, dried and cut into strips.

"I want fresh meat," Blue Jay said stubbornly. He was tired of Spotted Colt sounding wiser than he was. "We'll look for a place up these canyons," he announced, and waited for someone to argue with him.

"That is a good idea." Spotted Colt's expression was amiable; he was a man able to see a good idea even when it came from someone less wise than he. He didn't say that, but Blue Jay bristled.

They turned their horses up the mouth of a canyon, where they could see a deer trail. Blue Jay peered at the ground but couldn't see any human tracks. If there had been, they were a long time ago. Above them the canyon walls were studded with yucca, and pines grew farther up. Along the floor a thin trickle ran through a wide wash that he knew would fill in flood season. Grapevines entwined a tangle of stunted oaks, and the four stopped and crammed their mouths full of small green fruit.

The horses pulled them from the vines, slobbering green foam. A canyon wren flickered from branch to branch above, saying something to them in bird talk. Ahead, a snake slithered off a flat rock, and they heard its warning buzz in the scrub beside the wash. They went on, giving the snake a wide berth ("Hush, Brother," Mud Turtle said to it as they passed) and let the horses drink where the water in the wash spread out into a shallow pool.

There were tracks in the sand beside it: coyote and cat and the pointed hooves of deer. Hunter and hunted. Spotted Colt looked carefully. The cat prints were old. They were round, with four round toes, like a lynx's, but bigger. They made the hair stand up on his neck.

Farther up the canyon, where box elder, cottonwoods, and

willows would make a leafy shade in the summer, there were
traces of an old fence, as if hunters might once have made a
deer pen there. It was hard to tell, just some rotting branches
lying jumbled at the entrance to a side canyon that ran at an
angle from the bigger one. Spotted Colt saw something dark
and sharp embedded in the red earth, and he slid off Rainstorm
Horse and dug in the dirt around it. When he had worked it
loose, he held it out on his palm: sharpened flint, finely
worked, and too big for an arrowhead. A spearpoint, and as
good as anything the Buffalo Horn made. He put it in his
pouch.

Blue Jay got off Black Water Horse and felt in the earth,
too. The spearpoint would be lucky, and he wanted one.

Dances thought she could see the faint shadows of the deer
that had been run into the canyon, bounding on delicate legs
over the brush and stones, their dark muzzles and eyes shimmering in the chill air, bounding into the flutter of fallen
leaves. They had bigger ears than the deer she knew.

A few leaves trembled on the bare branches of box elder.
She followed the ghost deer into them, and they dissipated in
the cold wind. Above them, where the pines began, Dances
saw something else. She grabbed Blue Jay's shoulder. "Look!"
She shook him.

"What?" Blue Jay was still looking on the ground for another spearpoint.

"There." Dances shook his shoulder and pointed, and Blue
Jay raised his head.

High in the canyon wall was a cleft in the rock, beside a
stunted piñon pine, with a house inside it. The house had windows and a wooden ladder leaning against the wall, leading
to another level on top of the first. It hugged the canyon wall
as if it had grown by itself from the red stone.

Spotted Colt and Mud Turtle stared, too.

"Who built it?" Dances whispered. A house inside a cliff
face—a magical dwelling, high above everyone else, a lodge
in the sky. Who lived in it? The walls were of reddish yellow
stone, squared off and angular, the bottom level larger than
the top, made to fit neatly into the cleft.

"I have heard of Old Ones who lived in the cliffs," Spotted

Colt said. He sounded knowledgeable, but he was gawping with the rest of them. He closed his mouth.

Blue Jay scanned the ground again. "No one has been up this canyon in a long time." He swung up onto Black Water Horse. His sister had found something better than a spearpoint.

They picked their way up the side canyon, past the deer fence, craning their necks at the cliff. The house vanished and reappeared as they rode, screened sometimes by trees, sometimes leaping from the cliff wall in the afternoon sun, glowing like embers, cupped in living rock.

They followed the narrow rivulet that was all that was left of the water that had carved the canyon, and drew rein where it burbled out of the sand in a shallow pool. A tangle of scrub blocked their path. The walls rose sheer from the canyon floor here, out of snakeweed and greasewood bushes and the purple flowers of gray-green sage. Spotted Colt got off Rainstorm Horse and pushed his way through the brush. Dances darted after him.

"They must have had wings," Mud Turtle said, looking up.

"Eagle people," Dances breathed.

"No. See here?" Spotted Colt poked his fingers into a small indentation in the sandstone wall, just big enough for a toe-hold. Another had been cut in the rock above it, and then another, rising up the cliff wall. "This is how they got up there. A man from the cities told me once, a trader. He said his people used to live in the cliffs."

"We could live there!" Dances said. "For the winter!" In the sky, in an eagle aerie. She poked her fingers into the toe-holds.

"That would not be a good idea," Mud Turtle said. He was still sitting on Morning Star Horse.

"Why not?" Dances pulled off her shoes and put her toes in the first hole in the rock. It was worn smooth—with how many years of feet? With how many toes?

"People who would live in a place like this must have been magic," Mud Turtle told her.

"Yah, you are afraid," Blue Jay said. "I'll go up." His sister had found the magic people, so they belonged to him and Dances.

"There are probably ghosts," Mud Turtle said stubbornly,

but Blue Jay was getting off his horse. The horses were browsing on the brush and seemed indifferent to whatever might be up there. Laugher had lain down to nurse her pups.

Dances was halfway up the cliff wall, clinging by the hand-and toeholds, her dark braids swaying as she climbed. The steps were shallow, not enough for a whole foot, but they were set at an angle, so that the climb wasn't completely perpendicular. Halfway up the cliff they ended at a narrow ledge. A yucca grew on the edge, its dried blossoms shivering in the wind. Dances felt her way past it. The ledge was strewn with loose stone that rolled under her feet. The wind bit her here, splayed against the cliff face, and stung her eyes. She could see the walls of the house above her, bathed in the late afternoon light, glowing like honey.

The ledge narrowed some more and ran out. Another set of toeholds rose from it to the house in the cliff. Dances looked down and thought she saw something watching her from below. It was gray, and its mouth was open wide. She looked away and back again, and it was only Laugher, sitting in the dust while the pups tugged at her teats. She could hear Blue Jay coming up behind her. Dances put her fingers in the hand-holds and pulled herself up higher. Six steps and her nose was above the floor of the cleft, by the piñon pine that grew sideways from the rock. The house was built a little way back from the edge, she saw now, with a flat space making a narrow courtyard in front of it, just big enough to climb up on. Dances scrambled over the edge.

Spotted Colt watched her backside disappear above him and then her face reappear, wild with excitement, looking down at them. The wind that blew up the canyon ruffled her hair, and the afternoon sun lit her face. He was almost willing to believe she was one of the magical Old Ones who had built the house, that she might step off the cliff edge and walk in the air over his head to the other side of the canyon. The man who had told him about the cliff houses had said the Old Ones could do that.

Blue Jay was halfway up the cliff face now, and Spotted Colt followed him. He felt Mud Turtle glaring at his back. He knew Mud Turtle didn't want to climb the cliff, but if Spotted Colt did it, then he would have to. Spotted Colt heard Mud

Turtle sighing behind him and then the scratch of his feet in the toeholds below.

The rock was warm under his fingers and bare feet, as if something alive were asleep in it. Spotted Colt felt the canyon breeze ripple across his back, under his buckskin shirt. A butterfly drifted past his nose, borne on the wind, a flash of yellow and black, and a flock of birds wheeled overhead, curling like windblown cloth over the canyon.

Blue Jay pulled himself over the lip above, sending a shower of pebbles rattling onto the ledge. Spotted Colt followed him, hooked his elbows over the edge, and wriggled up. Mud Turtle was below him, edging his way along the ledge. He peered up at them resentfully and started on the last hand- and toeholds. When he was at the top he heaved himself over and lay panting on his stomach.

Spotted Colt turned his face to the breeze. "It's like being a bird," he said.

Mud Turtle rolled over on his back and sat up. "I am not a bird. And that is a long climb to walk up walls like a bug."

Spotted Colt looked out over the canyon. The low sun flamed along the red and yellow stone at the rim, a bright flare with the dark skein of birds against it. Below, the canyon fell into deep shadow, purple and blue. Inside the cleft, beside the house, were pictures carved and painted on the cave walls. A long plumed snake undulated along the back of the cleft, and beside it was a beetlelike figure with a long penis, holding a flute to his lips. Red handprints flanked them, and in the center was a spiral sun, rolling across the stone.

Spotted Colt made a gesture of respect at the figures. The plumed serpent was very old, and powerful. He represented life, the breath on the water. The flute player was said to have brought maize to human people. Dances gave him a greeting as she passed him, and Blue Jay and Mud Turtle did, too.

Beyond the pictures, in the corner made by the house wall and the back of the cave, a door made a sharp rectangle of shadow.

"Should we go in?" The men looked at the painted figures and at each other to see what they thought.

"That is what a door is for," Dances said. "To go in." She slipped inside.

Spotted Colt followed her cautiously. Something might still be living here, or something's spirit. The doorway was filled with the rubble of one of the stone walls, slowly collapsing in on itself. He imagined the whole house sliding slowly outward, slipping from its nest in the cleft, turning end over end, falling into the blue shadow. He looked down at the canyon again. It was an open mouth, edged with the white stones of its teeth, waiting to catch what fell. Dances' figure flickered ahead of him and vanished for a moment. Then it reappeared, eyes bright.

"There is a room in here!" she said. "Come quickly, before it gets dark!"

Beyond the doorway they found a room with more hand-prints on the walls and a roof made of poles. A seat of stones and mud ran around three sides, with another door in the fourth wall. Dances pounced on a black and white clay jar, not even cracked, that lay on the mud floor, a little dribble of some old grain spilling from its mouth. A band of undulating spirals, closed like the heads of ferns, ringed its middle, with slanted lines below that might have been rain, or mountains.

She peered into the neck of the jar, put it down outside, and poked her head through the other doorway. The second room was lit by a window, dust motes dancing in its shaft of light, and by light falling from a hole in the roof. It too was bare, and they could see the open storage pit beside the door with its stone lid lying broken beside it. The pit was empty. Only a few kernels of dusty maize clung to the bottom. Dances knelt and thrust her fingers to the bottom of the pit. She rolled the kernels between them.

"Where did they go?" she asked the grain.

"Down into the cities," Spotted Colt answered her. "That is what I was told."

"But why?" *Why go and live on the ground when you could be an eagle?*

"Because it is a lot of trouble to live up here," Mud Turtle told her. "No reason to climb up a wall."

"There would be if something was after you," Blue Jay said. "What?"

"Other people. You could see anyone coming from up here, and throw rocks on them if they tried to climb up."

"It would be easier to just go and fight them."

"Maybe there were more of them."

"They are a mystery," Spotted Colt said. "They are something to think on."

Dances wasn't interested in historical speculation. She knew what they had been. "They were magic," she said. "And their magic went away, and so they had to go, too." She put the kernels of maize in her pouch. The sun was falling behind the canyon rim, and the light in the room was full of blue shadows. If she half closed her eyes she could see them: a woman kneeling at the cold hearth, a little boy with a blue bead on a thong around his neck. Below on the canyon floor there would be a garden, with squash vines twining along the ground like green snakes, feathered serpents with leaves and yellow flowers blossoming from their mouths. There would be sunset-colored melons ripening in the sun, and tall, pale green stalks of maize.

There would be a patch of cotton plants that the white cloth of the cities came from. She tried to think what that would look like: green stems like the maize, maybe, with white threads growing from the pods. The little boy would wear a thin white shirt that would shimmer in the blue shadows of the room. Below him somewhere, men would hunt the big-eared deer. The air had been full of magic then.

Dances stood up. She ran her fingertips down the wall, feeling the smoothness of the plaster and the jagged edge where it had begun to fall away from the rubble that made the core. She went into the other room again and laid her hands against the handprints on the wall, fitting palm to palm, fingertip to fingertip. The men followed her, still arguing about who had lived here. Under the handprints she could see the faint outline of another flute player, and a coyote. The coyote looked as if it were playing: a puppy stance, head low, back end raised, as if the flute player were about to throw a stick for it.

Dances touched the coyote and then the little flute player. She ran her finger along his penis.

"Don't do that!" Blue Jay snatched her hand away.

Dances looked at the little flute player. "He told me to," she said, and Blue Jay dragged her out of the room, stumbling over the stones in the doorway.

"This is not a good place," Blue Jay said, when they were outside the house.

"I told you that," Mud Turtle said.

Blue dusk had filled the canyon. "We should go down now," Spotted Colt said, "before it's too dark to see. There was a cat by that water hole a few days ago."

One of the horses snorted in the shadows at the foot of the cliff. Far out on the ridge of the opposite wall a coyote yipped, and Laugher growled at it. Blue Jay nodded at Spotted Colt. Dances had walked away from them and picked up the black and white pot. Now she stood on the cleft's lip, arms wrapped around it. The breeze that blew up the canyon fluttered the loose hair around her face and the ends of her braids.

"Put that down," Blue Jay said. "It is time to go."

"I want it." Dances cradled the pot.

"You can't take it with you."

"Yes, I can." Her lip stuck out stubbornly. "I will carry it down."

"It doesn't belong to you," Spotted Colt suggested.

"They gave it to me," Dances said.

"Let her take it." Mud Turtle peered queasily over the edge of the cleft into the pool of blue twilight. "We should go down now. Why did I climb up here?"

"We will go first and catch you in a blanket," Spotted Colt told him and chuckled.

Mud Turtle glared at him. Dances clutched the black and white pot triumphantly as Mud Turtle lowered himself over the edge, feeling for the first toehold. Dances stood above him, leaning into the wind, singing to the pot. And then, as they watched, the ground gave way under her feet. She slid past Mud Turtle in a waterfall of pebbles, her dark braids whipping like snakes around her face. The black and white pot leaped out into the air, turning end over end.

Blue Jay flung himself at the canyon's edge, scrabbling in the loose stone, facedown, leaning out into the blue air. Mud Turtle lunged for her, clinging with one hand to the lip of the cleft. Spotted Colt knelt on the edge. They heard the pot strike the rocks on the canyon floor.

"Blue Jay!" Dances wailed. They could see her clinging to a yucca bush that grew from the rock a man's height below them, dangling above the ledge where the stretch of footpath ran. Her eyes were wide and dark, like obsidian, and rivulets of blood ran down her arms where the canyon wall and the spiny leaves of the yucca had clawed her. If she let go, she would miss the ledge and fall into the canyon's mouth.

Their arms stretched down, reaching for her. Spotted Colt grunted and wriggled farther forward. Mud Turtle looked miserably up at him and then down at Dances. "Come back up here and sit on my heels," Spotted Colt said.

Mud Turtle heaved himself back over the edge.

The ground gave way again under Dances. She whimpered, too frightened to shriek, and wrapped her arms around the yucca bush as the red sand slid away under her bare toes.

"Be still!" Spotted Colt shouted at her. Blue Jay was halfway over the ledge. Spotted Colt grabbed him by the arm. "Hold on to me, you fool. It will take both of us to reach her." He lay full length on the floor of the cleft, head and torso hanging into air while Mud Turtle held his heels. He got a grip on Blue Jay, fingers locked around Blue Jay's forearm while Blue Jay's fingers bit into his.

"Go down slowly now."

Blue Jay edged down the toeholds, his free arm reaching for Dances. The muscles in Spotted Colt's arm shrieked. He could feel himself sliding over the edge, Mud Turtle pulling the other way on his ankles, feel himself stretching, elongating like the painted serpent. Dances was trying to stand up now, to reach her hand to Blue Jay's. The sandstone cliff bit into Spotted Colt's chest, rubbing it raw. It was hard not to close his eyes, so that if she were going to fall into the air after the pot he wouldn't see it, wouldn't see her eyes, wide, the whites catching the last light as she fell.

Blue Jay edged lower, his bare toes clinging to the canyon wall. The yucca plant trembled, its roots giving up their grip on the sandy earth. A shower of fine dirt rained down the canyon wall like water turned to stone.

"Catch my hand."

Dances looked down once, a fleeting glance. As she did, Spotted Colt saw the canyon's jaws open and close. Then she grasped Blue Jay's hand and swung in empty air, her feet scrabbling for the toeholds, her free hand clawing at the red stone walls. Spotted Colt tightened his grip on Blue Jay's other arm, his muscles straining. Blue Jay's foot slipped from its toehold. He dangled, too, above Dances, swinging in the canyon wind.

"Pull us back!" Spotted Colt shouted at Mud Turtle. He felt himself slide backward, the stone floor ripping the skin from his chest. Blue Jay's feet kicked at the toeholds in the rock. Dances dangled, then dug her fingers into a crevice in the soft stone. Her feet dug at the canyon wall and found a niche. Blue Jay inched upward, and she lunged for a handhold and caught it. Mud Turtle pulled them back some more. Blue Jay's head came over the lip of the cleft. His face was bloody from the stone and his hand slick with sweat where it grasped Spotted Colt's.

Mud Turtle crawled across Spotted Colt, pinning him to the floor so he wouldn't slide forward. He knelt on Spotted Colt's shoulders and reached a hand down for Blue Jay's other arm, yanking him upward. His other hand caught Dances by the forearm and yanked her, too. They all fell over the lip of the cleft, floundering and scrabbling their way into the shadows, away from the edge. The rim faded with the last slide of the reflected sun behind the opposite wall.

Mud Turtle climbed off Spotted Colt, who lay facedown on the cool stone for a moment before he sat up. His chest was scraped raw, and he could feel where the skin had peeled off the bridge of his nose. His muscles fluttered under the skin, quivering of their own volition. He tried to stand up but his knees wobbled. His bones ached.

Blue Jay was cradling Dances, his bloody face pressed against her hair. She had closed her eyes and clung to him. She reached out a hand and patted Mud Turtle's shin where he bent over her. "Thank you," she said, eyes still closed.

The dusk drained off the canyon, and the stars came out. It was dark-of-the-moon, and the canyon bottom lay in a black pool. No one wanted to take Dances down the canyon wall in the dark, so Spotted Colt climbed down the wall to sleep with the horses, feeling his way and at the bottom putting his foot into the shards of the pot. He recoiled from them as if they had been alive, or had once been, before their fall. He mounded them into a little heap at the base of the cliff and put a handful of sage flowers on them. "Sleep," he told them.

This desert country grew cool at night, even in summer, as soon as the sun fell. It seemed unnatural to Spotted Colt. Now, in autumn, the night was icy. He made a fire with the sage-bark slowburner that they carried smoldering in a buffalo horn, and Laugher yawned at him when he curled up next to her and the pups for warmth. "Yaw-oop!" she said, opening her jaws wide.

In the morning he climbed back up and found the other three still sleeping, huddled together in a pile, Dances between Mud Turtle and her brother.

"Yah, if I was an enemy I could have climbed up with a knife in my teeth," Spotted Colt said disgustedly, prodding Mud Turtle with his toe. They all sat up in a hurry. "And all my bones ache, Dancing Buffalo," he said to Mud Turtle.

"You didn't slide over the edge," Mud Turtle said. "And all your bones are still in your skin."

"Hoo! I am blood brothers with your horse." Spotted Colt sat down, wincing.

Dances got up. Her face and arms were smeared with dried blood, and there were dark bruises where Mud Turtle had grabbed her and pulled her up over the edge. She whimpered as she stood.

"Good morning, Walks on Air," Spotted Colt said.

She smiled at him and bent to pat Blue Jay and then Mud Turtle on the cheek. Then she patted Spotted Colt, too. "You are all my brothers."

Spotted Colt supposed that now they were.

Dances limped away behind the house wall to find a private place to piss, while the men did likewise, and saw another door that they hadn't seen before. *Doors are to go in,* it said to her, so she went in. Inside, in the second room, Dances could see that the hole above her wasn't a place where the roof had fallen in. It was a door in the ceiling, and there was a ladder still lying on the floor against one wall. She propped it against the edge of the hole.

The rungs felt smooth under her hand, like the old steps cut in the canyon wall, polished by feet—old men and children and young wives, running up and down the stories of their magical house like squirrels. Dances stepped on the first rung. The ladder swayed under her, and she closed her eyes, fingers clenching the rung above, stomach sliding away from her. But it didn't give way, she didn't fall forever into the canyon, so she opened her eyes again and climbed up through the hole.

Above the log ceiling of the first floor there was another room, with bare plaster walls. A window opened in the outer wall and a flat trough ran down the middle of the clay floor away from it, with grinding stones set into its surface: three of them, worn deep and smooth with years of use. Dances wanted to kneel and grind the maize kernels from the bottom of the storage pit, but the handstones were gone. Only the basin stones remained, dusted with the pale shimmer of vanished meal.

Instead she closed her eyes halfway and watched the women who used to be here, a mother and two daughters, bending to the trough and rolling the handstones back and forth in their basins, backs and arms moving to the music of a flute. And now in the wall above the middle stone there was a niche set into the plaster, with something behind it. Dances couldn't see what it was—it was sealed with a layer of plaster—but it was there. It made a glowing outline on the wall, like the light seeping around the smoke hole of a tent. She opened her eyes all the way, and the mother and her daughters flickered out of sight. But the niche was still there, its outline imprinted on her eyes, like the green spots that came after looking at the sun.

Dances went to the smooth plaster wall and dug at it with her belt knife. The mud flaked away in little chips. She jabbed at it, gouging the blank surface with holes. A fine dust rose from the wall. The tip of the blade went deeper, and a chunk the size of her fist fell out. The knife poked into air. Behind the wall was a gap stuffed with cloth. Dances could just see the pale folds. She gouged the hole wider, and a rain of plaster fell on her feet. Dust rose from it like smoke, caught in the shaft of sunlight from the window. Gingerly she put her hand in the hole.

Her fingers touched the cloth, dry and brittle as ancient hide. Something hard was wrapped in it, she thought. Dances pulled more plaster from the edges of the hole with her fingers, coughing in the dust. It smelled like desiccated mice. She could hear the men shouting for her outside.

Whatever was wrapped in the cloth was wedged tightly into the niche. Dances pried at it with her fingertips. Under the dust she could see designs on the cloth—ears of maize faded to a thin greenish brown.

"Dances!"

She ignored the feet thumping in the room below her, the voices shouting through the hole in the floor.

"Dances!"

Single-minded, she worked the cloth-wrapped thing loose as Blue Jay stuck his head through the hole. Spotted Colt's and Mud Turtle's heads bobbed below Blue Jay's, necks weaving back and forth, trying to see what was up there. Blue Jay scrambled through, and Spotted Colt followed.

Dances unwrapped the bundle and drew her breath in. Inside was a wooden frame, painted with red and ochre paint and covered with feathers and crumbling husks of maize. She looked at the women who had been grinding meal to see what you were supposed to do with it, and saw that one of them was dancing, the frame on her head, among the maize stalks that grew through the floor. Then she danced through the wall and was gone. Dances set the wooden frame on her own head.

"Take that off!" Blue Jay lunged at her, but Dances skipped out of his reach.

"They gave it to me," she said stubbornly.

"That's what you said about that pot," Blue Jay retorted. "Then it pulled you over the edge."

Spotted Colt looked at the crypt in the wall. "Grave goods aren't a gift." He reached for the headdress. "Give it back."

"It isn't grave goods." Dances liked the feel of it on her head, the weight and the way it fitted around her brow.

"It is now." Spotted Colt looked at the empty room, the empty, dusty stones in the floor. "They've all gone away now, and that thing was theirs."

Mud Turtle nodded. "They are all dead in this place. Don't take that."

"Then why did they give it to me?" Dances looked as if she were going to cry. She wanted the headdress.

They didn't ask her how she knew it was a gift. "Some things it's not wise to take," Spotted Colt said gently. "Even when someone gives them to you."

Dances looked for the women who had been in the room, but they didn't come back. *Follow them*, the headdress said in her ear.

Spotted Colt reached out and took it off her head, and she let him. He picked up the cloth, which had fallen to the floor, and wrapped the painted thing in it, being careful of the husks and feathers. Then he put it back in the niche in the wall.

The men waited for Dances to go first, to be sure she wouldn't take it again. As she backed down the ladder she saw the cloth sinking back into the wall, behind the ragged edge of the plaster. Spotted Colt turned around and touched it with a fingertip. He said something to it before he followed her down the ladder, with Blue Jay and Mud Turtle behind him.

Dances put her foot into the first toehold and slid over the edge while they watched her, tensed to leap after her, but she didn't fall. The cliff face was warm with morning sun, and a blue lizard skittered under her hand. The rubble that had fallen from above the night before dusted the ledge, and she brushed it off with her foot, watching it drift into open air and splatter softly on the brush in the canyon.

One of the horses snorted, and Laugher gave a short, sharp bark that echoed off the canyon walls. In the daylight the mouth she had seen in the dusk was gone, closed behind a gray-green beard of scrub and sage. She started down the next toeholds. She could hear the men coming down above her, and Mud Turtle muttering.

When they got to the foot of the cliff, Dances saw the pile Spotted Colt had made of the shards of the black and white jar, under the drift of purple sage flowers. The flowers were scattered, as if something had been nosing among them. "What did you say to it?" she whispered to him. "To that thing we left up there?"

" 'Go back to sleep,' " Spotted Colt said.

Dances bit her lip. "I didn't wake it up. It was there."

"Sometimes it's better to pretend you don't see that."

The horses were pulling at their tethers, and they untied

them and led them to the pool where the spring burbled up. End of the Day Horse stuck her red muzzle into the water. Dances could see the muscles in her neck as she swallowed. The damp sand on the edge of the pool was marked with tracks, by paws that were just a little bigger than Laugher's. They circled the spring in a scattering of purple petals.

5

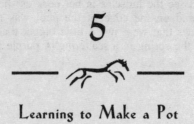

Learning to Make a Pot

THEY FOUND ANOTHER PLACE TO WINTER FARTHER UP THE mountains, in a cave in the tufa cliffs where a hot spring boiled up out of the rocks, sulphurous and steaming. Its waters soaked out the chill that invaded even young bones in the winter, and there was room enough in the cave for the four of them, the dogs, and the eight horses, tethered at the back in a makeshift pen.

The mountain slopes were studded with piñon pines, and they knocked the cones down with a stick and pried the nuts out. The deer ate pine nuts, too, and when they came to browse, Blue Jay and Spotted Colt hid behind a scree of rock and killed one with their bows. It snowed, and they buried the meat in the snow and hung the hide over the cave mouth. Dances cut pine boughs and made beds in the lee of the cave, where they slept wrapped in their buffalo robes, with Laugher and her pups burrowed in among them. The pups were half grown now, big-eared and hungry. The humans gave them the offal of whatever kill they made, and they devoured it, growling, and skulked to the back of the cave with the bones. Laugher had weaned them, but they still came sidling up to her at night, or when she lay down, and tried to nurse. She swatted them away with her paw, rolling them nose over tail down the hill. She was teaching them to hunt mice, and they hunted best on an empty stomach.

After a snowfall, the tracks of deer and rabbits and smaller game pierced the white slopes. Mud Turtle and Dances made four sets of snowshoes from saplings and scraps of the deer's hide, and the four left the horses behind and tramped through the high valley, hunting whatever moved, with the pups floundering behind them. They browsed ahead of the deer for the withered red bearberries that still clung to thickets lower on the mountain.

Something else, a long time ago, had lived in their cave— they found its leavings in the back, bones and old scat that made the horses snort. A big cat, maybe, they decided. But it had been a long time ago. The horses grew bored with it after a day, and the humans had no sense of it waiting in the shadows now, in the corners of the cave, the way the people who had lived in that other cave in the canyon wall had.

Mud Turtle and Spotted Colt were content with that, but Blue Jay, who came of a less solitary people, felt the emptiness of a Winter Camp with no noise and bustle, no children running between the lodges or old men to tell stories at night. Oddly, Dances didn't seem to mind, and Blue Jay thought uneasily of the ghosts in that other cave. They had seemed to talk to Dances, to be someone she could be friends with. He didn't try to explain that to the other men—they would have laughed, or made crossed-finger signs in case the spirits had followed her. Sometimes he thought maybe they *had* come along. When they went to cut grass for the horses, he thought someone watched her from the trees. It was hard work, digging the grass out from under the snow, especially when you didn't have hooves like Elk. When Blue Jay stopped to wipe his hair from his eyes, something moved in the shadows, but then one of Laugher's pups loped out of the dim leaves and nosed at his bundle of wet grass.

"Go and sniff out mice," he told it. It was Digger, the one that Mud Turtle had told Dances she could keep.

Digger sat in the snow and lolled his tongue out.

"Don't think I am going to feed you." Blue Jay chopped more snow away from the ground with the deer's shoulder blade and sawed at the grass below it with his knife.

"Yawp!" Digger yawned. His coat was a tawny gray-brown with a white front, and his ears stuck up like tents, bigger than Laugher's. His eyes were gold.

Blue Jay gathered the grass in his arms and dumped it on the hide they had spread in the snow. It was one of their tents, laid open. Down the slope, Dances was cutting grass, too, with Mud Turtle and Spotted Colt above them. With all the grass buried, it took all of them just to keep the horses fed. The deer fed on bark in the winter, and they had tried cutting some for the horses, who had pawed at that offering, blown down their noses, and declined to eat it.

Blue Jay yawned, his teeth chattering, and began tugging the hide back toward Dances' pile of grass. His feet were cold, his shoes soaked through with snow. Mud Turtle and Spotted Colt converged with them, dragging a second hide. They tugged and dragged them up the trail they had broken in the snow.

The cave in the tufa cliffs was warm and sulphurous smelling. They could see the steam rising from the hot springs up the rocky slope. The water pooled into a deep basin and then ran away down the mountain, where it met another stream, and then another, and finally flowed, they thought, into the wide river they could see in the distance.

Blue Jay squinted at the gray sky and the position of the sun. It was almost solstice, time to turn the sun around, tell it to start backward up the sky. "It's nearly time," he said to Dances. "I wish we had old Eats Air to tell us."

"Soon," Spotted Colt said, coming up behind him. "Tomorrow, I think."

"What if we're wrong?"

"No matter. We'll give it a push anyway. Everyone will push, so if we're late or early, we're just part of the dance."

At the solstice, Sun stood still at the lowest point in the sky, teetering and ready to fall forever behind the earth. If he did not begin his climb back up, there could be no spring, no rebirth, no world made new again. Therefore it was the duty of all human people to recognize that and tell Sun of their gratitude for warmth, for the growth of plants and game.

Across a darkening earth, fires went out and were relit, songs were sung, and the origin stories of the people were told. The Old Men and the shamans, who had watched the sky so long that they could make a calendar circle of stones by looking at the stars and not be more than a handspan off, told their people the stories of their coming to the earth: climbing up a pine tree through the four worlds, lifted out of the lake, pinched from river mud. Winter was the season of stories, the time to teach children in the red firelight, in the earth lodges of the Grass people, the houses of the cities, and all the other mysterious places beyond either.

Sun listened as Spotted Colt told the story of how the Dry River people came to be, and shook his fiery head. "That one can't remember two things at once," he said. "And the other is not much better. He forgot to tell how I made the sweat bath."

"He is good-hearted," Coyote said. He sat a little away from Sun, so as not to singe his tail.

"You would not know good-hearted from a hole in the ground," Sun said with a snort. The solar wind blew through his lips.

"You have a very fine house here," Coyote said, looking around.

"Stay away from my dinner and my magic leggings," Sun said.

"I wouldn't dream of stealing anything," Coyote said. "What do you think they are doing down there?"

"Doing me honor," Sun said.

"Really?" Coyote lay down and looked through a hole in the floor of Sun's lodge. "What are those new things? They aren't doing you honor."

"Who isn't?"

"Those pale ones."

"They're lighting incense," Sun said. "That's close enough."

"It's not the same thing at all." Coyote shook his head ruefully. "Not at all. They have some new ideas."

"Oh, really?" Sun squatted down and looked through the hole. His fiery hair hung down through it, and the snow melted. "There is no need for new ideas." He pulled his head back, and the earth froze again. The animals who had been waked from their winter sleep looked up groggily. They scratched themselves and yawned and went back to bed again.

"They will make the people in those cities listen to their new ideas and not to the stories," Coyote said.

"That is not good at all."

"These new things. They are very pale," Coyote said slyly. "I imagine they would blister."

"I'll think about that," Sun said.

When Sun had turned around, the days began to grow longer: slowly at first, just the hint of purple in the dusk where it had been black yesterday; then faster, until it seemed as if spring galloped over the earth. In the desert the snow had melted, and now the first spring rainfall painted the earth with flowers overnight, like a woman passing a brush along a cloth, scarlet and yellow and white. Mint and cress clogged the streams, and minnows darted among them like flakes of mica. The spotted fawns were born and stood on wobbly legs like waterbugs. The mockingbird men sat in the chaparral and sang all the songs they knew. The magpies began building their nests, decorating them with shiny stones and stolen red thread plucked from women's sashes. Mothers set their babies out to play with piles of clay beads in the sun. Even the peccaries had children and took them out to eat new shoots in the human people's gardens.

Green Gourd Vine took Magpie, Mouse, and Toad into the fields to throw rocks at the peccaries while the men cleaned last year's irrigation channels to water the new bean vines. The beans were just up, small, curling, springy shoots, as pale as water, unfolding their first four leaves. In the next field over, the new maize was up. Everything was climbing up out of the ground: maize, beans, squash, peppers, melons, cotton. The prairie dogs woke up and stuck their heads out of their burrows, sniffing the wind.

It was the prairie dogs who saw the Grass people first. When eight giant hoofed things came over the horizon, four of them with two heads each, the prairie dogs whistled in alarm and dived back into their holes.

The hooves shook the earth. When Green Gourd Vine looked up from the beans, her mouth dropped open. Magpie shrieked and ran to the city for Mother, while Mouse and Toad clung to their sister's skirt.

"It's people on those horse animals," Green Gourd Vine said, but her heart pounded in her chest. She had never seen horses or people who rode on them. Most people believed they were magic. These might do anything. Her skin tingled with terror and excitement.

The horses came closer, and now, trembling, she could see that some of them carried packs instead of people. Could these be traders? She felt dizzy. What magical things would they carry in those packs? Enchanted dresses, ever-full bowls, the secret language of birds? Green Gourd Vine looked over her shoulder to see if the Two Old Men were coming to deal with this, but she didn't see them.

The other men, who had been cleaning the ditches, were running across the field, waving their hoes like weapons. Green Gourd Vine looked back at them and then at the people on the horses. The air seemed to shimmer around them, limning them with mysterious fire. Her heart in her throat, she shook Mouse and Toad off and ran across the bean field. The men would never let her see the horse people if she didn't do it now.

"They took Green Gourd Vine!" Toad wailed as the men ran by. Her sister's white skirt flashed in the sun like the flicker of the mockingbird's wings. A lot of people were shouting now. The Two Old Men had come out of their houses and puffed across the courtyard that ran between Squash House and Turquoise House, out into the fields, with half the city behind them.

Green Gourd Vine stopped when she was ten paces from the horse people and stared. They stared back at her and over her shoulder at the city. A pack of dogs that had been trotting at their heels sat beside them now, big ears raised expectantly. Green Gourd Vine's heart was still hammering. There were three men and a woman on the horses, dressed in the buckskin shirts and leggings that the Grass people wore, their faces wild with tattooing, their long hair braided and twined with grass and feathers. The woman wore a buckskin dress, fringed at the hem, and hiked up around her so that her legs were bare almost to the hip. The men carried bows on their backs and round painted war shields slung behind them on the horses. And the horses—the horses looked at her with huge dark eyes and tossed their great bony heads. They were black and red and gray and spotted, bigger than deer, with round heavy hooves that had no split in them. A waterfall of hair tumbled down the backs of their necks, and their tails wore another fall of hair like a woman's. Green Gourd Vine held her breath, yearning to touch one. It snorted down its nose at her, and she shrieked and jumped back.

"Keep away from those things!" A man pulled her away. The men were clustered around the horse people now, breathing hard, clutching their hoes. Green Gourd Vine shook him off, rubbing her arm. The Two Old Men came puffing across the field. They stood for a moment, getting their breath back, while the horse people watched them silently. A murmur of voices rose and fell behind them, like bees.

"They are very wild-looking, are they not?" a voice said in her ear. Five Clay Pots was beside her.

"What do you think is in the packs?" she whispered back.

"Who could say?" He eyed the riders from the Grass with interest. "Magpie came to your mother with a wild tale about monsters, and so I had to come and see for myself, having no more sense than certain other people." His dark eyes rested on Green Gourd Vine with amusement.

One of the horse people raised his hands. He wore dark spirals tattooed on his cheeks and chin. "Our great-grandmother and great-grandfather were of your people," he said with his hands.

There was a collective intake of breath. They had heard of Six-Legged and Wants the Moon. This was where they had gone; these were the wild children they had bred.

"They were the Horse Bringers," the tattooed rider said. "Now we have come to their land to look for more horses. Will you give us hospitality?"

The Red Earth people thought hard. That was a serious question. When you made a man a guest you couldn't kill him afterward. Particularly if he was a relative. The Two Old Men put their heads together.

"We do not have any horses," Squash Old Man said after a moment, dodging the other question.

"We know this," the tattooed rider said. "The horses came from the river. That is where they live. We are told that spirits have come into your country with horses. Probably from these rivers. It is them we seek."

Squash Old Man had snapped his head back at the mention of spirits. "That is not good. They are not good." He waved his hands to indicate how very bad that was.

"We are not afraid of them." The tattooed man looked scornful. "Our great-grandfather was not afraid when he took the first horse from them."

"He went mad from them," Squash Old Man said, smacking his fist into his palm. It was hard to be certain these people were evil, but plainly they were misguided. It would be dangerous to let them call the pale kachinas into the city with their foolish quest. The Bean Canyon Old Men had said that the pale kachinas were crazy, not true kachinas, but something other, and worse.

"We will not bring any spirits here," a second rider assured him. His face was clean, and he looked more like a human person than the other, although of course all the Grass people were wild, and wild in their ways. "We ask only for food and a place to sleep for a few days. And the counsel of your Old Men, who know all things." The rider nodded gravely at Squash Old Man and Turquoise Old Man, and they looked somewhat mollified.

They whispered to each other while Green Gourd Vine stared at the strangers. It was hard, with hand talk, to be very precise. She didn't think even the Two Old Men were certain what kind of spirits these wild strangers were talking about.

"The people of Red Earth City do not turn strangers from their door," Squash Old Man conceded. "But what will these horse animals eat?"

"We will tie them to stakes, and they will eat grass," the clean-faced rider said.

Squash Old Man nodded, lips pursed. "It is true that we do not have the grain to feed such big animals as these."

Green Gourd Vine thought that horses must eat a lot; they would gobble down all the jars of maize in a few days, like the Shining Boy who ate and ate until his father turned him into a raven.

"Come," Squash Old Man's hands said. "We will give you a place to sleep, and when you have slept we will talk of why you must leave these spirits alone."

It was like being shut in a box. Blue Jay paced back and forth the length of the mud-walled room, stared at the stalks of maize and running deer painted on the walls, poked at the blanket-covered beds, sat for a moment on the seat that ran along three sides of the room, leaped up to stare out the window again. Earth lodges were for winter, when the warm thick fog of horses and dogs and people was a blanket against the storm. But who would shut himself in a box in spring? He could sniff spring out the window, overlaid with other, stranger smells that rose from the rooms below them. This room was on the third story of Turquoise House. It had been someone's who had died, he thought Turquoise Old Man had said, someone who'd had no daughters to move into it. They had climbed ladders up to it, which made Blue Jay uneasy, remembering the cliff house, and then a ladder down into it from the roof. Outside on the second-story roof was a high, flat courtyard where someone was drying pots. Below was the big courtyard of the city, divided by the thin stream that ran between Turquoise House and Squash House. On either side, more ladders led down into holes in the ground. As he watched, a procession of men wrapped in white cloth climbed down into one of the holes and disappeared.

Dances sat in the window ledge, one leg slung over it, dangling, with Digger beside her. His big ears were pricked up, and he seemed to be watching the men going down into the hole. The people here had brought them clay bowls of stew made with beans and wild turkey, and a plate of flat thin cakes rolled up like fingers. Then they had left them alone.

"I am going to sleep in the outside with the horses," Blue Jay said abruptly. "These are not real people. The men were making gardens when we came here."

"They are cloth weavers, too," Mud Turtle said. Men among the Grass did not tend gardens or make clothes.

"If I stay here I may start planting squashes." Blue Jay paced restlessly.

"We have only to stay long enough to find out where the

horses are," Spotted Colt said. "Your manhood may last that long."

"It won't," Dances said, grinning. "He's very suggestible."

Blue Jay cuffed the top of her head with his hand. "How can you stay clean, living in a box all the time? Stay here if you want to. I am going outside. There are probably bugs in those beds."

"No, don't," Dances said. "That would insult these people. And anyway, they are interesting to watch. Why do some of them live in holes?"

Blue Jay looked revolted.

"That's a holy place," Spotted Colt said.

"Oh," Dances said softly. She peered into the twilight. "What do they do in it?"

"Don't you go trying to find out," Mud Turtle said. He was lying on his back on one of the beds, hands folded placidly on his chest.

"Certainly not." Dances swung her bare leg back and forth outside the window. "I know how to behave."

"She is shameless," Green Gourd Vine's mother, Cattails, said. "She's nearly naked."

"They are different from us." Five Clay Pots looked across the courtyard at Turquoise House, where they could see the wild girl sitting in the window.

"She has black lines on her chin," Green Gourd Vine said. "How do they do that?"

"With an awl." Five Clay Pots stroked his fingers down his own chin. "They put the color under the skin."

Cattails made a noise with her teeth. "What do you expect from people who live in the Grass without houses?"

"How do you think we're related to them?" Green Gourd Vine asked her.

"We aren't. We are no kin to those people."

"Your grandmother's sister married the second son of young Out of Breath's mother's brother, and he was Six-Legged later on," Five Clay Pots said. "I think. I will have to check with the grannies."

"We are not kin to them." Cattails folded her lips tight.

"Do you think they would let me ride a horse?" Green Gourd Vine asked.

"No!"

Green Gourd Vine sighed. Cattails and Five Clay Pots were gossiping while they made flat bread over the fire and ate it. Her father, Squirrel, was in the next room, setting up his loom for a new blanket in the last of the light. Magpie and Mouse and Toad were in bed, asleep in a pile like puppies. You would think the new wild people weren't even there, across the court-yard in Turquoise House, except when her mother clucked her tongue and glared their way.

"She paints the part in her hair red," Green Gourd Vine said, so they couldn't forget about the wild people. "So do the men. I think it looks nice. Maybe I will try that."

"Only a slut would do that." Cattails didn't have to say why. Proper women wore their hair in coils over each ear as soon as they were old enough to be women. Not down their backs in braids with red paint in it. "And I know those skins are dirty. There are probably lice in them." She shuddered delicately.

Green Gourd Vine picked at the plaster on the windowsill. Beyond the wild girl she could see the men, mysterious in their fawn-colored buckskin shirts and leggings, fringed and decorated with dyed porcupine quills by some Grass woman. Their Horse Bringers had been rebellious children of Red Earth City. Strange, to have someone of your own people turned into legend in another people's history.

"Don't watch them," Cattails said.

The grandmothers disapproved. When Five Clay Pots went to them to get straight the lineage of the people that these strangers called the Horse Bringers, the grandmothers spat and said that any civilized blood had been diluted long ago, so it didn't matter.

"The grandmothers could be forgiven if they cannot remember," Five Clay Pots said craftily. "They are old and have lived long."

"It was the sister of the father of Old Red Ground Squirrel who was that boy's mother," Grandmother Little Feet said. She glared at him. "Her father was a flighty man, too. And the woman was kin to Beaver Tail, who was Turquoise Old Man then. Now go away."

The grandmothers did not approve of things done without their assent, even things done before they were born. They did not approve of horses, for which there was no use. And they did not approve of rumors of pale kachinas in Bean Canyon City. Things were moving too fast, changing like a shifting wind. Reluctantly they made room for the descendants of Out of Breath and Wants the Moon, because Five Clay Pots had shamed them. But the two others, even though they were clean-faced, were no kin to the Red Earth City, and these they regarded with deeper suspicion. Daughters were cautioned not to walk alone at night, nor listen to the notes of Spotted Colt's flute.

The young men found reason to neglect their looms and their bean fields and watch the wild girl ride the horses, flying over the ground with her hair streaming out behind her. They came home for their dinner dreamy-eyed, and their mothers put charms under their beds without telling them to drive away any thoughts of the wild girl.

For three days the city people fed them, but no one talked to them, despite Squash Old Man's promise. Twice Spotted Colt and Blue Jay went to the Two Old Men and twice they were told that it was not time yet—the men of the cities must confer in their sacred kiva before they could talk to the strangers. And then when they did talk, there was nothing to it. No ceremony, no pipe to smoke, just the Two Old Men saying that they had never seen any horses in Red Earth City since Out of Breath had found one and taken it away.

"There was more than one," Spotted Colt said patiently, again.

"Yah! These people are stupid!" Blue Jay said under his breath.

"No, just one," the Two Old Men said together.

"Then how could there be many horses now?" Blue Jay snapped, but they didn't understand him. He tried again in the words that had come down from Great-Grandmother. The Two Old Men looked as if a fish had talked. They looked like fish themselves, goggling and not saying anything, just moving their mouths like trout.

"It was a foolish one of our people," Turquoise Old Man said at last, "who took a horse into this city. Now there are the pale spirits who come into other people's cities. We think they own the horses. We are afraid they may come here looking for your horses."

"Where are they?" Blue Jay asked.

The old men didn't answer. They shuffled off, and Spotted Colt looked suspiciously after them. They weren't as old as they looked, and they knew more, but whatever it was, no one in this place was telling it.

Blue Jay ground his teeth. "Our great-grandparents must have been spirit people," he said to his sister. "They did not come from any people as stupid as these here." He sat down on the flat roof beside Dances and glared out over the city below them. The mud roof was warm in the sun, and the Red Earth people were like bees, crawling all over the three- and four-story houses and the courtyard between. They were in the gardens, hoeing among the hills of melons, in the houses weaving white cloth on their looms, on the roofs setting pots to dry in the sun. The whole city hummed like a hive. The sun caught the pieces of straw in the white plaster that coated the outer walls and made it glitter. In the courtyard below, a gaggle of children hid in the shadows of a rain jar and stared up at the strangers over its lip.

"We were told the Horse Bringers were children of this place," Blue Jay said, "and we are kin to them. But now I don't believe it."

Dances frowned. "The Horse Bringers came to us from the cities, but they were still spirit people, from under the river. They talked these people's talk, but it must have changed if they don't understand what you tell them."

"That is what I said, but the old man just said that Six-Legged was someone called Out of Breath who found a horse in the desert country. Then he said it was a shame to see a grandson of his clan with Grass people's marks on his face!"

If the Children of the Horse were not spirit people's children, Dances thought, then who were they? She was used to being more important than other people. "These people don't know where any horses are," she said scornfully. "Spotted Colt still thinks they do, but I don't. So how could they know anything else that is true?"

"Somebody knows," Blue Jay said stubbornly. "I will tell them how it really was and that they have to remember."

But all that happened when he did was that an old woman crossed her fingers and hissed at him, and a different woman, who looked like his mother, patted his cheek, tracing the spirals with her fingertips and shaking her head. "Poor child, to be brought up by those people when you are Old Red Ground Squirrel's nephew. Now those marks will never come off, and no one will let you marry their daughter."

"I don't want to marry their daughter!" Blue Jay said.

"Such a shame," the woman said. She shook her head and hurried off, carrying a basket of wet laundry.

"These people are fools!" Blue Jay kicked a loose stone against the rain jar, and an affronted toad hopped out of its shadow. He swooped down and caught it in his hand. "No horse," it said to him, and he dropped it.

Spotted Colt had no better luck. Old Rabbit Dancer had taught him that all things were worth looking at and knowing, and so he looked for horses by asking other things. He asked how cloth was made, and who had lived in the houses in the canyon cliffs, and who was the humpbacked flute player who danced on the walls of some of the houses in this place, too. He asked what they called the blue mountains in the south, and where the water in the stream ran to. And what were the strange monsters that people said had come to some other city with horses?

At the last question everyone folded their lips and remembered that they had work to do.

A man named Five Clay Pots, who Spotted Colt had thought at first was a woman, stayed when everyone else went away like water draining out of a jar with a hole in it. "We are afraid of those," he said to Spotted Colt. "It has been a bad year for spirit things. If you keep asking about those, they may come."

"Do they have horses?"

"Who knows?"

Spotted Colt studied the soft man, whom he knew to be one of the between ones, and so a powerful person. Five Clay Pots' thick dark hair was coiled over his ears in the loops that women wore. His heavy white skirt was embroidered with stalks of maize in red and green, and the white blanket over his shoulders was belted with a fringed red sash. His shoes were soft doeskin, sewn with shells and green beads. His walk was willowy, as graceful as a girl's, although Spotted Colt could tell from his face that he was older than that. He found that they were walking toward Squash House, as if Five Clay Pots were taking him somewhere.

Spotted Colt followed the soft man up a ladder to a first-floor rooftop. As they crossed the roof, a girl came out of the house beside it and stared at him. Five Clay Pots shooed her away with a motion of his hands, and she laughed at him. She wore her hair in the same coils that all the women made (like mushrooms in their ears, Dances said rudely) and a white skirt embroidered with blue suns and red and yellow lightning. The white blanket draped over one shoulder and across her chest was belted with a blue and white sash. A necklace of blue stones gleamed against her russet skin like little pools of water. She didn't go very far when Five Clay Pots shooed her. She scampered up the next ladder after them, and when Five Clay Pots motioned to Spotted Colt to sit down on the rooftop, where there was a wooden bucket of wet clay and a jar mold, she sat, too, at a little distance.

"Go away, you bad girl," Five Clay Pots said to her. Spotted Colt understood "go away"—it had been said to him often enough here. The girl laughed at him again and didn't move.

Five Clay Pots sighed. "When I was young, I was shame-less, too." He was silent while he greased the jar mold with fat from a small pot. Then he turned to Spotted Colt and began to talk with his hands and in words, one overlapping the other, saying the same thing, so that some of the spoken words began to sort themselves out for Spotted Colt. In between talking he pulled clay from the bucket and began to pat a base onto the mold. His hands slapped the clay rhythmically, like a dance with the new jar, making it rise up like the coils of a snake from the base of the mold. "You have come a long way to look for animals that I can see you can breed for yourselves."

He looked over the edge of the roof at the horses, grazing on the sparse grass beside the stream. Already they had eaten it nearly bare and would have to be moved soon. At first Dances and Mud Turtle had only hobbled them, but the horses had made their way to the edge of a melon patch and made a mess.

"They are all the children of First Horse and his wife," Spotted Colt said. "That is not any better for horses than it is for people."

Five Clay Pots nodded. He pinched off another ball of clay and rolled it into a long snake on his knee.

"And a mare has only one foal a year," Spotted Colt said. "They don't have litters, like dogs."

"Why do you think there are horses here?"

"Because there are," Spotted Colt said. "First Horse came from this country. And everyone talks of these monsters that have come with horses. Maybe they are more of the spirit people who brought us First Horse, and not monsters at all."

"And maybe what brought you First Horse was monsters, and they will come looking for his children." Five Clay Pots pinched the new coil onto his jar. It was a graceful shape, like the one Dances had found in the cliff house. "That is why everyone wishes you would go away, but we cannot make you go because the other two are kin to us. All the same, you have come in a bad spring."

Spotted Colt looked about him curiously. These people seemed to have everything they needed—the storage pits were full of grain and dried peppers and onions; the water in the stream was clear; a hunting party had brought home two deer yesterday and danced their thankfulness in the courtyard above the kiva.

Five Clay Pots smoothed the outside of his jar with a wooden scraper. "There are pale kachinas living in the Bean Canyon people's city. And the peccaries have come into our fields and eaten our food for two seasons now. Usually they live elsewhere. We don't know why they are here."

You couldn't see the coils of the jar at all now. It was perfectly shaped, as if it were a gourd that had grown. Spotted Colt pinched off a piece of clay from the lump in the bucket and rolled it between his fingers. It was cool, like live mud. "Maybe all these things are a sign," he suggested.

"And maybe the sun will set this evening." Five Clay Pots snorted, and the girl sitting on the roof with them giggled. "Everyone is trying to learn what they are a sign *of.*"

"They are a sign that you should give us the horses and we will take them away for you," Spotted Colt said.

"Then you will have to go to Bean Canyon City and get them, and I do not recommend it."

Spotted Colt thought of the white-clothed people they had seen last summer on the trail. Those had looked like city people, and they had been afraid of the horses. Spotted Colt thought now that was why they had run. He wondered uneasily just what it was that had come to Bean Canyon City with horses. For the first time he thought perhaps the horse spirits might be malevolent. There was no guarantee, actually, that if something gave you a gift, it meant well by it. Spotted Colt rubbed his chin. "I will have to think about that."

He watched Five Clay Pots finish his jar and start another one. Five Clay Pots didn't seem to mind. He chatted to him, with his voice and not with his hands, and Spotted Colt caught one word in five. He came back the next day at the same time, and Five Clay Pots was smoothing the outside of the jars with a slip of liquid clay. The day after, he put another layer of slip on. The next day he burnished the slip smooth with a round stone, and the next day he began to paint the jars, drawing fine lines with a paint stick. When he was finished, a black lizard coiled around the base of the jar, its nose a finger span from the end of its tail. Lightning zigzagged down around it from the lip.

Spotted Colt thought while the jars took shape and Five Clay Pots talked to him and the girl watched them. She came every day, usually with a piece of cloth to embroider or something else to do with her hands, a defense against accusations of idleness, Spotted Colt thought. The first day her mother came and shouted at her, and the girl got up and left. The next day when her mother shouted at her, she waved the embroidery in her hand, like a flag, and went back to stitching on it. The mother shouted at her again, Five Clay Pots shrugged his shoulders, and the mother left in a temper. She came back and shouted at her daughter every day, though.

"She thinks you are dangerous," Five Clay Pots said to Spotted Colt.

Spotted Colt bared his teeth. "I am. Everyone knows Grass people eat babies." The city people told other wild stories—about Grass people who worshipped evil spirits or never washed. These city people were shockingly ignorant.

Five Clay Pots shook his head. He held one paint stick in his teeth while he worked with the other. "Not babies," he said pointedly. He talked around the stick and waved the one in his hands. "Young girls."

Spotted Colt flushed.

"It is not a good idea to play your flute under some girl's window."

"I just happened to be there. Playing my flute."

The girl looked very busy with her embroidery.

Spotted Colt tried to pinch a pot out of the clay again. Five Clay Pots could do it in a few twists and pinches, a little pot as smooth and round as a green melon. When Spotted Colt tried it, the pot leaned wartily to one side. He mashed it into a ball of mud again.

Five Clay Pots clucked his tongue. "That is why men do not make pots. They have no patience."

It was hard to sit still. The wind blew little fingers of breeze along Spotted Colt's cheeks, and the young grass that rippled beyond the city walls gave off a green scent in the air. It was hard to sit still and think about the horse spirits and what you were supposed to do, when the grass whispered to you. He rose in one motion, uncoiling like a green shoot in the warm air.

The girl caught up to Spotted Colt beside Stream Young Man where he was untying the horses. "Can I ride one?" She waved her hands at him to translate the words.

Spotted Colt grinned. "Someone will be angry."

The girl shook her head.

Mud Turtle watched them go, with the girl on Grasshopper Horse and Spotted Colt leading her. He shook his head disapprovingly. Spotted Colt was supposed to be thinking about the things they had learned about the horse spirits, which he had come back and told them. Mud Turtle didn't care what

Spotted Colt said; he could tell what he was thinking about.

"We will have to think for him," Mud Turtle said to Blue Jay, feeling disloyal and desperate. They were sitting on the ground outside the city walls, where they didn't feel so much as if they were closed in a box of someone's old bedding. The dogs lay at their feet. "If we build a sweat bath, then he will come to his senses and sweat in it and clear his head. Bathing in the river the way these people do doesn't clear the head."

"That is why they are so stupid," Blue Jay said sagely. "They don't know how to be clean."

"I will take a sweat bath, too," Dances announced. Digger sat beside her, ears pricked, his tail tucked over his front paws. He had developed a white ruff, like someone with a cloth tied around his neck.

Blue Jay looked worried. "A sweat bath is not a good thing to do by yourself." It was something to do with others, so that if you stayed too long there was someone there to carry you outside.

Mud Turtle looked shocked. It was not something women did with men. This was why it had not been a good idea to bring a girl along. He looked at Dances' stubborn face and didn't say that.

"I will bathe after you," Dances said. She screwed up her nose at Mud Turtle. "And Digger can drag me out if I faint. And I will heat the rocks for the three of you."

Mud Turtle looked placated. She never listened to advice anyway. He heaved himself to his feet and stumped off to look at the scrawny willow trees that grew by Stream Young Man to see if any of them were suitable for bathhouse poles. Laugher and the other four pups followed him, gamboling through the spring grass.

"Go on," Dances said to Digger, but he didn't follow them. He sat beside her, ears up, watching whatever was going to happen next.

6

The Midden

GREEN GOURD VINE WATCHED THE WILD GRASS PEOPLE cutting willow branches and sticking them in the ground. They had gone outside the city walls to build what Spotted Colt told her was a house to take a bath in. She thought that couldn't be right, because you took a bath in water, but sometimes it was hard to understand what they were saying, even with hand talk *and* words. They used the wrong words as often as not, for one thing—not long after they had first come, the wild girl had kept trying to ask her where cattails grew and had appeared instead to be talking about something to do with feathers and rainwater. Green Gourd Vine finally figured out that she was bleeding and gave her a handful of cotton rags to use. Then the wild girl said that she had to go and sleep outside the city in her tent. Green Gourd Vine was puzzled by that— city girls just stayed in their own corner of the house and didn't cook food until their blood stopped—but she helped her set up the tent anyway, because the men would not.

The Grass people were a mystery to her. Five Clay Pots said they had their own customs, just as the Red Earth people did, but they seemed as strange as those of centipedes or loons in flight. Green Gourd Vine thought that perhaps you could expect no less of a people who flew on the backs of horses. The ride on the horse had been like clinging to Raven's wing. She felt as if she were taller than the trees, and when the horse began to run she wrapped her hands in its mane and held on while the ground swooped away beneath her. The horse bounced and jolted her until her teeth rattled, and then Spotted Colt shouted at it and it went faster still, and its gait smoothed out into a kind of rocking like a boat on a choppy river. The wind blew her hair back from her face, and she could feel the coils over her ears slipping loose from their thongs and blowing behind her. The horse's hooves pounded the ground like someone drumming. Spotted Colt was leading it by a rope that went through its mouth and ended in a long rein. His horse was speckled gray like a grouse's plumage; Green Gourd Vine's was a dusty brown. As the two of them drummed across the earth, she felt one of her shoes fly off and her hair stream out in the wind like the wild girl's.

She hadn't wanted to get down. When they came back to the city, she shook her head and smiled and wrapped her arms around the horse's hot, wet neck. The other two Grass men were talking to Spotted Colt, waving their arms and arguing with him, while the wild girl stamped her foot and shook her finger at him.

Spotted Colt looked up at Green Gourd Vine. "Sit here on him, then, but be careful he doesn't go off with you. I think he's too tired." He handed her the long rope rein.

The brown horse, whose name was Grasshopper, put his head down and snuffled at the trampled grass by the stream. Green Gourd Vine put the rein in her teeth and began to tie her hair back up before anyone saw her. Her skirt was hiked up around her thighs the way the wild girl's had been. Her legs itched with the hot horse sweat and hair. Her shoe was somewhere long gone. She wiggled the bare toes of her left foot. Maybe tomorrow he would let her go out on the horse and look for the shoe.

Beyond the planted fields the Grass men were driving their willow branches into the ground in a circle, bending them over and tying them down so that they made a round framework like the upended bottom of a pot. The wild girl was digging a hole in the ground ten paces away from it, piling the dirt in a mound between the hole and the willow circle. Green Gourd Vine thought maybe it was a fire pit—she was lining it with rocks. While Green Gourd Vine watched, the girl drew a line from the mound to the circle of willow branches, cutting it into the ground with a digger. The men dug another pit in the middle of the circle. They dragged the dirt out in baskets and spread it along the line she had drawn. All their tools came out of their packs. Green Gourd Vine wondered what else they had brought with them.

The dogs lay in the dirt, tongues hanging out, watching. They made Green Gourd Vine think of the coyote she had seen, the one that had talked to her in the bean field. It had told her to listen to the grass, but she had never been sure she had really heard that. It was easy to imagine things in the bean field at night. The grass didn't seem to be saying anything to her now. Where the horses had been tethered, there wasn't much of it left. Grasshopper Horse was nuzzling disconsolately among the trampled remnants. Green Gourd Vine swung her feet back and forth along his warm, hairy sides. Someone was watching her from the windows of Turquoise House, and she waved her hand at whoever it was. They would go tell her mother, and then she would have to get down. She laid her head along the coarse mane on Grasshopper Horse's neck, trying to soak up as much horseness as she could.

The Grass men had finished their frame of willow poles and were tying buffalo hides over them to make a little house. The buffalo hides had come out of their packs, too, and Green Gourd Vine envisioned an unending supply of mysterious things, a whole Grass village emerging from the bundles. The Grass girl had made a fire in the outside pit and put rocks around the edges—to heat, Green Gourd Vine supposed. The men took off everything but their breechcloths and left the clothes in a pile beside the packs. Then they pulled out bundles of pine needles and sweetgrass and dried sage—Green Gourd Vine caught a pungent whiff of leaves—and went inside the hut with them. The girl handed them a coal from the fire on a long spoon, and they closed the door flap.

After a while the girl picked up one of the rocks on a forked stick and went to the hut. She said something, and the door flap lifted up. She poked the stick inside the hut and took it back empty. Then she brought the rest of the rocks, carrying each one on the stick, and after them a hide bucket of water and a wooden cup. Green Gourd Vine watched, fascinated, but nothing happened after that. The girl poked at the fire and talked to her dog. The other dogs went to sleep.

It was dark in the sweat bath. The hides shut out the light, and the smudge of pine-needle incense and steam thickened the air until it was like being in a boiling pot. Steam still breathed from the stones in wraiths of hot mist. Blue Jay and Mud Turtle and Spotted Colt sucked it in until the dust left their lungs and the water rolled down their faces. Mud Turtle said another prayer and poured three more dippers of water on the hot stones in the pit—for the fire and the earth and the air. They boiled and hissed, and the steam filled the house until the men couldn't see each other. Blue Jay and Mud Turtle sat down with their heads between their knees, thinking prayers to Grandfather, He Who Always Is, asking for guidance, for purification, for forgiveness for things that displeased him, and waiting for Spotted Colt to come to his senses.

The door flap of the hut opened, and Green Gourd Vine saw steam billow out, dissipating in the dry air. The flap fell closed again. The Grass girl had sat down by her fire, hands folded in her lap, head bent.

Mud Turtle said a prayer and poured the seven dippers of water on the stones, for the six cardinal directions and for Grandfather who sat at the center of them. The steam billowed up and they thought on Him, envisioning Him as a flowing stream of water, giving life to everything. They thought on the willow poles, representing plants and creatures, men included, born in spring, dying in autumn, and living again with Grandfather in the Hunting Ground of the Dead. They thought on the sweat bath, its poles marking the four quarters of the universe, so that the house became an image of the universe, everything in the sky above and the earth below contained within it. Mud Turtle lifted his arms in the darkness.

*Grandfather, you have always been, and before you no
one has been. You where the sun goes down, behold me!
You where the Great Bear lives, behold me! You whence
comes the day, behold me! You where the summer lives,
behold me! Four quarters of the world, I am your relative. Give me the eyes to see and the wisdom to understand, that I may be like you. Let wisdom sweep away
ignorance. Look upon the living things that have come
up from your ground, the faces of your children without
number and the children in their arms. Look upon them
that they may face the winds and walk the good road to
the day of quiet.*

They thought on that while the steam soaked them through,
made them soft as cooked cartilage, their bones newborn.

Mud Turtle raised the flap again, and the soft, fresh air
poured in from the outside. Their mouths sucked it in. He
closed the flap and poured ten dippers of water on the stones,
and they thought on the stones.

The stones were Mother Earth, Only Mother, who showed
mercy to her children and from whom all fruits came. They
were the backbone and body of the earth, and the fire in them
a ray from the Sun.

*Hear us, O Mother, who gives food to her children. Re-
mind us in our ignorance to seek wisdom, in our haste
to seek thought. Remind us that the low door by which
we come into this house signifies our finite nature in this
world.*

They raised the flap one more time, staggering, leaning
against the willow framework of the house. Blue Jay's knees
shook and his face was ashy. Spotted Colt knelt at the door,
gasping, his hair plastered to his head.

The closing door dropped them into hot, wet darkness a last
time.

Mud Turtle ladled out the rest of the water onto the stones,
and, reeling, they took the bundles of sage and sweetgrass and

rubbed themselves with them, working the pungent scent into wet skin.

Spotted Colt's legs felt like cooked tendon, his arms heavy. He bent over, hands on his knees. Mud Turtle had opened the door flap, and the light beyond the shadow of the bathhouse dazzled his eyes. It rippled on the waters of Stream Young Man like fiery ice, a blinding sparkle that made his head swim.

The steam billowed out of the house, rising eastward on a faint breeze, dissipating in the desert air. An eagle circled above it, high up, and Spotted Colt's breath caught in his throat. Mud Turtle and Blue Jay ducked past him through the door, and he followed them. They raced across the trampled grass, making long, leggy shadows like herons, and plunged into the cold waters of Stream Young Man. The water was like ice on Spotted Colt's skin. He rose through it and stood with his mouth open, arms lifted to the spray that surged upward from their impact. The world was new, he was new again, clean, forgiven, a whole life ahead of him to live. He would live it properly; there was no doubt of that in the sharp moment of water on skin. Spotted Colt bent to the stream, gulping down mouthfuls of cold water.

When he splashed out of the stream, he saw the girl still sitting on Grasshopper Horse, watching him. She smiled and he smiled back. He climbed the bank and shook the water from himself and pulled his clothes on, dancing into wet leggings. A small child—a girl, he thought—raced up to Green Gourd Vine and said fiercely, "Mother says you are to get off that thing and come in right now!"

Spotted Colt pulled his shirt on, stuck his flute in his belt, and went to where Green Gourd Vine was still sitting stubbornly on Grasshopper Horse's back. The small girl child glared at him. He took the rein and held it while Green Gourd Vine slid down.

She patted Grasshopper Horse's hairy neck and touched his huge soft nose. "Tell him he is like the wind," she said to Spotted Colt. Grasshopper Horse licked her hand with a tongue the size of her foot, displaying long yellow teeth. She shrieked and jumped back.

"Mother *said* it would eat you," the child informed her. Spotted Colt was pretty sure that was what she had said.

"He likes salt," he told the older girl.

"Oh." Green Gourd Vine braced herself and held her hand out, palm up, teeth gritted. Grasshopper Horse licked it solemnly. She laughed.

The girl child tugged at Green Gourd Vine's skirt. "Mother said—"

Green Gourd Vine smiled at Spotted Colt again and ran toward the houses with her sister pulling on her sash.

Mud Turtle started to tell Spotted Colt what a bad idea it would be to have anything more to do with that girl, but Spotted Colt had turned away and was leading Grasshopper Horse toward the other tethered horses. He had wrapped the rein around his arm, and they could hear the notes of his flute, like a cloud of birds hovering around his head.

In the morning, Dances took her sweat bath. It hadn't made Spotted Colt any more sensible, but sometimes these things took time. And maybe she would find some wisdom in the steam that would tell her how to talk to him. She didn't want him bringing that girl back with them. That girl would tell the Buffalo Horn people how their Horse Bringers had grown smaller here, had only been children of the cities and not spirits, and that would be bad luck. Their spirits might be affronted and drive the horses away. Blue Jay thought so, too.

Blue Jay passed the stones in to her on the stick, and she prodded them into place in the pit. Digger sat looking hopefully at the hot stones, in case she was cooking something on them. Dances wasn't sure how he would like a sweat bath, but she had promised Blue Jay she would take him in with her. It was easy to stay too long and faint in the sweat bath, and people had died of that if no one took them out. Usually there were four women in a bath.

Dances opened the door flap again, and Blue Jay handed her the bucket of water and the dipper. The dipper felt old and smooth in her hand. It was Mud Turtle's dipper, and she thought it had been used in sweat baths for a long time. She ladled a scoop of water out of the bucket.

Grandfather, you made the flowing water.

She poured it on the stones. They hissed and the steam

billowed around her, like boiling air. Digger backed away
from it, whining.

Another scoop.

Grandfather, you made the air we breathe into our lungs.

She breathed the steam.

Another scoop.

You made the fire that lights the sun.

Another.

You made the bones of the earth.

The air in the house was thick now, like hot wet clothes.
Digger sat by the door, whining.

Dances crouched down beside the hot stones, her head between her knees. Digger put his nose in her hand.

"Go away!"

He nudged her harder, and she patted his head. "What do
you want, silly?"

"What do *you* want?" he asked her.

"I don't know," she told him, because it seemed reasonable
to talk to him here, in the sweat bath. She couldn't see him
very well through the darkness and the steam, just his eyes
glowing a handspan from her face.

"Well, no wonder you fell down the canyon."

Dances' head swam. She opened the door flap to let in air,
and Digger vanished in the shadows. She said another prayer
and poured the seven dippers. Digger reappeared. She thought
it was Digger. All she could see was the yellow eyes. The
steam made them waver and change in size and shape, so that
sometimes they were elongated like a snake's, and sometimes
they rippled as if they were under water.

"I want to belong," Dances said to the eyes. "I don't belong
here. None of us do. I want to find our horses and go home,
and not take any strange girls with us."

"You want all to be as it was, only with more horses."

"That's right."

"Hmmm," said the eyes. "I don't know if that can be done."

Dances felt light-headed. She opened the flap again to let
some steam out and air in. In the misty light she could see
Digger panting by the doorway. He didn't look as if he had
said anything.

When she closed the flap, the eyes said from the other side

of the sweat bath, "One time Uncle was coming along." They closed and slowly opened again. "Or he will be."

Dances looked at Digger. He had put his nose under the flap, out into the cool air, A thin line of sunlight leaked past him, limning his ears in yellow. She looked back at the eyes. They were round and golden and the right height for someone sitting on his haunches. "Are *you* Uncle?" she asked the eyes.

"Not mostly," the eyes said.

Dances' head throbbed, and she sat down again and put it between her knees. She put her hands flat on the earth that was the floor of the sweat bath. The earth was still cool, and she tried to suck the coolness into her skin. She wanted to run outside and plunge her whole body into the shining cool waters of Stream Young Man. But if she did that, the vision would go away because she was unworthy.

"Where are the horses, Grandfather?" she whispered. This was not He Who Always Is, but it was a piece of Him. All things were pieces of Him.

The eyes pulled a little piece of steam out of the air and rolled it into a ball. Dances could see that everything was rolled up into it—strange hairy animals with long curving teeth and hairy snakes where their noses ought to have been; odd little horses and tawny cats bigger than they were; human-colored people and pale ones the color of worms; horses like her own, brown and black, white and spotted; and things she didn't recognize: whirring things that sounded like angry bees, green light that moved on gray stones. All these things fell out of the ball of steam and ran into the corners of the bathhouse while Dances stood on her tiptoes, shifting her balance from foot to foot in case they ran over her bare toes.

"One day Uncle was coming along on his best horse." The eyes had a low, singsong voice, not quite like a growl. It sounded like Laugher's puppies when they rolled over and over in the grass, biting each other.

"Uncle was coming along, and he saw a pale-looking person riding a spotted horse . . ."

Dances looked at the ground to see if those things were there, too, but now there was only the singsong voice . . .

*   *   *

Uncle looked at the pale person and thought, "This person does not look healthy. This person looks as if he has been living underneath stones." He stopped his horse and waited while the pale person rode nearer to him. When the pale person got closer, Uncle could see that he had spots all over his skin, just like the horse. There was a smell in the air. It smelled a little bit like dead mice and a little bit like the midden.

"Ho," said Uncle. "Who are you?"

"I am Sickness," said the pale person.

"I can see that. You look like you need a sweat bath and a curing ceremony."

"It is too late for that."

"Well, where are you going?"

"I am going to take my sickness to the people who live in the Grass."

"Oh, you don't want them," Uncle said. "They are never sick."

"That is why I am going to see them."

Uncle thought about it. He didn't like the looks of this pale person. The horse looked all right, white with a spattering of black spots like raindrops. But the rider's spots were red, and they looked like sores all over his body. Uncle thought he looked terrible. And the smell got stronger. "Wellll," he said, "I don't think that's a good idea."

"Why not?" The pale rider flexed his bony fingers on the horse's rein.

"Well, you look hungry to me," Uncle said. "You look like you could use a good meal."

"That is true. I haven't eaten in a long time."

"Well, those Grass people, they don't know how to feed themselves, let alone strangers."

"I heard there are many buffalo in their country and the people there grow fat. That is the kind of people I want to visit."

"Oh, there are plenty of buffalo, but they can't catch them." The pale rider looked interested. "Why not?"

"They do everything backward. They are very contrary. They cook their meat in water and bathe in the fire." Uncle spun himself around on his horse's back, feet in the air, until he was sitting backward, facing its tail. "They ride their *horses backward, and so when they find the buffalo and try to chase them, they just get farther and farther away."*

"Have they always been like this?"

"Oh, no, just since the horses came. But now they are very backward. Just skin and bones now, most of them."

"I would like to find fat people."

"Well, I should think so. Let me think." Uncle scratched his chin.

"Do you know of any people like that? Fat people with good horses?" the pale person asked.

"Wellll. There are the people who live north of here. There are a lot of them, and they have so many horses and kill so many buffalo they live on nothing but back fat."

"Ah, that is just the sort of people I am looking for."

"Well, then, you should go that way." Uncle pointed in the right direction, stretching his arm over the Grass away from where his people were camped.

The pale person lifted the spear that he was carrying. Uncle saw now that it had a skull on the top of it. The pale person said, "I will go that way first, then. But afterward, I will come back and find the Grass people, too. I must visit everyone." He kicked his bony heels into his horse's flanks and began to ride northwestward.

Uncle turned his horse around to go and find his people and tell them to move their camp.

Dances could see the pale rider disappearing in the steam, his skin like a white toad, all blotchy with spots. She whimpered.

The eyes coalesced into a gray shape, hairy and canine. She could see now that it was Coyote. "And that is how Uncle saved his people from Death," Coyote said to her.

"But no one has horses except us. Did Uncle lie?"

"Maybe it happened some other time. Things are like that." Coyote had the steam ball he had made earlier between his paws, and she could see things crawling in and out of it.

"Happened when?"

"Tomorrow maybe. Sometime. Stories are happening all the time."

Dances was sitting on the ground by the pit, legs splayed out now, hands braced against the floor. The steam breathed around Coyote's ears. She felt light, as if she might rise up off the ground, float through the hides over the bathhouse, just keep going on up into the air, into the sky. If she lay down, the air would just take her.

Something was pulling at her, teeth digging into her arm, trying to drag her back out of the air. She batted a hand at it and felt a hot, rough coat. Digger growled at her and tugged some more, pulling her toward the door. She couldn't see where Coyote had gone.

Digger's teeth hurt her arm, and she scrabbled in the dirt, trying to get on her hands and knees. Digger had his backside through the door flap now, and then she heard voices, and Digger let go of her and hands reached in and pulled her out, bumping her over the rough ground.

"I told you!" Blue Jay's voice said.

The sun was a hot dazzle in her eyes. Blue Jay picked her up, flopping her over his shoulder, and waded into the stream with her. He dumped her unceremoniously in the water. The water was like being bitten, like Digger's teeth in her flesh, or the coyote's. Blue Jay held her by the shoulders while she floated, letting Stream Young Man carry her feet downstream, drifting in the current the way she had drifted on the air.

When they took her back to the city, the courtyard hummed with people. A trader had come and spread his packs out on the clay just past the Turquoise kiva entrance, and everyone was crowded around him, sifting through bags of shell beads and chunks of shiny, black obsidian, or fingering the soft skins of fox and raccoon or the red and black pots from High Up City where they used a different glaze. He had piles of bears' claws and elks' teeth and robes made from goose feathers. There were little jade figures with fierce faces carved by people in mysterious jungles to the south, and a pile of spotted cat skins with their heads still on. Red and blue birds squawked in wooden cages. A huge dried fish as tall as she was lay spread out on the clay, desiccated eyes staring, a spine projecting from its nose like a serrated knife. Dances stared at it, transfixed. It seemed no stranger to the things she had seen in the sweat bath, as if it had seen them, too.

"I bought it from the People Who Live at the Coast," the

trader said to her. "Knifenose Fish is very powerful."

"I can see that." The fish's mouth was open, as if it were leaping for the hook.

More people came out of their houses, bringing out things they wanted to trade—multicolored blankets, embroidered and painted cotton clothes, shoes sewn with blue beads, hair ornaments of turkey feathers. Five Clay Pots had a black and white jug balanced on his head and one in each hand. Cattails, the mother of Green Gourd Vine, came out, dragging a sack of dried maize and a string of peppers. Green Gourd Vine came with her. She found a pile of pink shell ornaments and held two up to her ears to see if she could see herself in the water of a rain jar.

The mother was arguing over the peppers with the trader's apprentice, a thin boy with a long, flat face like the jade figures. Spotted Colt slipped past her and peered over Green Gourd Vine's shoulder into the rain jar.

"Those are very nice."

She straightened up, smiling at him. The shells danced in her fingers, little spirals of nacreous light. They had been cut so they would go through a hole in the ear, in the way of the coast people.

She poked the end of one against her ear and shook her head to see how they would dance if she wore them. Her mother frowned at her.

Spotted Colt pulled out the eagle feathers he wore in his braids and smoothed them with the tip of one finger. He tapped the trader on the shoulder. The trader was a small man with a missing front tooth and an engaging smile that indicated he would sell you anything, even the assurance that the sun would rise tomorrow. Spotted Colt offered him the feathers and pointed at the shell eardrops. The trader frowned, indicating his reluctance to part with so valuable an item. Spotted Colt raised one eyebrow. His hands said, "These are from a sacred bird. Those are from a fish. But I will give you these feathers if you will add one of those painted flutes you have." The flutes were wood, elaborately decorated with red and blue flowers: courting flutes.

The trader said, exasperated, "I have just come from Bean Canyon City, where a man gave me a whole fox skin for one of those shells. They are very rare and hard to find, O prince of the Grass."

"The People Who Live at the Coast have piles of them outside their doors," Spotted Colt said. "All someone has done is file these so they will go in your ears."

The trader sighed. He inspected the eagle feathers. There were three, very good ones.

While he waited, Spotted Colt turned away from the flutes to show that he didn't care what the trader decided. Green Gourd Vine went to look at the spotted cat skins, dangling the shells from two fingers, as if she didn't know she still had them. Five Clay Pots watched them, arms folded in disapproval behind his stack of jugs. Spotted Colt could see him from the corner of his eye, see the trader thinking on his other side. "They are pretty," he said loudly to Green Gourd Vine by the cat skins, "but they are just fish shells. Leave them for an uglier girl who needs them more."

The trader moaned to indicate how badly he was being cheated, but Spotted Colt appeared not to hear him. The trader sighed elaborately. Spotted Colt gave his attention to a rock in his shoe. The trader sighed again. Finally he nodded at Spotted Colt, signifying agreement against his better judgment.

Green Gourd Vine closed her hand around the shells.

Spotted Colt turned back to take his pick of the flutes, spread out in a fan beside the birdcages. A red and blue bird cocked its head at him, looking back with a bright black eye. The bird sidled along its perch, ruffled yellow tail feathers, and opened and closed its beak. The beak was hooked and sharp-looking. Spotted Colt poked a flute into the cage, and it bit down on it hard. *"Awk!"* it said.

"A very rare and magical bird." The trader studied Spotted Colt to see if another trade was possible. "But for a prince of the Grass, a powerful possession." He cocked his head like the bird.

"I don't want a bird," Spotted Colt said. "I want horses. Now, if you have those to trade—"

The trader jerked his head up to look straight at Spotted Colt. "I saw those at Bean Canyon City, but those things that are living there own them, and they won't sell any."

"Ah," Spotted Colt said.

The trader looked sly. "Do you want to sell any of yours? I have seen the horses that the prince of the Grass has brought with him. It is only the second time that I have seen these creatures, and I would like one for my own, to carry my packs."

"Unfortunately," said Spotted Colt, "they do not belong to me." He put down the flute that the bird had bitten, ran his fingers over the rest, blew through one, put it down, and picked up another. Little notes like bright feathers fluttered out of it. He saw Green Gourd Vine's mother, Cattails, bearing down on them and Green Gourd Vine slipping away through the crowd.

"I could find you many pretty things to give to a young woman," the trader said. "Many pretty things for one horse."

"No." Spotted Colt tried another flute.

"I have a jade knife that was given me by a king in the south. It is very magical."

Spotted Colt blew a series of notes on the flute. This one had red flowers around the holes and spiral stems twining down its length.

The trader sidled closer. "*Perhaps* I could part with a spotted jaguar skin, if I had a horse."

"This is the one I want." Spotted Colt tossed the flowered flute in the air and caught it with one hand. He eyed the trader thoughtfully. "Be careful around my horses," he said with his hands. "They are heavy and their feet are hard." Aloud, he said as he passed Mud Turtle, "One of us had better sleep with the horses until that one has left."

"That would be you," Mud Turtle said, but Spotted Colt had already gone out of earshot. Mud Turtle saw him crossing the empty end of the courtyard with the new flute in his hand.

Dances watched him, too, with narrowed eyes. He was going after that girl with her hair puffed up over her ears like mushrooms. Dances swung her own long braids contemptuously. The fish looked up at her from its hide wrappings.

The trader could see that she wanted it. "Knifenose Fish will put you on the right path," he said. "He cuts a trail with that nose."

It would break if I packed it on a horse, Dances thought. It seemed to swim on the hide, leaping from dusty surf, nose pointing the way. She edged closer to the trader. "I will give you two dogs for it. Good dogs like this one." She pointed at Digger, sitting at her heel. Mud Turtle still had the other puppies. When the fish showed them the horses, he would see that she had made a good bargain.

The trader laughed. He bent his head toward her, conspiratorial. "Anyone can find dogs. This is a magic fish from the Endless Waters. You will have to find me something better than that."

"What? I have a good hide dress that is sewn with turquoise and red quills."

"Anyone can make such a thing." His fingers bunched themselves and then fluttered again, talking. "For a fish that knows the straight road—surely you have something else."

"No."

The trader whispered in her ear. "I need a horse to carry my packs."

Dances stared at him. "I am a Child of the Horse. We do not sell horses."

"A pity." The trader pulled something from the half-open pack beside the fish. "I could give you this, too, a magical thing from the creatures that have come to Bean Canyon City. A relic of their world." He waved it at her and snatched it away when she reached for it.

"Let me see that!"

Feigning reluctance, the trader laid it in her hand. It was a piece of cloth, not such as these people here made, but dyed a bright yellow and with a pattern of vines and flowers woven into the threads themselves. It was dirty and charred at one end as if it had been in the fire, but it shimmered beneath the dirt. Dances imagined the way it had shone when it was clean the way she imagined the fish before it leapt from the water onto someone's hook.

"I will give you this and the fish for one of your horses," the trader said.

Dances buried her face in the cloth, smelling it. It made her head reel. Embedded in it was the sour smell of sweat, and the ashy smell of old smoke, and other scents she didn't know, like leaves rubbed between the fingers. It was sewn at one end, and she thought maybe someone had worn it. "How did you get this?"

"I took it from the monster who wore it. In a great fight." The trader nodded his head, remembering the greatness of the battle.

He stole it from the midden, Digger said from the ground at Dances' feet. She looked down, startled. Digger nosed at the cloth, and she could see something in it now, in the shiny reflection where the sun caught the threads of the pattern.

Two men with pale skins were throwing things on a midden—a mattress and blanket, a white shirt, and a garment made of the yellow cloth. They said unintelligible words, like crows squawking. One of them reached into his clothing and then knelt beside a pile of tinder. Flame blossomed from the tips of his fingers. He threw the tinder onto the midden, and they backed away. Coyote looked at her out of the midden. Then it was dark and the trader and the peccaries were rooting at the edges of the rubbish.

"Why did they want to burn it?" she demanded of the trader, here, now, in this courtyard, and he backed away, eyes widening.

"Yah, you are a thief." Dances turned her back on him scornfully.

The trader waited until she walked off, the dog at her heels, and then he turned, heart pounding, to a Squash man with a pile of blankets. He saw the other blankets burning in the midden and heard the shouting when the pale monster people had seen him at its edge. Thunder had boomed around him like lightning striking a handspan from his ears, and he had run, clutching the yellow cloth. Their laughter had followed the thunder. Maybe it wouldn't be good to buy or steal a horse from a person who could see all that.

He began to inspect the Squash man's blankets. Behind him Dances darted through the crowd, snatched the yellow cloth, and ran.

Spotted Colt found Green Gourd Vine sitting on the warm ground just inside the edge of the melon patch. The melon vines had thick, hairy stems like ropes, with huge leaves like green plates. The afternoon sun made long shadows of them, dappling her face and shoulders until it was hard to see her sitting there. Spotted Colt slipped into the dim shade beside her.

Green Gourd Vine smiled at the shell spirals lying in her lap. They glowed in the melon shadows like moonlit fish. "Thank you." She said it out loud, and waved her hands to make it clear.

"You will have to get holes put in your ears," Spotted Colt told her.

"Five Clay Pots will do it. When he gets over being angry."

"Is he angry?"

"Oh, yes. But he thinks you are interesting, so he will get over it. He says it is a chance to understand Grass people. Mother says you are uncivilized because you can't weave cloth." *Mother says you are dangerous.*

"You are very strange people here," Spotted Colt retorted. "Men don't make clothes where I come from. Women do that."

"Women make clothes," Green Gourd Vine said. "Men make *cloth*. Then women make clothes."

"I don't see the difference. Men hoe the gardens here, too." Spotted Colt's lip curled, though he tried to stop it.

"Well, what do men do among your people?" Green Gourd Vine demanded. "They must do *something*."

"We hunt. We kill buffalo. We fight. We can't be ready to fight if we are watering squashes."

"Fight." Green Gourd Vine thought. "We don't fight. Unless maybe the Outsiders come and bother us, but mostly they trade with us these days. Why would you fight?"

"To steal horses," Spotted Colt said. "To get a reputation. How else does a young man make a name for himself?"

"He weaves a beautiful blanket," Green Gourd Vine told him.

Spotted Colt hooted with derision. "He courts a girl with a beautiful blanket." He shook his head.

"And how do you court a girl?"

"First," said Spotted Colt, "I make a reputation. I have somebody's hair on the end of my lance. I have many horses.

I give her father two and each of her brothers one."

"Somebody's hair?" Green Gourd Vine looked repulsed.

Spotted Colt put the flute to his lips. He blew a trio of notes. "I sing to her." He played a tune that wound itself, sinuous and beautiful as a green snake, through the melon vines. The broad leaves danced to its melody.

Green Gourd Vine chuckled. "She might listen to that," she said.

"And what would happen then?"

"He would take her a blanket. Then she would grind meal for him. Then he would move into her mother's house."

"Her *mother's* house?"

Green Gourd Vine nodded.

Spotted Colt looked appalled.

"What would a young man of *your* people do?" Green Gourd Vine asked him. "If he wanted to marry?"

"He would take her to his family, and they would set up a tent of their own next to his father's tent. Of course."

They both looked thoughtful.

"Someone has to leave their family," Spotted Colt pointed out. "How can a man hunt for his family if he goes where he doesn't know the hunting trails? Women can do women's work anywhere."

"And who helps the new wife when she begins to have babies?" Green Gourd Vine demanded.

"Her husband's mother."

"*His* mother? No wonder you people are fighting all the time."

"Only the men fight," Spotted Colt said. "The women stay home with their mothers-in-law and learn how to be good wives."

Green Gourd Vine shuddered. "Well, it is plain to me that our system is better."

Spotted Colt looked rueful. "We have a story, about a young woman who followed her husband—"

"We have a story about a young man who came to live with his wife."

Spotted Colt grinned. "There is more to see in the world than four mud walls." He played another little snake melody on the flute. It whispered among the melons and twined itself around her shoulders. It had a voice like the Grass.

Green Gourd Vine stretched out on the warm earth, her chin in her hands, in the green shade of the vines. "Tell me about these things there are to see." The white blanket that she wore over one shoulder gleamed like the shells. The other shoulder was bare.

"There is the Grass. It is wider than the Endless Water on the coast. The buffalo live on it, and we travel through it from summer to winter, and then we live in Winter Camp and sing songs until it is spring again. We feed our horses on the Grass, and they carry us across the world every year. We chase the buffalo and live on back fat and hump meat. We are a free people on the Grass."

Green Gourd Vine sighed. It sounded magical and enticing the way he talked about it.

Spotted Colt put down the flute and touched her forehead with his fingers. She lifted her head. He touched her throat. She thought of living in a tent in the midst of that emptiness, and the magic shimmered and vanished like a curtain of spray.

She ducked her head. "I'm afraid of it," she whispered. "Those people you have come with are the children's children of our people. Why can't you all just stay here?"

Spotted Colt rolled over on his back and looked up at the sky through the melon leaves. "In a house all year? Learning to weave cloth?"

"Well, no." Green Gourd Vine could see that.

"I have to find horses and take them home. That is why I am sent." He put his hands behind his head and turned his face to look sideways at her. "I would give you a horse to ride."

"I am afraid of your Grass," she whispered.

"And you think you are safe here because you have walls?"

"Mostly. No one has bothered us in a long time, since the Ancestors came down from the cliffs."

"What about the Outsiders?"

"Wellll . . . them, maybe. But they are afraid of the Ancestors, and so they are afraid of us, a little."

"The Ancestors?"

"The cliff people. Those were our grandfathers. The Outsiders think their ghosts are still in the cliffs."

"What about the whatever-it-is with the horses?"

Green Gourd Vine shook her head. "I don't know. Those things have moved into Bean Canyon City, but the Bean Canyon people are afraid to fight them, I think. The Outsiders are afraid of them, too. Maybe they are magic."

"They have horses, anyway."

Green Gourd Vine thought again of riding on a horse, the wind flying past her. If people could not have wings, horses were the closest thing. If she went with this man, he would give her a horse. She closed her eyes, envisioning it, and saw the Grass instead, endless, its blades bent over in the wind that blew all the time there, rippling like water. She saw herself sinking into it, floating off the horse's back, drowning, while the horse raced on.

Spotted Colt sat up. "We will have to go to Bean Canyon City, that is plain. I must talk to this trader again."

"The Two Old Men think the pale kachinas are dangerous."

"Five Clay Pots told me that. We have fought monsters before now. There are stories about that, too."

But when they went back to the city, the trader had gone. There was only a litter of straw packing and the shards of a broken pot scattered in the courtyard.

7

Foot-on-Trail

SPOTTED COLT KICKED AT THE RUBBISH, PERPLEXED. "DON'T they stay longer than that?" When traders came to the Grass, they stayed half a moon sometimes, bargaining and eating and telling stories and collecting others to tell elsewhere. Stories were part of a trader's unofficial stock. Even people who didn't buy would feed a visitor for the tale of what happened when the white elk came into Long Walker's camp, or the time that Hairy Feet had ridden a buffalo.

"Usually," Green Gourd Vine said. It was dusk and everyone had gone back inside their houses, so that the firelight shone from the windows in the white walls like squares of sunset. Cattails saw them and came scrambling down a ladder, running across the courtyard, her shoes slapping the packed dirt.

"Get inside!" she shrieked, running. "Where have you been? I didn't raise my daughter to go off like a slut with wild boys who buy her presents!"

Green Gourd Vine clamped her hand tightly around the shell eardrops. "Where did the trader go?"

"He left. I don't know why. He saw you and thought that all our girls are sluts, and he left maybe." Cattails' face was twisted furiously, and her hands were balled into fists.

Spotted Colt couldn't follow most of what they said, but the content was plain. Cattails grabbed Green Gourd Vine by the arm, and when Green Gourd Vine tried to pull away, Cattails smacked her with the flat of her hand on her bare shoulder. It wasn't very hard, but it made them both stop and stare at each other, mouths open in surprise.

Green Gourd Vine burst into tears, and Cattails did, too. "See what you made me do?" Cattails wept.

"I just went for a walk," Green Gourd Vine said sulkily.

"With *him!*"

"I like him!"

"He's from the *Grass!*"

"Yes."

"They eat babies there! They'll eat all yours and paint ugly marks on your face."

"None of that is true. Ask Five Clay Pots."

"Five Clay Pots is very ashamed of you. Five Clay Pots said to me that it is a shame that this man from the Grass has put a spell on you." Cattails' brows jerked together. "Maybe he has. Maybe he has put a magic on you so that you forgot your morals and your mother and how to behave. Let me see!" She grabbed at the sash that belted Green Gourd Vine's skirt and blanket.

Green Gourd Vine jerked away from her again, but this time the blanket came away in her mother's hand. Spotted Colt saw a flash of brown-tipped breast as Green Gourd Vine shrieked with rage and snatched the blanket back. She held it to her chest.

"You'll be sorry!" Green Gourd Vine screamed. "When women marry in the Grass they go to live with their *husbands!*" She turned on her heel and ran toward the house.

"You did this!" Cattails stuck her fingers out at Spotted Colt in a sign to keep off witches and ran after her daughter.

When Spotted Colt got home, they didn't say anything to him about the girl. Dances was cooking dinner, squatting by the fireplace with a long bone spoon in her hand. Mud Turtle said that the trader had loaded his packs on his dog travoises and his own back and been foot-on-trail by late afternoon. He didn't know why. "Maybe they are stingy here."

Blue Jay shrugged. "They are wrongheaded here, anyway. They think that our Horse Bringers were *their* people."

Spotted Colt sighed. It seemed to matter greatly to Blue Jay that legend be fact and not just holy truth.

Dances sat rubbing the soft doeskin of her shirt between her fingers while the stew bubbled in a clay pot that Five Clay Pots had given her. It was mostly maize mush, the way these people ate here, and peppers and a little dried antelope meat. "He has seen horses," she said. "He has seen the things that have the horses."

"Was he afraid of them?" Spotted Colt asked her.

Dances stirred the stew in her pot. "He wanted to buy one of ours."

"He asked me, too." Spotted Colt raised his eyebrows at Mud Turtle. "And have you counted ours?"

"I would have noticed a horse in his dog pack," Mud Turtle said scornfully. "That one was in a hurry. As if something scared him."

"What? These people are like puppies. That one was a wolf. I know. What would scare him here?"

Dances ladled out stew into clay bowls. "Eat this. Why do you care about him?"

They ate, watching the patterns that the smoke made on the plastered walls, how it made the painted deer leap in the firelight. Someone had been very clever with those, Spotted Colt thought.

"Are we going to Bean Canyon City?" Dances demanded.

"Oh, yes. Soon." Spotted Colt looked across the dark courtyard at Squash House. He thought he could see Green Gourd Vine's silhouette in a lighted window, but it was hard to tell. All the windows blurred together when he tried to count them, so many up, so many across, to the house where she lived. They would leave as soon as he had talked with her. Of course.

But because the trader had gone, the idea of Bean Canyon City, which had been so clear in Spotted Colt's head, turned sideways like a fish flipping and slipped into the soft summer morning somewhere behind the song that a mockingbird was singing on the lip of a rain jar. Another was perched on the ladder that led down into the kiva, trilling a rival repertoire. Spotted Colt rose early and sat at the window until he saw her come down the ladder from the first floor of their house, with a cloth sling for firewood in her hand. Then he went light-footed across the courtyard, dancing along the narrow plank that bridged Stream Young Man where he ran between the houses.

"Go away," she said when she saw him. "My mother will see you."

"I will pretend that I am your shadow." He stepped behind her and mimicked her pose.

Green Gourd Vine laughed. "Come along, then."

They crossed the bridge again, Spotted Colt imitating her every move. The rising sun was behind them and cast their true shadows out before so that she could see his. She raised her arms and danced three steps, and he did the same. She lowered her head and trudged along, darting her neck to either side like a turtle, and he did, too.

The city's firewood was stacked against the far wall of Turquoise House. Wood-gathering was the job of boys old enough to be trusted with an ax and too young to go hunting. The pile rose in an irregular stairstep, as neat as boys would make it when there were other things to do. Green Gourd Vine began to load wood into her sling, and he took it from her and stacked more in than she could have carried.

"I will take it back for you, and your mother will see that I am a fine young man."

"My mother will throw stones at you," Green Gourd Vine said regretfully.

"Then I will dodge. You can't carry all this." He hefted the sling over his shoulder. "What will you do all day today?"

"Grind meal with Mother and Five Clay Pots and Magpie."

"Inside all day, on a fine day such as this?"

"It's very pleasant," Green Gourd Vine said primly. "It is!" she protested, when he laughed. "Mouse plays the flute for us, and we all grind together and talk. We're teaching Toad. She has her own little grindstone and handstone. But she has to practically jump on it to crack the maize, she's so small."

He carried the wood over the bridge and up the ladder for her and deposited it at the second-floor door of her house. It didn't seem to be a good idea to bring it into the kitchen. Her little brother and sisters could carry some of it from there. The whole family was awake now; he could hear them murmuring and talking inside. One of the little girls was singing a repetitive song, rhythmic as a grindstone, over and over. Toad practicing, he supposed.

"And what will you do when you have done this fascinating thing all day?" Spotted Colt asked wistfully. He knew he should be loading his packs, but another day wouldn't do any harm. The trader had already left, after all, so there was no talking with him about it.

"It might be," Green Gourd Vine said, "that I will go out and see if the beetles have been at the beans again tonight. If they have, we will all have to go out and pick them off."

"But you don't all go and look at them?"

"Oh, no. One person can look at them."

So he went into the bean field, skulking around the edges like a thief, he thought, looking for Green Gourd Vine and hoping he wouldn't find her mother or father instead. His stomach fluttered like a bird's wing. He hadn't eaten dinner. Dances and Blue Jay and Mud Turtle had rolled their eyes when he left, but he had promised them he would load his packs in the morning for certain.

She was waiting for him, her blanket a pale splotch in the shadows, like a cluster of bean flowers against the trellised vines. The real flowers made a spatter of little white blotches behind her. There was no one else in the bean field, so maybe there were no beetles chewing at it. Or maybe she had just made up the beetles.

"Does your mother know you are here?"

"I hope not." She looked unrepentant.

"I felt that it was my fault when she called you bad names." Spotted Colt hung his head.

Green Gourd Vine sniffed. "Only if you are not an honorable young man."

He bit his lip. Was he? It was hard to say, out here in the bean field on a soft early summer night. "I have to leave and look for horses," he offered.

"In Bean Canyon City?"

"Yes."

She thought. "You could stay and let the others go. There are enough of them to find horses."

"Then how would I go home if I hadn't found horses?"

Green Gourd Vine smiled happily. "You could stay. My father could teach you to weave a blanket."

"You said"—Spotted Colt picked at a bean flower—"you said to your mother that in the Grass, wives go to their husbands' families."

"I didn't mean it!" Green Gourd Vine was shocked.

"Why not?"

"Go away from here? To where you have to live in a tent, and not have a garden or proper clothes or anything?"

"What do you mean, proper clothes?" Spotted Colt looked indignantly at his shirt and leggings. He had put on his best ones, embroidered with red and yellow quills, fringed, and painted with yellow suns for luck and happiness.

"Hide." Green Gourd Vine wrinkled her nose. "I couldn't bear to live in dirty hides."

"We clean them," Spotted Colt said, "with chalk and a brush. Who told you we didn't?"

"Mother. And anyway, I wouldn't know any of your people, and your mother would hate me."

"Not when she got used to you."

Green Gourd Vine looked out across the bean field, into the bare land beyond, the great distance that stretched from Red Earth City to who knew where? She had been to High Up City, of course, for Trade Fair, and to Bean Canyon City. But the Grass? She had only heard of it, immense and rolling, like a huge river with no far shore.

"If you wanted me for a husband, you would come," Spotted Colt told her.

"If you wanted me for a wife, you would stay here."

"If I wanted you for a wife and had a duty to my people, I couldn't stay here."

She glared at him, suddenly angry because things weren't easy. "Then go."

"You can think about me while I am gone," he suggested. "When we come back, you will have decided and then you can go with me. I will give you a horse to ride."

Green Gourd Vine thought of the wind in her face and her hair, and that it had been like being a bird to fly over the ground on Grasshopper Horse.

"A horse is better than a blanket," Spotted Colt said.

Not so respectable, certainly. "If you don't bring me a blanket, people *will* say I'm a slut," she told him. If he stayed long enough to weave her a blanket, then perhaps he would just go on staying.

Spotted Colt laughed. "I will bring you a buffalo blanket."

"No. A cloth blanket." It was important.

"I can't weave you a blanket," he said, exasperated.

"You would if you wanted me."

"No, I wouldn't."

Her eyes filled with tears. "But you want me to live in a tent! Go away, then!" She turned and ran from him, the way she had run from her mother.

The fish had shown Dances the way. She was quite certain of that. If she closed her eyes, she could see the road to Bean Canyon City. Dances clutched the cloth hidden in her shirt, drifting in the moonlight that came through her window. When they got there, it would find the horses for them. She felt tired with the long way they had come already, and her dinner had come up again after she had eaten it, but tomorrow they would find the horses. And the pain in her head and the queasy feeling in her stomach, which must be from not doing as they ought to, would go away. Dances slept, and dreamed of a road traveled by the fish, with Digger and the coyote trotting at her heels. She could see the herds of shining horses in the distance.

"Not everything means what you want it to mean," the coyote said to Spotted Colt out of the smoke of the fire he had poked up when he came in from the bean field. Spotted Colt spilled his stew. The bowl fell in the fire, and he leaped after it, splattering the floor with mess and ashes. When he had retrieved it, the coyote was still there.

Spotted Colt looked around him for his club. It was leaning against the wall with the coyote between him and it. Blue Jay and Mud Turtle had gone out on the roof to look at the stars when Spotted Colt came in, and Dances was asleep.

"I'll go with you," the coyote said.

"Go where?"

"Where those pale things are. Where you're going for horses."

"We don't want you," Spotted Colt said frankly. He wondered if Dances had called this thing up. She was the one who said she had talked to a coyote.

"I'll come anyway," Coyote said. "You may need me." He stuck his nose in Spotted Colt's bowl and drank what was in it, ashes and all. Then he disappeared into the smoke again.

He came back the next day while they were loading their packs. Spotted Colt saw him out of the corner of his eye while he was explaining to Green Gourd Vine why he had to leave. Her mother stood a few paces away from them, triumphant.

"I will come back, when we have found the horses."

Green Gourd Vine shook her head. "Some man will have brought me a blanket by then, I expect." Her mother said that these wild Grass people were like the peccaries that were spoiling the fields again, always wanting everything. They had probably brought the peccaries, her mother said. Green Gourd Vine didn't think Spotted Colt was to blame for the peccaries, but something had brought them, and Cattails preferred to blame the Grass people.

"They will go away, and you will find a decent man," Cattails said, as Spotted Colt walked away.

The coyote fell into step beside him. Spotted Colt wasn't sure anyone else saw it. "Don't you belong to the girl?" he inquired. Dances was still in the house.

"Not anymore," the coyote said.

Spotted Colt looked at him suspiciously.

"Look at that," the coyote said, and Spotted Colt turned his head, diverted.

Three peccaries were rooting in the midden in the middle of the city, their snouts digging up garbage and old shoes. A woman ran at them with a broom, and they turned on her, snorting. She retreated.

"They are bolder than rats," Spotted Colt said.

The hackles on Coyote's back raised until he was twice the size he had been. The peccaries looked at him and trotted off, but Spotted Colt saw one later, in the room on the first floor of their house, eating maize. The kernels fell from its lips in a spatter of slobber, and it snorted and grunted as it ate. When he shouted at it, it disappeared the way the coyote had done.

Coyote watched the peccary go through the same door he had used, with the human people's maize still dribbling from his lips. He got big enough to fill the sky and stood in Peccary's way.

"There isn't a lot of room here, Friend. Maybe you should find your own place."

Peccary snorted, chewing. He got bigger, too.

Coyote bared his teeth. "I will bite you on the behind if you are rude to me."

Peccary switched his tail.

Coyote was getting angry. "If you don't talk to me, I will bite you."

"I'm having dinner," Peccary said.

"You're always having dinner. You are as hungry as me, but you don't give anyone anything in exchange."

"Give them your backside," Peccary said rudely. "Nobody wants what you have to give anymore." He stuck his neck out and took a big bite out of the green squashes in the field. His hooves left deep holes in the soft earth.

"Why have you come to this place, anyway? And what is the matter with the girl?" Coyote asked him.

"Hungry," Peccary said. "Mine."

"What is?"

"Everything."

"No, it isn't. You should go away from here."

"I want it." Peccary's lips dripped squash pulp and slobber.

"Want what?"

"All of it."

"Yah, you are stupid." Coyote looked disgusted. "Nobody can have all of it, not even me. Go away or I'll bite you."

Peccary turned his back on him. He pulled up another big mouthful of squash vines, trampling the rest into the dirt with his sharp hooves. Where he had been was a mess of rubbish and torn ground.

Coyote bared his teeth, ran at Peccary, and nipped at his hairy backside. Peccary turned, snarling. They circled each other, Coyote's yellow eyes glowing, Peccary dribbling chewed squash from his lips. Coyote sank his teeth in the end of Peccary's bristly tail and bit the tuft off it.

"Eeeeehhhh!"

Coyote jumped back, leaving Peccary squealing and switching his wounded tail. He drew his lips back and spat the tuft out.

Peccary pissed in the squash vines and ran away. His little hooves made him look like a big man trotting on tiptoes, but they were sharp and broke open the new squashes as he went. Coyote stood panting, his head hanging low, tongue out. *Yah,* he thought, working his lips, *he tastes like rotten eggs. I will have to wash my mouth out.*

When Spotted Colt went back to the house, Blue Jay was trying to make Dances drink a willow tea. All afternoon they saw the peccary rooting in their food, or their beds, or just watching them, his hairy snout half visible behind the edge of a doorway. If they went toward him, he disappeared, so they knew he wasn't an animal peccary but something else. The dogs raised their hackles and growled at him, but they were afraid of him, too. When they found him defecating on Dances' trampled bed, with Dances shivering at the end of it, Blue Jay sat down and cried, scrubbing his eyes with his hand.

The peccary disappeared, leaving Digger barking furiously in the doorway.

"Stop it!" Spotted Colt said to both of them.

"I saw him," Blue Jay said. "I saw him after the sweat bath. I didn't say anything, because I didn't want to see him. I wanted to see First Horse, but he came instead!"

"Make him go away from my bed," Dances whimpered. "I don't feel good." She rubbed her temples with her fingers.

"He's gone. But something has called this." Spotted Colt felt the flesh on his arms rise up in little bumps. "If you saw him after the sweat bath, he has something to say. We should listen."

"I have listened!" Blue Jay snapped. "He just says, *'Mine!'* And you called him here, running after that girl who isn't our people!"

"What does she have to do with it?" Spotted Colt demanded. "I didn't see him in the sweat bath."

"Nor did I," said Mud Turtle.

"I didn't ask for him," Blue Jay whimpered. "And I saw him *after,* in the stream."

"Were you rude to him? What did you say?"

"I didn't say anything. He just stood there eating the steam from the sweat bath, and then he was gone."

"Did he do anything?"

"He belched."

"Yah, this is a joke," Mud Turtle said disgustedly. "A sweat bath is to speak with He Who Always Is, maybe even see him, not to see things like that. No wonder we cannot find horses."

"Any spirit may be a guide," Spotted Colt offered. "Maybe even this one. I myself have seen the coyote."

Dances sniffled. "He doesn't talk to *me* anymore." She fingered the front of her shirt.

"You shouldn't have talked to him to begin with," Spotted Colt said severely. "Maybe *that* is how all this started."

"He talked to me," Dances said. "And he isn't a dirty old peccary. I don't think he likes that peccary."

They looked at her curiously. "How do you know that?" Mud Turtle asked.

"I don't know," Dances said fretfully. "My head aches." She crawled under the covers again. The peccary's scat that had been on the blanket was gone.

It was only afternoon, and they had thought to leave for the Bean Canyon City in the morning, but Dances hadn't packed her things, and now she was asleep. Spotted Colt thought she was getting sicker.

"I am going to ask Five Clay Pots for something better than willow tea."

"Him!" Blue Jay was scornful. "And we have a medicine bag."

"And nothing in it has made her better."

"I don't trust these people. Like as not, *they* made her sick."

"When *they* are sick, they go to Five Clay Pots. Green Gourd Vine told me. Men like that make good healers. They are between and see things we don't."

"I will make her more willow tea," Blue Jay muttered.

*   *   *

"I will look at her," Five Clay Pots said. "Very likely she has just too much will, that one. Sometimes that makes a person sick."

He went into the next room and began to rummage among the pots and bottles and hide boxes and baskets that were stacked on a wooden shelf set into the plaster wall. Spotted Colt looked curiously over his shoulder. Bunches of dried plants hung from the ceiling, tied with red thread, and the air smelled dustily of herbs. Five Clay Pots took down a painted box and pulled out a white doeskin sack embroidered with wavy blue lines. He put it in a basket lined with blue cloth and chose three small red clay pots from the shelf. One had a head like a badger on the lid, and the other two were frogs. He opened one, and Spotted Colt caught the sharp smell of wintergreen oil. Five Clay Pots added two bunches of dried herbs to the basket and pursed his lips, thinking.

"Should I carry something?" Spotted Colt asked. The Dry River healers often used spells besides their potions. Sometimes spells called for large objects. One healer had a tooth as tall as he was, from an animal that Dry River legend said had had a tail at each end and teeth longer than a man.

Five Clay Pots consulted his basket. "This should take care of her. Come along."

Cattails met them in the corridor outside Five Clay Pots' house. "Where are you going?"

"The girl from the Grass is sick."

"You should let her alone." Cattails glared past him at Spotted Colt. "Let these people leave as they said they were going to."

"They can't leave while the girl is sick," Five Clay Pots said gently.

"They should leave now!" Cattails' mouth compressed into a thin, angry line. Green Gourd Vine was in her house weeping and wouldn't grind meal or cook or sew. Mouse and Toad had got into the honeycomb while she was supposed to be minding them, and Magpie had burned her fingers trying to make mush because Green Gourd Vine wouldn't.

Five Clay Pots touched Cattails' cheek with his fingers. He edged past her, his basket on his arm, his skirts brushing hers. Spotted Colt followed him without looking at Cattails.

Mud Turtle was sitting glumly in the corridor when they got there, his arms resting on his knees. "She's hot," he said. "Like a fire."

Blue Jay was sitting on the foot of Dances' bed, talking to her in a low, fierce voice. Digger lay beside him, his nose on Dances' feet. When they saw Five Clay Pots' shadow on the floor, they looked up. "You had better make her well," Blue Jay said.

"She will do that herself." Five Clay Pots knelt by the bed and put a hand on Dances' forehead. His eyebrows rose. "Get me some cool water."

"Anyone would take sick, being shut up in a box like this." Blue Jay paced back and forth in the little room.

"Get me some water!" Five Clay Pots snapped.

"I will." Mud Turtle rose from his seat by the door. They heard him climbing down the ladder to the courtyard, where the rain jars were.

Dances' eyes glittered, and her lips were cracked. Spotted Colt thought she looked worse than when he had gone to get Five Clay Pots. When Mud Turtle came back with a jar of water, Five Clay Pots dipped a cloth in it and put it on Dances' forehead. He held the jar to her mouth and told her to drink it.

"It will wash out the sickness."

Dances swallowed, wincing. She lay back down. She could see Five Clay Pots bending over her, his hair in those funny puffs that all the women here wore, his hands running over her body. She pulled the yellow cloth out from under her shirt and poked it into the bedding under her. She thought he might take it away if he found it. Odd shadows were running over the ceiling, like water moving. She looked for the coyote among them, but he wasn't there, just shapes like mist.

Five Clay Pots sat back on his heels. "She has a fever. Smoke may drive it out. Or steam. I don't know."

"Well, send for someone who does know!" Blue Jay snapped, stopping his pacing in midstride.

"Send for anyone you like," Five Clay Pots said.

"There isn't anyone who knows more," Spotted Colt said to Blue Jay. "Green Gourd Vine told me all these people go to Five Clay Pots when they have a sickness."

"Yah! Green Gourd Vine told you!"

Spotted Colt took him by the shirtfront. "Be quiet or I will knock your teeth down your throat."

"You made this sickness come! Playing with that girl. Uncle saw you putting it where it doesn't belong."

"Be quiet!" Five Clay Pots said.

Mud Turtle loomed over them. "Be quiet." He took Blue Jay by the shoulders and lifted him a little. "If not, I will sit on you."

"This is not a sickness I know." Five Clay Pots shook his head. "It is not the lung sickness or the bad water fever. It must be a sickness from the Grass that you have brought with you."

"Someone has put a spell on her!" Blue Jay said. "That is what has happened!"

Dances moaned. Her teeth were chattering.

"Make her well!" Blue Jay clutched at Five Clay Pots' arm. "Witch! Your people did this to her. You make her well!"

"Calling me names will not make her well," Five Clay Pots said, and Mud Turtle came from behind Blue Jay and pinned his arms to his side.

"Come." Mud Turtle shoved Blue Jay out of the room, to the kitchen.

"Let me go!"

"Sit down and behave or I will tie you up and take you outside." Mud Turtle sat him down on the bench that ran along the west wall, among a jumble of pots and griddles, and stood over him.

"She is dying!" Blue Jay howled. His face was red and slick with tears.

"Maybe not." Mud Turtle thought she might be.

"We should never have come to this place. Never have lived in these boxes. Our people always get sick in the winter, in winter lodges. How can people not die living in these places all year?"

"Hush."

Blue Jay was panic-stricken, flinging himself from the doorway into Dances' room to the window and back, shaking his fist and shouting out the window at the people in the courtyard, lunging through the doorway again to stare at Dances and Five

Clay Pots, until even Digger forgot who he was and growled at him.

The people in the courtyard below shook their heads. Everyone knew that Grass people were likely to go mad at any moment, but they wondered if this one might be dangerous now.

Five Clay Pots came through the doorway from Dances' room. He handed a tiny clay cup to Mud Turtle. "Give him this. And keep him quiet."

Mud Turtle came up behind Blue Jay and tipped his head back suddenly. "Drink. It will make your sister better." He poured the contents down his throat.

Blue Jay gagged and sputtered. He wiped his mouth and glared at Mud Turtle.

"The healer person says it will make your sister better," Mud Turtle said stolidly. Blue Jay and Dances were brother and sister, so that might be true.

"All right." Blue Jay wiped his mouth on his hand and sat down on the window ledge, quiet now. He closed his eyes and talked to He Who Always Is, and the Sun and Earth Mother and his ancestors, and anyone else he could think of, telling them why Dances needed to stay in this world. None of them answered him.

"The bathhouse is still there," Spotted Colt said to Five Clay Pots. "We could make a sweat in it again."

Five Clay Pots chewed his lip. "It might help the fever, but I don't want to move her." Dances' breath came in short puffs now, and her skin was hotter than ever and covered with raised red spots. "This is an evil thing. I have never seen anything like this."

"*Is* it a spell?" Spotted Colt thought of Green Gourd Vine's mother. She might do that.

"I don't know." Spotted Colt thought Five Clay Pots was thinking of that, too. "If it is, *you* should be sick," Five Clay Pots said, confirming that notion.

Dances began to shiver.

"Go and get me some cloths, ask Cattails for them, tell her I said to give them to you. Tell your Mud Turtle to make a fire in the kitchen and get some water. I want to make steam."

Spotted Colt bolted out of the room, frightened. "Make a fire and get some water," he said to Mud Turtle. Blue Jay was sitting in the window, his eyes closed. Spotted Colt ran across the courtyard to Squash House while the women who were washing their clothes in Stream Young Man stared at him. He shouted, "I am here!" at Cattails in the city talk as he went up her ladder, so she would know who he was. He pushed his way into her sleeping room. She came halfway down the ladder from her kitchen and stuck her fingers out at him again.

"Five Clay Pots says to give me cloths," Spotted Colt said with his hands.

"Go away."

"He says to give them to me." Spotted Colt started up the ladder.

Cattails squealed like the peccary. She retreated up the ladder and flung a pot down at him. It shattered on the floor. Spotted Colt cursed her. She threw a big cloth down at him.

"Give me more!"

A white blanket followed it, and then another.

Spotted Colt gathered them up in his arms. As he straightened, he saw Green Gourd Vine watching him from above. Cattails grabbed her arm and jerked her back, out of his sight. Spotted Colt bolted down the ladder and across the courtyard again, feet pounding on the bridge. He raced up another ladder and the outer stairs of Turquoise House and then along the flat roof and down into their house.

Five Clay Pots had set a jar of water on the fire, a jar with a pointed end that dug into the ashes, holding it upright. There were stones heating beside it.

Spotted Colt put the blankets by the fire. "She called me something bad, but she gave me these."

"Good. I have sent your Mud Turtle for the hides from your sweat house." Five Clay Pots was setting up a wooden framework over Dances' bed—a loom frame. Whoever had lived here had been a weaver; there were already bars in the ceiling to hold it.

"What have you done with Blue Jay?"

"He is asleep," Five Clay Pots said with his mouth full of wooden pins. "Unless I gave him too much. In which case he is dead."

Spotted Colt looked through the door at Blue Jay. "He is snoring," he reported.

"Excellent."

Mud Turtle came back again with an armful of hides, and Five Clay Pots hung them over the loom frame, weighting the ends with rocks so that they made a tent around Dances, with one folded up for a doorway. They shoved Digger outside, but he went back in again and flattened himself on the blankets, yellow eyes baleful.

Five Clay Pots put a big bowl by the bed and scooped the hot stones into it with a piece of deer antler. He set a bucket with more water beside it. "Is that water on the fire hot? Stick your finger in it."

Spotted Colt did so gingerly. "Hot, not boiling."

"Good. Dip the blankets in it. Get them as hot as your hands will stand them."

Spotted Colt took one of the blankets and gripped the handles of the jar with it. He lifted it off the fire and couldn't figure out how to set it down on its pointed end. Mud Turtle came and steadied it between his knees, his thick leggings absorbing the heat. Spotted Colt stuffed the blankets into the jar, one at a time, water overflowing on the floor. He carried them, dripping, to Five Clay Pots, who was pulling Dances' dress off while she batted feebly at his hands and Digger growled at him, hackles raised. Spotted Colt kicked Digger away and grabbed Dances' wrists, and Five Clay Pots yanked the dress the rest of the way off.

Dances' whole body was covered with red spots. Some of them were beginning to blister, making watery pouches like the ones that came from a bad pack strap or too tight shoes. She looked worse than she had before he had gone for the blankets, and her skin was leathery around the blistered spots. Naked, she looked frighteningly thin, her ribs showing and the hollows of her collarbone dark recesses in her body. She whimpered at them while they wrapped her in the hot wet blankets. Her hands clawed at the cloth, and Five Clay Pots wrapped the folds around them and tucked them under her.

"Hush, hush." He sounded as if he were talking to a child. "Hush and be still. Let the sickness go." He dropped down the hide that he had folded back and ladled water onto the hot stones in the bowl by the bed.

The steam rose up in a cloud the way it had in the sweat bath. Spotted Colt couldn't see anything in it, maybe because he was almost afraid to. But he hadn't prayed to it or given it respect; it was just steam. It might sweat out Dances' fever.

Dances' eyes were closed, and her dripping hair plastered itself to her face. Her mouth was half open. It was hard to tell if she was breathing or not. Spotted Colt thought that Five Clay Pots couldn't tell either because he knelt down and put his ear by her nose. The steam reeked of wintergreen and made the air thick and medicinal. It was like trying to breathe the uncombed cotton that Green Gourd Vine had showed him.

Spotted Colt could hear Mud Turtle pacing outside and Digger whining. The bottom of the hides heaved up, and Digger crawled back in and lay on the wet blankets.

Dances moaned and batted at the cloths with a hand she had managed to free from them. Something else batted at the hides, something almost as vaporous as the steam. Spotted Colt's head swam.

After a long time Five Clay Pots stood up and pushed the hides back and lifted all of them over the loom frame. Like Spotted Colt, he was dripping with sweat. His hands shook as he took a bundle of herbs out of his basket and lit it, waving the smoke over the bed. Dances' face was red with the heat; but Spotted Colt could still see the blisters on her face. Some of them had broken open. Her cheeks were hollow. Spotted Colt cast an uneasy eye through the door to where Blue Jay was snoring. As he turned back, he thought he saw something go past him, through the door.

Mud Turtle's hand closed around his arm, and he pointed. Dances' hands had stopped plucking at the blankets. They lay still on her chest, one of them palm up in an odd gesture, as if she had opened it to let something go.

Five Clay Pots put his own hand on her chest and took it off again. He put his ear by her mouth. Digger whined and jumped off the bed.

"Go and wake her brother," Five Clay Pots said. He closed his eyes for a moment. When he opened them, he said, "How do you bury your people?"

Mud Turtle started toward the bed.

"Not here." Five Clay Pots bent down and lifted Dances' body. "This one must be taken out of here quickly." He put her on a hide and rolled her up in it.

Spotted Colt picked up something that had fallen as Five Clay Pots lifted Dances. He straightened up with it in his hand, a rag of yellow cloth.

Five Clay Pots narrowed his eyes. "Burn it. Whatever it is, it's evil luck."

8

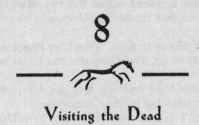

Visiting the Dead

THEY PUT COLD WATER ON BLUE JAY'S FACE TO WAKE HIM,
and when he saw the rolled hide he screamed at them.

"You did this! This place killed my sister! Why didn't you
wake me?" He dissolved into howling sobs, sitting on the
floor, legs splayed out, head in his hands.

"You wouldn't have kept her here," Spotted Colt said. He
thought of the wraith that had batted at the hides in the steam
tent and then slipped through the door. "I saw her go."

"This place made her sick! May it come and take you all,
too!"

Five Clay Pots looked uneasy. "This is a new sickness. If
it didn't come with you, it is a new sickness in the world
entirely."

Blue Jay threw his head back. "Dances! Come back!"

Five Clay Pots hurried over to him. "Be quiet! You do not
want her back, not now. Hush!"

"Dances!" Blue Jay wailed, hiccuping the name into his
sobs, his shoulders heaving.

Five Clay Pots shook him. His fingers dug into Blue Jay's
shoulders. "Do not call the dead."

Spotted Colt said, "The dead have gone. They don't come

back no matter how much we want them." He spoke half to
Blue Jay and half to Five Clay Pots, but he remembered the
ghosts that had appeared before the Dry Water people had
made their truce with the Buffalo Horn, and his certainty less-
ened.

"They may take us to *them*," Five Clay Pots snapped. "And
I am not ready to go. This thing that has killed her frightens
me."

So they burned the bedding, too, and everything she had
touched, with Blue Jay howling behind them.

Digger didn't follow when Blue Jay took Dances' body
away from Five Clay Pots and took it outside the city walls
to mourn. Instead he dogged Spotted Colt's heels like a
mourning shadow.

"Go away," Spotted Colt told him, but Digger wouldn't.

Blue Jay insisted on putting Dances up on a bier in the way
of the Grass people, and Squash Old Man and Turquoise Old
Man, after talking to Five Clay Pots, said they could not do
that here. So Blue Jay and Mud Turtle and Spotted Colt took
Dances, still wrapped in the buffalo hide, far out into the open
land on a travois pulled by End of the Day Horse, and built
her a bier there out of cottonwood branches.

Blue Jay wanted to give her End of the Day Horse to ride
on wherever she was going, but Spotted Colt and Mud Turtle
wouldn't let him and took his knife away.

"That is only for chiefs. And we haven't enough horses."

Blue Jay sulked. "We have more than we need without her."
He had stopped sobbing, but his throat was raw with it. He
lay down at the foot of Dances' bier.

"No."

"Then I will stay here and watch her," Blue Jay said craftily.
"Black Water Horse and I."

"You aren't going to give her Black Water Horse, either."
Spotted Colt took his arm and tried to get him to stand. Blue
Jay clutched the corner pole of the bier, wrapping his arms
around it. The bier swayed dangerously. Blue Jay put his head
on the ground, weeping silently now.

"You will be sick," Spotted Colt said. "Stop it. You can't
bring her back."

Blue Jay lifted his head. His eyes were red and swollen. "Why not?"

"Because they don't come back," Mud Turtle said. "My mother didn't come back and my father didn't come back and my little sister didn't come back. And they won't come back for you."

Blue Jay sat up, scrubbing his eyes. "People have gone to bring them back. Coyote went to bring his wife back."

"And he bungled it, and that is why we have death now," Mud Turtle said. "And anyway, that is only a story."

"How do you know? It was true once. There are lots of stories about people who went to bring a dead person home. There wouldn't be that many stories if it wasn't possible."

Spotted Colt sighed. "Most stories are about things that aren't possible."

Blue Jay stood up, his eyes glittering and earnest. He looked up at the hide-wrapped body on the bier. "She will leave in four days. I could go after her, stop her before she gets there, bring her home."

"She will be *dead*," Spotted Colt said. "Even if you bring her home, she will be dead. There are stories about people who did that, too." Husbands who convinced their wives not to take the trail to the Hunting Ground of the Dead, to turn around and come back to the village. The dead wives had rotted slowly, the stories said, until the husbands couldn't bear to sleep with them. That was what stories were for, to teach you what things were not a good idea.

"No, they did it wrong." Blue Jay looked at Dances' blanket-wrapped body again. "You can't just turn around. You have to go to the place where the dead live and talk to someone, and then they tell you how to bring her back so that she is alive again. That is how Coyote did it. He didn't love his wife more than I loved Dances." Blue Jay's voice caught. "I will go."

"How?" Mud Turtle asked.

"I will find out."

Spotted Colt handed Black Water Horse's rein to Blue Jay and waited while he mounted. He gave him End of the Day Horse's rein, too, and watched him as he started back toward the city, the empty travois bumping along behind. Digger put

his nose in Spotted Colt's hand. "Not everything means what
you want it to mean," Spotted Colt told him.

When they weren't watching him, Blue Jay went to Turquoise
Old Man and Squash Old Man and told them he wanted to go
to the place where the dead went; did they know how to get
there?

"Go away," Squash Old Man said. He said it with his mouth
and with his hands so that Blue Jay would be sure to understand him.

"I want to bring my sister back." Blue Jay was certain now
that he could. He couldn't think why he had not thought of
that when she first died.

"We don't want people coming back," Turquoise Old Man
said. "Go away from here."

"She died here," Blue Jay said. "I think she has to come
back here." That would be reasonable. How else would she
know where to go?

"No," Turquoise Old Man said.

Squash Old Man said something to two small boys who
were throwing stones into a circle scratched in the courtyard,
to see who could get the most in the middle. Their eyes opened
wide, and they left their stones and ran across the court. In a
little while five men came puffing behind them to where
Squash Old Man and Turquoise Old Man were sitting with
Blue Jay in the afternoon shadows that fell off the roof of
Turquoise House.

Squash Old Man spoke to them urgently. These men were
heads of the Holy Clowns, the Blue Clay and Rabbit Medicine
Societies, and the Sun House and Deer Lodges. They looked
with horror at Blue Jay.

"No one can go there." They said it together.

"I will," Blue Jay said. He added something rude to them
all in his own language and ran away.

"Weren't they going to leave?" Squash Old Man asked Five
Clay Pots.

"I hope so."

But they didn't leave. The brother of the one who had died
roamed around the city asking people where the dead went

and frightening little children. The other two followed, arguing with him.

"You can't follow the road to where the dead live because you can't see it," Mud Turtle said practically.

Blue Jay ignored him. He circled the walls of Red Earth City as if he could find a trail leading away from it, into the ground or the air. All they saw was the road to Bean Canyon City.

"And anyhow, you don't know what place she's gone to. Five Clay Pots says she went somewhere these people call the Skeleton House, where cities people go, up north under Blue Lake," Spotted Colt said. "Maybe she didn't go to the Hunting Ground of the Dead."

"I told you you should have let me send a horse with her," Blue Jay said.

"It is time to leave her." Spotted Colt looked toward where Dances was, out beyond the city. Five black birds circled on the thermals above her. "You can stop and talk to her on our way home, and tell her how we found horses."

"And then never see her again! How can I stop and tell her the news, if she is here? When will I pass this way again, once we have found horses and gone home? No, it would be much better to take her with us." Blue Jay looked stubborn.

"Then we will take the bones when we come back," Mud Turtles said. "And you can put her skull in a circle in the Grass, with her own kind."

"That is a fine idea," Spotted Colt said. "Why didn't we think of that? Now, let us go and find these horses that they say are in Bean Canyon City, before the monsters who own them move on somewhere else."

"Go yourself," Blue Jay said, unmoved by Spotted Colt's enthusiasm. "I will stay with Dances."

"There are not enough of us without you," Spotted Colt said, exasperated. "It may not be easy to get horses. And anyway," he added craftily, "if only Mud Turtle and I go, we will only bring back horses for Dry River. That is all right with us, of course, but you will disgrace the Buffalo Horn."

Blue Jay didn't answer him. He stood staring into the water of Stream Young Man as if it might pull him under, take him by some subterranean river to the Land of the Dead underneath Blue Lake.

Mud Turtle bent his head to Spotted Colt's ear. "Do you think he *could* go get her?"

"I hope not." Nothing good had ever come of that kind of thing. That was why there were stories about it in the first place, to teach you not to do it.

"He won't leave until he tries. Do you think we can do without him?"

"How long is a piece of rope?" Spotted Colt said. "How much use is a crazy person?"

Blue Jay spun around. "I am not crazy!"

"Yes, you are," Mud Turtle said stolidly.

Blue Jay's eyes glittered. He looked crazy.

"I don't think it's a road you can take in your body," Spotted Colt said to him gently. "The dead don't take theirs."

"I don't know how to get out of my body," Blue Jay said, as if it were a room with no door.

"Five Clay Pots might know." Spotted Colt weighed the unwisdom of that against the fact that Blue Jay wasn't going anywhere else; he might as well go to the land of the dead.

"Then ask him for me. Tell him we won't go away until he shows me."

"Maybe he doesn't care if we go away." Spotted Colt was reasonably sure that he did. Five Clay Pots was Green Gourd Vine's aunt—sort of—and he and her mother both wanted the Grass people gone.

"No one has ever done that, in my memory or the Grand-mothers'," Five Clay Pots said. "And I am not sure if it is still possible."

Spotted Colt sat on a bench in Five Clay Pots' weaving room with Digger lying on his feet, and they watched him spin cotton. The spindle was a rod with a flywheel disk jammed onto it about a third of the distance from the bottom. The cotton was wrapped around the rod, and it hummed and whirred in Five Clay Pots' hand. Men spun and wove the cotton, and women sewed it, but it seemed that Five Clay Pots was both, or either, and could do as he pleased. He had young Mouse with him and was teaching him to spin.

"But it was possible once." Spotted Colt prodded Five Clay Pots while Mouse scowled at him over his small spindle.

"You will snarl that." Five Clay Pots untangled Mouse's skein. "Stop and straighten it once in a while. It was possible once, but now it is dangerous, if it can be done at all. I would not send anyone on that road whom I wanted to come back." He sat with his legs folded under him in a puddle of skirts, the spindle end braced on the floor, its rod against his thigh. The sun that came through the open window lit his bent head and the swift flash of fingers as he rolled the spindle rod on his thigh, the thread shimmering and humming, twisting onto the rod in a cone above the flywheel.

"We have told him all this."

Five Clay Pots furrowed his brows at the humming thread. "It is hard to say what might happen. The Two Old Men told me I wasn't to help him."

"Then why are you talking to me?"

"Because I want to know what's in the Land of the Dead, of course."

Spotted Colt snorted. "You could go yourself."

"Thank you, no. Soon enough for that."

"But you'll send Blue Jay."

"I have no great attachment to Blue Jay. But I didn't say I would send him."

"Do you know how?" Spotted Colt demanded.

"I know how to send him *somewhere*. It all depends on who opens the door on the other side."

Spotted Colt nodded. It was as he had thought. You couldn't go in your body.

"If I send him and he doesn't come back, will you and that other one and your horses leave anyway?"

"Yes." Then Blue Jay could stay with Dances, which was what he had wanted.

"It is expensive," Five Clay Pots remarked. His fingers flashed and the thread hummed, while the white cone grew on the spindle.

"What do you want for it?" Magic was always expensive, and this was magic, of a sort.

"I will have to have a present to give the Two Old Men. Out of respect, for defying them."

"Of course."

"I don't know if it will work to send you to our Skeleton House, since you are Grass. It would be best if I had a present, too, so that the spirits know you are sincere."

"Of course."

Digger shifted on Spotted Colt's foot, opened his jaws, and whined. He closed them with a snap. Five Clay Pots watched.

"That is a fine dog."

"He wouldn't stay with you. He was Dances'."

Five Clay Pots winced at the careless naming of the dead.

"Now he says he is mine."

"I will take the others, then, the pups. One each for the Two Old Men and two for me."

"I would have to ask Mud Turtle. They are his." Spotted Colt hadn't expected him to ask for the dogs. "Why do you want them?"

"New blood is always good for a dog pack. These dogs are Grass."

"They are half coyote."

"So are we all." Five Clay Pots smiled. "In our secret hearts. Mouse knows." He ruffled the child's shorn hair. "Mouse watched them hunt his naming animal in the midden yesterday."

Spotted Colt had thought to offer him Dances' tent, which she hadn't died in and which was a fine one made of painted buffalo hides. "Well, I will ask Mud Turtle," he said, bewildered.

"Then you can give me the tent," Mud Turtle told him. Laugher would have more pups. She had more pups every year, sometimes twice. She was snoring in a corner behind the packs now, where these pups couldn't get at her to nurse, big as they were.

Digger sat on Spotted Colt's foot, but the other four were trotting across the courtyard, having inspected the midden and the empty mouse nest beneath it just to see if anyone had come back, on their way now to look at the women frying flat bread for dinner in the first-floor houses. They had made it their business to inspect all of Red Earth City, investigating grain bins and garden sheds. A man gluing a bow might look up suddenly to find a dog watching him, or a woman washing clothes find one nosing in her soap. Now they stopped to see if they could climb a ladder to the second floor where an odd noise, a rattle and a thump, was coming from a room above. One of them put two paws on the first rung and then the second, his back feet clinging precariously, before he fell off. Another tried it and got three rungs up.

"They will be climbing ladders by fall," Mud Turtle said.

Five Clay Pots said that they would send Blue Jay along the road to the Skeleton House (if indeed that was where he went) in the lodge that the Grass men had built for a sweat bath, because he couldn't go into the kiva, which was holy, and Blue Jay wasn't.

They carried the hides that Mud Turtle had stripped off it back down to where the frame still stood beside the river and tied them over it. Spotted Colt waited for the Two Old Men to come shouting out of the city at them, but no one came. There wasn't even anyone in the fields.

"When foolish things are being done, no one but Coyote comes along," Five Clay Pots said cryptically.

After Spotted Colt made a fire, Five Clay Pots burned a sticky resin that scented the hot air with pine sap, and set a little clay pipkin onto the coals to cook. Spotted Colt peered curiously at its contents, which looked unsavory, a mash of leaves and green-brown sludge. Blue Jay took his shoes and shirt and breechcloth and leggings off and unbraided his hair, all the things that would loosen the ties that held him here. Then he sat cross-legged with his eyes closed, thinking pure thoughts, which Five Clay Pots said would open the road to the Land of the Dead. Blue Jay hadn't spoken a word since Spotted Colt had told him that Five Clay Pots had agreed, not even to thank Mud Turtle for the dogs, which made Mud Turtle disgruntled.

"I can send him to the Land of the Dead," he whispered in Spotted Colt's ear. "And I don't need a pot of mush to do it."

"We need him," Spotted Colt said.

"He is crazy."

"Crazy or not."

Five Clay Pots was setting out a row of cups, the five clay

pots of his name, beside the fire, and pouring something into each of them.

"What is that?" Spotted Colt asked suspiciously. "I don't want to go, just him." He jerked a thumb at Blue Jay.

Five Clay Pots smiled, and Spotted Colt wondered if he and the Two Old Men simply planned to poison them all as a method of removing them from Red Earth City. Five Clay Pots said, "When using the ghost flower, it is a good idea to offer the spirits some, too, in case they get jealous. If it lets us see them, perhaps it lets them see us."

Spotted Colt decided he wasn't going to drink anything Five Clay Pots offered him.

Five Clay Pots picked up the pipkin from the fire by its handle and poured its contents into three of the cups on the ground. The other two he filled with water from a skin. He dropped more resin into the coals and produced a cloud of smoke that filled the room. It was dark in the sweat bath, even with no steam, and they saw him as a white form, ghostly as the guide he hoped to call up for Blue Jay.

"Now." Five Clay Pots tapped Blue Jay on the shoulder, and Blue Jay opened his eyes. "Drink this."

Blue Jay didn't argue with him. He got to his feet, tipped the cup, and drank its contents while Spotted Colt wondered again if he ought to stop him. Five Clay Pots handed Blue Jay another cup and then one of the cups of water, and he drank those, too, and it was too late to stop him, if Spotted Colt had been going to.

The stew in the cup tasted bitter, like greens picked too late, and made Blue Jay's mouth pucker. He gagged and swallowed and drank the second cup as fast as he could. Five Clay Pots handed him the third cup, and he washed the bitter taste down with the water. His throat burned and then felt dry, and he reached for more water. It tasted odd going down, sweet and oily.

Blue Jay stared at the walls of the sweat house, waiting for them to open and show him the road to the dead, but all he saw was Spotted Colt and Mud Turtle, and Five Clay Pots with another cup in his hand. It wasn't going to work, he thought crossly, and his knees felt wobbly, the way they had in the steam of the sweat bath. The ground began to undulate under his feet, and he sat down suddenly. *I'll rest,* he thought, and tried to tell Five Clay Pots that his medicine didn't work, but the words came out strangely, as if he had begun to speak someone else's language. And now he couldn't find Five Clay Pots, but he could just make out the road, running through the fading walls of the sweat house. *I'll rest first,* he thought, and lay down.

Blue Jay closed his eyes, and he swayed a little, as if a wind was blowing him like a maize stalk. Spotted Colt and Mud Turtle peered at him, waiting to see if he vanished. Blue Jay swayed some more, opened his eyes, staring past them, closed them again, and fell over.

Five Clay Pots stretched him out on the floor of the sweat house and put a cotton blanket over him. Blue Jay's hands were twitching, but nothing else moved. His breathing deepened and slowed until Spotted Colt had to put his ear to his chest to be sure of it. His skin felt clammy.

"What will happen now?" Spotted Colt asked.

"He will go. Or not."

"How will you know?"

Five Clay Pots took his belt knife out of the folds of his skirt and poked the sole of Blue Jay's bare foot with it. Blue Jay didn't move. "Well, he has gone somewhere."

9

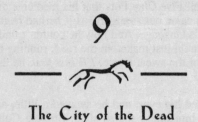

The City of the Dead

THE LANDSCAPE HAD CHANGED, AS IF BLUE JAY HAD walked a long way out into the empty country, but he didn't remember doing it. Red Earth City had vanished. He stood on a trail that wound between stands of cactus and agave plants and was very stony beneath his bare feet. Blue Jay looked around him for something to make sandals out of, but there didn't seem to be anything, so he hobbled along. He didn't see anything that looked like a lake.

The sun was hot, and the air was dry as dust. He turned a corner and found a woman sitting by the trail. For a moment he thought it was Dances, but then she turned her face toward him and he saw she was a stranger. There were deep lines around her eyes, and the skin of her neck was wrinkled.

"What are you doing here?" she asked him.

"I am looking for my sister."

"You aren't dead."

"I know that." *This woman is stupid*, he thought. "I am trying to find my sister Dances and bring her back with me, because she is not supposed to have died yet."

"How do you know that—that she is not supposed to have died?"

150

"Because she is a year younger than me. She is not old and ugly yet."

The woman sniffed. "Am I old and ugly?"

Blue Jay thought she was, but he didn't want to say so. "No," he said.

"Well, I am dead anyway," the woman said.

"What are you doing out here? Is this the way to the Land of the Dead?"

"It's just around that corner there." The woman pointed a hand at the next turn in the trail, where it disappeared into a thick scrub of mesquite and cactus. The hand was thin; he thought it might be just bones.

"Where?"

"There. Just follow that trail. I don't know if they'll let you in, though." She folded her bony hands in her lap again.

Blue Jay went on down the trail, walking backward, staring at the woman. He backed into an agave spike and yelped, turning around to see what had stuck him. When he looked again, the woman had gone. The trail got narrower until it was hard to tell where it went in the tangle of brush and cactus and agave. Everything was spiny and pricked his bare skin.

"Be careful!" a voice said from under a whorl of agave.

Blue Jay stopped and looked carefully to be sure it wasn't Rattlesnake.

A cricket peered back at him, shiny and black in the gray-green shadows. "Mind where you put your feet," it said. "What are you doing here?"

"I'm looking for my sister."

"Is she a cricket?"

"No, she's a human person."

"There's no one here but us."

"What about the Land of the Dead?"

"Oh, that's everywhere." The cricket gestured vaguely with a feeler.

"Where the human people go," Blue Jay said.

"Oh, I wouldn't try to go there."

Blue Jay lifted his foot. "Tell me where it is, or I'll step on you!"

The cricket scuttled farther into the agave. "You'll be sorry," it said sulkily. "No good comes of things like that."

Blue Jay got a stick and poked under the agave leaves with it.

"All right," the cricket said. "But don't say I didn't tell you. Follow the trail you're on, and you'll get there. Everybody does."

Blue Jay wasn't sure the cricket had actually told him anything. The trail got narrower and narrower, and everything poked or stabbed or grabbed him as he passed. He pushed his way along stubbornly and came out finally on the other side of the thicket, into a place where the ground was like obsidian, shiny and black. A coyote was sitting by the side of the trail.

"What are you doing here?" the coyote asked him.

"I am looking for my sister Dances, to take her back with me," Blue Jay said.

"Is she dead?"

"Yes."

"Are you?"

"No. I don't think so." Blue Jay wondered suddenly if he was, if Five Clay Pots had tricked him.

The coyote sniffed him. "You aren't dead. They won't let you in. I tried. My wife's in there, and they won't let me in either."

"Is your wife dead?"

"Yes. I almost brought her back, but they said not to touch her until we were back in our village, and one night I just couldn't stand it any longer and I put my arms around her, and she vanished." The coyote looked sorrowful.

"Then what are you doing here?"

"Waiting. To see if they will let me in again."

"How do I get there?"

"Just down that road," the coyote said. "You won't see anything until dusk. Just sit still, and when it's dusk, then you'll see them. Tell them to let me in again."

"All right, I will." Blue Jay went on along the trail, which ran through the black, shiny plain. There wasn't anything else there, no plants or other animals, just the earth with its strange dark surface, as if he were an ant walking on an obsidian arrowhead. In a while the plain ended in a sheer cliff. Blue Jay stood on the edge and saw a stream and green grass and trees down below, but there was no way to get down there.

There was one tree growing out of the cliff face, its branches just reaching up to the lip where he stood. He wondered if he could climb down it.

When he lay down and looked over the cliff, he saw that there was a vulture sitting in the tree. It was black, with a bald head and a ruff of white feathers.

"What are you doing here?" the vulture asked him.

"I am looking for my sister Dances. I want to take her home with me."

"Oh, no. Not allowed." The vulture sounded mournful.

"Are you in charge here?" Blue Jay demanded, leaning over the cliff. "Why isn't it allowed?"

"Oh, too many of you. Way, way too many." The vulture sighed lugubriously. "If we let you go back, the world would fill up with you. And you make such a mess."

"Doesn't the Land of the Dead fill up?"

"Oh, they're very light. Just bones." The vulture peered up at Blue Jay, extending its neck from the dark hunch of its shoulders, ruffling its collar of white feathers. "There's too much of *you*. Either you aren't dead yet or someone hasn't cleaned you properly."

Blue Jay backed up. "I'm not dead."

The vulture opened its beak thoughtfully. "Then you had better go home."

"I have come to get my sister," Blue Jay said stubbornly. A tear rolled out of his eye. "We are first friends, since we were babies. She caught a new disease in the cities, and it killed her."

"Ah." The vulture seemed to know about that. It cocked a red eye up at Blue Jay. "You will die, too, eventually. Patience is important," it added. "We wait."

"I have to take her home," Blue Jay said. "Back to the Grass. If I don't, I'll go to the Hunting Ground of the Dead when I die, and she'll still be here."

"You know a lot of foolish ideas," the vulture said. "Not so much about being dead. I suppose you'll do it anyway, so I might as well take you down there." It sighed.

"Can you do that?"

"Certainly. Just climb on my back."

Blue Jay looked down dubiously. It was a long way to the

bottom, and he didn't like the idea of touching the vulture. But it clambered farther up the tree toward him, pulling itself along with its beak, and spread its wings to make a canopy that Blue Jay could climb down. It was very big, bigger than vultures in the live world. Blue Jay slid onto its back. Its feathers were warm and oily and smelled faintly of carrion.

"Hold on." The vulture spread its wings. Blue Jay gripped the collar of white feathers around its neck. Its head was perfectly bald, covered in red, wrinkled skin. It launched itself from the tree in a ponderous flapping of wings while Blue Jay clung to it, terror-stricken. The noise of its wings sounded like thunder. Then suddenly it spread them wide to catch the thermals, and they were floating silently in the sunlight. They soared, sailing on the air currents like a boat on water, giddily swooping over the landscape below. Blue Jay could see the river like a shiny strip of cloth, and willow trees growing out of its banks. He couldn't see any people or houses.

"Where are they?" he asked the vulture.

"Patience, live person." The vulture soared over the riverbank, dropping slowly in graceful swoops. A little way above the ground it let its feet down and descended with another awkward flapping.

Blue Jay slid off its back. As soon as they ceased moving, the world grew perfectly silent. The sun shone, but it was as if the landscape had been sealed up in a drop of amber. Nothing stirred among stones and sticks and fallen leaves along the riverbank. No bug people sang in the bushes, no mice rustled in the leaves. Not even a breeze stirred the branches above him. This world was perfectly still. Only the vulture moved in it.

"Are we there?"

"*You* are."

"There's no one here."

"Sit down and wait. The world is reversed here. Their night is your day, and your night is their day."

That didn't make sense to Blue Jay, but in all the old stories, when a vision spirit told someone to do something, that person should do it. Bad things happened to people who didn't obey a spirit's instructions. Blue Jay sat down obediently on the riverbank and watched dry leaves and bits of dead stick float by.

"Well, I'll be going now," the vulture said.

Blue Jay felt uneasy at being left here in this silence. "Where are you going?" Even a vulture was better company than no one.

"Oh, there's a lot to do," the vulture said. "Always a lot to clean up, especially these days. Work, work, work." It lifted off the ground with a heavy flapping, then beat higher into the sky until it was only a dark silhouette soaring above him. It grew smaller and smaller and then winked out in a flash of sunlight, and Blue Jay couldn't see it at all.

He didn't know what to do, so he went on sitting by the riverbank as the vulture had told him to. It was so quiet that he felt as if he too had been sealed in amber, embedded in perfect silence. The sun slid down the sky while he sat staring at the water, the only thing that moved.

Finally, after a long, long time, as the sun dropped behind the mountains, he saw something flutter in the water. At first he thought it was only another stick, but then he saw that it was a fish. As he watched, small brown fish began to swim in the clear twilit current and crayfish to scuttle across the bottom, waving their pincers. A faint sigh stirred the trees.

Blue Jay looked up. The air looked thick, like glue cooking in a pot. He thought he heard voices: the faint murmur of women talking, the shrill shriek of children. A dog barked, and someone shouted at it. He stood and turned around and around in a circle, looking for them.

Gradually they began to coalesce out of the air, growing thicker and thicker, more solid, until he could see them: people very like the people of Red Earth City, in white clothes, women carrying clay pots on their heads, men with hunting gear over their shoulders and dogs at their heels. Birds chattered in the trees.

"Look! It's a live person!" The voice was soft and excited.

Blue Jay turned to find a small child two paces behind him, staring, the fingers of one hand pointing, the thumb of the other in its mouth.

"What do you want here?" A man who looked important, like a chief, strode over to Blue Jay. Blue Jay thought for a moment that he saw through him, saw the white bones underneath the skin, but then the man was solid again, standing hands on hips in front of him.

"I am looking for my sister," Blue Jay said. "Her name is Dances."

"How did you get here?" He was almost as soft-voiced as the child.

"The vulture brought me. And the coyote asks if you will please let him in again," Blue Jay added, remembering his promise.

The man ignored that. "Well, I am Flycatcher. Your sister is married to me."

"Married?" Blue Jay's voice reverberated through the dusk. They all turned and stared at him, hands over their ears.

"Yes, she's over there." Flycatcher pointed. "You can go and talk with her, but don't be so loud." Flycatcher's voice was almost a whisper.

Blue Jay saw a cluster of houses, stacked one on top of another like the ones at Red Earth City. A woman was making pots outside the first one he came to, and he saw it was Dances. Her pots leaned to one side, as if they had had too much cactus juice.

"Dances!"

She looked up. "Blue Jay? What are you doing here?"

"I came to find you." He stared at her, trying to see if she was transparent the way the others had been, but she looked as solid as she always had.

"Did you die?" she asked him.

"No. I told you, I came to take you home with me."

"Oh, dear." Dances' mouth was a round O of dismay. "But I am married to a man here."

"How can you be married? You are dead. He's dead!"

"Well, the world does go on," Dances said, "even if you're dead. Neither of us ever married anyone in the live world, so we thought we would do it here."

Blue Jay stared. This didn't sound like his sister at all. Maybe she was lying. Dances was always telling fibs, making jokes on people.

"You're joking with me."

"I am not. Here, hold this pot up while I try to see why it's leaning." She sighed, exasperated. "They always lean. I just can't get them straight."

"Well, why are you trying? It's too dark anyway." Blue Jay didn't bother with the pot. He looked around him at the village. There were turkeys gobbling in the courtyard, their necks bobbing up and down. A fat old dog snored under a ladder behind her. Firelight flickered on the inner walls of the houses, illuminating the rooms above him. Before the sun had gone down there had been nothing here.

"It's the only daylight we have," Dances said. "Between when the sun goes down and when it's full dark."

"I thought this place was under a lake," Blue Jay said fretfully. "Where's the lake?"

"When you came down the cliff," Dances said, "you went under the lake. This village is at the bottom of it."

"I didn't see any lake. And how can there be a stream here if we're in the water?"

"Silly, I didn't say we were *in* the water. We're *under* it, the way one world is under another."

"Well, I ought to be wet," Blue Jay said. "I tried to send you a horse, but they wouldn't let me. I don't know how we'll get back again."

"Silly, I can't go back."

"Yes, you can," Blue Jay said stubbornly. "You don't want to be here married to some ghost."

"I *am* here," Dances said. He noticed that she spoke as softly as the rest of them.

"Well, I'm going to take you back," he told her loudly, drowning her sibilant protest.

"Shhhh!" Dances waved her hands at him. "Don't shout like that."

"I'll shout if I want to!" Blue Jay bellowed.

The village shuddered as if there had been an earthquake. He watched the mud houses and the people shimmer and crack open like eggs, and disappear. A pile of bones and rubble lay at his feet.

Blue Jay looked where Dances had sat. There was no sign of the pot she had been making, or the clothes she had worn. There was only a bleached skeleton sitting incongruously in front of the ruined walls, its legs crossed under it. Blue Jay touched the skull with his fingertip, and it toppled from the neck. The rest of the bones collapsed in a heap with a soft sigh like rain falling.

He backed away, horrified. All around him the village had vanished. The men coming home from the hunt were only scattered femurs and vertebrae, the ring of dancing children a still circle of bone.

"Come back!" Blue Jay shouted, but no one moved.

The night was cold now, with the fires gone. Blue Jay shivered in his loincloth, his teeth chattering. He started to run, but it was too dark to see anything. He tripped over a pile of bones and flung himself away from them, shrieking. Finally he huddled in the lee of the tumbled walls and waited, freezing, for the dawn.

He slept eventually, numb with cold, and woke to find even the ruined walls and the skeletons of their inhabitants vanished, faded into nothingness with the light. There was no sign of the vulture, or the coyote, or the woman from the trail. He sat down with head bowed, where he thought he remembered that Dances had sat, and waited for dusk to fall again. He wasn't sure they would really come back. Maybe he had imagined them all.

By noon Blue Jay's stomach was growling. He got up to look in the stream, hoping for a fish, but there was nothing there but dead leaves. The water moved downstream sluggishly, as if this place thickened it and held it back, so that it must fight its way past to wherever it was going. Blue Jay looked up in the air, hoping the vulture would come back, but nothing moved above him either. By nightfall he was thoroughly hungry and frightened.

The sun sank down behind the mountains in a pool of gelatinous orange like fish eyes, and the people came back as the dusk did, forming out of shadows at the corners of his vision. He closed his lids tight for a moment, and when he opened them he could see the village, the walls of the houses solid against a gold and scarlet sky, smoke rising from the cook fires. Blue Jay got up and went back to where Dances had sat. She was there again, patting her pot.

"Well!" she said. "That was a terrible thing to do. I told you not to shout."

"I'm sorry," Blue Jay said contritely.

"We are very quiet here," Dances told him. "We like it quiet. When there are loud noises, we can't stay."

Someone in the house behind her was cooking meat on a spit. He could smell it. Blue Jay's stomach growled again. He hadn't eaten since he had come to this place.

"That's my husband's aunt cooking," Dances said. "Fly-catcher, my husband, brought home a fat deer yesterday."

"I am very hungry."

"Well, I will feed you if you will promise not to make loud noises."

He nodded and she got up, leaving her pot, which looked a little straighter than it had yesterday. She came back out with a clay bowl filled with chunks of roasted deer meat. A breechclout and a pair of sandals were tucked under one arm.

"Put these on. It isn't decent to come here like that."

Blue Jay tied the breechclout around his hips. It was white cloth, the kind that these people wove from cotton fibers, with a design like red mountains painted around the hem. It felt like wearing a skirt. The sandals were woven yucca that laced over his instep. He tied them on his sore feet, and Dances handed him the bowl of meat. The meat smelled wonderful, better than anything he had ever smelled. He picked up a piece greedily and stuffed it in his mouth. He ate a second piece and a third, and three of the flat maize cakes that Dances brought him, sopping up the meat juice with them.

"I didn't know that dead people ate," he said, struck by a sudden thought between the third piece and the fourth.

"Well, of course we eat. Everybody eats." Dances' husband came and sat down by Blue Jay, and she brought him a bowl, too. The aunt didn't come with her, but Blue Jay thought he could see her, peering at him from the edge of a window. He stuffed the last piece of meat in his mouth and watched Fly-catcher. He could understand what Flycatcher said, which was odd, because Blue Jay couldn't understand the people who lived in cities when they were alive. Flycatcher was a solemn young man, with the air of authority that important people wore. If Dances had to marry someone, certainly it should be a chief, Blue Jay thought. But she couldn't stay here.

"I don't know how you got here," Flycatcher said. "But if my wife wants you, you can stay. You can hunt with us today."

Blue Jay thought this wasn't the time to talk to Dances again about leaving, about going back to live people with him. He would wait until Flycatcher wasn't there. "It's dark," he said.

"This is our day," Flycatcher said. "You come with me. I'll lend you a bow."

Flycatcher gave Blue Jay a bow and a quiver of arrows, and they set off, with the other ghosts, up the trail that led out of the town. Blue Jay stumbled in the darkness, but the others seemed to know where they were going. He followed behind the last of them, trotting to keep up, afraid of being left and waking in the strange, still wood. There was nothing else to do but follow. He couldn't see to track, and in any case, learning the terrain of a strange hunting ground took time. There was much studying involved in knowing where the deer lay at night and where they watered and where the rabbits came out to feed. He thought about it and wondered if all the animals here were dead, too.

The men up ahead of him were talking to each other in whispers. He couldn't understand them, but they sounded excited. Two of them ran ahead of the rest, their white clothes making a milky trail in the woods, like their white bones. Blue Jay heard crashing in the underbrush where they were driving the deer. The others followed more slowly, and he came behind them, resisting the urge to wrap his fingers around the last man's shirt and hold on.

Then they all began to run, whispering through the dry leaves ahead of him as he panted to keep up. The last man vanished in the woods, and he couldn't see them anymore. "Wait!" he called, but no one answered.

Blue Jay floundered among the black trees, turning in a circle, trying to see where they had gone. Which way was the village? He stumbled into a clearing where a dead tree lay and looked up at the stars, but they were all strange, patterns he had never seen before. He started to shout for the ghosts and stopped himself, afraid of what might happen.

Then he heard them, coming back through the trees, their

footfalls light as wind. They were laughing and carrying sticks over their shoulders, but Blue Jay couldn't see anything on the sticks but two beetles tied on with grass.

"Where did you go?" Flycatcher asked him cheerfully. "We killed two fine deer."

"Where are they?"

"On the poles," Flycatcher said.

They are making fun of me, Blue Jay thought. *Well, two people can do that.* He was silent the rest of the way back to the town. When Flycatcher handed the two dead beetles to Dances, he pretended that he didn't see anything amiss. These people were stupid, and they played stupid jokes.

Blue Jay sat down grumpily to show Dances that he didn't like her husband making game of him. Flycatcher had gone away with the other men without paying any more attention to him. After a while Blue Jay began to smell fresh blood, and he looked to see what Dances was doing. A fat buck was laid out on the ground in the firelight in front of the house, and Dances was skinning it.

"Where did that come from?"

"Well, you killed it, silly."

"I didn't kill anything. They lost me in the woods."

"Well, Flycatcher killed it. You came home with it." Dances didn't sound as if she wanted to quibble over it. She pushed the hair out of her eyes and set at the haunch with her skinning knife.

"They brought home dead beetles!" Blue Jay frowned at her. "They made a game of me." Two old women had come to help, and they looked at him curiously.

"It looks like a deer to me," Dances said tartly. "It might look like a deer to you, too, if you came and helped us with it." Skinning was hot, hard, dirty work.

"Bah, you're always telling lies." Skinning was also women's work. He wasn't going to do it while they made fun of him.

He sat and sulked, but presently, when he smelled deer liver cooking, his stomach clenched and said that it wanted some. Dances brought him a piece, and he ate it, the juices running out of his mouth.

"Do you still think it's beetles?" she asked him.

"I don't think this is beetles. I think your husband brought back beetles, and you had that deer kept somewhere, to make a game of me."

"Yah, you are not so important that we spend all our time hiding deer to make you look a fool! You can do that by yourself," Dances said disgustedly. She wouldn't talk to him for the rest of the night.

Blue Jay sulked while he watched his sister and the two old women cut up the rest of the deer. The aunt was a wrinkled crone with hair as gray as thunderhead clouds. She looked old enough to be dead. Flycatcher and the other men were playing a game with black and gray pebbles on a clay board by the fire, laughing softly, their mouths smeared with deer grease. What the ghosts didn't eat the women cut into thin strips and laid out on a stone to dry. The offal they gave to the dogs. Then they dragged the deer hide down to the stream to soak. Dances and Flycatcher's aunt wrestled it over the bank and pegged it to the bottom with bone stakes to keep the current from carrying it off.

By this time the sky was beginning to lighten, and Blue Jay watched to see what would happen when the sun came up. The ghosts seemed to shimmer in the graying air already, and the flames from the fires grew pale and cold. While he watched, his sister and the old woman grew transparent, still standing in the stream, until he could see the water through them. They climbed out just as the sun tipped its eye over the mountain to the east. The world folded in on itself in the flicker of an eye, and when he looked, there was only a trail of bones along the stream bank.

Blue Jay looked into the water, but the deer hide was gone, too. They must be ghost deer here. Behind him the town had vanished again, and the men around the game board were only a ring of skulls and rib bones.

Blue Jay snorted angrily. They made fun of him and then they turned into bones. An idea occurred to him. He sidled over to the skeleton men before the sun was full up and they vanished entirely. They lay in heaps of bones, each with his skull resting in a pile of ribs and vertebrae, legs and arms sprawled about as if they had each turned to bones with the sunrise and fallen where they sat. Where did they go? Blue

Jay wondered. Where did their spirits go when their bodies turned to bones? Never mind, they would be back with the sunset, and they would see what happened then. He began to rearrange the piles of bones, picking up what he thought was Flycatcher's skull and setting it amid the vertebrae of a man called Red Eye. Red Eye's skull went on Thornbush's ribs, and Thornbush's to Flycatcher.

We'll see how she likes that, Blue Jay thought. *She's always telling lies. We'll see how she likes having her husband's head on some other man's shaft. Hah!* He lay down beside where the fire had been, to sleep and wait for the night.

Blue Jay woke, yawning, when the air grew cool. The ghosts were there, transparent but growing solid. Dances and the old aunt came up the path from the stream as if they had just finished pegging out the hide. The men were standing up, shaking out their clothes, which had come back with their flesh. They staggered a little as they moved, and then one fell down with his face in the stones along the edge of the fire. The fire was burning again now, too.

The man said a bad word and stood up, looking at his hands and feet with a puzzled expression. He examined them more closely. The other ghosts were doing the same.

"I am not right," one of them said.

"Those are my feet, Thornbush."

"Well, I am wearing them."

"Flycatcher has Red Eye's."

"We are all put together wrong."

Blue Jay began to snicker. The ghosts danced around each other, pointing at their feet and hands, tugging at their heads as if they were trying to take them off. Blue Jay snorted. They didn't notice him, so intent were they on this mysterious redistribution. A hooting laugh escaped him, louder. The ghosts were pulling at each other's arms and legs. In their white clothes, waving their legs about, they looked like cranes dancing. Blue Jay whooped with laughter.

"Be quiet!" Dances rushed up to him, glaring. "Did you do this?"

"Of course not!" Blue Jay chortled. "There must have been

an earthquake in the night—in the day—when you sleep, I
mean. It rolled the bones together."

"How do you know that?"

"I don't. I was asleep. But there might have been."

She gave him a long, angry look and went inside her house.
Blue Jay followed her. "I'm hungry." He seemed to be
growing hungrier than usual here.

"I'll make you maize mush," Dances said grudgingly.

"Dances, aren't you glad to see me?"

"Of course I am." Dances stood in the middle of her kitchen,
hands on her hips. "But you shouldn't be here. I didn't mean
to die and leave you, but now I have, so that is the way things
are."

Blue Jay sat down sadly on the mud bench that ran around
two sides of the kitchen walls. This place looked like the
houses at Red Earth City. The mud walls were plastered with
white and red clay, and aspen roof beams held up the ceiling.
Bunches of dry grass hung from the beams, giving off a mysterious onion smell, making the air musty and pungent. A shelf
above his head was lined with red and yellow baskets, painted
clay bowls, and a pot of spoons and wooden whisks. Storage
baskets and clay water jars stood along the south wall. Above
the jars the white plaster was painted with a red deer running,
an archer with drawn bow behind it. Dances wore a white skirt
and a blanket of woven cotton, like the city people's.

"At least you ought to be with *our* dead people."

"That's what happens when you leave home. You end up
dead somewhere else."

"I made you a bier. I didn't put you in the ground the way
these people here do."

"I don't think it matters. Maybe I wanted to come here. I
don't know."

"Why would you want to do that?"

"Flycatcher is here."

Blue Jay snorted again, thinking of Flycatcher walking
around on Red Eye's knock-kneed legs. Outside they were still
falling down, their bodies unfamiliar and unwieldy. "For
him?" His voice was scornful.

"You learn things when you are dead," Dances said. "I was
young and ignorant. Now I am not. You tell those people in

Red Earth City that there will be more people dying of what killed me."

"What was it?"

"I don't know, but the coyote said so, when I was on my way here."

"He said his wife is here." Blue Jay hadn't seen any coyotes.

"Everything that is dead is here. Coyotes don't live in houses. She is where coyotes live."

"Are those deer we are eating dead? And the turkeys?"

"Everything but the vulture, I think. He comes and goes."

"That is very strange."

"If there is an alive world, why should there not be a dead world? All those dead people have to go somewhere."

"Five Clay Pots told me the Outsiders think the dead people go into the wind."

"Maybe theirs do," Dances said disapprovingly. "We live in houses." She licked her finger and touched it lightly to a flat stone in the coals of the kitchen fire. "This is ready. Get me some meal from that basket in the corner."

Blue Jay took the lid off the tall basket and looked in. There was nothing but a handful of dry leaves in the bottom. "There isn't anything in here."

"Of course there is. I filled it this morning."

"It's just leaves."

Dances made an exasperated noise with her tongue and went to the basket. She grabbed a handful of the leaves and put them in a clay bowl. While Blue Jay stared at her, she poured water on the leaves and stirred them up with a bone spoon.

"I'm not going to eat leaves."

Dances shook her head and didn't say anything else. She stuck a dipper into the bowl and poured out a dipperful of something pale onto the hot stone, spreading it with a wooden blade. The smell of cooking mush filled the kitchen. When the flat cake was bubbling, she picked it up by the edge with her fingertips and flipped it quickly.

"How did you do that?" Blue Jay demanded.

"Here." Dances pulled the flat cake off the stone and rolled it up between her fingers. She handed it to Blue Jay.

He peered at it. It was maize cake. He bit the end experimentally. It tasted like maize. When he looked in the clay bowl, there was maize mush in there, too. "Ah, you are always playing tricks on me!" He ate the cake quickly in a few gulps and glared at Dances. Since she had been with the dead people she had become foolish. "Don't you miss End of the Day Horse? Don't you remember being a Child of the Horse?" He tried to shake her by the shoulders and will her to remember.

"No," Dances said shortly. She cooked him another cake and he snatched it off the griddle before she could roll it up, hungrier than he had been yesterday.

The light had faded outside until the sky was full dark, a deep vibrant blue shot with pinpoint stars. Fires burned in a long line in front of the houses, and the ghosts heaped wood on them until red and orange flames shot into the dark air. Inside, the little hearth fires gave off a yellow warmth that pulsed in the open windows like something breathing.

"Here." Dances took a small deer-hide box off the high shelf. Its lid was painted with a red and white spiral, unwinding forever in slow circles. Inside was something brown and shiny that she held out to Blue Jay. "Field Mouse gave me this, for you, before we left. She said it must be magic—it looks like a bird." She dropped it in his palm.

Blue Jay turned the little stone over. "I didn't know you had this. How did you bring it here?"

"It followed me." Dances shrugged. "When I got here, it was here. These people saw it and said it meant I should marry Flycatcher."

"Well, I never saw it before."

"Well, I never showed it to you. Field Mouse said it was for you, only she was too shy to give it to you, the stupid hen."

Blue Jay tried to remember Field Mouse. Her face wavered in the corner of his memory, a little girl with shiny dark eyes and wispy hair. She had pretty hands. He looked at the stone. How could it be here when he hadn't sent it? And how did Dances cook dead leaves into cake? It made his head hurt, and he was still hungry. The cookfire gilded Dances' ears and nose, and the jumping flames made the buffalo horns tattooed on her chin dark and mysterious.

Flycatcher came through the door. "Are these my feet?" He stood in front of Dances, demanding her attention.

"I think so. There is the scar on your toe."

"Everyone was all mixed up," Flycatcher said.

Blue Jay snickered.

"That child with one eye who came last dark-of-the-moon says there is a dead buffalo a little way up the valley. We're going to go and get it." He looked at Blue Jay as if he were a bug that Dances might want out of her kitchen. "We can take him with us."

Dances said, "Yes, show him the buffalo."

Blue Jay followed the men out into the night again. The moon was only half full, but it gave a watery gleam to the grass that grew by the stream bank as it meandered up the valley. Blue Jay thought of buffalo back fat and hump meat, and his mouth watered. His stomach growled. He wished he had asked Dances for another cake.

The men carried coils of yucca rope over their shoulders to drag the buffalo with, and three small boys scampered after them. Flycatcher fell into step beside Blue Jay. "How long are you going to stay here?"

"That's hard to say." Blue Jay could just see Flycatcher's white teeth in the moonlight. "How did you get your right feet on again?"

"Someone was very careless," Flycatcher said disapprovingly. He didn't sound as if he were going to tell Blue Jay how they did it.

They walked on, following the stream. The ghosts' footfalls made no noise in the grass. Blue Jay's own steps sounded very loud to him, loud enough to shake the ground. The boys scampering ahead of them were pale dots bobbing like luna moths above the grass. He saw a coyote looking at him from beneath a bush, its yellow eyes like coals in the darkness, and he wondered if it was the wife of the coyote he had seen among the agave and black rocks.

The men ahead of him stopped, and Blue Jay ran into their backsides. They all stumbled amid a flailing of bony arms and bows and spears swinging wildly. The feathered shaft of an arrow protruding from someone's quiver poked Blue Jay in the eye. They untangled themselves and gathered around a fallen tree trunk.

"There is the buffalo," Flycatcher said. "It's a fat one." The ghosts began to tie their ropes around the tree trunk.

"It's a dead tree!" Blue Jay said loudly, but they didn't pay him any notice.

The small boys were dancing around the bare crown of the tree, breaking off short branches and waving them.

"Look out, now," Flycatcher said, shooing them off. He twisted the rope through the base of the branches and knotted it. "All right, now, pull."

Blue Jay stamped his foot. "It's a dead tree! And you will take it home and Dances will tell me it's a buffalo! Yah! I am not going anywhere with you." He sat down in the grass. "You have not treated me well at all."

"He is crazy," one ghost said to another, making a gesture at his head.

"It wasn't right to let a live person in," the other said.

"Yah! You are all stupid!" Blue Jay shouted at them. "Boo!" He yelled it as loudly as he could, and they all fell down in heaps, white bones gleaming under the moon.

"Hah!" Blue Jay said. "I'll teach you to play tricks on me." He went to a pile of bones and picked up the long femurs, the tibias and fibulas, and swapped them with the ulnas and the humerus and radius bones. He swapped another skeleton and then another and stood back, giggling. The dead tree lay among them, tangled in rope that faded away as he watched it. Blue Jay made a face at the bones and ran away down the trail.

"Where are the others?" Dances asked him when he got back to the village.

"I don't know. They lost me on the way. They never wait for me."

Dances looked at him suspiciously, hands on her hips. "Did they find the buffalo?"

"It was a dead tree!" Blue Jay said. "You all play stupid tricks on me here."

"Maybe we don't play tricks," Dances said shortly. "Maybe you don't see."

She fed him, but she wouldn't talk to him for the rest of the night. When the men didn't come home, she chased him angrily out of the house. "You have done something! Go and sit by the river until they come back!"

Dances wasn't the same, Blue Jay thought mournfully. Being dead had made her different. Surely if he took her back to the live world, she would be the same again; she would be his sister, his constant companion, his best beloved. He lay down by the river and put his head on his arms and slept as the sun oozed over the mountains.

The world of the dead was a fly in a drop of honey, bones embedded in amber. The sun crawled from one side of the sky to the other, flowing slowly like surf solidified into stone. Blue Jay had begun to feel it. While the light shone, his limbs were heavy, his flesh almost too weary to move. He got up once to piss and nearly fell, stumbling over his own feet on the riverbank. He lay down again and waited for the nightfall, eyes open on his pillowing arm like a dog watching a door.

At last the bright crescent of the sun sank behind the mountains. Blue Jay felt his limbs lighten as if he were weightless as the ghosts. He stood, feet now not quite touching the dry grass. He looked at the village and saw smoke coming from the houses, but Dances was still inside. Blue Jay turned the other way quickly, running lightly over the grass to where the dead tree had lain. He wanted to see the ghosts when they woke up with their legs on their shoulders. That would teach them not to make game of him.

When he came near, Blue Jay slowed and then dropped to his belly, wriggling through the grass like a coyote. He could see the branches of the tree's crown above a shallow rise in the ground, and he poked his nose over cautiously. The ghosts were there, talking in a furious whisper. They looked as comical to him as giant, upended babies. Most were standing on their hands, like great birds, their legs sticking out of their shoulders, huge feet flopping at the ends. One or two were trying to stand on their feet, heads poking out between their thighs, rear ends wobbling helplessly in the air. Blue Jay buried his nose in the grass, shaking with silent laughter. All around them the little ghost boys danced, doing handstands. They wished *their* hands had been put on their bottoms.

The ghosts' angry, sibilant words were impossible to hear, but Blue Jay could see them, smudges rising above their heads, whipping round and round, coalescing into a dark spiral, like a dust storm. The ghosts stamped on their handsfeet and cursed him. The words rose higher, darker. Blue Jay began to feel queasy in his stomach. He backed away, wriggling on his belly while the grass waved all around him in the wind of the ghosts' anger. Their hands grew until they were wide as plates, and they stamped up and down on them, waving their long legs like branches in the wind. The air gathered around their words, and now he could hear them, a tornado roaring in his ears. Blue Jay stood up and ran.

The ghosts' words chased him across the grass, their shadow running ahead of him like a dark funnel. Blue Jay looked over his shoulder and saw it looming, bending toward him, waving long dark arms with hideous feet on the ends. He ran faster, his heart pounding in his chest, his feet heavy on the ground now, as if his shoes were stone. He stumbled at the stream bank amid a scattering of fist-sized stones that hadn't been there before, and his ankle turned under him. He righted himself, limping, hopping painfully, lumbering on toward the village. What if Dances wouldn't let him in?

It was nearly full dark now, and the roaring in his head and the hammering of his heart drowned out the tornado behind him. Blue Jay limped into the village, yelping with every step, and flung himself through Dances' door.

"Hsssssh!" Dances put her fingers to her mouth. "Be quiet, Most Noisy."

Blue Jay whimpered.

"What is the matter?"

"I have turned my ankle. It hurts." It was silent outside now.

"Let me look at it." Dances pushed him onto the bench on the kitchen wall and knelt down beside him. "Well, that is swollen. You ought to be more careful."

Blue Jay winced as she prodded the swelling.

"I'll put some salve on it and bind it for you. What were you doing?"

"Nothing."

Dances opened a clay pot of something vile-smelling that was a greasy, dark brown. She smeared it on his leg while he gagged.

"What is that?"

"Piñon pitch salve."

"It smells like rotten meat."

Dances shook her head. "You don't belong here." She wound a strip of soft deer hide around his ankle and pulled it tight, pinning it with a bone needle.

"Come home with me, then. That's why I came here."

"I can't go there with you."

"Why not? The coyote took his wife home. Or he would have, if he hadn't forgotten and touched her before they got there."

"I think someone always forgets and does that." Dances peered at him in the dim light. "You don't look good."

"I'm all right."

"I can see through you."

"How?" Blue Jay bent over and then stood up, trying to look over his shoulder.

"I don't know how. I just can."

"I'm hungry," Blue Jay said.

"Well, they'll be bringing the buffalo."

"I told you, it's a dead tree."

Dances made an exasperated noise. "You don't see."

They heard talking outside, and she went to the door. "They're here now. It's a fat one."

"Aren't you afraid to eat it?" Blue Jay asked sarcastically. "Who knows what it died of?"

Dances giggled. "Is it going to kill us?"

"Maybe. If root rot is poisonous. Why do you play these games?"

"Watch." Dances went through the door to where the men had dragged the tree up in front of the houses. They pulled off the ropes, and she took a knife and began cutting into the bark. When she cut into it, the tree turned into a buffalo.

Blue Jay came out and stared at it. "How did you do that?"

"This is our food. It's not like your food."

Blue Jay poked the shaggy buffalo hide with a forefinger. It felt real. He stared into the glazed eye as if it might tell him something. The buffalo was cold, but it didn't smell rotten. He couldn't see what had killed it.

"Sometimes they just come," Dances said. "I think maybe somebody gives them to us in the live world. Not buffalo usually. Mostly it's deer and antelope."

"But you kill food here, too."

"Oh, yes."

She didn't seem concerned by any of it, or by why food looked like beetles and dead sticks until she touched it. Maybe only he was seeing the buffalo. Maybe they really ate dead sticks. Blue Jay's stomach cramped. The food here tasted all right, but he was always hungry.

The hunter ghosts glared at him. "Someone has been careless," Flycatcher said to Dances, with a jerk of his head at Blue Jay. "Our arms were all on our hips and our legs on our shoulders. It was very uncomfortable."

Dances snapped her head around at her brother. "They will get tired of you if you keep this up."

"I didn't do anything," Blue Jay said sullenly. A snort of laughter escaped him in spite of himself. "But they were very funny, dancing on their hands, with their feet bouncing around."

The other ghosts began to talk to each other. Flycatcher spoke in a low voice, and Red Eye and Thornbush nodded. They eyed Blue Jay.

"I didn't do it," Blue Jay said.

"You are a nuisance," Flycatcher said.

"And we can see through you anyway," Thornbush added. "You had better go home while you still can."

"I'm all right."

Red Eye peered at him. "It may be too late."

"He can't stay here. If he dies here, he won't be properly dead. He'll have to go and sit outside with the coyote."

Blue Jay stood up straight in front of them. He took Dances' hand. "I came to get Dances. I am taking my sister back with me."

"Oh, you can't do that."

"I can if she wants to." Blue Jay looked at Dances pleadingly.

Dances hung her head. "I don't want to," she whispered.

Blue Jay put his hand under her chin and made her look at him. "Why not?"

Tears rolled down her cheeks. "I'm dead. Nobody would marry me there if I came back with you. They'd be afraid of me."

"I wouldn't be."

"Well, I can't marry you!"

"You didn't want to get married!"

"I do now. You will, too. And then you would leave me, and everyone else would be afraid of me."

"You love him better than you do me," Blue Jay said stubbornly, turning his head to glare at Flycatcher. Flycatcher smiled at him.

"Maybe so." Dances shook her head. "I don't know. It's all different here. Blue Jay, go away! Go home before you have to stay here!"

"But when I die, I'll go to the Hunting Ground of the Dead and you'll be here!" Blue Jay wailed.

"You won't mind, then," Dances said with certainty.

"I will."

"Then you shouldn't have brought me here. Go away now!" She backed away from him a step. She didn't look like his sister. There was something different about her face. He could see the bones through it. The other ghosts moved forward, coming between Blue Jay and Dances.

"Dances!"

They closed in between them until he couldn't see her.

"You should leave," Flycatcher said. He smiled again, pleasantly, as if he were bidding a favored relative farewell.

"Wait!" Blue Jay said desperately.

They paused. He could see through them all now, one behind the other, with Dances at the very back.

"Where do you go?" he asked. "At daybreak. Where do you all go?" Maybe he could follow.

"We go where it's dark," Flycatcher said. "Our world is dark."

"Some other place?"

Flycatcher shrugged. He looked as if he couldn't explain it any further.

"But you go on living?"

"We . . . are."

"Dances!" Blue Jay called again.

"No," Flycatcher said.

The rest closed in on him, driving him before them. The old aunt waved a bone spoon at him; it might have been her own bone. Even the little children and the dogs were almost transparent now, skulls showing through their skin and fur. It made them look angry.

"But I am a Child of the Horse!" Blue Jay said. "I am descended from important spirits!"

"That doesn't matter here."

They pushed him ahead of them until he found himself suddenly at the base of the cliff. The vulture was waiting for him, perched high on the limb of a dead tree. Its white ruff and bald head shone in the moonlight.

The vulture extended its neck, peering curiously at Blue Jay. "You should have left sooner, live person."

"I didn't want to leave," Blue Jay said resentfully. "They chased me."

"You should thank them." The vulture settled itself on its branch, fluffing its feathers. "But no one ever does," it added.

Blue Jay turned to see the ghosts vanishing, moving away from him over the dry grass, bones and faces faintly luminous in the darkness. "Wait!" he called, but they didn't. In a moment they were only a milky tide, flecked with dark, receding across the ground.

The vulture bent its dark head. "And did you find your sister?"

"She wouldn't come." Blue Jay felt dizzy with the betrayal of that.

"Ah." The vulture considered. "What are you going to do now?"

"They told me to go home."

"Hmm. I suppose you'll want me to take you."

Blue Jay looked upward at the cliff edge. It disappeared into the night, with only the sudden appearance of stars oto tell him where it ended.

"Get on," the vulture said irritably. "If you stay here you'll just make a mess I'll have to see to. Go and die where you're supposed to." It spread its dark wings and dropped down from its perch in the dead tree. Blue Jay's head felt swimmy, and the stars began to whirl above him. "Get on!" the vulture snapped. "Hurry!"

Blue Jay grabbed a handful of dark, oily feathers and pulled himself up on the vulture's back. He could feel the ridged sinews where the wings attached to the backbone. It still smelled of dead meat. It turned its head to look at him, cocking one red-rimmed eye. "Hold on," it said. Its foul breath made his stomach heave, but he wrapped his arms around its neck and laid his face dizzily against the greasy feathers. The huge wings began to beat, pushing the air downward, and he felt them lift from the ground. The black cliff slid beside him as they angled up its face, the fires of the City of the Dead winking out as if the water he couldn't see had closed over them. He expected the vulture to light at the cliff top, but it didn't. The dark heavy wings beat the air until it caught a thermal above the desert. Blue Jay looked down and saw the coyote still waiting by the black stones, motionless and silent as a statue. In the agave clump he could see the cricket and its relatives scurrying back and forth, eating dung and dead leaves, turning everything back to earth again. The dead woman sat bonily by the trail, her hands folded in her lap.

"What is she waiting for?" Blue Jay asked the vulture.

"Crickets," the vulture said.

The air was hot and smelled of the vulture's breath. Blue Jay leaned his head against the dark neck again, his stomach rising. His feet and thighs felt suddenly light, and he realized that the breechclout and sandals that Dances had given him were gone, faded with the City of the Dead. Maybe they hadn't been clothes at all but dry leaves, whispers of dead grass, beetle carapaces, shiny and empty as the sunlight. The hot wind blew on his face, and he closed his eyes while the great wings held him up on invisible air.

"Get off," the vulture said, rippling the sinews of its shoulders. It banked in the air, tipped one wing low, and Blue Jay grabbed at the dark oily feathers as he fell. They slid through his hands. The vulture shook its wing a little, like a dog shaking off water, and he lost his grip entirely.

Blue Jay dropped down through the thick air, spinning around and around like a leaf. High above him he could see the vulture climbing the thermals again, growing smaller in the sky. He looked down and saw the ground rush toward him. All around him were faces, bony faces transparent against the blue sky. He saw Dances and Flycatcher and the old aunt, Red

Eye and the small child who found the buffalo, all faces on the wind, eyes made of stars. They opened their mouths to speak to him, but no sound came, and the ground spun closer until he fell away from them, past Dances' bones on her bier, and through the hide roof of the sweat house into the darkness of his body.

10

The Pale Kachinas

"HE'S DEAD." MUD TURTLE POKED A FINGER INTO BLUE JAY'S ribs. They were sunken as a cleaned fish, and his skin was pallid.

"No, he isn't. He's still breathing." Spotted Colt didn't like the look of it, though. And Five Clay Pots had gone away and left them there with a dead, or possibly enchanted, person.

Mud Turtle put his ear to Blue Jay's mouth. He frowned, wet the outside of his ear with his finger, and tried again. "Maybe," he conceded. He laid his head against Blue Jay's bare chest. "Ummm," he said. He pulled the blanket back over him.

Spotted Colt sat down cross-legged beside Blue Jay, and his head nodded. It was dim in the sweat house, and magic made him sleepy. They had taken turns for four days to watch Blue Jay do nothing but lie there. He hadn't even peed in his sleep. That couldn't be good for him.

"What do we do if he is dead?" Mud Turtle asked.

"Put him up on a bier with his sister," Spotted Colt said, yawning. "There's no lack of buzzards here." Already the dark shapes had swarmed over the body on the bier, perching on its poles when they were sated. The local people gave it a

177

wide berth, and Five Clay Pots said fastidiously that Grass people were uncivilized. Spotted Colt thought that burying bodies in the dirt was uncivilized.

"Ummm," Mud Turtle said. He asked the same question every day and was never happy with the answer.

Blue Jay could see them watching him. They were dim shapes in the fog that enfolded him, lumpy outlines like buffalo over his head. He tried to sit up, but his arms wouldn't move. His legs felt like stone, holding him to the ground. A fierce bright ache shot through his temples. He could still see the road to the dead, running faintly through the thin walls of the sweat house, through the moonlight and cactus to where Dances was. He could follow it, he knew. Get up out of his body again and follow it, and not come back. This time he wouldn't need the vulture to take him there. He wondered if he ought to, but there was no one to tell him.

"I think he moved." Mud Turtle looked fixedly at Blue Jay.

Spotted Colt got up stiffly. He lifted the flap of the sweat house to let in some light. Blue Jay's eyelids fluttered at the sudden brightness, and a trail of spittle ran from the corner of his mouth.

"He's either coming back or going away again." Spotted Colt dipped a cloth into the bowl of water that Five Clay Pots had left and wiped it across Blue Jay's forehead. Blue Jay's lips parted.

The light was a fierce white brightness, brighter than the thick amber daylight of the dead. It burned his eyes with its fierceness. His lips were dry and cracked, and his stomach hurt. He opened his mouth, and someone squeezed drops of water into it. He moved his tongue against his teeth.

"Are you dead?" the someone asked him, a curious voice from a long way off. He thought at first that it was the vulture again and said, "No!" because his stomach said it didn't want to be dead.

The someone dropped more water into his mouth.

"He's waking up," Spotted Colt said.

"He still doesn't look good to me." Mud Turtle prodded a finger through the blanket. "And he has a bad smell."

"Here we are!" Five Clay Pots bustled through the open door flap with a covered clay bowl in his hands and a cloth sack over his arm. "Is he awake yet? Oh, that's good. Very good. Now, then." He set the bowl down and unpacked his sack as he talked. "He'll be hungry, but he mustn't have anything but thin broth to start."

"I think he's dying," Mud Turtle said.

Five Clay Pots cocked his head at Blue Jay. "Hmmmm. Maybe. Give him some water from this." He handed Spotted Colt a waterskin from his sack and pulled Blue Jay's blanket back to look at his chest. "Goodness, you're thin. Did you see the Land of the Dead? What was it like?"

"I don't think he should talk yet," Spotted Colt said.

"Well, if he's dying, I want to know." Five Clay Pots pulled the blanket back up and took the lid off the clay bowl. "Drink some soup now. It's been four days since you ate."

"I ate buffalo," Blue Jay said, pushing the words out past his parched lips. "And deer meat." His stomach cramped at the smell of the broth.

"Dead people's food." Five Clay Pots clucked his tongue. "That won't feed a live person."

"You did go there," Spotted Colt said.

"I . . . went there."

Spotted Colt lifted Blue Jay's head while Five Clay Pots spooned some broth into his mouth and Blue Jay swallowed.

"What was there?"

"Bones."

"Just bones?"

Blue Jay thought about Dances and Flycatcher, and the piles of bones that were left when he shouted. "I'm not sure. Sometimes they were people."

"Did you talk to them? Did you bring your sister back?" Spotted Colt looked uneasily about the sweat house, and Mud Turtle made a sign with his fingers.

"She wouldn't come." Blue Jay closed his eyes, and his breath slowed and grew shallow.

"Eat this." Five Clay Pots held the spoon under his nose again. Blue Jay opened his mouth and swallowed. Some of the broth ran down his chin. Five Clay Pots set the bowl down. He put his hands under Blue Jay's shoulders and lifted, and

Spotted Colt held him up until they could prop him against the poles of the sweat house.

"Are you certain she didn't come?" Mud Turtle asked uneasily.

"She wouldn't," Blue Jay said again. "I think I was foolish to go."

"Well, when we have learned we are foolish, we are on the road to being wise," Five Clay Pots said. "Now, open your mouth and drink some more of this, and tell us about the City of the Dead."

"It is dark. A city of night. In the daytime there is nothing there."

"How did you get there?"

"I don't remember." Already the road was fading like a dream. He looked down at his naked body. "I had clothes there. A breechclout and sandals. Dances gave them to me. There was a stone, too . . ."

"Be glad you don't still have them," Five Clay Pots said briskly. "If you had kept them, you might have stayed."

Blue Jay shuddered. That seemed a dreadful possibility to him now. "How long was I there?"

"Four days," Five Clay Pots said, spooning broth.

Blue Jay swallowed the last of the broth and closed his eyes. "I'll sleep now," he murmured.

They stretched him out again, and while he slept, he dreamed of Dances. She was standing outside the City of the Dead, and then she was standing beside her bier. It was hard to tell, and even though she was smiling at him, she faded as he watched her.

He woke up and told Spotted Colt, "She has married somebody there," and went back to sleep.

When he woke up again, the Two Old Men and the heads of the Holy Clowns, the Blue Clay and Rabbit Medicine Societies, and the Sun House and Deer Lodges were standing over him.

"I have seen the Land of the Dead," Blue Jay said.

"You must go away now," the Two Old Men said with their mouths and then again with their hands. The priests of the Holy Clowns and the medicine societies and the lodges all nodded.

"They say you have to go away," Five Clay Pots told him helpfully.

"Why?"

"He isn't well yet," Spotted Colt protested.

"He has opened up a road," Turquoise Old Man said, "and it will not be closed again until he has gone. We told you not to help him," he said severely to Five Clay Pots.

"Sometimes it is good to know what is on the other side of a wall," Five Clay Pots said. "And they have given us four fine dogs to express their gratitude."

"Hmmph!" said Squash Old Man.

"I have seen the road," said the chief of the Holy Clowns. "It goes through the wall of this skin house and into the desert yonder." He pointed the way that the skeleton road had run. Blue Jay couldn't see it anymore now himself.

"We must close the road," said the chief of the Deer Lodge.

"Quickly," said the chief of the Blue Clay.

"Before ghosts come down it into our city," said the chief of the Rabbits.

"The road will close behind them when they leave," Squash Old Man said. "We will bring you your packs to this house here. There is no need to go back into the city."

"They are leaving," Cattails said with satisfaction. "That Grass boy with the tattoos on his face went to the City of the Dead after his sister, and now the Two Old Men have told them to leave."

Green Gourd Vine stared at her mother. "He went where?"

"And Five Clay Pots helped him, the old fool! There'll be ghosts and bones and who knows what all in our houses now, and dead people going just anywhere. But at least they are leaving. Five Clay Pots says the ghosts and dead people will follow them when they go, and not stay here. I think he just wanted to know what it was like there. He always wants to know everything before he needs to."

Green Gourd Vine sat silently, stunned and thinking. After a thing like that, of course the Two Old Men would make them leave. She wondered if Five Clay Pots had known that and done it on purpose. She fingered her earlobes. Five Clay Pots had put holes in them with a bone needle the way she had asked him, while her mother fumed. Green Gourd Vine had put the shell spirals through the holes and admired the effect in a water jar, but her ears were very sore. Five Clay Pots had given her a flask of salve to rub into them. "If you have the ornaments you don't need the young man," he had said briskly.

Out her window, Green Gourd Vine could see the Grass men loading their packs on their horses. The horses' hides gleamed in the sun like water on stones. *He won't come back,* she thought. Beyond lay the bean and squash fields that the peccaries had trampled. The littlest boys stood around the edges of the fields now with piles of rocks to throw, taking shifts, day and night. The hunger of the peccaries was like a rooting snout all around Red Earth City.

"*They* will go, too, now that those Grass people are leaving!" Cattails said. "If you are lucky, the young men will forget that you ran after that Grass boy, and one of them will bring you a blanket this winter."

"I don't want a blanket," Green Gourd Vine said rebelliously, but she kept her voice low enough that Cattails couldn't hear. It didn't matter what she wanted. Unless she was going to be like Wants the Moon, who had run off with the horses long ago, then she would have to let a boy give her a blanket or she would have no daughters to take care of her when she was old.

Blue Jay swayed from side to side on Black Water Horse's back, but he wrapped his fingers in the dark mane and held on. End of the Day Horse trotted beside him, looking perplexed that there was no one to ride her. Gray Cloud Horse and Bites If You Aren't Careful Horse followed on their leads. Blue Jay looked up as they passed Dances' bier and bit back the tears that welled in his eyes. She was married in the City of the Dead and would not come back, and being a Child of the Horse had made no difference. This land was not like their own.

"We will find the horses when we come to this Bean Canyon City," Mud Turtle said sympathetically. "And then we will come and take her bones back to the Grass. Maybe her spirit will come with them."

Blue Jay shook his head. "Leave her here. She is married here, married in the skeleton place. She can't come."

Mud Turtle cocked his head at him. The Buffalo Horn boy still looked thin enough to have come from the Skeleton House himself, as indeed he had, where all the food was air and illusion. But there was something in his eyes that was different. Maybe if you went to the Land of the Dead and came back you were older then.

Spotted Colt kept his back to Red Earth City, no matter how much the skin between his shoulder blades itched with wanting to turn around and see if Green Gourd Vine was watching him go. A wind-carved willow with its feet in Stream Young Man whispered to him as they passed, and Digger, trotting beside Rainstorm Horse, looked up and said to him clearly, "That is not a good place. We should have left sooner."

"Don't talk to me," Spotted Colt said crossly. "I don't want to be talked to by dogs."

Digger's tongue lolled out as if he hadn't said anything. He turned away from Spotted Colt and stuck his nose in a hole that belonged to a burrowing owl.

From her window, Green Gourd Vine could just see Spotted Colt's faint form lean down and drag the dog up by the neck ruff, and then they were gone, winked out into the dry red stone in the blaze of sunlight that shattered its surface if you looked too long.

The young men from the Grass had been gone five days when the pale kachinas came to Red Earth City.

The boys who had been set to watch for the peccaries saw them first, a dark line of horsemen and walkers coming out of the afternoon sun. When they came near, the boys saw that their skins were white as the underbelly of a horned toad. They dropped their stones and ran for the city walls, eyes wide as fish ponds. They told the Two Old Men, who sent for the lodge and medicine society priests and the Holy Clowns, and they all hurried across the bean field as they had when the Grass people came.

Green Gourd Vine heard the commotion and thought maybe the Grass men had come back, so she darted out of the house with a look over her shoulder for Cattails and ran for the bean field, her skirt hiked above her knees, her heart pounding. Mouse and Toad and Magpie appeared from nowhere and danced along beside her.

"What is it? What is it? What is it?" Magpie sang.

"It is pale people like the ones in Bean Canyon City!" Toad said eagerly.

They could hear Cattails calling them from behind, but no one stopped. And then suddenly they could see them, and Green Gourd Vine stopped with her hand to her mouth and snatched at Mouse and Toad. Her toes dug into the warm earth, and her legs felt unable to move. The pale kachinas were spread out across the edge of the bean field like a row of dancers getting ready to dance a new dance into Red Earth City. She pulled the little ones to her, and Magpie clutched her skirt.

"Are they magic?" Toad whispered.

They were as pale as water, skin so colorless Green Gourd Vine thought she could see through it. They were shaped like men, but it was as if some mysterious hand had emptied a true man's body and put something altogether different into it, so that only the outer edge was the right shape. The walking kachinas had shirts of leather. The ones on the horses wore hard gray shirts like turtle shells. The shells were dusty and dented, but the sun glinted on them, and the chief among them had designs carved into his, and a feather in his hard, shiny hat. Dark hair grew all over his chin.

Just behind him was another pale person riding on a small, strange animal, like a horse only with long rabbit's ears. This one wore a blanket of black cloth and a wooden thing around his neck, not nearly so wonderful as the chief beside him, but he had an air of importance and heaviness about him. He spoke sharply to a man on foot, who touched his forehead in what must have been a gesture of respect.

The man in black frightened Green Gourd Vine even though she couldn't see any weapons on him. Some of the others carried sticks slung over their shoulders or tied to the seats that were strapped to the horses' backs. Sticks would be no match for bows, she told herself.

The Two Old Men were talking to the pale kachinas and to

a man who had come with them who looked as if he were
from Bean Canyon City. The Bean Canyon man was listening
to what the kachina in the shiny hat said, and then telling it
to the Two Old Men.

"They ask you for something to eat and water for their
horses," the Bean Canyon man said.

Squash Old Man nodded solemnly. That was hospitality.
That was required, whether kachinas asked for it, or beggars,
or men from the Grass. He sighed quietly. They had just got
rid of the men from the Grass. Maybe these wouldn't stay
long.

"And a place to sleep," the Bean Canyon man said.

"We are honored."

Turquoise Old Man looked sideways to see what the priest
of the Deer Lodge thought, but he couldn't tell. Deer Lodge's
face was blank, just like Blue Clay's on his other side.

Squash Old Man beckoned to Green Gourd Vine's father,
Squirrel, and said, "We will give them the empty house beside
your wife's, underneath Old Lady Antelope's house."

Squirrel nodded. That house had been empty since the
woman who lived in it had died without any daughters. It was
a very fine house, with two sleeping rooms, a weaving room,
and a big kitchen.

"Do these people eat human food?" Squash Old Man inquired. If they were kachinas, they might eat smoke or bones.

The Bean Canyon man spoke to the leader, and the leader
threw his head back and laughed. It made a loud, roaring
sound. He said something over his shoulder to the others, and
they laughed, too.

"They eat meat," the Bean Canyon man said. "And bread.
Your women can cook for them."

"The people of Red Earth City offer you hospitality."
Squash Old Man spoke formally to the leader in the hard shell
shirt.

"There must also be grain for the horses." The Bean Canyon
man inserted himself between them.

"There is grass," Squash Old Man said.

"These horses eat maize."

Squash Old Man nodded, but he frowned at the Bean
Canyon man. Hospitality required that the visitor be given

what he asked for. But good manners also required that he not ask for things that were unreasonable.

The pale person on the long-eared horse said something that sounded like birds squawking, and the Bean Canyon man said to Squash Old Man, "We will go into your city now. We are very hungry."

"Those are not kachinas!" The chief of the Holy Clowns glared at the important men gathered around him in the kiva. "I am certain of it now that I have seen them up close."

"Then what are they?" Squash Old Man asked irritably. The Holy Clowns were sometimes as vague as a drift of wind, their heads in the clouds, talking to birds. He was chief of the Summer People, who governed the city until the equinox. If the people of Red Earth City upset the kachinas, everyone would say it was his fault.

Turquoise Old Man coughed. "We can't be sure yet. Therefore it may not be a good idea to give them everything they ask for." Turquoise Old Man had seen the pale people eating, and they ate a great deal for kachinas. But those colorless skins must be magical. Or monstrous. He was beginning to suspect the latter. They had showed him things, cups and plates, made out of shiny hard stuff, some watery, like bits of moonlight, and some the color of the sun. The Bean Canyon man said they were looking for more of that mysterious substance. Turquoise Old Man thought it might be a kind of shiny rock, especially when the leader showed him a finger ring set with transparent stones like colored ice. He was sure those were rocks. Kachinas wouldn't want that. Monsters might. Kachinas, if you treated them with respect, would be benevolent. Monsters were unpredictable.

"They are looking for those shiny dishes," Deer Lodge said. "I do not know what they are."

Blue Clay snorted. "Nor do I know what good they are."

"Well, they aren't of any use," Turquoise Old Man said, as if that proved his point. "They are beautiful, certainly, but they would get far too hot in a fire. And these pale people are not traders."

"Then what are they?" Squash Old Man was growing exasperated. Everyone knew what they weren't. No one was prepared to say what they were, except for himself, and no one agreed with him.

"The Bean Canyon people say they can make magic with those sticks they carry. The Bean Canyon people say they shoot flame."

"Hah! That I would like to see!"

"They eat a great deal," Sun House Lodge said grumpily. "And so do their horses."

"That man from Bean Canyon says that these people set great store by those shiny things," Blue Clay said craftily. "They think there is a city in the desert where the people have those things."

"It would be a good idea to send them there," Sun House Lodge agreed.

"Where?" Squash Old Man demanded. "There is no such place, or I would have heard of it."

"If they are looking for it, then they will not be here in our city," Blue Clay explained. "Very likely that is what the Bean Canyon people have done, sent them to us."

"Bean Canyon people are not to be trusted!" Squash Old Man said, outraged.

"We should ask the true kachinas," the head of the Holy Clowns said. "And Grandmother. And see what they have to say."

The other men nodded. If the kachinas said to drive these creatures out, then they would not have to worry about hospitality. And if they said to send them to look for shiny stones, that would be just as good.

Squash Old Man set his lips in a stubborn line. He could see Grandmother in one of her bodies making a nest in the corner of the Hole to the Underworld. Grandmother would speak to *him,* he thought, and tell him that hospitality was more important than fear. The Hole to the Underworld was a narrow trench with a wooden cover near the end of the kiva, in front of the Kachina House. It marked the place where the people had emerged into the world above, and Grandmother often made her home there. Grandmother Spider knew what was woven into the life of every village. From her web in the corner of the universe she saw everything. Squash Old Man knelt in front of the fire pit and laid a wrapped stick of sweet-

grass incense on it, and three little lumps of copal, tree sap
bought from the traders who came up from the southern jungles. The smoke twisted into a lazy spiral above the coals,
sweet and heady.

The priests of Blue Clay and Rabbit began to chant. They
wrapped their voices around the smoke, braiding it, made a
web to reflect the web of the universe that was anchored to
each stone and pine tree. Turquoise Old Man thought he saw
her, great gray legs splayed on the strands. Behind her was
something that might have been the true kachinas, tall, top-
heavy, beaked, with heads like pots. They danced solemnly,
never speaking.

A little wind whisked down the kiva entrance, kicking up
the fire. The coil of smoke dissipated, the web melted, the
woodsmoke made them cough.

"Grandmother says that we should treat guests with respect," Squash Old Man said.

Turquoise Old Man hadn't seen that.

Squash Old Man folded his arms. "They are guests."

Rabbit nodded. He hadn't said anything until now. But these
pale people looked too strange to be earthly. Offending them
for no reason was dangerous. Besides, he wanted to touch one
before they went away, to see if that colorless skin was warm
like real people's.

The Holy Clowns looked dreamily into the last of the copal
smoke. Grandmother floated in it, drifting on her web. "All
thread gets used," she said to them.

They nodded to her. Very likely something would happen
now. When something happened, it was their job to interpret
it for the people. Sometimes they could stop things from happening, but not always. They thought that this was one of
those unstoppable times.

Toad crouched on the roof outside the house where the pale
kachinas were living. She hid behind the water jar because
they simultaneously thrilled and frightened her. Their voices
sounded like mellifluous frogs, exotic and unintelligible. If she
lifted her head, she could just see them through the window,
their bleached faces floating in the dim room, edged with firelight. Toad stared, her dark eyes just above the window's edge,

dark hair lost in the dusk outside. She wondered how they had lost their color. Maybe they had been left too long in a sunny window and their colors had faded as cloth did, although Toad had never heard of that happening to people. Generally people got darker. One of them, she saw, had a very bright red face, like raw meat, and the skin was peeling off his nose. Maybe they had been scalded, and when the skin peeled away it was pale underneath, like boiled fish.

The scalded one stood up and Toad ducked, but when he didn't come to the window, she raised her head again cautiously. They were all kneeling on the floor now, and the scalded man, who wore a black blanket, was talking to them. The other men scratched themselves and shifted uncomfortably on the hard floor, but they didn't get up until the black-blanket person told them to. Then they all picked up their sticks and slung them over their shoulders. This time they did come to the door, and Toad flattened herself behind the water jar.

The pale people climbed down the ladder and marched across the courtyard without speaking to anyone who was walking there in the evening air. Instead they talked to each other in low voices, pointing at the walls and roofs of the city. Toad thought they were rude, but maybe they had never seen a city before. Red Earth City was far grander than Bean Canyon City. She flitted after them as they crossed Stream Young Man to where their horses were hobbled in the dusk, eating grass that Squash Old Man had had cut for them. The horses switched their tails and nuzzled at the sacks of maize that the Bean Canyon man had demanded. The pale men poured some out into piles on the ground for them and took the packs off the horses' backs. Toad slid into the shadows of Old Grandmother Little Feet's rain jars. The pale men slung the packs over their shoulders while the man who was the leader gave them directions. The rest of the men carried the packs across the stream, stumbling under their weight. There were too many for one trip, and they left three on the ground to come back for.

Toad held her breath as they filed past her. What was in the packs? It could be anything. Spirits or magic. Unimaginable things from the other side of the sky. Once they had come back for the rest she would never know. Toad darted forward. She could look before they got back.

Toad crouched beside the black-robed man's long-eared horse, her nose full of its hot, wet, salty smell, and pulled at a pack, fumbling with the heavy leather straps and the cold smooth fastening that was like a pin. The horses snorted over her head, but she kept working at it. The pin came loose, and Toad pushed the leather flap open, burrowing her hands into the things inside like someone plunging them into a stream of mysterious water. The pack spilled out things beyond comprehension: a cup and a small box of the shiny moon-colored stuff; a white cloth embroidered with many colors; two tall shiny posts with holes in the top; sheets of thin hide between red leather covers; cylindrical, waxy things like smooth sticks. Toad sat on the ground before the treasure, openmouthed. She didn't know what any of it was for, which made it all the more magical and wonderful.

She heard a shout and saw the men coming back across Stream Young Man with torches. Toad froze, caught and guilty, the shiny box in her hands. The man in the black blanket shrieked, pointing his arm at her. A man with a shell over his shirt lifted his stick and leveled it. Toad thought of magic and curses and ran.

The sound was like a thunderclap, reverberating in the courtyard and drowning out the pale men's shouts. Toad heard something go past her ear like an angry wasp, while the sound bounced from wall to wall around her. A flock of turkeys flew up, gobbling hysterically, and raced about on the rooftops. Toad looked over her shoulder and saw the long stick in the turtle man's hand blossom with red fire at the end as another boom crashed and bounced across the courtyard. A water jar beside her cracked open, and its water gushed onto the dirt.

Toad couldn't move. Her mouth was open like a fish's, her arms and legs numb. She stared at the turtle man and the stick and the smashed jar, and began to hiccup.

The leader of the pale men said something, and the turtle man put his stick down. The black-robed man with the scalded face was still shouting. The leader snapped something at him, and he stopped, clamping his mouth shut. The leader strode over to the opened pack, scooped the contents inside, and yanked it closed. He pushed it roughly at the black-blanket man and gestured to two of the others to pick up the rest. He paid no attention to the people who had stopped to stare or the ones who had run from their doorways or onto their roofs. The pale visitors strode back across Stream Young Man and shut themselves up in their house.

The courtyard buzzed like a hive into which someone had thrown a rock. Green Gourd Vine and Cattails counted the little ones and looked frantically for Toad. They found her sitting hiccuping beside the smashed jar, her clothes soaked through and her teeth chattering.

Cattails picked her up and wrapped her in the blanket she was wearing over her own shoulders. Green Gourd Vine stared at the water jar, her fingers to her mouth. She had seen the fire explode from the end of what she had thought to be a stick.

"Toad! Are you all right?"

"I wanted to see, to see their pack," Toad snuffled, burrowing into her mother's arms.

Cattails caught her breath. "Never. You are not to go near those men. Those are monsters. Squash Old Man ought not to have let them into the city."

"Well, now they must leave!" Squirrel came up on Cattails' other side and inspected Toad. "I have said so to Squash Old Man. Now I am going back to say so again." He hurried away.

Most of the people of the city were milling in the courtyard, restless and uneasy, unwilling to go back in their houses and cook dinner and weave cloth as if the world were still normal, uncertain as to what else to do. The Holy Clowns came out of their houses, not even dressed, in white shirts and loincloths like anyone, and inspected the broken water jar. Squash Old Man went to pound on the wall beside the pale people's door to protest, but they pushed the hide flap aside, poked a fire-throwing stick at Squash Old Man, and closed it again.

"You will make them angry," the Bean Canyon man said.

"*We* are angry!" Squash Old Man retorted.

"That doesn't matter," said the Bean Canyon man.

*   *   *

The sound of the gun was like a stone dropped in water, hurling its ripples against the walls, smashing at the whitewashed clay and retreating, smashing and retreating, always returning, paler but not diminished. When human ears thought they could no longer hear it, the mice heard and crept from their nests in the storerooms to eat dried beans, stomachs twisted in sudden, piercing hunger. The maize heard it and began to sprout strange, new leaves and new, inedible pods. The crows heard it and circled over the rooftops, cawing, catching the sound in their dark throats. The peccaries trotted purposefully toward the melon fields on their sharp hooves and tore the vines to shreds.

"We should tell them where to find these things they want," Turquoise Old Man said. "Blue Clay is right."

"Lie to them?"

"If necessary." Turquoise Old Man folded his lips tight.

Squash Old Man peered out the high window of his house. The walls and rooftops on both sides of the courtyard were bathed in the warm yellow light that spilled from windows and doorways. The smell of cooking bread and venison drifted on the evening breeze. The pale people were dark silhouettes against their windows across the courtyard and the Red Earth people nervous shadows on their rooftops. He had been wrong, but he didn't know what he could have done that would have been right. Not to have let them into the city would not have worked at all, not when they had sticks that shot fire and stones. Squirrel had found the hard ball that had shattered the water jar. Rabbit said that it would kill a person if you shot it into him. Squirrel was furious because the thing had been shot at his child. He had threatened to go into the pale people's house with a spear, and Deer Lodge had stopped him because Squirrel belonged to the Deer Lodge and was Second Man there. After that, First Deer Lodge had promised that they would meet in the kiva about it and decide what to do. If it had been a man of Red Earth City, he would have had to pay maize and beans to Squirrel and be shamed publicly. Squash Old Man was afraid of what would happen if they tried to make the pale people do that.

"Tell that man from Bean Canyon to come here," Squash Old Man said, and Turquoise Old Man nodded. It was not his place to fetch people for Squash Old Man, but Squash Old Man had just admitted he was wrong. That required politeness in return.

The Bean Canyon man came cautiously, looking over his shoulder as if to remind them that the pale people might come behind him. "The pale kachinas are very angry that you have disturbed their belongings," he said.

"They are not kachinas."

"They can order fire," the Bean Canyon guide retorted. "Can anyone but the kachinas do that?"

"They have nearly killed a child of ours with it," Squash Old Man said.

"Those things are called guns."

"They are very dangerous," Squash Old Man said severely. "We cannot have them in our city."

The Bean Canyon man nodded. That was what the Bean Canyon Old Men had said, too.

"So we will tell them where they can find these things they are looking for, and then they can go away."

The Bean Canyon Old Men had said that also, but the guide only nodded. "I will bring them to you in the morning."

Dawn comes early to the desert, seeping through the dry air like a fog made of light, and turns the walls of the cities to honey, and the land to scarlet and rose. The pale people got up in it, stretching and spitting, and went outside to piss. They didn't ask where, just did it in the courtyard. Then they called their guide and set out for Squash Old Man's house.

Green Gourd Vine was coming home with a jug full of water when they crossed her path. One of them grinned at her, and she stopped and stared at him, anger over Toad fading in her curiosity. He had a face the color of a salmon, changing abruptly to white above his eyebrows where his hat had sheltered him. His hair was dirty and pale as straw, but what stopped her in her tracks were his eyes. They were blue. Green Gourd Vine goggled at him. He had blue eyes, like pieces of turquoise.

The blue-eyed man said something to her, and his grin widened.

Green Gourd Vine didn't understand him. "My sister is sorry she opened your packs," she said, thinking that if he were a kachina he would understand her. "She is only a baby."

The blue-eyed man spoke to the rest of them, and they all laughed, except for the black-robed man, who frowned at Green Gourd Vine. The blue-eyed man took a step toward her and reached out his hand. Before Green Gourd Vine knew what he was doing, he had grabbed her by the arm and put his face against hers. The water jug fell and cracked open. His other hand grabbed her breast and squeezed. Green Gourd Vine struggled in his grip, screaming as soon as she could pull her face away from his. He gripped her wrist tighter as his mouth covered hers. She kicked him in the shins, and he jerked her arm hard. She sank her teeth into his lip, and this time he pulled back, yowling.

Green Gourd Vine brought up her other hand, balled it into a fist, and punched him in the face. When his grip loosened, she twisted away and fled, sobbing, out the opening between Turquoise House and Squash House and into the bean fields. She could hear someone shouting after her, but she didn't stop; she just kept running.

"That was not a right thing to do," Squash Old Man said severely to the pale monsters. "Not even for monsters." Green Gourd Vine hadn't come back, and Cattails was wailing outside her house. Squirrel was raving. First Deer Lodge had knocked him down and was sitting on him until Squash Old Man could get the monsters away. "We will tell you where to find these things you look for, and then you must leave."

While the Bean Canyon guide translated, the black-robed man said something to the leader, who nodded his head and made shushing motions at him, as if to say, "Later, later." The black-robed man subsided sullenly.

"We are looking for the cities of gold," the leader said through the Bean Canyon guide.

"What is gold?" Squash Old Man asked.

"This." The leader held up a little box. "Have you seen cities made of this?"

Squash Old Man inspected it solemnly. What fool would

build a city out of this? "Oh, to be sure," he said. "To the north and west, beyond the canyons where the Ancestors lived, there are whole cities with walls of this gold. They are all set with those shiny stones that you like."

11

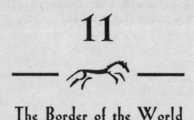

The Border of the World

GREEN GOURD VINE DIDN'T STOP AT THE EDGE OF THE BEAN
field. She kept going, plunging blindly over the irrigation ditch
and through the tall whispering stalks of the maize rows,
scrubbing her mouth with the back of her hand. She could
taste the pale person's blood on her tongue, and she spat with
every other step, trying to get it out of her mouth. The maize
was higher than her head and nearly ripe. It crackled as she
ran, a green sound like biting into a plum. Pollen from the
disturbed tassels dusted the air and clung to her hair and hands.
At the edge of the maize she burst from the crackling stalks
and saw the peccaries.

They were knee-deep in the melon vines, and they turned
their hairy snouts to her, bigger than they had been. Green
Gourd Vine fled again in the opposite direction, abandoning
the tangled stems and the round yellow fruit, broken open, to
the peccaries snorting between the rows. She found the path
that the women followed when they went berrying, and when
that ended out of sight of the city among thick shrubs of bearberries, stripped now, their leaves crisping in the late summer
sun, she went higher still, up the foothills on a trail the hunters

196

took in winter when deer moved up the slopes to eat piñon nuts.

The coyotes saw her go and sniffed the air curiously. City people were a sociable lot who lived in dens together. They didn't usually travel alone. The coyotes followed her for a little way to see if she was carrying anything to eat that she might put down and forget. When they decided that she wasn't, they went on about their business, which was a dead elk that someone had told them about.

Green Gourd Vine stopped at the crest of a ridge to catch her breath. She didn't know why she was climbing up here, but it seemed as if the higher she climbed the less she could taste the pale man's blood and spit in her mouth. She found a handful of withered berries and ate them, then pried the nuts out of a fallen piñon cone with the tip of her belt knife. A trickle of a stream ran from a spring high up the mountain, or the last of the season's snowmelt maybe. It was only as wide as her hand, but she knelt and scooped the water up in her cupped palm and drank some and washed her mouth out.

Then she sat down on a flat rock, warm from the morning sun, and thought. Maybe now Squash Old Man would make the pale people leave. Maybe they would be gone when she went back. And maybe they were like the giant that Coyote killed, which was so big that everything walked into its mouth unawares, thinking it a cave. That was more likely, she thought despairingly. She pulled her blanket aside and looked down at her left breast. There was a bruise starting, five dark spots like fingertips. Green Gourd Vine sniffled. The pale man had hurt her, and none of the other pale people had even tried to stop him, and the one in the black robe had given her an evil look. *I won't go back until they've gone,* she thought with her eyes closed. *Not until tonight, certainly.*

The coyotes came trotting back down the path, because the thing they had heard about from the buzzard people had turned out not to be a dead elk but something else, and it wasn't dead yet, and they didn't like its looks, anyway. They saw her sitting on the rock and stopped.

Green Gourd Vine opened her eyes and saw them.

"Go away. I am not good to eat."

"Maybe." The coyotes seemed to be thinking.

"I am too big, and I will throw rocks at you." She picked one up to prove that.

"There is a thing on the other side of the ridge," the coyotes said. "Maybe you should go look at it." It was always just as well to have someone else look at things for you that weren't dead yet.

Green Gourd Vine eyed them suspiciously. She wasn't sure they were really talking to her. Maybe she was hearing it in her head. They sat side by side, tongues lolling out, big ears pricked toward her.

"We'll tell you a story," one of them said. It seemed to have got bigger, and now she could see it sitting behind the other two, three or four times as big as they were. "This hasn't happened yet."

"Then how can it be a story?" Green Gourd Vine asked crossly. Her mouth still tasted funny, and she spat again.

"We are what we eat," the coyote said. "You be careful."

"Then you are a beetle," Green Gourd Vine snapped. "Or a rat snake."

The coyote yawned. Its mouth opened wider and wider and wider until she could see rabbits and moles and a horned toad and a porcupine in there. There was a road. You could almost walk down it. Green Gourd Vine started to get up, then pinched herself and sat back down. The road disappeared.

"Well," the coyote said, when it had finished its yawn, "this all happened sometime next year, or maybe later. Coyote was coming along, going from village to village with the news. He met a man from—" The coyote thought. "From High Up City, and he told him, 'There is a new person coming along. He has long legs and many new things, most of them bad.' "

"We don't want him," the man from High Up City said.

"That is too bad. He is coming anyway. He is clever like me. I am going to all the tribes to tell them."

"Yah, go away and tell it to someone else," the man from High Up City said. "There is no one like that here."

So Coyote went along to the coast, and he met two women pounding acorn meal. The people there eat acorns and things from the sea. They sew shells on their clothes. When they die, they go across the water in a cloud of blue fire.

"Who are you?" the women asked him.

"I am Coyote," Coyote said, "and I have come to tell you about a new kind of person who is coming along here. He will be here any day now. He is pale like a worm, and he will come in boats."

"We do not want any worm people in boats," the women said.

"He will come anyway."

"What will we do?"

"He is the Long-White-Bone-Man. Whatever he says to you, you must say no."

"We will do that," they said.

Coyote went along again to the place where the people live in houses thatched with grass, and he came to three more women digging camas bulbs. "There is a new person coming," he said.

The three women took him to their chief, and Coyote told the chief, "There is a new person coming along."

"We have seen all the people there are," the chief said. "We have seen the Coast people and the people of the cities, and the wild people of the Grass and even the people from the south with the flat noses who bring jade and spotted cat skins to trade. If there was another kind of person, we would have seen him."

"You have not seen anything yet," Coyote said.

He went along some more and came to two boys of the Grass people. They were skinning a buffalo they had killed. They offered Coyote some of the back fat.

"Thank you very much," Coyote said. "I have come to tell you about a new person coming to hunt the buffalo."

"Who is this person?"

"He is clever like me, and so he will catch many buffalo." Coyote ate the back fat and licked his lips.

"There are many buffalo," the young men said carelessly.

"But none quite so fine as this one, O Hunters of the Grass." Coyote looked pointedly at the buffalo carcass and licked his sharp teeth until they gave him another piece, and the liver as well. They had wanted it for themselves and so they were cross, but it is not wise to refuse Coyote gifts when he asks you for them.

"My thanks to the Hunters of the Grass," Coyote said. "I will tell you what to do when the new person comes."

"What is that?"

"When he gives you new things, give them back. When he gives you new things, do not take them."

"We already have all we want," the young men said.

"No, you don't," Coyote said.

The young men piled the buffalo meat in the hide and tied it with ropes. They went back toward their village, walking and dragging it behind them.

Then Coyote went south and saw a medicine priest gathering plants in the jungle. The people in this place have flat faces and like to count things. They build cities out of stone.

"Who are you?" the medicine priest asked him, making signs with his hands.

"I am Coyotl. I am going everywhere to tell people that a new person is coming, who is clever like me and pale as the snow."

"We don't know snow," the medicine priest said. "It is always warm in our cities."

"You will know it when he comes. He has no grandfathers or grandmothers."

"Then Jaguar will eat him."

"Only some of him," Coyote said. "I ate one of him, and when I spat out the bones, more of him leaped up from them, many and many new pale people."

The medicine priest looked troubled. He had scars all over his face and chest. They should have protected him from things like that. "Then what should we do?"

"I don't know," Coyote said.

"What kind of story is that?" Green Gourd Vine asked. "Is this new kind of person the same as the pale things that are in my city?"

"Maybe," the coyote said.

"Can you make them go away? They are dreadful people, and I don't think they are kachinas. Kachinas used to be our ancestors, and these pale people were never related to us."

"How do you know?"

Green Gourd Vine was insulted. "They are ugly, like the

stomach of a frog. And they have no manners."

"They are something new," Coyote said.

"New is not better. *Can* you make them go away?"

Coyote looked irritated. Green Gourd Vine thought maybe he couldn't.

"Where did they come from in the first place?"

"The sea told me about them." Coyote scratched behind his ear, looking at the sky. "Maybe. Maybe it was the horses. I don't remember that."

"Did *you* bring them here?"

"Those Grass people wanted horses."

"You don't want what you haven't seen!"

"How do you know? Do you want to see one of the pale people?"

"I saw one," Green Gourd Vine said. "He put his mouth on mine." She scrubbed her hand over it again.

"This one is dying," Coyote said. "I think."

Green Gourd Vine thought about that. It would be interesting to see one if he couldn't grab you. She looked past Coyote at the falling slope of the mountain and the next range rising behind it, green-furred with pines and capped with a bare, striated mesa of pink and white rock. The top edge caught the afternoon light and glowed yellow as egg yolk. She thought of the shiny yellow stuff the pale people wanted, and wondered if that was what it was made of. She didn't know anyone who had been up that high. If that was what the pale people were looking for, and they saw it, they would never go away. "Where is this person?" she asked the coyote.

He seemed to have shrunk back into one or both of the coyotes who sat watching her. They didn't say anything, just stood up and trotted away down the trail. Once the female turned and looked over her shoulder at Green Gourd Vine to see if she was coming.

Green Gourd Vine followed, half reluctant, half curious. She had never had coyotes talk to her before, except for the one in the bean field before the Grass people came. She thought he might have been one of these.

The coyotes followed a narrow ledge that clung precariously to the cliffside just where the little stream spilled over the edge in a miniature waterfall to a channel that ran away downhill

between steep sides of red and tawny rock. The water pooled
into a green pond at the foot of the waterfall before it flowed
on, and Green Gourd Vine could hear its voice burbling
among the stones. Pebbles rattled from beneath her feet,
bouncing their way down the cliffside and plopping into the
green water. She went carefully, trailing the coyotes as they
flowed along the cliffside like gray and yellow shadows,
blending with the sunlit stones. The coyotes scrambled up a
steep bank, and she followed, climbing on hands and knees.
They trotted across the top of the ridge again, where the land
flattened into a tabletop of white peppergrass flowers and tall
spines of yucca. Across the canyon made by the stream's channel, a house of the Ancestors was set like an acorn in a wood-
pecker's hole into the cliffside. There it was dissolving slowly
into the earth again, ringed by crumbling walls that slid into
dry dust and sifted in silent rivulets over the edge. Green
Gourd Vine said a prayer to the Ancestors as she passed. The
Outsiders were afraid of the cliff houses and thought there
were ghosts in them, but the people of the cities acknowledged
a kinship with the grandmothers and grandfathers who had
lived there like eagles in their nests.

When she turned back, the coyotes were tail tips disappearing over the edge of the mesa. The sun pooled on the
ground like a jar pouring out bright water. It was midafter-
noon, and her stomach was growling with hunger. She picked
a handful of yucca fruit and ate it raw, wiping sticky hands
on the peppergrass. Then she went after the coyotes, pulling
her skirt and blanket around her to keep them from the spiny
yucca leaves and thornbush and greasewood that grew thicker
and thicker as she went. As she neared the edge of the mesa,
she saw that someone besides the coyotes had been there before her. The brush was broken and trampled as though something had stumbled through it, blundering across the mesa in
a path that wove from side to side. She could see faint prints
of a shod foot and a place where the person had fallen once,
grabbed a handful of greasewood, and staggered on. Where
the coyotes had disappeared over the mesa's edge, a trail went
down again, narrow and precipitous, with the edge of a flat
ledge showing at the bottom of it. Halfway down, two black
buzzards perched in the scrubby trees that grew from the cliff-

side, and above them two more circled patiently on the updraft.

Green Gourd Vine scrambled down the trail, loose stones sliding under the hard soles of her shoes. The buzzards in the scrub flew up in a ponderous flapping of dark wings and lit on the cliff edge. When she had passed, they settled to roost in the scrub again, patient and ominous.

The trail curved around a bulge in the mesa's wall. Green Gourd Vine edged along it and on the other side found the coyotes sitting side by side, big ears pricked interestedly at a man who lay on his face on the rock shelf.

The ledge was halfway from the bottom of the canyon, the width of a man's height and a bit more, and twice as long as that. At the far end it sloped down in a not-quite-sheer drop through a tangle of yucca and greasewood. The man lay where he had tried to drag himself into the shade of the overhanging cliff. There were flies crawling at the edge of his mouth, but Green Gourd Vine thought she saw his back rise and fall with slow, ragged breaths. He wore one of the hard leather shirts that the pale men in Red Earth City had, with leggings of dark material under it and black boots that came up to his knees. His head was bare, his thinning gray hair plastered to a pink scalp. The coyotes sat side by side, watching him, while the circling buzzards dipped their wings on the thermals, beady eyes cocked at the ground.

Green Gourd Vine looked warily for one of the sticks that shot fire and stones, but she didn't see anything but a leather bag tied to his belt. He was lying half on it. She edged closer and poked the still body with her finger. When he didn't move at all, she knelt down next to him, peering at his face. His chin was covered with hairy gray stubble. One cheek was pillowed on the sand, and the breath rattled in his throat.

This one was no danger, she thought, and the coyotes were right—he was dying. He must have got lost from the people who had come to Red Earth City. She got up and went around the body to the feet and lifted one of them by the instep. His boots were black leather, fine but very plain. As she tugged one halfway off his foot, he mumbled something and flailed one arm. Green Gourd Vine stopped, frozen, but he fell back on the ground again, and she pulled the boot clear of his foot.

She set off up the trail to the mesa top, carrying it, retracing her way to the waterfall. Where the stream spilled over the lip she clambered to the edge of the water and rested, studying the boot, turning it over and over in her hands. It was dusty and scarred, but the stitching was as fine as anything the women of Red Earth City could make. She put her face into it, inhaling the strange smell, salty with human sweat but with other overlying odors like an unfamiliar pattern on a strange loom. The water bubbled cold and fast at her feet, boiling over the stones along the cliff edge, spilling into the canyon below in a gush of exuberant foam, like children tumbling down an otter slide. She took a long drink, then caught the running water in the boot and said thank-you to the stream. Then she went back, carrying the boot carefully down the path to the ledge.

The buzzards were still waiting in the trees and the coyotes still sat side by side, like watchers at a dance, so Green Gourd Vine supposed he was still breathing. She knelt down and turned him on his back. He was hideously ugly, scalded red and hairy, and his breath stank. Green Gourd Vine wrinkled her nose. She lifted his head with one arm and poured water from the boot into his mouth with the other. Most of it went over his face, but he swallowed some of it, sputtering and gasping. She poured a little more down him and laid him back on the ground.

The sun was low in the sky by now, and Green Gourd Vine thought that she couldn't get back to the city by dark. It might not be a good idea to be out alone in the night. She was a child of the desert but not of the open spaces; she felt more secure here on the ledge, even with buzzards and coyotes. She eyed the coyotes thoughtfully, but they hadn't moved. Her stomach growled. She untied the leather sack from the man's belt, picking carefully at the knots, ready to leap up if he moved. His breath rasped in his throat, but he didn't speak.

Green Gourd Vine retreated to the end of the ledge with the sack and opened it. There was a smaller pouch inside with two stones in it; a sharp knife of some substance she didn't recognize; a piece of wood carved in a shape like a roof brace with the figure of a man tied to it; and a string of stone beads ending in another little figure on crossed sticks, like the big one. She stared at the beads and the big figure and didn't like them. The knife cut her forefinger. Green Gourd Vine sucked the end of her finger and sat on the edge of the flat ground, swinging her feet over the canyon and thinking. She would have to give the pale man some food if she didn't want him to die. Maybe she should have brought some yucca fruit from the mesa top. And she didn't have a fire drill. She sighed. In the morning she would have to do something about those things if she wanted to keep him. Already he seemed like an unwieldy pet, a tame bear or an elk calf. Still, she felt a sense of ownership. The coyotes had given him to her.

She took off her blanket and laid it over him, and then pulled her skirt open so that she could wrap herself up in it. The sun went down behind the canyon rim, and the sky darkened into deep blue-black. The stars came out. She watched the arm and heart of the Chief of the Night grow bright in the sky. The Chief of the Night was so big that he took up the whole sky on every side of the world. When people in Red Earth City could see his arm and heart, his feet were beyond the horizon, shining on the Grass, and his head had already set in the Endless Waters. There were other constellations within him: Long Tail and the Fawns and the Pot-Rest Stars, the Meal-Drying Bowl and the Hand, and the milky sweep of the Backbone of the Universe. She wondered how the pale man had got lost among them.

Green Gourd Vine's teeth had begun to chatter as the sun fell. She wrapped her skirt tighter around herself, but it didn't help. *He'll freeze,* she thought, looking at the man lying under the blanket. So she got up and went slowly to him and lay down next to him, pulling the blanket over them both. He felt hot, as if he had a fever, and her eyes closed in his warmth. Something else warm settled on her feet, and she knew that the coyotes had lain down with them. A dark whirring fluttered to the ground. The heavy arc of the buzzards' wings bowed over them, shutting out the stars and the cold wind that whispered up the canyon. Green Gourd Vine curled in their living cocoon and slept.

In the morning he was cold. Green Gourd Vine woke to find the man beside her stiff and solid as ice. She shrieked and flung herself away from him, snatching back her blanket. She stared at him, heart pounding, wondering what madness had made her lie down with him. The coyotes were gone, and the buzzards were only dark shapes still circling patiently overhead. They had never been here, she had dreamed a dream, and now this pale man was dead, and the others in Red Earth City would blame her for it. They would find him and find her footprints. She had gone mad, dreaming that she had lain down with coyotes and buzzards. Maybe she had caught a madness from him, the same madness he had died of. Green Gourd Vine put on her skirt, wrapped her blanket around her shoulders, and knotted her sash with shaking fingers. She saw the man's pouch lying on the ground. The man tied to the crossed sticks inside it was probably magical. He might go and tell the pale men in Red Earth City about this one here. She snatched up the pouch and flung it over the edge into the canyon below.

The buzzards saw it fall, but noted only that it didn't seem to be food. They didn't care about the pale man's spells. Magic does not work on buzzards. They dropped lower in the sky, regarding the woman watchfully. When she had scrambled away along the path that edged the mesa wall, they settled down on the ledge in a dark shudder of wings.

Their beaks plucked out the cold eyes, and their claws perched on the stiffened shoulders. They tore away the linen shirt and the breeches, beaks working under the leather jerkin. After a while the coyotes came. They drove the buzzards up into the air above the corpse, snapping white teeth at them. When they began to tear at the chest, the buzzards settled again, on the other end, unruffled. Coexistence was possible. One foot was already bare of its boot, and so they began on it first.

No one in the troop of pale men who had come to Red Earth City missed the man on the ledge at all, because he had run away from another expedition entirely, after knifing a sergeant over a gambling game. But Green Gourd Vine didn't know that. *They will think you killed him,* the wind whispered in her ear. *His ghost will follow you,* the yucca said. *The man on the sticks will curse you,* the greasewood told her. *He had already marked you,* said the five fingerprints on her breast.

You cannot stay here with no food and no fire, said her stomach. Green Gourd Vine thought. She could go to High Up City, where the Trade Fair was held every year. No one had said there were monsters in High Up City yet. But who would take her in? She had an uncle who had married a High Up City woman and gone to live there. Maybe he would ask his wife if she could live with them. But then Green Gourd Vine would be a stranger there, without even a house, and no one would want to marry her or weave for her. The prospect unfolded itself dismally before her eyes like a blanket unrolling off a foreign loom.

I will go there anyway, she thought stubbornly, chin up. *I will go to the hot springs first and soak off the curse from that pale man's things, and then I will go to High Up City. If I don't starve first.* Her stomach rumbled loudly. She picked the last of the yucca fruit from the few scraggly plants that grew on the mesa top and turned in a slow circle, orienting herself. The hot springs were northwest, on the way to High Up City. Old women went to soak in them for their bones, and sometimes they left food and blankets there for the next visit. They might still be there if the coyotes hadn't eaten them. The hot springs were maybe a morning's walk from where she was, a day's walk from the city, another day in the other direction from High Up City. *I won't starve by then.*

Behind her she could see the buzzards landing, and more coming in, specks turning to flapping wings to descending shadows, the word going out on the air currents: dinner. She turned and began to trudge up the slope, zigzagging along a path already worn into the warm stone by generations of feet. In the old days, the days before even the Ancestors, the people who lived in caves in the valley of Water Old Man went up the mountains every winter, to the high slopes where the piñon pines grew and the low sun warmed the mountain flanks. There they stayed through the winter and turned the sun around at the solstice. Sun Coming Back was danced in a cave, her father had told her, which was why nowadays kivas were always cut into the earth. The People Before the Ancestors had known that to bring light, you must first have dark.

Green Gourd Vine almost thought she could see them as she went—old men in skins and naked children, women with packs on their heads, gray dogs who looked more like wolves than today's dogs did, half-seen shadows walking before and beside her. A faint flute song drifted in the air, not quite heard, like an eddy of dust on the wind.

As she neared the hot springs, the smell of sulphur filled the air like rotting eggs. Green Gourd Vine wrinkled her nose. When she was little, she had gone with her grandmother to carry her journey bag and her sun shade when she went up to the springs to soak her bones. Grandmother would sit in the hot pool, her wrinkled breasts floating on the surface of the water, her long gray hair undone and rippling out around her like moss. Grandmother dozed while Green Gourd Vine perched on the edge and held a piece of stiff hide over her head with a pole so that her scalp didn't burn through her thin hair. The hot springs were supposed to take off curses, too, the way they took off aches, and people who thought that witches were after them sometimes went to wash spells away in the sulphurous water. The water boiled up from the heart of the earth and would be more powerful than the man tied to the crossed sticks.

It was hot at midday, and she felt lightheaded by the time she got to the top of the trail, where the spring bubbled furiously out of the rocks. The water steamed and burbled, a voice from the center of the earth, and then seeped slowly down into other, lower pools, still hot but no longer boiling. A stinking white and yellow crust covered the surface, like scum on a stewpot. The rock here was bare, just red stone with the paths from pool to pool worn in it. The sun blazed off the yellow and red and white cliffs across the gorge. A cave in the rock opened just above the lowest of the pools, and Green Gourd Vine crawled in to see if there was anything left there. She found a tattered blanket and a journey bag that had once been full of dried meat and bread. Now it was empty, the end bitten off and shredded. *I am not hungry,* she thought.

She laid her skirt and blanket on the stones beside the lower pool and put her shoes on top of them. Cautiously she stuck a bare toe in the water. It was as hot as stew. She yelped and took her toe out, but after a moment she tried it again. As she eased in, steaming water rising past her ankles and then her calves, it began to feel better. Slowly Green Gourd Vine slid into the pool and lay like a turtle with only her head above the surface. She scrubbed her skin with her hands, washing off the fingerprints on her breast. She could feel them flaking away like caked mud. If the man tied to the crossed sticks had cursed her, that fell away, too. She closed her eyes, chin on her breast, sleepy with the heat.

"You had better get out of there before you cook."

Green Gourd Vine opened her eyes. Standing over her were the men from the Grass. Blue Jay and Mud Turtle politely turned their backs, and Spotted Colt held out her blanket and skirt. She blinked groggily.

Spotted Colt knelt down by the pool. "Phew! You are right," he said to Mud Turtle. "It must be good for you, to smell so vile."

"Good for the lungs," Mud Turtle said. "And the bones."

Spotted Colt pulled at Green Gourd Vine's arm. "But it is no place to sleep."

Green Gourd Vine sat up slowly.

"Come along."

She stood and wrapped herself in her blanket. Her fingers were wrinkled like old fruit. She pulled her skirt around her and knotted her sash, her head spinning. When she bent over for her shoes, she fell over and ended on her knees, hands braced against the stone.

"Here." Spotted Colt stretched her out on the rocks and gave her some water from his waterskin. "How long were you in there?"

She looked at him blankly.

"When did you last eat?" He put his fingers to his mouth. She shook her head. The red and white and yellow striated stones of the gorge were beginning to spin, revolving slowly over her head. Spotted Colt took a piece of dried meat from the bag at his belt and broke a bite off. She chewed and swallowed. Behind the men she could see the horses standing on the trail, and Digger and his mother beside them, watching her curiously.

"They said you were up here," Spotted Colt said. He said it with his hands, but his fingers were a blur against the revolving mountains. Green Gourd Vine shook her head. She didn't understand. Spotted Colt picked her up and set her down just inside the cave, where it was shady and beginning to be cool with the afternoon breeze. He gave her some more water. "Are you by yourself?"

Green Gourd Vine nodded. Now that she was in the shade, the rocks weren't spinning. Outside the cave she could see Mud Turtle taking off his breechclout and leggings, and then his bare backside disappearing into the sulphur pool.

"We saw your tracks," Spotted Colt said. "The dogs wanted to follow you. What are you doing up here alone?"

Green Gourd Vine bit another piece off the dried meat and gulped it down with a swallow of water. "The pale kachinas came to our city, only they aren't kachinas, they are some kind of monster, and I found one back down there"—she waved an arm vaguely—"but he died, and they will think I killed him, so I can't go back. I am going to High Up City," she added.

"Alone?"

She nodded forlornly.

"Those pale people are there, too. We had word from a trader on the trail. They are not good people to be around."

"Then where will I go?" she wailed.

"With me." Spotted Colt put an arm around her and settled her so that she was leaning against his shoulder.

Green Gourd Vine whimpered.

"We have an extra horse."

"Leave?"

"You already left. Isn't the Grass better than living with those pale people in your city?"

"I don't know."

"It's better," Spotted Colt said. "If you don't think so, next year I will bring you home." If the pale people had got in her city, he thought, next year it might not matter.

Digger came into the cave and lay down at her feet. He put his nose in her lap the way the dream coyotes had done.

"I will tell you about the pale people," Green Gourd Vine said urgently. She talked in simple words, using her hands, too, so that he would be sure to understand. "They are like— like mushrooms. They pop up where you don't want them, but once they are started there, they stay."

"Do they have horses with them?"

"Oh, yes. Not the one that died down there. He didn't have a horse. Maybe it ran off. But the ones who came to my city, they had horses."

"Maybe we can take horses from them. Maybe that is what we will do."

"No! No, no, no, no! Not in my city! I can't go back! And something terrible will happen if you go back there. No, no!" She turned around so that she could grip him by the shoulders, shaking him into attention.

"All right, then," he said.

"Not in that city anymore," Mud Turtle said, too, when Spotted Colt told him about it. They camped for the night up the mountain from the hot springs, in a high meadow where they could see anything coming at them. Mud Turtle gave Green Gourd Vine Dances' tent, which Blue Jay had given him in exchange for the pups, and set it up for her, patting her on the head when he found her sitting beside it crying.

"It would be a bad idea to go back to that place," he said to Spotted Colt. "Those are not good people, and anyone can see us coming."

"They have horses," Spotted Colt said.

"Fine. We will go back there," Mud Turtle said. "And she will probably stay." He nodded his head at Green Gourd Vine, sitting miserably beside the tent.

"She is going to stay with me now," Spotted Colt said firmly.

"Then she will tell us how to find this Bean Canyon City, and we will go there. And you had better make Blue Jay give her his sister's clothes. She can't ride a horse in that cloth skirt."

In the morning Spotted Colt said so to Blue Jay, who sulked and then gave in.

"She didn't die in them, and she doesn't need them in the House of the Dead," Spotted Colt said gently. "This girl does."

In Dances' tent, Green Gourd Vine pulled the soft hide dress over her head, smoothing the leather with her fingertips. It was very beautiful, embroidered with dyed porcupine quills and fringed along the hem and sleeves. She looked dubiously at the leggings. Spotted Colt had said she would need them until her skin grew used to horsehair; otherwise she would have a rash in a most uncomfortable place. He had been delicate about it, but she knew leggings were men's clothes, even on the Grass. She thought these might be his. She picked them up, imagining herself like the wild girl, flying on the red horse's back. She imagined herself in Red Earth City, wearing fringed leggings, and put them back down again.

"Hurry up in there," Spotted Colt called. "Do you know how to put them on?"

Green Gourd Vine stepped into the leggings and tied them around her waist. Spotted Colt smiled at her when she sidled out of the tent. Her hair was still done in squash blossom puffs, and she had put her blanket on, too, over the dress and leggings.

Mud Turtle had cooked maize mush in a basket full of hot rocks, and he gave her a bowlful in a turtle shell. Green Gourd Vine scooped it out with her fingers, ravenously, but she frowned at the turtle shell. "I could make you clay bowls," she said when she had set it down, as if that would make these wild men civilized, as if all it took was clay bowls, and Spotted Colt would cut off his long hair and learn to weave blankets. "All I need is some good mud and a bit of sand," she added hopefully.

Mud Turtle chuckled. "Clay bowls break, child."

"Oh."

Blue Jay handed her End of the Day Horse's rein. "You can ride this horse until we go home. Then I have to give her back to my mother."

He seemed to be trying to be kind, and Green Gourd Vine nodded, but her eyes were filling with tears. The only word she caught was "home." Home would not be Red Earth City anymore; not a solid point on the landscape, but a moving place on the river of Grass. She would float in a tent on that river. She looked up at End of the Day Horse, who seemed higher than she had yesterday. Green Gourd Vine's backside still ached from yesterday's ride, and the insides of her thighs itched, as Spotted Colt had said they would.

"You'll get used to it," Spotted Colt said. He took her

around the waist and boosted her up gently, so that she hung over End of the Day Horse on her stomach. He shoved, and she wriggled, kicking her feet, until finally she swung her leg over and pulled herself upright.

"I'll teach you to get up on her with more care for your dignity," he said, "but you can't do it in so many clothes."

Green Gourd Vine shook her head and pulled her blanket tighter around her. Spotted Colt swung lightly onto Rainstorm Horse's back.

"Ride out," Mud Turtle said. They turned the horses toward the tree-covered slope to the north, where a trail crossed the peak and went down again to Bean Canyon City. Green Gourd Vine had drawn them a map in the dirt, marking Red Earth City and the hot springs, Bean Canyon and High Up, and the trails between. They went single file now, the packhorses ambling behind them in a line and the dogs trotting between, with Blue Jay at the end. Green Gourd Vine clutched End of the Day Horse's mane with both fists, but Blue Jay held his rein lightly in one hand and a bow with a nocked arrow in the other.

Green Gourd Vine saw the border of her world as she crossed it. It was a house, as big as Squash House at home, and it enfolded the meadow like a soap bubble. As they approached its wall, it trembled and vanished, and they rode through into the sea of wild land outside. In its outer seeming this outside country still wore the skin of the mountains that she knew, but the bones had shifted under that surface, and now she could see something else there that she hadn't recognized before. She still didn't know its name, but she thought it knew hers. The buzzards and the coyotes who watched them go, from the high thermals and from the chaparral scrub, knew it, too. It didn't have a name, because they did not speak words, but if they had they would have simply called it Everything. Life. The many roads of the web.

The wild land closed around Green Gourd Vine and around the man who had died on the ledge. In a few days his body was picked clean. The shreds of the cloth shirt and breeches fluttered in the brush along the canyon wall. The coyotes had eaten the boots and jerkin. A buzzard, pecking at the skull, rolled it farther and farther from the body until at last it bounced down the steep slope at the end of the ledge, rolling and hopping through the greasewood. It came finally to rest on the canyon floor beside an anthill, and the ant people hurried out to clean it, and eventually a horned toad moved in. The larger bones the coyotes took back to their den, where they were raising a family.

The string of beads and the man on the crossed sticks spilled from their pouch as they fell, plummeting to the canyon floor, and landed in the brush by the streambed. The beads and their little man hung there, glinting in the sun, until a magpie found them and took them home to decorate his nest. The larger man fell clean through the brush, and the crossed sticks lodged between two stones among the oval leaves of a young cactus. The wood rats who lived in the cactus came out and looked at him, but he only stared at the sky. He wasn't something they could eat, and Wood Rat Woman said to leave him alone, but Wood Rat Man said that he would do to shore up the north wall of their house, and so he dragged him into their burrow.

All that remained on the ledge was a scattering of vertebrae and ribs and a metal belt buckle.

12

Bean Canyon Vanishes

It took two days to go to Bean Canyon City because the world had changed and Green Gourd Vine lost the trail. And when they got there, they could see that there were guards set up all along the edges of the fields, even in the lower fields that were half a day's walk from the city.

They tied the horses out of sight in a clump of oak and thornbush and lay with their noses poking over the canyon rim. Below, they could see the city strung out along Bean River. The straw in its walls caught the noon glare and reflected it back in a splash of fire so that it glinted and shimmered in the white air. The guards stood each within sight of the next in the fields below. "I don't like this," Mud Turtle said. "They are waiting for something, and it would not be good if it was us."

"Well, they have seen you already," Green Gourd Vine said. "We are not stupid people here in the west. They may just be guarding the fields from the Outsiders."

"Who are they?"

"Wild people like you. They raid here at the end of the summer when our maize and beans are ripe. They have no morals."

"Are you sure these people here have seen us?" Blue Jay asked her.

"They saw us yesterday," Green Gourd Vine said, "with this many guards out." She thought of the way the Grass people had walked into Red Earth City, and the pale people behind them. Red Earth City should have put out guards. Maybe the pale people had taught the Bean Canyon people that.

"We need to know where they have their horses," Mud Turtle said, single-minded.

"They will be as afraid of you as they are of the pale people," Green Gourd Vine said. "They will think you are more pale people, riding on horses."

"Then we will have to go away again, and come back at night."

"By a different trail." Blue Jay nodded.

"The way we did when we stole horses from you at Three Trees," Spotted Colt said to Blue Jay.

"The way we raided you at Salt Lick," Blue Jay said.

"Yah, we saw you coming at Salt Lick."

Blue Jay grinned. "And going. With your horses."

Spotted Colt laughed. He grinned back. It was the first time Blue Jay had smiled since his sister died. The black specks that had circled on the thermals everywhere they rode spun away into the blue sky. He clapped Blue Jay on the shoulder. "With our people riding together, no horse is safe."

"When you have decided whose is bigger, we will have to find the horses," Mud Turtle said.

"They will be there," Spotted Colt said happily. "What else would they be guarding?"

To Green Gourd Vine their voices sounded less and less like the cries of birds and had begun to sort themselves into words. "You have not seen the pale people," she said to Spotted Colt. "They are guarding against *them*, maybe, if they have gone away. To keep them from coming back. They have sent them to *my* people!" she added bitterly. "And they won't let *you* in." And then because the world had changed, precisely because of that, because she had already been swallowed up, she said, "But they would let me in."

"You?" Spotted Colt cocked his head at her. Her face was

stubborn, her chin out. His heart fell. "You will stay with these people if you go there."

Would she? Green Gourd Vine thought. How could she say, now that the world had changed? "If the pale people have been there once, they will come back again, and no one but a fool would stay and wait for them," she said. That much seemed true, and could be said aloud. "So likely I must go with you, but first I can get into Bean Canyon and see if there are horses."

Spotted Colt's heart was in his eyes now. He could feel it leaping this way and that inside him. He started to tell her so when Mud Turtle's finger poked his ribs, so he only said, "Very well, Most Wise. We will wait for you."

Behind a bush, Green Gourd Vine took off her leggings and her buckskin dress with the fringe and the porcupine quills and put on her old clothes. They looked tired and rumpled and dirty, but that would tell the Bean Canyon people that she had been on the road. She had no other story to tell them but the truth, and it would serve, as it had with Spotted Colt, if she told only the right parts of it, like picking the ripe ears of maize from a stalk. The three men waiting for her on the canyon rim were green ears, likely to cause the Bean Canyon people indigestion and heartburn, and best left out of it.

She skirted around the canyon's edge, angling downward at its mouth to the river floor and then up the stream to Bean Canyon City on the proper trail that visitors would take, where everyone could see her coming. The guards in the lower fields greeted her with polite suspicion and handed her on to the guards in the upper fields, who passed her along to Summer Old Man, who was actually a young man with a broad, pleasant face and a crooked front tooth.

"Where have you come from, Niece?" he asked her. "Niece" was a term of respect for any unknown young woman.

"From Red Earth City." The Bean Canyon people spoke nearly the same language, with a strange pronunciation to some of their words, but intelligible. "I have run away from pale people who came there."

"Ah." Summer Old Man didn't elaborate, but his eyes told her what she wanted to know, that he had sent the pale people there. "We have heard of them," he said carefully.

"They are not here?" She looked nervously around her. The white walls of Bean Canyon City sparkled in the sun, pleasant and homey. The houses were four stories high, and even five in places, although not so large as in Red Earth City. Three women and two men were building an addition onto the roof of the near end of Summer House, likely for a daughter and her husband. The courses of dressed red sandstone were already laid for the walls, and the men were setting cottonwood rafters across the top. The women ran lightly up and down the ladder from the ground, and then up the narrow stairsteps that went two stories higher, with bundles of brush on their heads. Green Gourd Vine thought of building herself a house here, a little rooftop house like this one, three roofs above the ground, with a ladder she could pull up when anyone tried to come in.

"Have you seen them out there?" Summer Old Man asked, after a time when he didn't answer her question, to let her know that he didn't want to. Green Gourd Vine could make him tell her by asking thrice more—questions asked four times must be answered—but that was not something to do when you could get the answer another way. "No," she said. "I was running."

"We have seen those horse things they ride, up on the canyon rim today," Summer Old Man said craftily. "*You* didn't see them?"

"I don't like those," Green Gourd Vine said. "I don't like those at all. I don't want to see those." She pulled the blanket away from her breast and showed him the bruises. "This is what they did. So I ran." She started to cry, which was easy enough. Let loose, the tears flowed down her dusty cheeks, making little rivulets on her skin. She hiccuped and buried her face in the blanket.

Summer Old Man looked up at the people working on the new house. "Froglet!" he shouted. "Hop down here."

A young woman hurried down the steps and then down the ladder to the ground. When she started across the courtyard toward them, Green Gourd Vine saw that she had a hopping gait like a little bright toad, because one foot dragged a bit. It didn't slow her down. Green Gourd Vine peered from the blanket folds as she stopped with a hop in front of Summer Old Man.

"This girl has come from Red Earth City," Summer Old Man said. "Something bad has happened to her there." He looked uncomfortable, probably because he had sent the pale people to her city himself.

"I'll take her to Mother," Froglet said. "We're about to stop anyway, until the men have the poles tied down." Above the rafters went a layer of smaller poles, running in the other direction, and then branches smaller yet, and then twigs and brush, each course crossing the last. It made a roof you could dance on. A roof you could live on, cook, and sleep, and make pots on.

Froglet took Green Gourd Vine's arm. "Come." She tugged at her and Green Gourd Vine followed. Froglet's round mother was coming down the ladder to see what was the matter. "This girl came from Red Earth City," Froglet said. "I think she came by herself." Her eyes were wide at the idea of that.

"Tch! Poor thing! There are wicked things loose in the world." The older woman's expression was motherly. "I am Berry, and this is my daughter Froglet, and my other daughter Ripple and Froglet's husband, up there on the roof with my husband. Come into our house."

Green Gourd Vine let them lead her up the ladder and the two flights of stairs, and then down the ladder again into a cozy room with a hearth at the center and walls lined with shelves full of pots and baskets and spoons and the men's hunting spears and bows. The door in the roof and one high window let in light. Two other rooms led off this one, one facing the front wall, with another high window, and the other a dark storeroom at the heart of the house. A doorway drawn on the opposite wall with charcoal showed where the door to the new room would be.

"That will be my husband's and mine," Froglet said chattily, as they sat Green Gourd Vine down by the hearth and gave her water from a jar in the corner. The smaller jug used to fill the jar from the rain barrels or the creek sat on the floor beside it, cold and damp and dripping water for the little toad who had somehow found his way up three flights, maybe in a load of wood, and was allowed to stay and eat flies. "Right now we are living here in my mother's house with Ripple. She is going to get married next year as soon as her boy has finished her blanket. I'm not supposed to say that yet, but everybody knows it."

"And when did you have anything to eat last?" Berry asked Green Gourd Vine when Froglet paused for breath. "Well, I thought not," she went on, when Green Gourd Vine didn't answer. She bustled about and produced rolled flat bread and a bowl of soup left from their dinner. "I suppose you came all that way yourself!"

"I ran away," Green Gourd Vine said, disliking the idea of lying outright.

"Were those pale people there?" Froglet asked.

"Hush!" Berry looked uncomfortable. Frightened, maybe.

"Have they been here?" Green Gourd Vine asked her.

"They are not here," Berry said, lips compressed.

"Is that why there are guards in the fields?" Green Gourd Vine asked.

"Father says they may come back," Froglet said. "Father says they are an evil magic and they will come back unless we fight them."

"Be *quiet!*" Berry rounded on her daughter. "It's a wonder Swimmer married you, you talk so much," she added, trying to turn it to a joke when Green Gourd Vine stared at her. "Well!" she said briskly. "Now you have eaten, you will be tired and want to sleep. I will make you a bed in the storeroom where it's dark and no one will bother you."

And I can't hear you talking, Green Gourd Vine thought. She stood up, yawning. "That is kind. May good things come to your house, Mother."

"May good things go with you when you leave," Berry said. She looked at Green Gourd Vine's dirty clothes. "When you have slept, Froglet will give you some clean clothes and take you down to the river so you can wash yours and bathe."

After we have decided what we're going to tell you, Green Gourd Vine thought. It wasn't so different from her deciding what she was going to tell them. Everybody had lots of truths, and they separated them by size and color like kernels of maize. Yellow ones to tell everybody, red ones to tell somebody, black ones you told nobody.

Berry spread a pile of blankets in the storeroom. Green

Gourd Vine lay down, inhaling the familiar musty smell of maize and mice and dried beans. Everything in Berry's house smelled like Cattails' house. She had to tell herself that the pale people had been here, as they had been in her town, and neither was hers now. When Berry left, she heard voices in the next room, talking low, and she wriggled into the shadows near the door.

"If they are the pale people come back, why haven't they come down to the city? They knew the way well enough before."

"Because Summer Old Man has put guards in the fields."

"Our guards can't shoot fire."

"Maybe these pale people can't, either."

"The last ones could. Why should these be different?"

"Why should they not? We don't even know what they are. Maybe there are different kinds of them."

"I think that Red Earth girl knows what they are. I don't believe she didn't see them."

"She was afraid, poor thing." That was Berry.

"And maybe they sent her here to spy for them."

"The way we sent Water Strider to show them the road to Red Earth?"

There was an embarrassed, sullen silence.

"Maybe these aren't pale people," Froglet said. "No one has got close enough to see."

"I got closer than anyone else! I saw the horse things."

"There have been horse things before. I heard that the buffalo hunters have horse things."

"Well, it was not buffalo hunters in our city for the last four moons, throwing their garbage on the floor and eating like shrews. And walking around lordlywise, telling us what to give them."

The voices grew loud and angry until someone said "Shush!" and they quieted. Green Gourd Vine edged back from the door. The guards were to keep the pale people out, not horses in. The pale people had been here, but they were gone now, and they had taken their horses with them. They wouldn't leave horses here. They were not fools. If they left horses here, the Bean Canyon people would sell them, or eat them.

I could stay here now, Green Gourd Vine thought, afraid
again of the wild land and the night. *If I don't go back, Spotted
Colt will know there are no horses here, and he will get tired
of waiting for me and leave. Then I could live here.*

And the pale people could come back. Another thought
came to her. *Will come back. They are like the peccaries. If
there is anything left to eat, they will come back for it.*

They are not back yet, she said crossly to that thought. *And
I am too tired to leave this place today.*

"She won't come back," Blue Jay said to Spotted Colt. Spotted
Colt was on his belly looking over the canyon rim at the ant
people below in Bean Canyon City, trying to see which one
was Green Gourd Vine.

"Get down!" Spotted Colt said. "They will see you."

"They have already seen you. Your head is sticking up like
a melon." Blue Jay sat down beside him.

"Get down!"

Blue Jay wriggled down on his stomach. "Look—I could
drop this rock and hit that one down there." He pointed at an
ant person digging clay out of the riverbank.

Spotted Colt snatched the rock.

"I know. Let's sit up here at night and make noises. They
will think it's ghosts."

"We are not children. There—I think that's her."

"She won't come back. You could get old up here. She's
used to living in a hive like bees. In boxes." Blue Jay shuddered, remembering the House of the Dead. Every time he
remembered the rooms in it, they were smaller.

"She *said* she would come back."

Blue Jay shrugged. "What does it matter? There are girls
on the Grass."

"I want this girl," Spotted Colt said stubbornly.

"They are all the same."

"You didn't think that about your sister."

"My sister was different." Blue Jay's face twisted, like
someone who had been hit in the belly, so that Spotted Colt
felt sorry he had said that.

"This is just a stupid hive girl," Blue Jay said viciously. "If
you want a place to put it so badly, go steal one of those."

He pointed down at the women washing clothes in the river. They knelt on a rock in midstream, the white clothes flowing out from their hands like foam on the water.

Spotted Colt felt less sorry for him. "You don't know anything. Those dead people didn't teach you anything."

"They taught me not to want what I can't have," Blue Jay said sullenly.

People below them were pointing up at the canyon edge now. Spotted Colt grabbed Blue Jay by the arm and pulled him away. "Now they have seen us. That is your fault!"

The men below them were shouting, and Spotted Colt and Blue Jay broke into a trot. Mud Turtle was waiting with the horses in their camp on the mesa top, out of sight of the city in a stand of bent piñon pines.

"They saw us," Spotted Colt said. "Knows Everything sat on the edge and wanted to throw rocks."

"Most in Love was trying to see that girl. Maybe tonight he will play the flute for her."

"Are there horses in that city?" Mud Turtle asked them, ignoring the rest.

"Maybe," Spotted Colt said. "Green Gourd Vine hasn't come back yet."

Blue Jay snickered.

"What are you laughing at?"

"She will come back when pine trees grow turquoise."

"She will come back," Spotted Colt said stubbornly.

It was not hard to live in Bean Canyon City and be a daughter to Berry, except that Berry's husband, Hunting Owl, didn't like her. He looked at Green Gourd Vine a long time with unblinking eyes, like his namesake, and said, "Who are those people with horses on the mesa?"

Green Gourd Vine shook her head. "Wild People. I don't know where they are from."

"How did you get past them to come in here?"

"I ran." Green Gourd Vine's lip trembled. She felt now as if she really had run away from the Grass men as well as the pale ones. Everything seemed to have hands outstretched to snag her; wild hands, clawed, eyes glowing at her out of the night. She had almost forgotten watching the world change. It changed back so easily in Berry's warm house.

"If they are Outsiders, they would have caught you."

"Leave the child alone, Owl," Berry said. "She's been frightened."

Hunting Owl gave her another long owl-look and sat down at his loom.

But except for Hunting Owl, it was like living in the rush of a burbling stream in Berry's house. Froglet and her sister Ripple chattered all the time, telling everyone everything that had happened or might happen, and Berry bustled about the house, making flat bread and wonderful-smelling pots of dark beans and bowls full of onions and peppers and cress from the stream. No one expected Green Gourd Vine to eat her meat half raw or sleep in a tent with snakes crawling in and dogs with fleas. Berry had two dogs, mournful-eyed bitches whom Ripple and Froglet bathed in the river, holding them under with just their noses sticking out until all the fleas floated away. They washed their clothes with yucca soap and dried them on the rocks, and made coiled pots with fine sand and clay dug from the bank. They painted the pots red and white, with borders of lizards and maize ears, and fired them in a buried kiln. Hunting Owl and Swimmer, Froglet's husband, finished the roof of Froglet's house, and the women plastered the walls with mud and painted suns and dancing deer and a river full of fish along the walls. In the afternoons the men combed and carded the white cotton that grew in a field up the canyon and spun it into thread. They wove it into cloth on the big loom in the main room of the house, and Berry sewed it into skirts and shirts and sashes embroidered with red and yellow. In the afternoons the women ground meal at the grindstones set into the floor while Berry's nephew played his flute for them.

Green Gourd Vine remembered the rhythm of the grindstones. She had ground meal at home with her mother and Five Clay Pots and her little sisters, back bent to the stone, back and forth in time to Mouse's flute, passing the meal from one sister to the next, grinding it finer each time until it would stick to a polished stone. If she closed her eyes, she could imagine that it was Cattails and Magpie and Toad and Five Clay Pots grinding meal in Cattails' storeroom. She could go back before there were peccaries in the fields or Grass men in the city or pale kachinas on the roads.

But when she opened her eyes, there were stranger women grinding meal where her mother ought to be, and a silent owl-eyed man glaring at her from his loom, and a wild Grass boy up on the mesa wondering why she hadn't come back to him.

"I am going to go down there." Spotted Colt stuck his belt knife in its sheath and slung a waterskin over his shoulder.

"They will eat you," Blue Jay said. "Ants on a mouse. There is only one of you. Mud Turtle and I are not coming."

"No one asked you."

Mud Turtle folded his arms over his chest the way he did when he was thinking about a recalcitrant horse. Then he would go and talk in the horse's ear and it would follow him. He didn't think Spotted Colt would follow him if he talked in his ear. "Your father Horse Stealer sent us to find horses, not girls," he said mildly. "We have been gone over a year already."

"Then another moon will make small difference."

"We could tie you up," Mud Turtle said thoughtfully.

"For how long?" Spotted Colt raised his eyebrows. "Eventually you would have to untie me. Then you would be unhappy."

"I will be unhappy when we go home and your father finds out you have brought back a girl instead of horses."

"Nobody said instead of."

"It will be if we stay here till Leaf Fall. The horses will have gone clear to the Endless Water by then."

"She is finding out where they have gone."

"Maybe she isn't going to tell you!" Blue Jay snapped. "And they have gone to Red Earth City if they aren't here."

"Then why don't you go back to the Red Earth City?" Spotted Colt demanded. He turned to Mud Turtle. "*You* said that was not a good idea to go there, but maybe we should let him. It will give him something to do."

"Maybe," Mud Turtle said dubiously.

Blue Jay bit his lip, not sure whether he had won or not. If he went, he could see Dances. "I will ride back there and look," he said to Mud Turtle, "while you persuade Most in

Love not to go down there and say 'I'm a stranger who wants to steal your women, kill me.' "

But when Blue Jay got there, riding fast, Dances was gone. There were scattered bones at the foot of the bier and shreds of hide wrappings. There were no horses in the city, either, and no pale people, but a great many hoofprints leading north and west. When he got back to the camp on the mesa, Spotted Colt was gone, too. He felt as if when he turned around, the horses would be gone, and then the mesa.

"You were to keep him here!" Blue Jay said accusingly.

Mud Turtle shrugged. "I can push a rope into the air, too."

Blue Jay sat down and looked into the clear air hanging above the canyon. It was like cold water poured from a jug. The trees were turning yellow, their leaves blowing across the canyon like butterflies. Moving-on time. On the Grass, the Buffalo Horn would be going to Winter Camp. If he and Dances had not come to this place, they would be packing Mother's dresses and baskets, mending her tent and snow-shoes, and teaching the young horses to pull a travois. There would be Buffalo Horn girls who would lie down in the red and yellow leaves with him. Dances hadn't known about those, but they didn't matter because he only slept in the leaves with them. It was Dances he talked to. *Who will I talk to when I go home?*

Autumn was like an ache in the heart. While they waited for Spotted Colt, the aspen leaves danced on their trees, blew loose, and vanished in the wind. The last crickets hid in the corners of the tents while the geese flew overhead, honking mournfully. *I liked the little Horse Child, too*, Mud Turtle wanted to say, when he saw Blue Jay brooding, but it didn't matter, because it hadn't gone far enough to talk about, and she wouldn't have had him anyway. In the meantime, Laugher found a porcupine and came to Mud Turtle trembling, her mouth full of quills. He pulled them out, begging her pardon guiltily with each twist.

Digger had gone with Spotted Colt, and, working their way through a ravine to the back of Bean Canyon City, they found a rattlesnake sunning itself in the last of the afternoon light.

It lifted its flat head and stared at them, coiling into a snake basket with a buzzing tail.

"No trouble, Brother," Spotted Colt said to it, giving it a wide berth. Its slitted yellow eyes watched them, glittering in the low sun.

The snake was the only one who saw them. The Bean Canyon people had posted guards, but they were not used to watching for one man alone, and Spotted Colt was used to stealing horses. He saw some women in the cotton field, picking the last pale tufts that sprang from the open bolls. It was hard to tell in the dusk whether one was Green Gourd Vine. Farther up the canyon more women with baskets slung on their backs were picking peppers from a patch of frostbitten bushes.

Spotted Colt slid through a tangle of grapes, the fallen fruit squelching under his feet. The women were across the stream from him, so he slipped along the bank where the chaparral was thickest, freezing when a dog hunting mice in the cotton lifted its head. Digger froze, too, a gray dusk-shape at his heel. The wind was the wrong way, and the dog didn't bark. Spotted Colt saw Green Gourd Vine among the peppers. Her head caught the last sunlight as it spilled over the canyon rim, making an aureole around her black hair. The peppers glowed like coals in the basket on her back.

The other women had moved away from her, talking among themselves. Two of them were Hunting Owl's sisters. Green Gourd Vine gave a black look at their backs.

"I suppose Berry will give her a house," one of them said, just loud enough for Green Gourd Vine to hear. "She will give anyone anything. There's never enough food in that house, she gives it to anyone."

"That's a blessing!" Froglet said, but they sighed and patted her head.

"Your mother doesn't know when to stop."

Green Gourd Vine sniffed. Spotted Colt put his hand out of the dusk and touched her arm. She gasped.

"Ssshh!" the dusk said.

A tongue licked her instep, and she stifled a shriek. "What are you doing here?" she hissed back at them, heart thudding in her chest. "You frightened me."

"What are *you* doing?" Spotted Colt countered. "How long

does it take to be sure there are no horses? Have you looked under all their beds?"

"Hush, they'll hear you!" Green Gourd Vine looked fearfully at the women. She felt Digger's frost-tipped fur against her leg. The dogs would smell him and bark. "Come away."

She pulled Spotted Colt into the shadows of a leaf-shorn willow. The bare fronds brushed against his face. He said, "You weren't going to come back, were you?"

"It isn't that easy."

"Not to come away with me. I suppose not."

"I was afraid to when I was at home," she said frankly. "Then when I had nowhere to go, it seemed safer with you. Now . . ." She bit her lip.

"If all you want is to be safe," he said sullenly, "stay with these people. Live in a box."

"Tents feel to me as if they will blow away in the wind." She watched the leaves scudding through the dusk. She touched his arm miserably. "You feel that way, too."

"As if I would blow away?" He snorted. "Men of the Grass do not break their promises."

"What about your people? What about when you take me back there? To your mother?"

He grinned. She could just see his teeth, white in the falling darkness. "My mother says I should get married."

"She didn't say you should get married to a woman from the cities."

"No," he conceded. "But she didn't say not to."

"She didn't think of it," Green Gourd Vine said with certainty. "She would have if she had thought of it." Her mother had certainly said it. She missed her mother now, dreadfully.

Spotted Colt's fingers closed around her wrist. "You are arguing for argument's sake. I don't want you to marry my mother. Do you think I would let her be cruel to you?"

"No . . ."

"Then you don't want to leave here. It isn't my mother at all. Or the Grass, or the horses. Or me."

"I could maybe belong here," she said tentatively. "I don't know about the Grass. Or tents. I wouldn't belong there."

"You don't belong to places!" Spotted Colt said, exasperated. "You belong to people! Husbands and wives belong to each other!"

"My people belong to places."

"Your people are prairie dogs! Building houses out of dirt. No, wait, I didn't mean that!" But she was already running away from him, up the stream bank. Digger stuck his cold nose sympathetically into Spotted Colt's hand. Spotted Colt cursed and kicked a stone into the river, where it fell with a plop like a surprised frog. He hadn't said he loved her. That was what he had meant to say.

Green Gourd Vine stopped when her basket strap came loose and the peppers spilled on the path. She bent angrily to pick them up, and more fell out. "Yah!" She stamped her foot, kicking them as Spotted Colt had the stone. Then she scrubbed her hand across her eyes. The pepper juice stung like fire inside the lids. She flung the basket on the ground and knelt by the river, splashing cold water into her burning eyes. The women ahead of her were out of earshot on the path up the canyon, and she cursed them for leaving her behind. She dried her dripping face on her skirt and gathered up the peppers again. Digger was nosing among them—she could just see ears and a brushy tail in the dusk—and she cuffed at him until he went away. Then she set off up the path clutching the basket in her arms.

It had got very dark. As soon as the sun dropped below the canyon rim, night flooded in, pooling at the bottom like black water. The path was stony, littered with rocks washed smooth by the river, and she kept slipping on the loose stone. A pair of eyes glowed yellow in the cattails by the water. She hurried. "All thread gets woven," the eyes said, and she threw a rock at them.

When she came into the square of light that shone down from Berry's window and climbed the ladder to Berry's roof and down into the warm, firelit room, Hunting Owl looked at her with disapproval. He was sitting at his loom, weaving in the firelight, a blanket with a jagged pattern of red mountains and green arrowheads.

"This woman is well enough to leave us now," he said.

"When she has built a house for herself," Berry told him, pulling the husks off onions by the fire.

"I'll help her," Ripple said. "I like her. She has shells in her ears."

"Civilized people do not have holes in them," Hunting Owl said.

"Customs differ, Owl," Berry told him.

Hunting Owl sniffed. "People in Red Earth City have never behaved well."

"*I* want a man from there," Ripple said. "Maybe he will let me have shells in my ears."

Her father reached out an arm without leaving his loom and hit her above the ear. It was not very hard, but it was a smack. Ripple's lip quivered.

"No child of mine does as those people do. We are proper people here in this city. They are not." He shot another look at Green Gourd Vine and went back to weaving.

That night Green Gourd Vine dreamed that she was trying to climb down the ladder into a house and every time she did the house changed, became different in some uninhabitable way. Once it grew smaller, so that only her foot and ankle fit. Then it turned into a badger's den, and the next time there was a family of spiders inside, all weaving. When she tried again, it was full of water. Whatever had changed the world had changed the Bean Canyon people, too, so that they didn't know her. Or maybe it had only changed her.

In the morning when she got up, she couldn't see them. They were like fog people in the corners of the rooms, misty shapes like clouds walking. And the walls were translucent, like sheets of mica. She could see the shape of the canyon walls and the trees along the mesa top through them.

So she got up to piss, and before she could change her mind she just kept walking, past the transparent boys bringing in the firewood and the girls with water jars on their heads and the misty guards in the bean field. "I am going home," she said to all of them, and no one tried to stop her. If a Red Earth girl came and left again, it wasn't their business, and besides, Berry's man had said not to trust her. Better to not trust her outside the city than in.

She could see Mud Turtle, waiting for her on the canyon rim. He looked solid and sleepy, wrapped in a buffalo skin beside his watch fire. He yawned and stretched his arms over his head as she climbed the last few steps, as if he had just now noticed her, but she thought he had been watching her all the way up.

"I can't see them," she said. "They have turned into fog people."

"That is very likely." Mud Turtle didn't seem surprised.

"Why?"

"You are different now. Maybe they can't see you either."

"They couldn't." She looked back. Bean Canyon City looked like a pile of flat stones tilted together in the leaf-bare canyon below her. She squinted her eyes, trying to see the outlines of the houses, but their shapes were cracked and askew, as if someone had hit them with a hammer, or as if she were squinting into the sun. The fields must have been somewhere, but she couldn't find them. She could make out the uncleared chaparral that grew around the edges, and the tangles of frost-blackened grapes, but not the neat rows of beans and peppers or the tall brown stalks of maize waiting to be cut for mattresses.

Spotted Colt woke and came loping across the mesa. He stopped when he was twenty paces from her and became dignified.

"It happens to people," Mud Turtle said as he came up to them. "They can't go back. It is like putting a turkey back in an egg."

Spotted Colt came and put his arms around her. "I would rather have a hen than an egg," he said into her ear. He brushed it with his lips. "And you will have to sleep in my tent now. A coyote ate a hole in yours last night."

13

The Wolf Trail

THEY CAMPED AT EVENING A DAY'S RIDE FROM BEAN Canyon City in case the Bean Canyon people should think better of it and come looking for her. Blue Jay, scouting, found another high meadow with a creek running through it and grass for the horses, and Mud Turtle said they should stay there and think for a while, until they thought of where to look now for the horses that seemed to stay always just out of their reach.

Spotted Colt made no objection to that, and Mud Turtle and Blue Jay listened to his flute playing in his tent, from dusk until the stars that were the Girl and Her Brothers had crept above the northern horizon; and after that giggles and silence. Mud Turtle rolled himself in his buffalo robe and considered hunting and training young horses and other things that did not involve women. Blue Jay took his own flute out and played softly, thinking.

When she woke late in the night, Green Gourd Vine heard the flute, like an echo of Spotted Colt's. She poked Spotted Colt in the ribs. "How do I know we are married?" she demanded.

"Because you have slept in my tent." Spotted Colt felt sleep-

232

ily under the blankets. "If you have forgotten, we will do it again." He sounded hopeful.

She tucked her knees together. She knew she was married, but it was important that the wild Grass boy knew it, too. "Grass boys don't ever sleep with girls they are not married to?"

"All the time," Spotted Colt said cheerfully.

"Then how do I know—"

"They don't take them to their own tents!" He sounded horrified. "When you take someone to your tent, you have married her."

The noise she made with her teeth was skeptical.

"Look." He sat up, too, pulling the blankets around his shoulders. "I knew a man who did that once, because it was raining and the girl's mother was in her tent. He had to keep her."

"You ought to give me a blanket." She poked at the one covering them. It was the one she wore in the daytime, spread over his buffalo hide.

"We don't do that."

"Well, what do you do? Besides make girls sleep in your tent, with a story about dogs eating theirs?" She prodded Digger with her toe, and he snorted sleepily. It wasn't a story, though. She had seen the holes.

He tucked her into his arm, and she didn't protest. It made her skin tingle pleasantly. Earlier he had been in a hurry, and she hadn't known for certain what to do. She had watched dogs and turkeys—she wasn't ignorant—but dogs weren't people, and turkeys even less so. Five Clay Pots said people were the only ones who liked to do it all the time, not just at certain seasons. Coyote had given that to people, Five Clay Pots said, to annoy them. Gifts that looked very good to begin with had that way of being more trouble than you expected.

"I told you," Spotted Colt said to her, kissing the hollow of her neck. "I give your father horses."

"My father doesn't want horses. And he isn't here."

"Then I give *you* a horse."

"Really?"

"Of course. I am a chief's son. It isn't right that my wife not have a horse."

"All right. Do it now," she said. "I want to be sure I am married."

"I only have two horses with me. And you have End of the Day Horse to ride already."

"I want your horse instead of Blue Jay's." She gave him a sideways glance. "I don't want to get to your people and find out I have married him by mistake."

Spotted Colt chuckled. "Then I will give you Grasshopper Horse, and we will put the packs on that End of the Day Horse instead, although I think she will be insulted. She's a prideful beast."

Green Gourd Vine smiled at that. "Are horses prideful?"

"Certainly. They're like people. They know when they are important." He tucked her closer into his arm and flipped the tent flap open so that they could see the sky. The cold air bit at their faces, and they could see Digger's breath rising from the foot of the bed of skins and buffalo blankets. The sky was clear, dark black, lit with a round moon and pinpoint stars.

"The stars will be different where you live," she said.

"Not so much. We live a little north of your cities, but the people I know are still in the sky." He pointed to the seven stars in the north. "There are the Girl and Her Brothers."

Green Gourd Vine leaned her head close to his to see what he saw. "We call them Long Tail. Your stars all have the wrong names."

"Wrong for whom?"

She rested against his shoulder, but there was a little crease between her brows. "If even the stars change their names, how will I know where I belong?"

"You belong with me."

"Just us two?" At home, if you married, you married a whole family, a whole city, a vast clan of aunts and uncles and nieces and nephews and grandmothers.

"Sometimes. In summer we are all together once or twice to hunt buffalo. In Winter Camp sometimes there is just one family to a lodge. Maybe the lodges are together, maybe not."

I might like that, she thought. Maybe it meant she wouldn't have to live with his mother. She pointed lower down the sky. "What do you call those? The three bright ones in a row."

"The Three Deer," he told her softly. "Old Rabbit Dancer

taught them to me, one night when the sky was like this, clear as obsidian. I was five years old. They were the first stars I learned, after the Girl and Her Brothers and the Star that Stands Still."

"We call those three the Fawns."

"Well, then," he said, "that is close enough."

"Five Clay Pots taught me," she said with a little sniffle. "I was teaching Mouse and Toad. Magpie knows them already, all their names." Her voice faltered.

He kissed the hollow of her throat, remembering a woman who had been a captive of the Dry River people. She had grown ill of the homesickness and had died, stubbornly refusing to live with them no matter what they did for her. "Heart, I will give you children to teach the stars to. Your stars and mine."

"Tell me some more of your stars."

"Those in the midst of the Wolf Trail are the Rabbit—three bright ones and the two smaller ones." He took her forefinger and traced the Rabbit's haunches.

"What is the Wolf Trail?"

"Where the stars are thickest, where Wolf Star went down to earth. That band where they lie thickest across the sky."

"That is the Backbone of the Universe," she said, "and you are ignorant."

Spotted Colt smiled at the way the moonlight rippled on her bare shoulders, like water, and at the warmth she gave off in the crook of his arm. "When a man dies he takes the Wolf Trail south and comes to where the spirits live."

She shook her head, correcting him, trying to order his world so she could understand it. "You said when your people die they go to the Hunting Ground of the Dead and hunt buffalo." Everything he told her was jumbled and untidy. How could she trade what she knew for new truths that shifted under her feet?

"One is a story," he said comfortably. "The other is what we believe. Maybe the story is a way to what we believe. We don't understand these things yet because we aren't dead. Maybe both are true."

Green Gourd Vine considered the sky. Five Clay Pots had said that the stars knew their own names. What people called them was just for convenience, so you didn't have to keep saying, "the third star from the left with the two little ones beside it." She pointed at the zigzag of lights that Spotted Colt had called Rabbit. "We call her Spider," she told him. "She is weaving the Backbone together."

"I met a man once who called those Land of the Widows," Spotted Colt said dreamily. "He came from the Endless Water."

Green Gourd Vine craned her neck past the tent flap. The Meal-Drying Bowl and the Pot-Rest Stars had set and wouldn't come back until spring. The legs of the Chief of the Night were above her now, his head far to the north. There might be stars above the Endless Water she had never seen.

Spotted Colt put his hand on her breasts, under the buffalo robe that she had wrapped around herself. She felt his fingers exploring, warm and pleasant. He bent his face and kissed the tip of the left one, and something shot through her like the snap of spark that came from rubbing fur and then touching someone.

Spotted Colt wasn't thinking about the stars now. He was sprawled on the bed, nuzzling her breasts and kicking at Digger with his foot to make him move. Digger rolled onto his back and snored, and Green Gourd Vine snorted with laughter.

"I didn't want that dog," Spotted Colt said. "He gave himself to me."

"Then he is yours," Green Gourd Vine told him.

"He is half coyote."

"I know. I think he talks to me."

"Don't talk to him."

"He knows my talk," she told him. "Better than you do."

Spotted Colt rolled over and grabbed Digger. He shoved him out of the tent and dropped the flap. Darkness flowed around them. "He can talk to Mud Turtle. He hears horses, he might hear dogs."

"Poor Mud Turtle."

"Don't feel sorry for Mud Turtle. He owns more horses than anyone in the Dry River, even my father, who is the chief. I told you, he talks to them, and then they follow him. That is why we own horses that used to belong to the Buffalo Horn people. Lie down, Heart."

He pulled the buffalo blankets up over both of them, and she felt his hands exploring under the fur, small animals nuzzling her skin. Through the smoke hole of the tent, one star looked down at her like a white eye.

In the morning Mud Turtle and Blue Jay woke them before dawn and said it was time to ride. Spotted Colt cursed them as he stumbled out of the tent, but when he looked at the graying sky he didn't argue.

"Snow," Mud Turtle said. "That Five Clay Pots person told me it can surprise you here. I don't want to be surprised in the open."

Green Gourd Vine cocked her head at the thick sky of cloud like heavy uncombed cotton. "Snow," she agreed. "It's early."

"We need a Winter Camp," Mud Turtle said. "If there is snow now, it is too late to look for horses."

"They won't go anywhere, either," Spotted Colt told him.

"We're too close to that city. And I don't want to dig an earth lodge with four people and no proper tools. We should go to last year's camp. I have been thinking about this, not lying legs-in-the-air all night."

"Last year's camp isn't far." Blue Jay studied the crest of the blue mountains that nearly touched the low cotton sky. He held his fingers out. "Three days if we hurry."

Green Gourd Vine was afraid of that sky, of being out in the open in snow. She put on her leggings, and Spotted Colt boosted her up on Grasshopper Horse. They loaded her packs on End of the Day Horse, who looked affronted until Mud Turtle talked in her ear. Gray Cloud Horse and Bites If You Aren't Careful Horse carried the rest, and Killed a Snake Horse dragged the tent poles. Laugher and Digger trotted now ahead and now behind, snuffling at the ground and making side trips to see if they could catch a rabbit or dig a ground squirrel out of its hole. The dried meat they had brought from Red Earth City was nearly gone, and they knew they would have to hunt soon. But first was Winter Camp, a place to settle, to dig in for the cold.

The snow held off until they got there. They left a little trail of crumbled tobacco and Green Gourd Vine's prayer sticks behind them to thank whoever was responsible. No one had been in the camp since they had left it the winter before, although Spotted Colt checked it carefully to be sure that Cat or Bear hadn't moved in. The hot spring that bubbled out of the ground nearby was not as odoriferous as the sulphur springs, but its water soaked away trail aches and made bathing a pleasure.

A light snow fell their first night in the caves, and in the morning the world was powdered with it, white and glistening as frozen meal. They led the horses outside and watched while they snorted at the new snow and dug the stiff grass out from under it with their hooves. This was what it would be like living on the Grass, Green Gourd Vine thought. Except that your cave would move every few days, like a turtle. The men went out to hunt for the deer whose tracks they could see in the snow, leaving her to water the other horses and cut pine branches for beds in the cave. She made hers and Spotted Colt's as far away from Mud Turtle and Blue Jay as she could, but that wasn't very far. She had never minded hearing her father and mother at night, but now she felt frozen at the thought of Mud Turtle and Blue Jay hearing her. They weren't relatives, not brothers and uncles but strangers into whose house she had come to live.

Then the men came back with a great bustle and noise and a deer they had killed, as well as two rabbits that Blue Jay had hit with his throwing stick. The dogs danced around her while she cleaned them, poking their long gray noses into the carcasses while she swatted them away. Finally she threw them the offal, and they gulped it down noisily, no-manners, and sat breathing warm dog breath at her and waiting for more.

Whistling, the men worked a pile of stones loose from the slope and dragged them up to the cave on a hide. They dug a fire pit near the mouth, where the smoke would mostly blow outside, and lined it with rocks, fitting them together with fussy precision. Green Gourd Vine thought of Hunting Owl and Swimmer building the walls of Froglet's house. When they were through, they laid a fire for her to cook a haunch of the deer's carcass over. She put it on a spit, and Spotted Colt and Blue Jay sat beside it and played their flutes to the evening sun, braiding the music into the fire smoke and the meat smell. At the back of the cave, the horses stamped their

feet and snorted softly. The flute notes and the honey light of
the fire and the grassy horse smell made a warm magic in the
cave that Green Gourd Vine thought reluctantly might draw
her to its center, a warm, lazy magic of firelight and food.
After dark, when the four sat around the fire, Blue Jay told
them the story of the Flying Head, which Green Gourd Vine
knew, too, and so it was easy to follow the words. He told it
well, with fierce faces and bared teeth as the Head gobbled up
all the people in its path, roaring when it fell into the river to
be swallowed by a pike. There was a comfort in the familiar
tale, which Five Clay Pots had scared her with every winter
of her childhood. Edging closer to Spotted Colt, Green Gourd
Vine told them the story of how the Governor of the Yellow
Kachina People stole the wife of Tiny Flower, and how he got
her back. Then Mud Turtle told the story of the Rattlesnake
Brothers, and Spotted Colt told how Coyote gave away his
blanket to a rock and tried to take it back again.

When he had finished and the rock had chased Coyote
through valleys and riverbeds and flattened him into a rug,
Spotted Colt stood up, yawning. He eyed the bed of branches
at the far end of the cave. Without saying anything, he got a
coil of rope from his packs and tied the branches into a mattress that wouldn't come apart. Then he drove a stone wedge
into a crack in the ceiling above it and tucked in the edge of
one of his tent hides with it to make a curtain. Mud Turtle
and Blue Jay said something to each other at that and chortled,
but he paid them no mind. He took Green Gourd Vine by the
hand and led her behind their curtain.

Spotted Colt's mouth tasted like deer meat, hot and faintly
sweet. The cave was dark, only the faint red glow from the
eye of the fire seeping around their hide. On the other side
Mud Turtle and Blue Jay were talking, and the horses were
sleeping standing up. Green Gourd Vine lay down on the
branches, inhaled their sharp resinous scent, felt their needles
cushion her beneath the buffalo rug. Spotted Colt pulled another buffalo rug over them and began peeling off her riding
leggings and doeskin dress, the clothes that had been the dead
Grass girl's.

"I don't know what I am," she whispered. "I have shells in
my ears and hide clothes and I am sleeping in a cave."

"You are an onion," he said in her ear. "Layers and layers." His hands slipped the last layer off.

Maybe that was it. There was the Red Earth layer, and the layer that ran away to sleep in a cave, and soon there would be the Grass layer, and somewhere inside all of them the layer that wore shells from the Endless Water in its ears. All at the same time, one over the other, like ghost selves. She tried to explain that to him and got tangled up in the lack of words.

He seemed to understand. "All people are like that. That is what the elk said to me when I became a man."

"The elk?"

"My spirit. He told me that when he came to me."

"Oh." She was still not sure if he had actually talked to an elk or if he had gone out into the Grass to see a vision, which Mother said the wild people did. She thought it might be either. "All people are layers?"

"I think so." He put his arms around her gently, cradling her. "That is how I love you, and my mother, and my tribe, and my horses, and Mud Turtle, all at the same time. But you mostly, right now."

He kissed her mouth again, and that little snap of spark ran through her again and settled somewhere just below her navel, where it felt him stiffening. All the layers flowed together into one that knew what it wanted, the way a story comes together at the end, so it can't end any other way. This is what it would be like when she lived on the Grass, she decided; like living in a story.

All that night the two of them hid behind their hide curtain, trying to be quiet, laughing and shushing each other, and in the morning they got up yawning and dreamy.

After that, for a while, it was an enchanted life, like living in the story of the girl who married the blue snake or wedded fire and went to live in their magical house.

The next days were sunny. Green Gourd Vine found wild onions and dug them up, and they pried the nuts out of piñon pinecones and toasted them on a flat stone in the fire. When it was dark, they ran laughing down to the hot spring with Mud Turtle and Blue Jay and plunged in, sending a spray of steaming water into the air, sinking like turtles until only their noses stuck out, while the dogs stood on the edge and Laugher barked at them. Digger didn't bark, but when the moon rose, he put his head back and sang to it.

Green Gourd Vine washed her hair with yucca soap in the hot pool and combed it by the fire, making a crackling, sparking magic with its long black ends. In the daylight she soaked the deer hide and cleaned it with the scraper that Spotted Colt made her from one of its leg bones. Singing, she rubbed the brains into it and rolled it up beside the fire. She sang to Spotted Colt a flute song that Red Earth men played for women grinding meal, and he played it back to her while she unrolled the hide and kneaded it into supple folds. Mud Turtle and Blue Jay made a set of stones for Wolves and Deer and played with them by the fire, betting each other buffalo hides they hadn't killed yet and horses they didn't have. Green Gourd Vine tied the hide around a cone of tent poles and built a fire inside to smoke it. While she was waiting, she found some soft red stone and crushed it to make paint. And painted leaping deer and blazing suns and the humpbacked flute player who has maize in his pack and a penis as long as his flute, along the walls.

In the mornings, she cooked mush made from piñon nuts and dried deer meat dehydrated in the cold sun, and served it to the three of them, sitting down cross-legged beside them when their bowls were full. She watched them while she ate, eyes bright on their faces, mysterious, magical men from another world. She took care of them all indiscriminately, even though it was only Spotted Colt she slept with. If they had sniffles, she mothered them and rubbed their backs in the hot pool. When the snow fell, they huddled inside the warm, lazy cave and told each other stories and got ready to turn the sun around at the solstice. And then she and Spotted Colt went behind the hide again. She liked that part best, feeling his warm skin on hers under the blanket, his hands making her skin tingle. At night, sometimes in the afternoon, Green Gourd Vine and Spotted Colt got into their bed behind the hide and mapped the hollows and crevices, the round contours of each other, recording hip and thigh bone, breast and shoulder blade in memory, painted in mind like the pictures on a calendar hide, this circle for lips on a round breast, this arrow for the phallus of the humpbacked flute player.

All life was magical, and Green Gourd Vine could pretend that it would always be like this, just the four of them in their warm cave. Until Blue Jay ground the Wolves and Deer stones against each other in his fist and threw them across the room, spattering them against the painted sun. He stood up, swaying on his feet. "I can't breathe!"

"What is the matter?" Green Gourd Vine crouched by the wall, picking up the stones, her eyes startled wide.

"I can't breathe in here. I am going hunting."

"But it is going to snow." She looked worriedly out past the hide at the cave mouth. The sky was dark and thick.

"Not a good day to hunt." Spotted Colt got up from his place by the fire, where a moment ago he had been cuddling Green Gourd Vine.

Mud Turtle stood. "I will go with him."

"Nothing will be out in this weather."

"It doesn't matter." Mud Turtle rummaged in his packs. "*I* will be out."

Green Gourd Vine tried to give him the Wolves and Deer stones. She held them out in her cupped hands, but he didn't take them. "But it's nice in here," she said to him, bewildered. "Like your Winter Camps at home."

"This is not a Winter Camp!" Blue Jay snapped. "This is a cave, a hole in the rock! What do you think we are?"

"It's not—?"

"For Winter Camp, we have earth lodges," Mud Turtle said gently. "Houses dug into the earth, roofed like your houses are—do you think we are bears? They have smoke holes over the fire pits and proper quarters for the horses, and beds far enough apart that we do not have to listen to someone—" He stopped, pulling the buffalo robe off his bed. "We will be out of meat soon. Best that Blue Jay and I hunt."

"There is weather coming," Spotted Colt argued. "It is not hunting weather."

"It doesn't matter." Blue Jay spoke tightly, between his teeth. He had put on his boots and buffalo fur blanket and was pulling snowshoes from his pack.

Green Gourd Vine set the stones down in a little heap by

the fire, frightened. "It is not safe, this weather. The snow will eat you."

"Not me," Mud Turtle said. "Too old and tough."

Blue Jay put the snowshoes in a horse pack, the small kind that rode in front of him on Black Water Horse's back. His eyes were glittery as black water themselves. He picked up his bridle and shouldered past them.

"But—"

"Let them go, Heart." Spotted Colt put his hand on her arm. But he went and argued with Mud Turtle himself in a low angry murmur. Mud Turtle answered him back in the same voice, shaking his head stubbornly. When Blue Jay came back leading Black Water Horse and Morning Star Horse, Mud Turtle took his rein and stumped out of the cave after Blue Jay. They swung up on the dark backs and headed down the valley, black as crows against the white ground, with Laugher bounding along after them like a leaf blown on the wind.

Green Gourd Vine watched them, biting her lip.

"They are angry at us, Heart," Spotted Colt said.

"I know. But I thought it was nice here, like a story."

"Oh, it is. But it's our story. They have to find one, too. That's what they're looking for, not deer who have sense enough to stay denned when it snows."

Blue Jay was still muttering, scanning the crisp snow for the delicate, pointed prints of deer, that it was meat they were after. Mud Turtle knew better, but he went along anyway. Spotted Colt was like a puppy with a new bone with that girl, and it was tiresome. Any adventure would be better, even one that came on the white shoulders of the snow. The sky was dark and cottony, low over their heads with dark snow beasts waiting in its folds. The sun barely pushed its way through it.

The deer had been out earlier in the day, before the sky darkened so. A trail of prints ran from a stand of piñon pine down the edge of the stream, past the hot springs that still bubbled noisily under their white blanket.

"We can see where they den," Blue Jay said over his shoulder. Black Water Horse snorted in answer to his voice and the burbling voice of the hot springs.

"Best not to follow too far," Mud Turtle said, but he was

content to let Blue Jay lead the way for a while. Mud Turtle would make sure they didn't get out of sight of the high humped ridge that crouched above their cave.

"What does Most in Love know?" Blue Jay said surlily. "This isn't his country."

"It's the girl's. We might have listened to her, but we didn't." He sounded so matter-of-fact that Blue Jay laughed.

"Yah, you are tired of them, too."

"He and I are Horse Brothers. But he had to marry sometime. I will marry very likely, when we go home. I have enough horses now to give a girl's father and brothers."

"Buffalo Horn horses most likely," Blue Jay said as they picked their way down the steep stream bank, following the deer, but Mud Turtle only grinned.

"Why are *you* not married?" Mud Turtle asked him after a while. "An important Child of the Horse, and all?"

Blue Jay was silent, but he knew the answer. Dances wouldn't have liked it. Why wouldn't Dances have liked it? For the same reason that he didn't like any of the men who talked to Mother and Freckled Rat about her. Freckled Rat said that wasn't nice, but they weren't that way; they just didn't need anybody else. The thought caught in Blue Jay's throat along with the memory of the ghost husband, Flycatcher. Blue Jay had looked, when he came back to the sweat house, for the little bird stone that Dances had given him in the Land of the Dead, but he had never found it, not even among her packs. If he went back there maybe he would find it.

"This is far enough," Mud Turtle said, as if hearing that thought, the way he heard horses talk.

"Go back, then."

Mud Turtle thought about it. If Blue Jay wanted to get lost in a blizzard and die, then he and Spotted Colt would bring back all the horses. If they found any. And the Dry River people would have all the reputation, and the Buffalo Horn none. And old Rabbit Dancer would look at him while he explained how he had lost the Buffalo Horn boy in a blizzard and it was not his fault about that, and he would see straight into Mud Turtle's heart. Mud Turtle sighed. "Maybe we will find them down there," he said. He pointed to a stand of bare cottonwoods shivering in the canyon below them. Their snow-frosted trunks were laced with old creepers and wintry scrub among drifts of fallen leaves. He could see the marks on their bark where the deer had browsed. Laugher pricked her ears hopefully, scenting the wind.

Blue Jay turned to answer him, and Black Water Horse slipped on a stone. Mud Turtle saw them fall, dropping suddenly from the trail, sliding down the snowy, rock-strewn slope, horse and rider together, rolling and tumbling like stones themselves. Black Water Horse screamed, legs thrashing, and Blue Jay disappeared in the flailing legs.

The deer, who had been there all along, leaped from the tangled vines like arrows and shot across the snow-covered ground. Laugher started to run after them, and Mud Turtle, picking his way to the bottom, shouted her black angrily. She came, reluctantly, and sat at the bottom of the trail, not going near the place where Black Water Horse lay still, his neck twisted at a horrid angle, grotesque and monstrous as a kachina. Mud Turtle looked for Blue Jay and saw him, pinned under Black Water Horse's flank, his head in a drift of reddening snow.

"Is that your blood?"

Blue Jay opened his eyes. He tried to lift his arm to his head but it wouldn't move. Mud Turtle knelt next to him and felt his head. His fingers came away sticky and warm. Mud Turtle cursed under his breath. He tried to shove Black Water Horse's inert body off Blue Jay. He tried to pull Blue Jay from under him. Nothing moved. Blue Jay's eyes closed again. Mud Turtle wasn't sure he was breathing. A few flakes of snow fell on Black Water Horse's dark hide as he watched.

Spotted Colt got up from the bed at the back of the cave, stretching. He felt warm and sated, sinuous and sleek as a weasel. Green Gourd Vine was singing to herself in the bed, brushing out her long black hair while the wind whistled past the cave mouth, biting his skin. Spotted Colt pulled the thongs from his own braids. He would ask her to brush his hair, too, just for the feel of her fingers in it. Then they would make soup over the fire, and Mud Turtle and Blue Jay would come back, without a deer most likely, to say they had been foolish, and then all would be well. And maybe Spotted Colt could remember not to fondle his bride in front of them.

He pulled back the hide at the front of the cave, to go out and piss, and stopped. The air was thick with falling snow, blowing on a bitter wind, so that he could not see an arm's length in front of him. Digger got up from his place by the fire and whined, looking into it.

"Heart!" Spotted Colt felt the heat and weasel-sense of satiety and comfort leave him.

Green Gourd Vine came out from behind their hide. Her hair whipped around her face in the wind that came through the cave mouth.

"Heart, they are out in that."

Blue Jay could feel the snow closing his eyelids. If he looked up, he saw the whirling endless white of the storm, and the flakes fell in his eyes, cold and stinging. If he closed them, it was so easy to let the snow pile up on them. The warmth in Black Water Horse was ebbing, and both his legs had gone numb. Mud Turtle had given up and left—how long ago?— to get the others to come and help lift the weight of the horse from him.

And then the snow had gotten thicker, pale as the new people. The horse monsters. On the Grass, people had only heard of the Horse Bringers, Six-Legged and Wants the Moon, grandparents of the Children of the Horse. No one had talked of pale people coming with them. Blue Jay wasn't sure how that had happened, whether the horses truly came from the pale people, or the cold, pale people somehow came from the horses, giving birth like damaged mares, like wounds breeding maggots. He seemed to see them now, rising from the snow, pale as ghosts. Maybe they were ghosts, like the ones that had plagued the Buffalo Horn people and the Dry Water camps. Ghosts of old misdeeds. There they were now, walking out of the snow at him, telling him he had been wicked to Buffalo Horn girls, letting them think he might marry them when all he wanted was his sister. Wicked to have kept her from it, so that she had to die to marry. Wicked, and now the snow ghosts would eat him.

* * *

Mud Turtle let Morning Star Horse go where he wanted to, hoping he could smell the others in the cave. The snow made a white curtain around him, blinding as the inside of a cloud. Once Mud Turtle had been inside a cloud. He had gone to find his vision spirit on a high peak and was waiting there when the sky suddenly lowered. Mockingbird came out of it, ruffling gray-and-white feathers, and after that Mud Turtle had been able to talk to horses, and to most other animals, too. He asked Morning Star Horse where they were going now, but Morning Star Horse had no answer. He could only go toward whatever faint scent of grass and dry cave was carried on the wind, if it wasn't a false scent, blown off some distant mountain by the gale howling across the valley; if they didn't drop with the next blind step from the edge of a bluff into the silent, waiting snow. Mud Turtle could barely see Laugher's gray shape popping up ahead of him and disappearing again in the driving white curtain of the storm. He called to her, and her head appeared for an instant, crowned with a patch of snow between her ears. Her breath made little clouds like steam boiling off a stewpot. She floundered through the snow, a wet, gray fish leaping, and he followed her, followed Morning Star Horse's nose.

The snow had begun to drift into the cave now, the cold breath of winter leaving little encroaching trails of white to dust the floor. Spotted Colt was crouched over a piece of hide and Green Gourd Vine bent over him, her long hair brushing his shoulders. "What are you doing?"

"I am making a torch that won't go out." He sliced the hide into a half circle with the sharp obsidian blade of his belt knife.

She had been afraid that he was going to go look for them, and then she would be by herself, alone in this cave when none of them came back. "I will go with you."

"No. Someone has to stay here and keep the fire going, so we can see the light."

"The fire won't go out."

"That is because you will stay and tend it."

"No." She looked at him stubbornly, lip out. He didn't look up to see it.

Spotted Colt folded the piece of hide into a cone and poked holes in the edges with a bone awl. He knotted three lengths cut from a roll of sinew into the holes and lashed the cone to a stick. The stick he lashed to a torch, leaving the cone high enough that it wouldn't put out the flame or catch fire, but would keep off snow. Satisfied, he lit the torch with a piece of wood from the fire. The flame blazed up, casting long, sudden shadows on the cave walls.

"Hold this while I get Rainstorm Horse."

She held the torch, admiring the ingenuity of it, and its utter uselessness. "You can't see through the snow with this," she said to him.

"No, but they can see me." He looped Rainstorm Horse's rein over one arm and held out his hand for the torch.

She shook her head, terror welling up in her eyes. "I will come."

"You will not."

She backed away from him. "You will not leave me here by myself."

"Heart, it won't help if you come. The horses don't like the snow and you don't ride well enough. Give me the torch."

"No."

He looked at her, exasperated, not knowing what to do and feeling foolish. He didn't want to wrestle her for it, but only a bigger fool would take her out in this. The wind howled, driving snow past the hide curtain, whipping around his booted feet.

Mud Turtle bent his head, trying to keep the stinging snow out of his eyes. He thought Laugher was still with him, but he couldn't be sure. She was just a gray shadow among the other shadows that chased each other through the blizzard. He wondered if he would die out here. And if he did, if Spotted Colt would get home. If Spotted Colt got home, maybe he, Mud Turtle, would be remembered. His fingers were numb. His nose ached. He had come to find horses, to get a reputation. But then there had been the little Buffalo Horn girl, whom he had yearned for even while he knew she wouldn't have him. She was proud, and he was ugly. Now his Horse

Brother was married, and Mud Turtle wondered why he had thought someone would love an ugly man. He had horses. He could marry many women. But he wanted one to love *him*, not his horses. Laugher loved him, but Laugher was a dog.

Laugher's head bobbed up at his heel, emerging from the snow in a spray of wind-driven slush. She yelped once and plunged into the drifts ahead of them. Morning Star Horse lifted his wet head and whickered. Ahead of them, faintly, Mud Turtle thought he saw a flicker of light. It might have been a will-o'-the-wisp, a spirit light come to lead him astray. Or Blue Jay's ghost going home through the storm. Mud Turtle set Morning Star Horse's head for it, anyway.

Spotted Colt confronted Green Gourd Vine across the fire pit. She danced just out of his reach, torch in her hand. This was not what he had expected. He had expected to go out in the storm and find Mud Turtle, who was his Horse Brother, and maybe he would die doing it, but that was as it should be. It was not as it should be if his wife came with him and died, too. And in any case, he was more likely to die with her than without her, since he would be hampered trying to take care of her; but if he told her so, she would be insulted, he could tell that.

"Give me the torch," he said again, and she just shook her head, stubborn, lip stuck out. He could see it now.

Rainstorm Horse lifted his head and whickered, and outside, muffled by snow, another answered him. Spotted Colt spun around. Green Gourd Vine came around the fire, waving the torch, nearly setting fire to the curtain as she pulled it back. Now he could have taken it from her.

"Here!" Spotted Colt shouted into the storm. "Mud Turtle! Blue Jay! We are here!"

"We are here!" Green Gourd Vine echoed him. A shrill bark came out of the snow, and Digger yelped back.

They could see movement, something white moving in the whiteness of the snow: Morning Star Horse, snow-encrusted, with Mud Turtle huddled on his back.

"Come inside from the wet." Spotted Colt helped Mud Turtle down. He was stiff and nearly fell. Laugher dropped beside the fire, tongue hanging out, snow melting off her frozen coat.

"Where is Blue Jay?" Green Gourd Vine asked.

The snow was colder than it had been. Warmed by the fire, Mud Turtle's face and hands ached with the returning cold. Ahead of him Spotted Colt rode Rainstorm Horse with the city girl beside him on Grasshopper Horse. They had had a brief, fierce argument over whether she should come, until Mud Turtle had said that it would take all three of them to lift a dead horse. So here she was, huddled in a buffalo blanket, clinging to the horse's back. They were probably all going to die anyway, Mud Turtle thought morosely, and she might as well die with them as starve in the cave. He wished they had untied the packhorses so that they wouldn't starve, too, when their human people didn't come back for them. He said so, and Spotted Colt shouted angrily at him to be quiet.

Spotted Colt was trying to see Laugher in the snow ahead of him. They thought she might be able to take them back to Blue Jay, but it might be just as likely that she was going somewhere else. Mud Turtle said she wasn't. It irked Spotted Colt, depending on what Mud Turtle said a dog told him. Spotted Colt had stolen horses and fought the Buffalo Horn and never been touched. He was the fortunate one, the magical son, the charmed warrior. Now he was following a dog through the snow because neither man could bring himself to let the Buffalo Horn boy freeze. Spotted Colt's new wife might freeze instead because of it. He didn't know how all that had happened. It hadn't been part of his plan.

The wind picked up in a vicious gust that blew stinging ice down his neck. Rainstorm Horse floundered through a drift, and ahead of him Laugher disappeared in the driven snow. They hadn't gone far from the cave, Mud Turtle said, when it had happened. But in their blindness now, it would be so easy to pass within an arm's reach of the place and never see. Panicked, Spotted Colt called Green Gourd Vine's name, and she called back to him out of the white blindness, the torch a glimmering ghost of light that came and went.

                    *   *   *

Blue Jay couldn't feel his legs now, or his hands. The white-ness danced around him like women swaying, swinging the fringes of white dresses. If he could move his hands, he could catch them, pull them to him. They would lift him up and take him into the heart of the storm. And then a woman did dance out of the snow. It was Dances, her white snow dress embroidered with frozen lakes and the wind that blew in from the outer reaches of the Wolf Trail.

"I brought you this. You left it," she said. He saw the little bird stone, gleaming in her palm.

"It wouldn't come with me," he said. "It stayed behind."

"That was your dream. This is mine."

Did the dead dream?

"That Field Mouse girl will be waiting for you. Give her the stone."

No—as long as he didn't marry, he could keep Dances.

No! She shook her head, adamant.

Why had he thought that? It seemed a foolish notion now. Was that why Spotted Colt and Green Gourd Vine had made him so angry?

Dances stood over him, hand on her hip. She was barefoot, but even the snow could not make her colder than she was. The little bird-shaped stone fell into his palm.

When she left, she took the snow with her. The wind stilled abruptly, and the last flakes fell out of the frozen air. The sky overhead was black as obsidian, glowing in the east with the milky, cold circle of the moon. It washed over the snow-blanketed land so that it, too, glowed, light enough to see the bark on the bare trees above him, and the ragged outlines of their torn leaves.

Black Water Horse was a frozen weight on his legs, his broken neck buried in the snow, body a white mound like the roof of an earth lodge. Blue Jay twisted his neck, but all he could see overhead was the wheel of the stars, and to either side the unbroken blanket of the snow.

"There he is!"

At first Spotted Colt saw only a tangle of fallen limbs under a bare tree. Digger plunged past him, pawing at the snow, and one of the limbs became a horse's hind leg.

They slithered down the buried path. Blue Jay's eyes were closed, and he felt cold as the snow.

Green Gourd Vine put her ear to his mouth. "He's breathing!" Its sound was uncertain, ragged, breath that might stop at any moment. His mouth was blue in the moonlight.

They dug the snow from the body of the horse with their hands and pushed at its dead weight together. It didn't budge. Spotted Colt and Mud Turtle took it by the legs and heaved. They tied ropes to the stiffening legs and then to the live horses and drove them forward. The body shifted slightly. Blue Jay moaned. Green Gourd Vine wedged her hands under Blue Jay's shoulders. Mud Turtle smacked the horses on their rumps, and they lunged forward again. Black Water Horse slid an arm's length. Green Gourd Vine grabbed Blue Jay by the armpits and pulled him free. They landed together on her back in the snow, and Spotted Colt and Mud Turtle came running back for them.

"He's cold. He's frozen."

"Put him up in front of me." Mud Turtle heaved himself stiffly onto Morning Star Horse, and Spotted Colt lifted Blue Jay up to him. Mud Turtle wrapped both arms around him, his buffalo robe enfolding them like a tent.

"Look." Spotted Colt pointed back the way they had come. In the moonlight they saw the humpbacked ridge lifting itself toward the sky, and below it the dark hollow of the cave mouth.

"Not far," Mud Turtle said into Blue Jay's ear as Morning Star Horse lurched forward. "Not far."

Green Gourd Vine put her heels to Grasshopper Horse's ribs. His heavy gait jolted her spine, and she hung on fiercely. Behind her she could hear Spotted Colt shout, but she ignored him. He couldn't move fast, leading Mud Turtle and Blue Jay, and there were things to do to get ready. A man of Red Earth City had frozen once, in her childhood, and that year's Squash Old Man had found him. She remembered the Deer Lodge priest building the fires, and how they had warmed him.

When the men came to the cave mouth, she had put one of the tents up inside the cave and made a fire in it beside a pile of blankets. The tent leaned as if it had palsy, but it hadn't fallen over. Spotted Colt saw what she was doing and tightened the ropes.

"Get him inside," she told them.

They carried Blue Jay into the tent, leaving the horses to shiver beside the outer fire. Green Gourd Vine whistled the dogs inside the tent, too, and took her clothes off, paying no attention to the men, except to snap at them both, "Undress!"

They stripped wet clothes off and pulled Blue Jay's stiffened, icy leggings from him, and then his shirt. His fist was closed over something, and they couldn't uncurl his fingers, so Spotted Colt cut his shirtsleeve with a knife and tugged it off. They laid Blue Jay on the blankets and lay down beside and over him, enfolding him in human warmth. Green Gourd Vine wrapped the blankets over them all like a bundle. They could feel Blue Jay shivering, so they knew he was still alive. Green Gourd Vine snapped her fingers for the dogs, and they crawled under the blankets, too.

"Yah, they are wet!" Mud Turtle said.

"So are you," Green Gourd Vine said with a quiver of laughter. It was hard to be solemn when they were all wrapped naked in a blanket together.

"I am not hairy," Mud Turtle said with dignity.

"You are heavy," Spotted Colt said. "You are lying on my leg and it is going to sleep."

Outside the tent they could hear the horses stamping their feet and blowing down their noses. Inside it smelled overwhelmingly of wet dogs. The heat of the fire was soporific, seeping slowly into their skin. Blue Jay's breathing deepened, settling into a rhythmic drone of exhaustion and pain, but in the firelight his lips had got some of their color back.

"Do you think his legs are broken?" Mud Turtle asked in a whisper.

"Why do you always think of things like that?" Spotted Colt hissed. "We will be lucky if he doesn't lose his ears and his fingertips."

"They will be easier to travel without," Mud Turtle said stolidly. "I am thinking practical thoughts."

"I don't think they are broken," Green Gourd Vine said.

"Um," Mud Turtle said, but he listened to her. She had pulled Blue Jay from under Black Water Horse and ridden back to make the fire, and she wasn't so fine she wouldn't get in bed naked to save him. It might be that women from the cities were not as useless as Mud Turtle had thought.

She cradled Spotted Colt with one arm and Blue Jay with the other. Spotted Colt could feel the curve of her backside where it fit into his belly and tried not to think thoughts that would make him stiffen against her. The feel of her made him want to even now, in bed with Mud Turtle and a frozen Buffalo Horn man and two dogs. *I am not the magical son,* he thought. *I know nothing. I did not save this man. It was my wife and a dog. All life is uncertain.* Oddly, that didn't bother him. He pressed his cheek against Green Gourd Vine's hot shoulder and dozed.

She felt his face against her back, warmly comforting. *One day I will be alone,* she thought. Women almost always outlived their men, unless they died having babies, and her family's women never did. *By then I will be able to stand that. I will be a Grandmother, and wise. And right now, I have him.* It seemed enough, cocooned in the steamy tent with a moist dog nose under her elbow and someone's foot entangled with hers.

Blue Jay heard their voices as if they came from a long way off. His fingers and toes ached, and his ribs hurt when he breathed, but he was conscious of a warm weight enveloping him that made him in his delirium remember being carried at his mother's breast. The fingers of his right hand were curled tight around something. He unclenched them painfully and touched it with his thumb. The little bird stone. It had come with him. He tried to remember Field Mouse, and her face came more clearly to him. Memory slid back and she was there: a half-naked baby girl helping him dig fish bait, a solemn ten-year-old giving him a blue feather for his horse's tail, a big-eyed adolescent dancing at her puberty dance, the same year that Dances came of age; always in Dances' shadow. She stepped out into the light now, a grave young woman watching him talk to Grandmother Weevil's girl, with whom he had lain in the tall grass the night before they left. (He hadn't told Freckled Rat, who would say it would bring him bad luck.) Grandmother Weevil's girl would be married by now. He thought Field Mouse might not be.

Behind her he saw Dances watching him. (Mud Turtle saw her for a moment, too, strangely comforted.) Then Dances lifted her hand and turned into mist, and Blue Jay knew she wouldn't come back, even if he died now. But she had been there. That would have to be enough. Would be enough. He closed his eyes and found that he could keep Dances under his lids, a glimmer of light that wouldn't blind him.

14

The Long-White-Bone-Man

BLUE JAY SAT FLEXING HIS FROSTBITTEN FINGERS IN THE FIRST patch of spring sun. Only the tip of the middle left one was gone, with the tip of his right ear. Mud Turtle had sat on him while Green Gourd Vine cut the blackened flesh off and held a hot coal to the raw spots. He remembered that, vaguely, mostly just a memory of thrashing and cursing them while they held him down. But the ear and the finger had healed clean. The other fingers ached when they got cold, but he could still draw a bow with them. Green Gourd Vine said he was lucky he could do that.

Water dripped from the stones above the cave mouth, melting snow that made little rivulets in the muddy ground. The horses had been staked out to graze on the new grass that was trying to poke its head through the slush. The four humans had done their part to turn the sun around at the solstice, and it was riding higher in the sky each day now, having decided after all not to slip forever beyond the horizon. Blue Jay wondered what would happen if some year no one danced the Dog Dance to bring it back. Would it just drift away into the sky, growing smaller and smaller, leaving the world in perpetual winter? Or did the sun care what they did? Did it have its own appointed course, and did people only think they might shift it one way or the other, while the sun went on, magnificent in its unconcern? Blue Jay frowned at the melting snow. Those were things that Spotted Colt and Mud Turtle talked of; Dry River people always thought on peculiar and dangerous things. Now they had him doing it.

He got up and looked at the sky. It was nearly the Spring Rain Moon: time to find horses and go home. They were almost two years gone. Maybe they would be legend among their own people by now.

Green Gourd Vine came skidding up the icy path from the stream with big handfuls of new cress. She gave him a sprig of it. The taste was hot and icy at the same time, and he chewed slowly, relishing it. She put her hands on her hips and bent backward, stretching. He eyed her belly suspiciously, but she didn't show any signs of being pregnant. They would never get home if she got big-bellied halfway there, he thought, mildly irritated at the prospect, even though she hadn't done it.

Green Gourd Vine gave him another piece of cress. "It's good for your digestion. You look bilious," she informed him.

"I am bored," Blue Jay said fretfully. "I am beginning to think about things that make my head ache because I have nothing to do."

Morning Star Horse whickered and tugged at the end of his tether. He rolled his eyes at End of the Day Horse.

"Your mare feels the same way," Green Gourd Vine said. End of the Day Horse was hiking her tail and sidling back and forth just out of reach of Morning Star Horse.

"Yah, slut," Blue Jay said. He took her tether and moved her farther away from the stallions.

Mud Turtle, who was cleaning stones and mud out of Killed a Snake Horse's feet, looked up as Killed a Snake Horse tossed his head, too, and whinnied. "They will have had to winter somewhere, like us," Mud Turtle murmured. "Now they will be bored and wanting to get out, like us. Maybe they will start looking again, too?"

He said the same thing to Spotted Colt and Blue Jay and Green Gourd Vine when they sat down to eat morning mush together.

"Who?" Blue Jay demanded.

"The peccaries," Mud Turtle said. "Those pale people." He turned to Green Gourd Vine. "What is it that they want?"

"They want shiny rocks and that bright clay they make bowls out of," Green Gourd Vine said. "That is what they told the Two Old Men."

"They are crazy," Blue Jay said.

"That doesn't matter," Spotted Colt said. "Crazy people make sense to themselves. Mud Turtle is thinking a thought here."

"And where will they find those things they want?" Mud Turtle asked.

"They won't. Except maybe for the rocks. There is quartz in the mountains. But we never saw this other thing before."

"But they are looking for it? And the Bean Canyon men told them that it was in Red Earth City?"

"I think so." She spat over her shoulder. "They are snakes."

"So what will the Red Earth men do?"

Green Gourd Vine frowned, puzzled.

Spotted Colt laughed suddenly. "They will do the same thing. But they can't send them back to Bean Canyon. Where would they send them?"

"They are more honorable than that!" Green Gourd Vine said. "*My* people would never send monsters to someone else's city."

"Not to a city, maybe. But elsewhere? Where do these Outsiders live that you talked of?"

"Northwest. Beyond the canyons where the Ancestors' houses are. They come south and raid us when they want to steal things, but mostly they live to the northwest."

"What are they like, these Outsiders?"

"Grabby. They take anything they want. And they live in brush huts like wood rats. They have teeth like dogs."

"Have you seen one?"

"Once, but he was dead. And I saw a woman once, that someone stole. She ran away again as soon as he quit tying her up. She was afraid of his house. Five Clay Pots tried to teach her to grind meal, and she bit him."

"They are wild people?"

Green Gourd Vine thought. "I don't know. I used to think

Grass people were wild people, but now I see that you are not. So I don't know about the Outsiders now. But I would not have one in my house."

"They sound like the Red Bow people." Mud Turtle said. "Maybe they have killed these pale people by now."

"They might." Green Gourd Vine looked morose. "If they have, they will have taken the horses. It would not be good for the Outsiders to have horses. They will raid my people every moon if they do."

"I think the pale people are harder to kill than they look," Mud Turtle said.

"I found one dead. Remember?"

"I don't think Outsiders killed him," Spotted Colt said. "I think the desert killed him."

"Maybe the desert will kill them all!" Green Gourd Vine thought of the story that Coyote had told her, of the Long-White-Bone-Man. He sounded unstoppable, something foretold and inevitable in the future, like winter.

"The horses are antsy," Mud Turtle said. "So are we. It is time to get out of Winter Camp. Isn't it possible that the pale people will feel the same way? That they will be foot-on-trail? That maybe they have wintered with the Outsiders, since they were gone from Red Earth City when Blue Jay went back to look?"

"Who knows what monsters will do?" Blue Jay protested. "Maybe they flew up into the trees for the winter."

"Without their horses? I have never met a horse who could fly."

"Now that would be useful." Spotted Colt grinned.

"You wouldn't like it," Blue Jay said, remembering the vulture's back, and how far it would have been to fall.

"Pay attention!" Mud Turtle growled. "Child, do you know where these Outsiders winter?"

Green Gourd Vine nodded.

Green Gourd Vine thought she did—you know how to find the thing you fear—but the world was very large and she had never actually been there. They rode for half a moon to the north, but they didn't see any Outsiders or pale people. Blue Jay, who was the best tracker among them, went out to look for prints of horses or grass that had been grazed, while the rest camped and argued over where to go next. Green Gourd Vine was tearfully apologetic that she couldn't find their camp.

"I'm not afraid of them, truly." She looked pleadingly at Spotted Colt. "Well, I am, but not when we have horses and I am with you. But they move all the time. They are wanderers. And I have only heard the old men talk, or people who have traded with them. Once I knew a man who had been a slave there, until he ran away and they couldn't catch him. Mostly people don't come back when they find the Outsiders."

"Hush, Heart. I know. We don't think you are hiding them."

"I wanted to help," she said morosely, because she was afraid of them, and was terrified to find them, and so she felt it her duty to do it anyway.

Blue Jay came back. "There are tracks," he said. "North of us, in a wash. But old ones. If we didn't make them ourselves," he added.

Mud Turtle and Spotted Colt scanned the skyline. "I don't remember this country. Those tracks aren't ours." Spotted Colt was fairly sure of that.

"Well, then, we should go there." It seemed as good a choice as any. Morning Star Horse and Killed a Snake Horse were still dancing around End of the Day Horse, and now Rainstorm Horse had got interested, too. Mud Turtle smacked them all on the nose with his fist, and they looked affronted. He readjusted End of the Day Horse's packs.

Spotted Colt nodded. "We will go to the hoofprints."

Green Gourd Vine swung herself up on Grasshopper Horse, the way she had learned to do now, and rode close to Spotted Colt. If there were hoofprints, there were horses, and then there were pale people, even if there weren't Outsiders. One seemed more than dreadful enough to Green Gourd Vine. Both were an unspeakable thought.

But when they got to the wash, it ran through a flat, high valley and there was no human person in sight, nor any sign that there had been except the prints, which faded into dust ten paces away. Only the ones that had been protected by the lip of the wash were still intact. They were old, as Blue Jay had said. Green Gourd Vine relaxed.

While the men inspected the hoofprints in the wash, she

rode to the trickle of a stream that was still left in the riverbed that the wash flowed into, to fill their waterskins. She couldn't see the water, but she could hear it, burbling quietly to itself, and Grasshopper Horse could smell it. It was dry country here; water was something to be conserved and taken where you found it. Green Gourd Vine's lips were parched, and her skin chafed with the blowing dust. She had ceased wearing Spotted Colt's leggings and now rode as the wild girl had, with her dress hiked around her thighs. Her legs and feet were coated with dust. Maybe the water would be deep enough to bathe in. Grasshopper Horse, who was coming into season herself, was cranky and fidgety and kept turning her head, despite the smell of water, trying to go back to the others. "If I can't have babies foot-on-trail, neither can you," Green Gourd Vine told her, and kicked her soundly in the ribs. Grasshopper Horse snorted and tossed her head, but she went the way Green Gourd Vine told her to.

The stream was nearly dry, but it pooled in one place into a deep green pond, fed by a slow trickle that trickled out again at the other end. Green Gourd Vine could see that the pond had once been much larger and might be filling again now, fed by the spring rains and the snowmelt from the high country. She slid off Grasshopper Horse with the waterskins over her arm and a good grip on Grasshopper Horse's rein. She put her foot on the rein and pulled her dress over her head, leaving it in the sand. When she kicked her shoes off, the stones were hot under her feet. She sank into the green pool, holding the rope while Grasshopper Horse stuck her nose in the water and drank.

The ripples pooled out from Grasshopper Horse's lips. Green Gourd Vine patted the surface, making her own ripples to run up against them. They bounced off each other, crossing and recrossing in an aqueous pattern, interlaced like a basket of water. Green Gourd Vine pulled the pins out of her hair and let it float on the water. She ducked her head under and came up blinking at the sun reflected off the droplets on her eyelashes.

Grasshopper Horse jerked her head up, twitching the rein out of Green Gourd Vine's lax and dreaming fingers. Green Gourd Vine sat up with a splash as Grasshopper Horse started away. Cursing, she plunged out of the pool after her. Grasshopper Horse trotted a few paces, dragging the lead, looking east into the sun. She whickered. Her ears pricked forward like Digger's when he saw a rabbit. Green Gourd Vine stumbled behind her, dripping and naked, and grabbed the rein as Grasshopper Horse started off again. From the distance Green Gourd Vine heard an echoing whinny, faint as a bird's call. She dragged Grasshopper Horse back to the pool, her hand tight on the rein, while Grasshopper Horse fought her.

Green Gourd Vine snatched up her dress and the waterskins as Grasshopper Horse whickered again. "Be quiet!" She clamped her fingers hard on Grasshopper Horse's bony nose. Clutching the dress and skins, she swung onto the horse's back and dug her heels in.

The men looked up to see her riding hard across the sand, her wet hair flying behind her, shoeless and naked. She slid off Grasshopper Horse's back and dropped the waterskins. "There are horses out there!"

Mud Turtle took Grasshopper Horse, who was still looking backward and whickering quietly. He turned his back politely while Green Gourd Vine tugged the dress over her wet skin.

"Where are they, Heart?" Spotted Colt asked her gently. Blue Jay was shading his eyes, looking east.

"That way. I heard one whinny. This horse smelled them, I think, and made a noise. Then some other horse answered." Her hands shook as she tugged and dragged at the doeskin dress. "I couldn't think of anything but to run."

"A good plan," Mud Turtle said. "We will all run, for a while, and hide somewhere until night. Then we will see what these horses are."

"Do you think they heard Grasshopper Horse?" Green Gourd Vine looked frightened. "Whoever is with these horses?"

"Maybe. But they may not think of us. They may think of more of their own kind. That one you found dead maybe. In any case, it would be a fine idea to go back and brush out our trail, once we are camped."

Mud Turtle and Spotted Colt seemed very certain of what to do, and not at all afraid. Blue Jay wanted to go now, right now, and find the horses, steal them, and ride home. But he was outvoted and went with the others, irritably looking over his shoulder. They camped at the mouth of a canyon, where they were screened from view but could see anyone coming. There was a trail out the other end, too, if they needed it. Blue Jay and Mud Turtle went back to brush out their tracks. Spotted Colt put up the tents trail-style, with fewer poles, so they could be taken down in a hurry, and made a fire out of sight of the canyon mouth. The horses were tethered, not hobbled, to keep them close.

"What can we do without?" Spotted Colt asked no one and everyone, surveying the packs.

"Tent poles," Mud Turtle said. "We can cut new ones."

"If we get a chance to stop," Spotted Colt said.

"Travel light, travel fast," Blue Jay said.

"We're teaching you how to steal horses," Mud Turtle said to Green Gourd Vine.

They rooted through the packs and discarded anything that could be replaced.

"What am I going to cook in?" Green Gourd Vine wailed as they threw out the baskets. It was bad enough cooking in baskets with hot rocks instead of in proper pots you could put on a fire.

"We won't be cooking." Mud Turtle pawed into the next pack. "This is the hide with the hole in it. Let Coyote have the rest of it, and maybe he'll help us." He tossed the hide aside.

"This blanket is nearly bald." Spotted Colt inspected a buffalo skin. It was Blue Jay's buffalo skin. Blue Jay dug into another pack and threw out a pair of shoes that belonged to Spotted Colt and had a hole in the sole.

When they were finished, they had cut their packs from three to two, and those they repacked so that they were three again, lighter now. Mud Turtle reinspected the harnesses until he was certain each horse could run with a pack and not lose it.

Green Gourd Vine watched with interest, almost forgetting that these preparations were being made so that they could go and steal horses from monsters and Outsiders. Plainly Mud Turtle and Spotted Colt and Blue Jay stole horses all the time—mostly from each other, she supposed. They had an aura of excitement now that she hadn't seen before. They glowed with it, like a tent at night with a fire inside, as if the thievery made them brighter, stronger, cleverer. She remembered Spotted Colt talking about how the young men made a reputation. It had sounded fierce and strange to her, and frightening. City people didn't raid each other, and lived in fear of those who did. But now that she was on the raiders' side, some of that fierce excitement spilled over, like sparks rising from a fire, and she felt it burn her skin.

She had thought Spotted Colt would be restless the day before they were to raid the pale people, but instead he slept all day like a log, inert, deep in sleep, not even snoring. At nightfall, he opened his eyes and stood up almost in one movement, fully awake. The horses seemed to know something was happening, too. They danced sideways on their hooves, taut with energy.

When it was full dark, they tied the loaded packhorses in a line and rode silently out of the canyon toward where Green Gourd Vine had heard the horse whinny. They put her in the middle, with Spotted Colt in the lead and Blue Jay on Gray Cloud Horse just behind her. The dogs trotted silently beside them, and they moved slowly, keeping in the shadows of brush and the sides of dry washes.

The night was never still. If you were quiet you could hear the bug people going about their business, singing in the chaparral; the silent *whoosh* of an owl going by; the scuttle of mice in the sand; the yowling, growling song of a cat in the distance. Green Gourd Vine had been afraid the horses would make noise, but Mud Turtle talked to all of them before they mounted, and they seemed to know what he said.

When they neared the east end of the valley and the dogs found the scent where Green Gourd Vine had said they would, it led up a steep slope to a jumble of brush huts in a stand of aspens. They were ragged, messy structures, like broken wasp nests, with two banked fires burning among them. From the smell, the midden was in among them, too. Green Gourd Vine wrinkled her nose. They expected to find the people asleep in the camp where the strange horse was, but they could see men walking about and hear shouting through the trees. Spotted Colt froze, and the rest stopped behind him.

"Maybe it is a dance," Green Gourd Vine whispered.

The firelight glinted off one of the men, and they saw that he had on the kind of shiny shirt that the pale people owned. He was the one doing the shouting, stamping back and forth, raging in a voice that sounded like wood splintering. His face looked ghostly, like a mushroom, in the dim light.

Two more men stood by one of the fires, their hands behind their backs. They had normal-colored skin and dark hair bound up with thongs. Their clothes were mostly made of skin, although one of them wore a blanket that came from the cities. It was torn and dragging on the ground now. The firelight showed a necklace of blue stones around his neck. While they watched, the pale man grabbed the necklace and tore it off. He looked at it, shouted, and threw it on the ground in disgust. The other man didn't move.

"They are tied," Spotted Colt whispered.

"They have no shiny rocks or that bright clay." Mud Turtle shook his head. "These are not wealthy people. Look at their huts."

Green Gourd Vine pressed her lips into a line. She refused to feel sorry for these people.

"Be still." Spotted Colt put a hand on Mud Turtle's shoulder. Two pale people were dragging the Outsiders out of their huts. Three more stood with their sticks pointing at anyone who might want to argue. The firelight gleamed on the shiny length of the sticks, which were not wood at all but something harder, colder, more deadly. At a little distance, the black-robed pale man watched silently, his face only half lit by the fire, dark planes of glimmer and shadow, arms folded across his chest. His fingers played with the crossed sticks that hung from his neck. Green Gourd Vine remembered the crossed sticks and hanging man that the dead one had carried, the ones she had thrown into the canyon. The black-robed man didn't seem to be part of whatever was going on. He just waited.

The Outsiders that the pale men had dragged from their huts, and the two tied beside the fire, were silent, sullen, eyes dark and angry under dark brows. When the pale men shouted at them, they muttered something low and angry and shook their heads. They looked like buffalo bayed up against a cliff face, lowering and angry, and dangerous.

The four in the shadows of the trees watched silently. It might be, as Green Gourd Vine had said, a dance, but it was a dance of no good omen. The pale people were dancing with the Outsiders the way they had danced with the Bean Canyon people and with Green Gourd Vine. If the Two Old Men of Red Earth City had not sent them this way in the fall, they would have danced with Red Earth City the same way. Outside the glimmer of the fire, the woods were dark and still, as if everything in them was hiding from the Long-White-Bone-Man.

Mud Turtle peered through the darkness, looking for the horses. If there were pale people here, there were horses. They had learned from the cities that pale people did not walk, or at least their leaders didn't. The lowly, the leather shirts, might walk, but the shiny shirts did not; nor did the black-robed man who had the horse with the long ears.

"They will be nearby," Mud Turtle whispered. "I am going to look for them." He slid down from Morning Star Horse and handed his rein to Spotted Colt. "I will talk to them a little maybe."

Spotted Colt nodded, and Mud Turtle vanished in the trees.

The people in the camp were still shouting. The leader of the pale men stood in front of the man who had worn the turquoise beads, who was likely the leader of the Outsiders. Pale Man was a head taller than Turquoise Beads and stood very close to him. Turquoise Beads stared past him as if the pale man wasn't there shouting and spitting in his face. The other pale men were pawing through the empty huts now, throwing things out the doors in a jumble, skin clothes and cooking baskets and a baby in a cradleboard. The baby landed upside down in the dirt, and the mother rushed toward it, screaming. She snatched the baby up and inspected it, spitting vicious, angry words at the pale men who came after her and tried to grab her again. She clutched the baby to her chest.

They turned away from her and grabbed another woman by the arms, a younger one. One of them put his hands on her breasts, and then up under her dress. After a little while of that, they pulled her into an empty hut. She thrashed her legs and bit them, but they got her all the way inside. Green Gourd Vine could hear her screaming.

She sat on Grasshopper Horse shaking, and Spotted Colt reached over and took her hand. "They are just Outsiders," Green Gourd Vine said between her teeth.

Spotted Colt wondered if the pale people had been here all winter, thinking the Outsiders would show them the shiny rocks and the bright clay in the spring; and now there wasn't any. There had never been any. He tried to decide how many horses they probably had, and what they would do if their horses were stolen. They would still have the sticks that Green Gourd Vine said shot fire, but you couldn't ride on a stick, so far as he knew.

"They will be like mice," a voice at his heel said. "Always more. They are a new kind of person."

Spotted Colt looked down and saw Digger, dim in the shadows, ears pricked to listen to the pale people. "Not yet. Not where I come from," he retorted.

"No, not yet."

15

Into the Sun

THE SKY WAS BEGINNING TO LIGHTEN IN THE EAST BEHIND the trees, and Spotted Colt had begun to fidget by the time Mud Turtle came back. The pale people didn't seem to know they were here, but he thought the Outsiders did. The Outsider chief had looked their way twice.

"There are twice ten horses tethered in some spruce trees above the village," Mud Turtle whispered.

Blue Jay's eyes widened. That was more than they had thought. But it meant there were more pale people than they had thought, too. While they considered that, the sun came up past the horizon's ridge in a quick flash, like an arrow shot between the trees. They blinked and backed deeper into the shadows of the aspens. The air around the village was growing paler, and they could see faces clearly now. There was blood on the Outsider chief's mouth. They had best keep him tied until the end of the world now, Green Gourd Vine thought. If they let him go, he would kill someone. Outsiders were fearless, quick and vicious as weasels, and more willing than most to die if they could take their enemy with them.

"I have talked to these horses," Mud Turtle said.

"And did they tell you how long these pale people are going

to stay here mistreating this village?" Blue Jay whispered back.

"Horses don't know things like that. They said the grass here has been bad all winter."

"Will they let us take them?"

Mud Turtle shrugged. The people of the plains had learned long ago that horses were not dogs—even the best trained would go with any man who came along with a handful of grain. "They are horses like ours. They will go with whoever drives them."

"If we wait till night, these pale people may go away, on our horses," Blue Jay said.

Spotted Colt nodded thoughtfully. How long would they stay once they were sure there was no treasure here? Until their tempers wore off? It was hard to say how long that might be. The black-robed man was talking to the leader now; it looked as if they were arguing. The black-robed man seemed to want something that the leader didn't care about, but the leader looked as if he didn't want to say that. The black-robed man snarled something at him, and the leader nodded (*Yes, yes, all right*) and made a symbol against his chest with his fingers, one line downward and another line across it.

The sun was high enough now to show the Outsiders' village. It was a sad camp, Spotted Colt thought. These people were wanderers, but not like the Dry River or the Buffalo Horn. He didn't see any dogs in the camp, and their brush houses were unkempt, branches protruding like badly shorn hair. Their clothes were deerskins, but plain and ill made, not the quilled and painted finery of the Grass. No wonder they raided the cities with all their wealth of cloth and pots, and pits full of grain. He could see why Green Gourd Vine was afraid of them. Like the Grass peoples, their wandering life had made them fighters. They would be a constant threat, always hungry and always on the horizon.

Now they stood glowering as the invaders tore the brush huts apart like dogs who have waited outside a den until their patience is gone and begin to dig it open. The pale men would be intent on that for a while.

Spotted Colt and Blue Jay looked at each other and nodded. They signaled Mud Turtle and Green Gourd Vine with their

hands, and carefully they picked their way out of the aspens
and down the slope. As they passed the midden, they saw
Peccary rooting at its edges, and the dogs growled at him. He
looked up as they went by and snorted, then put his snout to
the ground again. They could see the tracks of his little hooves
all around the camp.

A protruding boulder, big as one of the brush huts, clung
to the stony hillside below the camp, and they stopped in its
lee. "You wait here with the packhorses," Spotted Colt said
to Green Gourd Vine. "When you see the horses coming, run.
These will follow you. You can let their leads go."

Green Gourd Vine thought about waiting here while they
went into the Outsiders' camp and left her.

"You will only be trouble if you come with us," Spotted
Colt said frankly. "Here you will be useful."

She nodded. She was afraid of the Outsiders' camp, even
if it had given her a certain satisfaction to see them mistreated
by the pale men. She was afraid of Peccary. She was afraid
of being left alone. If she was going to live on the Grass, she
would have to not be afraid of things like that. At least not of
all of them at once. "I will stay here."

They were gone up the trail again almost before she finished
speaking. She huddled in the shadow of the boulder, where it
was still cold with the morning mist, and waited.

The mist wreathed the aspens, hanging like drifts of cobweb
among their pale green leaves. The three moved through it
silently, ghosts in the trees. They were downwind of the pale
men's horses and those horses had not smelled the Grass
horses yet. They had left the two in season behind with the
packs. Blue Jay rode Gray Cloud Horse, who was the color
of the mist.

They passed well out of sight of the Outsiders' village, but
they could hear the shouting and, once, the sharp report of one
of the sticks that shot fire. The Grass men had never heard it
before, but they knew what it must be and stopped instantly,
hearts in their mouths at the sound. Their horses threw up their
heads and danced frantically in the wet drifts of last year's
leaves. It was like a thunderclap, cleaving the trees and the
village. They would not have been surprised to find the Out-

siders' camp split open by it, the ground cracked and gaping, and demons crawling up from its depths.

In the midden, Peccary paused, chewing on a rotten clump of berries that had gone bad. His little eyes narrowed, and he flung his tail up.

Green Gourd Vine heard it where she hid behind the boulder, and the packhorses and Grasshopper Horse started, nostrils quivering, flanks heaving with the surprise of it. Terrified that the pale people had shot at her people and not the Outsiders, whom no one would miss, she tried to talk to the horses the way Mud Turtle did: *There now, Foolish, it is only noise.* They quieted at last, but when a crow cawed in a spruce tree higher up the slope, they flinched and swiveled their ears, rolling dark eyes back toward where the dreadful sound had come from.

The horse stealers could see the pale men's herd now among the spruce trees, ghostly brown and black shapes with here and there a pale hide shimmering like a scrap of mist. These horses didn't seem to have minded the thunderclap of the pale men's stick. They nuzzled at dead leaves and stalks of the dried grass that had been their feed, snuffling along their picket line. The pale men had tethered them by leather harnesses about their heads to a rope that ran from one tree to another, through rings on the harnesses. They lifted their heads as the Grass horses came through the trees, and snuffled interestedly.

"Peace, brothers," Mud Turtle said quietly. He pulled his belt knife out of its sheath.

The horses looked at the dogs once and ignored them. They knew dogs. They snuffled at Mud Turtle's hands as he went down the line, cutting the picket rope at each end. He spoke into their ears as he went, running his hands down warm flanks, pulling the rope loose from their halters. He paused at the long-eared horse that was a horse and wasn't quite, and then turned him loose, too. There was no telling what he was, but there was no point in leaving him behind. The horses began to wander away through the trees, figuring out freedom. Spotted Colt and Blue Jay were waiting for them. Mud Turtle swung up onto Morning Star Horse.

As the sound of hoofbeats drummed through the trees, the men in the camp knew finally that they were being robbed.

They shouted unintelligibly, like angry crows, and a thunder-clap of sound echoed in the aspens from the sticks that shot fire.

The Grass riders bunched the horses in a herd and drove them hard, skirting the camp as widely as they could on the sloping ground. The horses ran wild-eyed with the long-eared animal among them and the Grass riders yipping at their heels. The dogs darted among the pounding hooves, ears flat, nipping at any who straggled.

A pale man plunged out of the camp and leveled his stick. The blast echoed in the trees and Rainstorm Horse reared in fright. The pale man upended the stick, doing something to the bottom of it, and Spotted Colt drew his bow. The arrow he loosed bounced off the pale man's shirt. The pale man ran for Spotted Colt. More were coming behind him. The pale man drew a long knife and lunged at Rainstorm Horse's belly. Rainstorm Horse plunged sideways, and Spotted Colt swung his war club over his head. It came down on the pale man's bare head. His skull caved in, a depression like a puddle in the ground, filling with blood. Spotted Colt thought about stopping to take his hair—a trophy unlike any other seen on the Grass—and thought better of it. The others were coming at them fast.

The herd was at full gallop now. Green Gourd Vine saw them coming and loosed the packhorses, sending them down the trail before her. Grasshopper Horse slithered in loose stone, but Green Gourd Vine hung on. Behind her she could hear the thunder of hooves and the voices of the Grass men.

As they passed the edge of the camp, another pale man leveled his stick, and the blast knocked Morning Star Horse to the ground. Buffeted by the sound, Mud Turtle felt him drop from under him, collapsing in a shower of blood and torn flesh. Mud Turtle rolled sideways while Morning Star Horse thrashed, screaming, and shuddered into a red stillness. Limping, his lungs hurting, Mud Turtle caught the halter of a red roan, one of the pale men's horses, and flung himself up on its back. He bent low over its neck and hung on, talking into the red ears. Blue Jay ran the pale man down on Gray Cloud Horse as he tried to make his stick shoot again. The man slipped, shrieking, under the pounding hooves. His shirt was only leather, and it split open and shredded. Blue Jay made Gray Cloud Horse rear and come down on him again before he rode on.

The broken man on the ground writhed, reaching for his stick, while another picked it up and knelt, balancing the weight on his knee. Another clap of sound, like rocks cracking, the ground opening, the howl of demons. Blue Jay felt something slap hard against his arm. He dug his heels into Gray Cloud Horse's flanks, and they followed Mud Turtle and the stolen roan down the slope.

The rest were running free now, spreading out across the valley below the hillside. Spotted Colt and Blue Jay swung wide, to either side, bunching them up again, the dogs darting in and out. The stolen horses snorted and settled into a steady gallop. Running was what they knew how to do—running, and carrying people. It didn't matter who, so long as someone told them when to run and when to stop. Mud Turtle's stolen roan turned easily when he leaned to one side, pressing its flank with his knee. The packhorses were on the edge of the herd now, with Grasshopper Horse among them. Green Gourd Vine was still on her back, her hair come loose from its pins and streaming out behind her like the horses' tails. Spotted Colt was holding them on the left flank. Mud Turtle looked to the right at Blue Jay and saw blood streaming down his arm. Blue Jay looked pale, but he was riding upright. Gray Cloud Horse was holding the right flank of the herd. Mud Turtle called to Spotted Colt over the drumming of the hooves and pointed at Blue Jay. Spotted Colt shaded his eyes and looked. He nodded. They kept running.

Coyote watched the running horses from the top of the hill beside the pale people's camp, and from inside Digger, in the dust of the herd. He felt very pleased with himself. They had stolen the horses from the monsters, just as in the legends about himself, in the days when he stole Summer and cut up the heart of Terrible Monster. Now the horses would breed, and there would be more horses. All the people of the Grass would have horses. And he had thought it up.

Another bang came from the camp below, and Coyote ducked without meaning to, scrunching his head down into his shoulders. Then he shook himself, embarrassed, pretending that he hadn't even heard the bang, although his big ears were stiffened, listening to see if there was going to be another one.

Spider was sitting in a berry bush, spinning a web in the new leaves to catch bugs that came looking for spring sap. "Why did you let them in?" he demanded of her.

Spider chuckled. "I thought you thought them up."

"I thought up the horses."

"That is like thinking up dogs without fleas."

"Well. Anyway. Now they will be able to hunt more buffalo. That part is good."

Spider shrugged two of her eight shoulders. Coyote would brag all day when he was trying to convince himself that he had been clever. She went on spinning.

The thieves ran until the horses were flecked with foam and they had put more than a day's travel between them and the men on foot. There was no discussion as to which way to go now. They looked at the sun and went east. East into the morning, and east into the Grass.

At afternoon they stopped. Green Gourd Vine got Mud Turtle's medicine bag and looked at Blue Jay's arm, unwrapping the blood-soaked cloth he had tied around it. The stone had gone clean through the way it had gone through the water jar.

Blue Jay stared at it wonderingly. It was a magical wound. In some way it made him magical, too.

"You're lucky it didn't go through the bone," Green Gourd Vine said.

"Could it do that?"

She thought of the water jar. Its sides were two fingers thick. "I don't know what it could go through. Whole people, maybe."

Blue Jay touched the hole in his arm with a fingertip. He would have a badge now of the time he fought the monsters in the west. When he was old, children would come to look at his scar. Blue Jay smiled slowly. He would be legend, not as a Child of the Horse with the now-dubious ancestry of the Horse Bringers, but in his own right. He was Blue Jay, who went west and fought monsters and came home to tell of it. He would be more important than Freckled Rat. "I will have to marry this year," he confided to Green Gourd Vine. "It is time."

"Whom will you marry?" She smeared both sides of the wound with salve while he clenched his jaw.

"Field Mouse maybe," Blue Jay said through gritted teeth. "That is who my sister said I should marry."

Green Gourd Vine thought of the wild girl. "Sisters are wise," she told him. She tied a clean cloth torn from her skirt around his arm.

Mud Turtle was talking to the stolen horses. He had already counted how many were mares—only six. The long-eared horse was still among them.

"What are you?" Mud Turtle asked him, scratching him around his big ears.

The long-eared horse blew down his nose.

"Are you a horse?"

The long-eared horse looked at him sideways.

"I'll call you Rabbit Horse," Mud Turtle said. "Whatever you are, you are the only one there is, so no one else has one."

Rabbit Horse nodded his head at that.

Mud Turtle rubbed his ears a last time and went on to talk to the roan he had ridden. He put a spare bridle and rein on the roan, and it didn't mind them, but he was still grieving for Morning Star Horse, Spotted Colt thought, watching him wander among the new horses with Laugher at his heel. Mud Turtle was kin to his horses and dogs in a way that most people weren't. Mud Turtle would keep the long-eared horse because it was an oddity, too. They were all oddities now, Spotted Colt supposed.

When the horses had rested, they went on, at a slow steady trot now, and didn't stop until nightfall. *Home,* the air said, as it blew around their ears. *Home.* The smell of grass blew by on the wind. Maybe it was only imagination and longing, but Green Gourd Vine thought she smelled it, too. A little whisper of magic came with the grass smell, just a faint sibilant murmur, a slight illumination limning the riders and the shadowy shapes of the horses so that you might think they would glow at night if you saw them moving across the darkened prairie.

It stayed with them as they grew smaller and smaller and winked out into memory where the desert met the long grass.

EPILOGUE

WOLF EYE, CHIEF OF THE TRIBE WHOM THE CITY PEOPLE called the Outsiders and who called themselves the People of the Wind, saw the pale men fall under the war clubs of the horse strangers and took note of the fact that once they had shot their sticks they had to put more magic in them before they would work again, a fact that the pale people had been at pains to conceal from Wolf Eye's people all winter.

The horses were gone now, and the pale people were shouting angrily at each other. Wolf Eye poked with a toe at the spill of turquoise beads scattered at his feet. He could still feel the raw place on his neck where the pale leader had jerked the string from it. The woman they had dragged into the hut was sitting in the dirt outside it, sobbing and pounding viciously at the ground with a skinning knife as if it were the pale men's skulls.

The invaders carried the two dead men, one of whom wasn't quite dead yet, into the center of the camp and put them down. The trampled man writhed like a bug that was half squashed. The black-robed one, who was some kind of priest and who had been bothering the People of the Wind all winter, ran up with his bag and made motions over him with his hands while he moaned. It didn't do any good, though, Wolf Eye saw. The priest put something on the man's forehead, and something else in his mouth, but he died anyway. The priest chanted over him some more, and over the other one, even though any idiot could see that *he* was dead, but they didn't get up.

Wolf Eye twisted the ropes that bound his hands. No one tied up a chief of the People of the Wind and lived very long afterward. He could see One Ear beside him, thinking the same thing. The pale men had no horses now, and Wolf Eye knew they didn't like to walk; they broiled easily in the sun, their flesh cooked like roasted fish, and the hard shells they wore were heavy. Wolf Eye looked at One Ear.

The pale leader came back and shouted at Wolf Eye. Over the winter Wolf Eye had learned a little of their language, so that he didn't need the interpreter who had come from the cities and spoke the People's talk with a horrible accent. The interpreter had tried to steal extra food from the People's store when the winter got hungry, and the pale men had let Wolf Eye kill him. That was when they were still pretending to be guests. Now they were demanding to know who had taken their horses. The pale leader was so angry his face had turned red. He shouted at Wolf Eye and drew back his arm to hit him.

That was when the woman who had been sitting in the dirt jumped on the pale leader's back and pushed her knife into his throat before anyone could stop her. Blood spurted out, splattering Wolf Eye, and the woman had cut Wolf Eye's hands loose and nearly cut through One Ears' rope when two of the pale men shook off their surprise and pulled her away. She was only a woman that someone had raped. No one had thought she would do anything. The pale men leveled their sticks at the People, who had picked up their spears. The People's eyes were dark and menacing now.

One of the pale men, their second leader, snapped a command. His men picked up a rope and began to drag the woman toward a tree.

"Enough!" Wolf Eye's roar filled the camp. His people took a step toward the pale men and then another, teeth bared.

"Stop!" Second Leader held up his hand. No one stopped.

"We will shoot you!" The pale men waved their sticks menacingly.

The People came on. The sticks roared, and several of the People fell in their tracks. No one else stopped.

"We will shoot again!" The People were nearly on them. The pale men looked frightened, upending their sticks and trying to pour magic into them.

The woman looked into the faces of the men who were trying to decide whether or not to let go of her and run. She spat. One of them hit her hard across the face, and then they dropped her arms and fled, stumbling down the slope past the midden.

The People were nearly on the rest of them. A pale man dropped his stick and pulled out his long knife. An arrow stuck in his throat, and he staggered backward, fingers clutching at it. The People leapt on them, growling like cats. The pale men's long knives killed many, but there were more People than pale men, and they swarmed over them, clawing and biting and stabbing with their spears and belt knives until the pale people were rags on the ground.

The black-robed man had stayed crouched over the dead ones, but when he saw how the wind was going, he got up and ran, too, holding up his skirts. One Ear drew his bow, and the arrow sang down the slope. Black Robe fell face forward, the arrow shivering in his back like a prayer stick. He got up again, clawing at the dirt, and stumbled a few feet more. The People let him go. Peccary watched him swerve by the midden, staggering in looping curves, eyes glazed. He snuffled at the tracks a moment and snorted.

Wolf Eye gave an order to his people. They picked up the pale dead men, threw their bodies down the slope, and threw their weapons after them. Wolf Eye thought about keeping the sticks that shot fire, but his shaman said not to; they were foreign magic and he might shoot himself with them. So they threw those down the slope with the rest. Their own dead they buried at the center of the camp and then moved out, leaving it to them. Their spirits would live there until they went away on the wind. The spirits of the pale men, on the other hand, f they had any, would wander, since they hadn't been properly buried. The People of the Wind moved out in a hurry.

The two who had run lasted three days. The sun was unseasonably hot for that time of year, and their feet blistered in their boots and their lips blistered and cracked on their faces. After a while they lay down and didn't move anymore, and a while after that the wild half-coyote dogs who trailed the People of the Wind for their leavings (but didn't come closer because the People of the Wind ate dogs) found them and ate them.

"There," Spider said, "I told you they were edible."

Peccary moved on, because there were more of them in the cities along Water Old Man, and more coming from the south.

Coyote sat on the hill in Sun's hot breath, figuring the angles.

"If I were you, I would go into the Grass," a small bug said from an aspen leaf.

"No," Coyote said, "I think I will stay here for a while and see what I can give these new people in exchange for the horses, and that disease."

And so he stayed, and gave them race riots and bad teeth and the diseases that come from greed. And also invention and art and curiosity, and the capacity to see him sometimes, just out of the corner of our eye.

"But what about the horses?" the boy asked insistently. He didn't care about dead Spaniards four hundred years ago.

"The horses lived in the Grass, and for a while it was a magical world."

"For a while." The boy sighed. Magic never lasted.

Coyote sighed, too. He brightened. "There's always a new story; someone just has to make it up."

"Would that make a difference?"

"Everything makes a difference. Spider will tell you."

"Always," Spider said from a corner behind the bar. She moved one delicate foot, and they saw the web shimmer on the horizon, floating above the street outside. "Paint it. Dance it. Tell it. But remember, you don't know how it's going to turn out."

AUTHOR'S NOTE

THERE ARE ALWAYS PEOPLE TO THANK, AND IN THESE BOOKS I always owe thanks for stories. Many of these have as many variants as Cinderella, and I have added my own. But I first learned of them from the following sources.

The water origin of First Horse is adapted from a number of Plains traditions that tell us that horses first came up from under the waters of a river—usually when a human was offered a gift by a supernatural power and made a wise choice. Blue Jay's visit to the land of the dead has its origin in a Chinook story called "Blue Jay Visits Ghost Town" in *American Indian Myths and Legends,* edited by Richard Erdoes and Alfonso Ortiz. Additional details, particularly the Orpheus parallel, in which the rescuer must take the dead wife back to earth without looking at her or touching her, come from other accounts of visits to the dead in the same book, and particularly from a Nez Percé story told in *Trickster Makes This World* by Lewis Hyde. Coyote's prediction of the coming of the Europeans is a Brule Sioux story told in *American Indian Myths and Legends* (with the Coyote role given to Iktome, the Spider Man, another traditional trickster). And finally, the tale of Uncle and how he outwits Sickness comes from a Kiowa

280

story that I read years ago and cannot find again, so my thanks must be thrown onto the wind, along with my apologies, with the hope that they will land on the author in whose book I first met Sainday, Uncle of the Kiowa.

Additionally, I have to thank as always Elizabeth Tinsley of Book Creations; and Lucia Macro and Krista Stroever of Avon Books, patient editors all; and the staff of the Hollins University Library for endless renewals and strange interlibrary loan requests.

And finally, I want to thank Richard Dillard for Wile E. Coyote.

Coming in Spring 2001
The next book in Amanda Cockrell's
unforgettable saga

THE HORSE CATCHERS

The Rain Child

Only from Avon Books